I was born in Taunton to an English father and Italian mother, and raised in Bristol where I still live. Married to Rebecca with two sons, Ben and Leo, I retired recently from my role as a GP practice manager and have used my new found freedom to fulfil a lifelong ambition to write a novel.

Beltane's Child

Stephen R. Hartnell

Beltane's Child

Vanguard Press

VANGUARD PAPERBACK

© Copyright 2024
Stephen R. Hartnell

The right of Stephen R. Hartnell to be identified as author of
this work has been asserted by him in accordance with the
Copyright, Designs and Patents Act 1988.

All Rights Reserved

No reproduction, copy or transmission of this publication
may be made without written permission.
No paragraph of this publication may be reproduced,
copied or transmitted save with the written permission of the publisher, or in accordance
with the provisions
of the Copyright Act 1956 (as amended).

Any person who commits any unauthorised act in relation to
this publication may be liable to criminal
prosecution and civil claims for damages.

A CIP catalogue record for this title is
available from the British Library.

ISBN 978 1 83794 056 1

This is a work of fiction. Names, characters, business, places, events and incidents are
either the product of the author's imagination or used in a fictitious manner. Any
resemblance to actual persons, living or dead, or actual events is purely coincidental.

Vanguard Press is an imprint of
Pegasus Elliot Mackenzie Publishers Ltd.
www.pegasuspublishers.com

First Published in 2024

Vanguard Press
Sheraton House Castle Park
Cambridge England

Printed & Bound in Great Britain

To Rebecca

Thank you to my wife and family for their support and encouragement; to Rebecca Megson-Smith, my writing coach, without whom I could never have written this book; my critical friends, Gemma, John, Raj and Wayne, for bringing tears to my eyes with their compliments; and also to those who wrote the books that inspired my story, specifically Adam Ardrey and Simon Andrew Stirling. Thank you to Vicky Gorry and Chandray Isaacson at Pegasus Publishers.

Contents

Background 13
How Will I Be Remembered? 21
The Ashes of Deceit 28
A Father's Wrath 39
The Birth of a Prince 46
The Rise of Morcant Bwlch 57
Safety in God's Hands 67
A Sanctuary Despoiled 74
A Saviour Comes 85
Enemies at Every Turn 101
Out of Sight, Out of Mind 115
Lailoken 123
Initiation 130
A Prince in Waiting 136
Aedan the Uther 149
The Horsemen of Manau 160
A Call to Arms 172
A Mentor's Plea 182
The Battle of Arderydd 192
Aedan's Gambit 202
The Game Begins 210
An Understanding of Equals 222
Invasion 229
Delgon 238
Columba's Acceptance 249
Gwenhwyfar 261
Greedy Eyes Look West 274
A Mother's Advice and a Sister's Respect 282
The Pieces Move 302
Becoming Pendragon 310
Kingdom of the Scots 324

Background

Before embarking on my historical justifications, I must apologise to Arthur fundamentalists who might be outraged by my particular take on his story. But as I note below, the facts available to us are scant and unless something historically concrete comes to light, we have a lot of open ground to play with. If Bernard Cornwell can get away with it, so can I.

Many of us recognise Arthur as a legendary king of Britain who was a leader of the post-Roman Britons in battles against Saxon invaders. The basis for the Arthur story we know so well is thanks to Geoffrey of Monmouth, who told the story in his twelfth century *Historia Regum Britanniae*. Geoffrey depicted Arthur as a king of Britain who defeated the Saxons and established an empire. The many elements and incidents that are now an integral part of Geoffrey's story include Arthur's father Uther Pendragon, the magician Merlin, Arthur's wife Guinevere, the sword Excalibur, Arthur's conception at Tintagel, his final battle against Mordred at Camlann, and his final resting place in Avalon. The story was further embellished by the French writer Chrétien de Troyes, who added Lancelot and the Holy Grail.

There are also several poems attributed to Taliesin, a significant character in this book, a poet or bard said to have lived in the sixth century. The poems also refer to Arthur including *Kadeir Teyrnon* (*The Chair of the Prince*), which refers to 'Arthur the Blessed'; *Preiddeu Annwn* (*The Spoils of Annwn*), which recounts an expedition of Arthur to the Otherworld; and *The Elegy of Uther Pen[dragon]*, which refers to Arthur's valour and is suggestive of a father-son relationship for Arthur and Uther that pre-dates Geoffrey of Monmouth.

Other early Welsh Arthurian texts include a poem found in the Black Book of Carmarthen, *Pa gur*, in which Arthur recounts the names and deeds of himself and his men, notably Cai and Bedwyr. There was also the Welsh prose tale, *Culhwch and Olwen*, included in the modern Mabinogion collection, which contains a much longer list of more than 200 of Arthur's men, with Cai (Kay) and Bedwyr (Bedevere) again taking centre stage. Other texts such as *Annales Cambriae* links Arthur with the Battle of Badon and also mentions the Battle of Camlann, in which Arthur and Mordred were both killed.

As I have found, for anyone researching the Arthur story, there are a huge range of books on the market to consume, books often disparagingly described as pseudo-historical by historians. All these books follow a well beaten path: the twelve battles written in Nennius' *History Brittonum* including the most famous battle of all, Badon; where they might have taken place and when, invariably followed by trying to identify who the most likely historical figure Arthur is or might be based upon.

Badon becomes a major problem for Arthurian writers because it tends to skew timelines and ruins the many different theories. The clearest evidence of when Badon happened can be found in the writings of a cleric by the name of Gildas in his polemic *De Excidio et Conquestu Britanniae*. In this work he excoriates the leaders of the time for their sins. He talks about the Battle of Mons Badonicus and how it relates to his own birth, but tellingly, he doesn't once mention Arthur. Instead, he lauds a man by the name of Ambrosius Aurelianus as the leader of the resistance to the Saxons. So the problem here is why Gildas neglects to mention Arthur if Arthur is considered to be a major player. Now, Arthurian fundamentalists try to find various excuses but the easiest, for me, is that when Gildas wrote his *De Excidio* he didn't know of Arthur's existence. Furthermore, as there are so many different sites with Badon in their name throughout the length and breadth of Britain, there is every possibility that there was more than one battle of Badon.

In terms of where the battles Nennius speaks of were, I have taken the view that armies in the Dark Ages were unlikely to march over huge distances; after all, they were predominantly on foot and would have to pass through the lands of many kingdoms, often unfriendly, to get to where they needed to go. As an example, in the battle list, there were battles in the Caledonian Wood (Scotland), the City of the Legion (Chester or Caerleon?) and Badon (possibly outside Bath in Somerset) which seems impractical.

So I concluded that the Arthurian battles had to have geographically taken place reasonably close together. Also, the battle sites had to be congruent to where a particular foe would approach from or be based. The contortions of authors trying to site the battles made it difficult to take seriously what I was reading until it struck me: what if the battles were close together but against different foes.

It was not until I read *Finding Arthur* by Adam Ardrey and *The King Arthur Conspiracy* by Simon Andrew Stirling that I found my answers. Those books brought my attention to and identified Artuir mac Aedan, who lived in southern Scotland in the latter half of the sixth century, as the likely Arthur of history. Between the two authors, they made the argument that all the battles could be placed within a couple of days walking distance from each other. Additionally, they theorised that battles could have been fought against both the Angles and the Picts rather than just the Saxons (or Angles). Modern day Scotland, therefore, for me, ticks all the boxes.

The Scottish slant brings me to one of the most famous Welsh poetic references and strangest to Arthur which comes in the collection of heroic death-songs known as *Y Gododdin*, attributed to sixth century poet Aneirin. One particular stanza praises the bravery of a warrior who slew 300 enemies, but says that despite this, 'he was no Arthur'. What makes *Y Gododdin* interesting is that their kingdom lies to the south of what is now Edinburgh. So why would a Scottish tribe revere someone whose major exploits were in southern England?

The twelve battles of Nennius' writings will play a major part in my books, but this book only covers the first one, the battle on the Glein. I have set it on the River Lyne, south of where the Battle of Arderydd is said to have occurred (in the parish of Arthuret) north of Carlisle. There are, of course, many possible sites for the Glein but I liked the argument that two Ls makes the sound cl/gl, hence Llyne becomes Glein.

As for the other battles described in this book, there are historical references to Dun Breatain (today's Dumbarton), Delgon and Craigmaddie Moor. It is unclear whether Arthur fought in these engagements, although it is assumed that he did. At least two of the encounters would have been in support of his father, Aedan. The battle of Delgon is pivotal in the history of Dalriada or Dal Riata and probably took place on the Kintyre Peninsula. From my visit to the area, I settled for a place near West Tarbert by a golf course on the B8024 looking out towards the Sound of Jura, a pinch point where Aedan's force could have been held by his uncle, Conall. The terrain, too, allows for cavalry to be hidden in the surrounding hills.

The other battles mentioned in a number of sources were difficult to build into the narrative but the order I chose made the flow of the story that resulted in Aedan becoming king of Dalriada more straightforward. To further help the timeline, I moved the Convention of Drumceatt forward a year. Interestingly, some sources suggest Arthur could have been present at Drumceatt and even involved in an incident involving the Sacred Cauldron of Dymwch, thought to be one of the treasures of Britain. I toyed with this story but thought it would only complicate the story. Nonetheless, the story of the Sacred Cauldron was too good to miss out so I have placed it later in the story.

Through reading Ardrey and Stirling, it became apparent that a number of well-known names could be reasonably attributed to the area of Scotland where I decided to set my story. These include:

Gwalhafed (Galahad)
Gwenhywfar (Guinevere)
Drystan (Tristan)
Gwallog ap Lleenog (Lancelot or Galahad)
Myrddin (Merlin)
Morgant or Morcant (Mordred)
Muirgein (Morgana)

I apologise that I have not always been consistent with the names. I battled with myself for months and came up with a rather uneasy compromise, choosing the Welsh names except for Galahad. I'm still unsure this was correct.

Characters such as (Saints) Columba, Serf and Dewi along with Urien, Rhydderch, Aedan, Domelch, Clydno ap Eidyn, Peredur (Percival) and Taliesin certainly existed as probably did Crierwy. Crierwy is a wonderful character who is a figure in the *Mabinogion* and the *Hanes Taliesin* and considered a daughter of the enchantress Ceridwen. The Welsh Triads name her one of the three most beautiful maids of the Isle of Britain.

The Arthur stories tell us that Ygerne/Igraine is Arthur's mother. There is a school of thought that the name actually means lady, so it is probably a title rather than a name. After some thought I decided to acknowledge the connection and made her the Lady of Strathclyde and Aedan's second wife. Whilst talking of Aedan's loves, I also felt that Crierwy's connection to Lake Tegid or Bala and Loch Lomond, and her presence when Arthur's sword was thrown into the lake, made her the likely candidate for the legend's Lady of the Lake.

Angle leaders such as Aethelric and Hussa are also known to have existed.

One of the great challenges of researching individuals was the constant issue of name changes. Lailoken changed to Myrddin, Crimmthan to Columba etc. Another problem was the use of nicknames. This was, and has been, a particular problem when it came to Aedan mac Gabran who was also known as Gorlasser (Gorlois?) and Gwyther (meaning wily and tantalisingly similar to Uther). This was also the case when looking at Gwallog. Gwallog, apparently, means hairy. Does that mean he was hairy or was he actually called Gwallog/Hairy? I chose to stick with Gwallog as being his real name (ap — or son of — Lleenog). This works well as there was a Lleenog (possibly the root for Lancelot) who lived a generation before this story is set who was probably his father. I considered making Gwallog Galahad but I felt it added additional complication, and anyway, Gwallog, who has a pivotal role in the story, strikes me as a great knightly yet tragic figure who deserves to have the Lancelot status.

Characters such as Aeronwen, Arthmael, Cormons, Faolin, Senan, Nessa, Tearlach and Dugald etc are completely fictitious. Cormons, in fact, was the unusual name of an Italian cousin of mine.

Spoiler alert: I have chosen to adopt Morgant Bwlch as my Mordred. I am unconvinced at the familial aspect of the Arthur story and found that this individual seemed to be a particularly nasty piece of work whose machinations and similar sounding name made him an ideal candidate for Arthur's nemesis. I hope you agree. I do touch upon the incestuous potential but I felt the whole idea was highly unlikely.

Initially I chose Beltane because of the Pagan importance it has connected to the celebrations and the sexual excitement generated from the 'partying'.

What also piqued my interest was the surprisingly simple explanations for the magical elements to the Arthur story. Firstly, the throwing the sword into the Lake: it was considered that throwing a sword into water once their owners were dying or dead was an offering to the gods; secondly, the disguising of Aedan (Uther) can be argued away by covering himself in ash from the Beltane fires so that Crierwy would not recognise him; lastly, taking the sword from the stone was a ritual when becoming a protector of the people. It is easy how these things can be easily turned into something more than they actually were.

Most of the names used in this book are of Welsh origin. To help the reader pronounce them, a crash course in the Welsh alphabet is recommended. In summary, most letters are pronounced as the Latin or small letters, e.g. *a* as in hat, *b* as in boy and *c* as in care. So Crierwy is pronounced Kr-i-er-wee. The Welsh alphabet does have additional sounds to the English, e.g. *ch* as pronounced in loch, *dd* as in thin, *ff* as in off, *ng* as in long, *ll* as in cl (Llanelli), *rh* pronounced hr and *th* as in thin. As an example, Muirgein would be pronounced m-u-ear-ge-in. I hope Welsh speakers will forgive me for ruining such beautiful names.

Also, I have adopted both Gaelic and early translations of place names, where I could find them, such as:

Camlann is now Camelon near Falkirk
Strevelin is now Stirling

Eidyn is now Edinburgh
Dun Breatainn is now Dumbarton
Pertneck is now Partick
Dunpelder is now Trapain Law
Ebruac is now York

Finally, I wanted to discuss the Druidry/Shamanic rituals. Trying to write about these in an understandable and relatable way was a real challenge and I'm not sure I fully did it justice. Research helped outline a particular process for initiating followers into the Cult of the Cauldron. The images of the salmon of wisdom, tattoos and remaining alone in coracles at the centre of the lake probably happened. I borrowed some rituals from modern Shamanic induction, specifically being buried alive in a process of rebirth. I have since been informed that the original method was being closed in a cave — a very distinctive Christian ideal?

It is also said that initiates changed their names once the individual was initiated, e.g. Gwyn became Taliesin and Lailoken/Menw became Myrddin (discussed above). It is suggested that Crierwy may also have changed names but the whole thing became rather complicated and confusing.

Shamanic practice includes a process called 'journeying' where a person imagines or pictures travelling to a lower or upper world. Having tried it, I can share the realness of the images of animal spirit guides. The symbol of the bear which occurs on occasion was brought in to explain Arthur's name, i.e. Arth is considered to mean bear.

For all those who are acquainted with Shamanic or Druidic practices, I apologise for any inaccuracies and pray forgiveness for oversimplifying or unwittingly disrespecting its significance.

As I said at the outset, this is my interpretation of one of the great stories. For me, the geography, the people, etc fit well into Lowland Scotland.

Arthur was Arthur mac Aedan, son of Aedan, son of Gabran. He was an Irish Scot, a man born through deception, a Scottish warrior who became a warlord and legend. Enjoy!

Prologue

How Will I Be Remembered?

It was quiet now, the sounds of battle but a memory. The setting sun, like a veil, was drawn over the worst excesses of battle. There was a chill in the air, a sure sign that autumn was almost upon them.

The murders of crows picked at the cadavers of fallen men, a sharp reminder of the meaninglessness of the human body and the cheapness of life.

Arthur, the great battle leader, the hammer of the Angles and of the Picts, and a disciple of Arawn, breathed heavily, leaning against his shield. His wound from a wooden spear wracked him with pain and he had to grit his teeth through each new wave of torment.

"The aftermath of battle is not pretty," Bedwyr muttered.

"That's true," Arthur gasped.

Arthur looked about him; the bodies lying around them were many and stretched away in all directions. The battle had been bloody and desperate, men he had come to know and respect, their eyes expressionless, now lay dead, their mortal coil severed. He sighed. He was filled with a heavy and profound sadness. Arthur winced again from the pain as the healers picked him up and carried him to a tree where he could sit in relative quiet and comfort, away from the stench and death, if that were at all possible.

Arthur gazed at his friend. He knew he was dying; the blood flowed too freely and it could not be stopped by the healers who stood about him, conferring in low ominous whispers. Arthur rolled his eyes. Linen strips wrapped around the wound had all too quickly reddened with fresh blood. "I think, my dearest friend, that our time together on this earth is drawing to a close," he whispered.

"You will be well again, Arthur," Bedwyr assured him. "You are a man of stone."

"You're a bad liar, my friend, or a man who has lost his faculties." Arthur grimaced.

"You must rest now and sleep," Bedwyr offered.

"Sleep? No, my friend, if I close my eyes to sleep, I fear I will never awaken and there is so much to say before and after I send you away."

"Send me away?" Bedwyr questioned. "What will you ask of me?"

Arthur nodded and breathed deeply. "You must take my sword, Celeborn, and give it to my mother to throw into the waters of Loch Lomond as my final offering to the gods."

"Arthur—" Bedwyr started.

Arthur held up his hand. "Bedwyr, you are the man I trust above all others. Take my sword and tell my mother of my fate."

Bedwyr wanted to argue, but seeing the determination on Arthur's face, nodded reluctantly. He picked up the sword lying next to Arthur's right hand. Arthur sank back again, looked at the sky and sighed with relief. He lay quietly for a while and Bedwyr shuffled uncomfortably, wondering if he should stay or go.

Arthur closed his eyes. His mouth was parched; he could taste the blood that trickled from a deep cut across his cheek. He pointed to a skin filled with water and Bedwyr duly obliged, gently tipping the skin to allow the water to dribble into Arthur's mouth. Arthur choked a little but then drank greedily. Bedwyr wiped Arthur's wet chin.

"Thank you," he groaned. "I am told Gwallog fell," Arthur continued, his voice only just above a whisper.

"Yes, Arthur. He died the hero he was," Bedwyr confirmed, "and," he continued, "Cynon killed the bastard Morcant."

"Good, it is done then." Arthur grimaced. "Death's sleep will be more restful. Is my uncle safe?"

"He is wounded but it is superficial. You'll be reassured that his looks remain."

Arthur smiled. "I am glad." He paused and Bedwyr saw a cloud cross his face before he continued. "Gwallog was a good man, he didn't deserve to fall here in a war he, and you, opposed. I should have listened more but

I couldn't see past my pride and my... jealousy. I owed him much and thanked him too little."

"You are too hard on yourself; he made his choice, as did I," Bedwyr soothed.

Arthur grunted and sighed deeply. "I have done some terrible things, Bedwyr. In my dreams I see the faces of frightened men put to the sword to satisfy my lust for revenge. The screams haunt me, Bedwyr. What happened to me, what did I become?" He shook his head sadly. "I was a Druid of the Cauldron, a disciple of peace, and I become a disciple of revenge and a bringer of death."

Arthur looked at Bedwyr, his eyes full of sorrow and regret. As Bedwyr began to speak Arthur shook his head. There was nothing more to be said but to Bedwyr's surprise, Arthur asked a further question. "Tell me something, Bedwyr, how will I be remembered?"

"You will be remembered forever as a great warlord. And your name will echo throughout the ages," Bedwyr assured him.

"Forever?" Arthur chuckled. "I can't ask for any more, I suppose. Fame, it would seem, is always assured if you die in battle rather than dying in your bed." Arthur smiled sadly one last time. "You should go now, my friend," he whispered. "Make haste. Aed and Gawain will take me to Iona where I can lie with my forebears. They and Muirgein will make sure that trickster Columba allows my burial."

Bedwyr stood up stiffly. His limbs ached and the cuts on his arms and legs stung. He signalled to a man close by to fetch him a horse. "I will do your bidding, Arthur." Without thinking he reached out and stroked Arthur's cheek as a man strokes a lover's face at a time of parting.

Bedwyr nodded and turned away then as tears pricked his eyes. He was determined he would not let Arthur see his distress. He grasped the sword, wrapped it in a linen cloth, and strode towards where his horse was being readied. He mounted the horse but as he turned to leave, Arthur called after him. "And Bedwyr, please pass on a message to my mother."

"Yes, Arthur?"

"Tell her I'm sorry."

Nodding, Bedwyr rode off without looking back.

Bedwyr rode hard through the night, and as dawn broke, stopped to rest by a waterfall, known as the Loup. He led his horse to the water's edge and allowed it to drink its fill. He sat against a rock. He was numb; his body was stiff and screaming to rest. Exhausted beyond endurance, he sat quietly gazing at the sunrise before his eyes slowly closed.

Resentment swept through him as he remembered Arthur ignoring the words of advice he, Gwallog and others had given to him. But then he wondered if it had been his wife who had been kidnapped, would he have done any different?

The disappearance of Gwenhwyfar had enraged Arthur to a level of madness which Bedwyr had never seen in any man. Gwenhwyfar's betrayal, as Arthur saw it, tipped his friend from an already tortured paranoid man into one who had lost all sense of reality, a man overtaken by hatred and spite. Even when it became clear she had not betrayed him, he pushed on regardless, driven by demons Bedwyr could never comprehend. As he considered this, sleep overtook him.

He awakened sometime later with a start after a fitful sleep, dipping his head into the flowing waters of the Loup to help him overcome his torpor. He rubbed his face vigorously but then noticed there was still blood on his chest, arms and hands. He shrugged; there would be plenty of time to wash. A further dip into the frigid water rid him of the last feelings of dizziness and nausea his sleep had brought on. He stood gingerly and stretched his back, groaning loudly before mounting his horse. He looked up into the sky and let the sun warm his face. He checked the sun's position and decided it was time to move on despite an almost overwhelming desire not to. He banished the thought, and with renewed determination, he swung his mount westward. With luck, he thought, he would arrive on the shores of Lomond before sunset.

Riding hard throughout the day, stopping only for refreshment, he finally set eyes on the waters of the loch. Its beauty always filled him with awe but this time his overwhelming sadness left his heart heavy and made his head pound. His hand dropped to the hilt of the sword Arthur had given him and he sighed deeply before nudging his horse forward.

He followed well established paths and dropped down to the loch's shoreline. At last, he caught sight of the settlement presided over by the priestess of the Cauldron, Cerridwen's representative in the living world, and the lodgings built on the crannog that stretched out into the loch. As he entered the settlement and trotted among the round huts that were scattered about him, he looked around, his head foggy as if full of sheets. A short, square, bearded man with unkempt hair and a look that suggested that he'd seen too much and too many winters, drew him from his reverie with a challenge.

"What is your business here?" he said with a note of threat.

"Good day, friend," Bedwyr replied ignoring the man's challenging rudeness. "I am Bedwyr, companion of Arthur, son of the Lady of the Lake. I must have an urgent audience with the Priestess Crierwy. Take me to her?"

"And why would she want to speak to you, an armed stranger who has clearly seen action recently?" The man rejoined, casting his eyes over Bedwyr's bloodstained, mud-stained, war ragged attire.

Bedwyr sighed inwardly trying to control his rising anger. "I have news of her son," he said finally.

The man looked suspiciously at Bedwyr but Bedwyr continued. "I am no threat to the priestess, friend."

At that moment a woman appeared from a roundhouse directly behind where the guard was stood. "News? What news?" It was a voice Bedwyr knew well.

He turned towards the sound of the woman's voice. "Lady Crierwy?" he said nervously.

"Bedwyr is that you?" Crierwy said with surprise. "My goodness, you're a man now." She studied him a moment and continued, "You look terrible."

"Yes, Lady, there has been a battle. At Camlann," he said flatly.

Crierwy regarded him for a few moments and Bedwyr couldn't help shifting under her gaze. "Arthur?" she asked falteringly.

"I'm sorry," Bedwyr began.

She closed her eyes and sucked in a deep breath. "No," she whispered stumbling slightly as she grasped for a thick wooden pole close by.

Bedwyr slid awkwardly from the horse and strode quickly to where Crierwy stood and helped her regain her balance. He reached out for her hands and she, surprisingly, didn't object. He helped lower her, with the help of the guard, down onto a stool and they sat together for a while without speaking. When the guard moved away, she broke the silence. "How?"

"He was betrayed—"

She didn't let him finish the sentence. "He sent you? He must have been still alive when you left."

"Yes, Lady, but I fear he is not long for this life. He sent me to you to give you this," he said gesturing to the sword, Celeborn.

He took the sword from the linen cloth and passed it to her. "He is being taken to Iona. They hope that Muirgein can cure him but it is doubtful that anything can be done, even if he can make it to the sacred Avalon."

Crierwy nodded slowly. "My poor boy," she mumbled. Despite her pain she quickly composed herself, her dignity clear to see. "So much death," she said to herself. She cleared her throat. "Thank you for coming here, Bedwyr, and telling me. I can think of no one better than you. You were always a good boy... sorry," she stammered, "a good and honourable man."

Bedwyr flushed. "You give me great honour," he said.

She smiled sadly, sighed, and with great effort scrambled, none too elegantly, to her feet. "My bones become weary, Bedwyr," she said. "Anyway," she groaned, "come now, we have a solemn task to perform."

Bedwyr nodded and stood to follow her.

Crierwy beckoned to the squat, square, bearded man to prepare a coracle. He acknowledged her and duly dragged a coracle to the water's edge without any apparent effort. Bedwyr stepped into the craft and stretched out a hand to help Crierwy aboard. Once Crierwy had taken a seat, Bedwyr slowly and wordlessly pushed off. They laid Celeborn between them and Bedwyr rowed slowly towards the middle of the loch.

As they rowed, Bedwyr took in the magnificent sunset; the clouds were punctuated by holes through which the rays of the sun cast magical, ghostly lights that danced upon the surface of the water. When they had reached the middle, Crierwy instructed him to stop. Complete silence surrounded them. Along the shore the lights from Crierwy's settlement brightened as the day light faded. "Help me stand, Bedwyr," Crierwy said wearily, "and pass me the sword."

With the sword in her hand she called, "Kleena! I bring this gift to you as an offering from my son whose life's thread will soon be cut. Accept him to your bosom and bless his friend Bedwyr who has brought this offering to you."

Crierwy took a deep breath, and after a few moments of hesitation, she threw the sword in a high arc across the waters. It turned over once, and as it hit the surface, the blade caught the last rays of the sun before sinking immediately. For a moment the glare of the light blinded Bedwyr and it seemed to him as if a hand had reached up from the waters to catch the blade.

"Was that a hand I saw stretch out of the water and catch it?" he gasped.

"Now that would be a story, my dear Bedwyr." Crierwy smiled. "I've heard it said that water nymphs frequent this place so who knows. Now, come," she breathed, "let's go back to shore, our task is done. And you must be hungry."

He nodded his thanks. It was then that he saw an eagle soaring high in the sky. He watched it for a while until he heard, from somewhere deep in the forests surrounding the loch, a bear roaring. He couldn't help but smile.

Chapter 1

The Ashes of Deceit

The day had started brightly; the lands around the point of Tantallon had been drenched in early spring sunshine. Nonetheless, as the hours passed clouds had begun to bubble up in the west.

Taliesin wandered aimlessly through the encampment admiring the preparations but also soaked up the adulation from the attendees who had recognised him as the coming man in the bardic traditions. "It won't rain, brothers and sisters," he trilled as he noticed people gazing at the sky. There were looks of scepticism on the faces of those who acknowledged him but they reacted to him amiably enough.

Taliesin set himself down next to Crierwy who had found herself a comfortable spot beneath a handsome, if slightly wizened, oak tree. He sensed people staring at him and he felt a smug swelling in his chest. He was sitting with the most beautiful woman in all the kingdoms north of the Great Roman Wall of Hadrian. The envy directed at him spread like delicious warm waves washing over him. Crierwy pretended not to notice. She was acutely aware that they were celebrities, she a priestess and Taliesin the new King of Bards. She felt irritation at the people's looks and the way Taliesin reacted to them. It was something she had never really grown used to but being the Priestess of the Cauldron acted as a useful shield to protect herself from any unwanted attention.

The encampment was awash with rumours that the Lord Prince Aedan of Manau would be attending the night's festivities. Aedan had, on many occasions; made his interest in Crierwy very clear, despite the annoyance it gave Domelch, his wife. Crierwy had succeeded in deflecting his intentions but it was no simple matter keeping away from him.

Despite knowing this, Taliesin appeared oblivious to her concerns. As far as he was concerned, his very presence was enough to ensure her chastity. But Crierwy was all too aware that Beltane was a night when the rules of marriage and relationship were best described as relaxed, thus the festival of fire and fertility was guaranteed to be celebrated with total abandon.

Aedan's attendance at the feast made her anxious and she was tempted to leave but she understood that her absence would be remarked upon and would reflect poorly on her. Nonetheless, it nagged away at her that Aedan might take advantage of the chaos that would inevitably ensue once the shackles of propriety were shaken off. However, despite her nervousness she was confident she could and would rebuff him if necessary.

As the day wore on and the sky began to darken, the clouds began to clear as Taliesin had predicted. Aedan duly arrived with his entourage of a dozen warriors and a couple of servants. He slipped off his horse languidly and stretched his back and legs. Looking around at length, his eyes fell on Crierwy. To her surprise he simply nodded in her direction and then made his way towards one of the cauldrons where vegetables were being cooked. He peered inside and she could see he was savouring the smells and congratulating the women who were more than happy for this celebrity to taste the food. She barely noticed Taliesin chatting amiably to her about nothing in particular as she watched the scene.

After some minutes, Crierwy lost sight of Aedan and his followers and she felt able to relax, but to her surprise and no little annoyance, she felt a pang of disappointment. Perhaps she had been presumptuous and he had given up on her. Did she really feel rejection? "For goodness sake," she muttered irritably. She sighed, disappointed at her youthful arrogance and slapped her hip. Taliesin simply stared and after a pause continued his ramblings.

Large pots were dotted about the encampment and hanging over fires. Like the pot nearest to Crierwy, root vegetables were tossed in along with herbs and spices. The warm rich smells of the vegetables and freshly baked bread filled the air and added to the feelings of warmth and wellbeing that swept across the celebrations.

Just like the increasing volume of ale, the music too was intoxicating and people were standing and swaying in various states of reverie to the hypnotic drumming. Bards set to work on the growing number of people, telling stories of deeds from long ago. To no one's surprise, least of all hers, Taliesin became the primary contributor and centre of attention. Roars of approval met his poetry and stories.

The bonfires were lit by the time the last rays of the sun slipped below the horizon, creating an unworldly orange light over the growing throng. Excitement grew as the paddocks, where the animals were being kept, were being prepared to be opened. The restless cows circled and nudged into one another reminding Crierwy of roiling waters. They lowed pitifully at first but their anxiety grew as the bonfires flared and crackled about them and the people gathered more closely to their enclosures.

When the gates were finally opened the bellowing cattle were funnelled between the bonfires and guided through the camp and out towards the summer pastures. This was always a time of danger as the cows had been known to stampede and cause grievous harm to some of the more impetuous men who believed they could sidestep the oncoming rush.

But once the cows cleared the area, the younger men could concentrate on the fire leaping, the drumming becoming more incessant and intense, the dancing frantic in and around the birch trees. Men and women of all ages whipped themselves up into a frenzy in praise of the goddess of spring, Ostara.

The men scooped up the embers and rubbed them into their faces and over their bodies. Some of the more foolish younger men, urged on by their friends, practised fire walking to prove they had won the blessings of the ancestral spirits, believing themselves to be impervious to the scorching heat. Needless to say, as Crierwy grimaced, judging by some of the unearthly screams from some, it hadn't ended well. The stricken youngsters' more kindly friends dragged them away from the crowd and dowsed their feet with water and applied balm brought to the celebrations by those more experienced in the stupidities of drink.

The drinking continued apace, the conversation more animated, and carnal passions grew. People's natural reserve was being shed; young men and women danced naked without embarrassment or care. Suggestion became action and more and more people disappeared from the encampment and deep into the woods. Those with the last vestiges of control ran through the shadows scooping up festive greenery with the intention of decorating the nearby village, but whatever plans they had quickly gave way to lust.

Crierwy looked on. This was, she knew, when all red-blooded males were made Bel and every woman his divine consort Anna. Despite her self-control she felt a raging passion in her body, her blood felt as if it were on fire. Taliesin had disappeared and she was alone. She ached for company and someone to share the moment. She started to laugh hysterically, overtaken by the constant infectious drumming and lost to unbridled joy that overtook her. In her reverie, she hadn't noticed or even cared when someone covered in ashes sidled up to her. They danced together and he held her gently and then swung her around. She shrieked with joy and excitement as her feet left the floor as she was spun around faster and faster. "Stop!" she cried. "I'm going to be sick! Stop!"

The man slowed his spinning until he reached a gradual halt and they both fell to the grass laughing. She sighed loudly, feeling the dizziness subside only to be overcome by a different dizziness, a feeling of drunkenness but unlike anything she had experienced. His flattery touched her and she gladly allowed him to stroke her face, arms and shoulders. Crierwy's consciousness was slipping as the effect of the mixture of ale and the hallucinogens fed to her by this stranger began to take hold.

"Do I know you or are you a stranger?" she giggled. "Or perhaps…" she started looking at the stranger with a kind of awe. "Are you Bel? Have you come for me?"

He smiled and whispered, "Yes, if you want me to be."

Before she could stop herself, she blurted the words, "I do."

Her Bel smiled at her and picked her up in his arms before carrying her to a line of trees at the edge of the clearing. She could see all around them men and woman were in each other's arms, tearing at each other's clothing, having sex. No one cared that they were surrounded by other couples. Seeing others having sex, in twos and threes and more, excited her more.

But this man, Crierwy saw, acted differently from the others. He was gentle; he continued to stroke her face and hair, constantly reassuring her so that any doubts she may have had were banished completely. Slowly he slid his hand inside her linen dress, cupping and stroking her breasts. She didn't protest as he pulled up the hem of her dress and slid gently inside her. She moaned and sighed as his body rose and fell before he cried out, his body rigid as he climaxed. As his passion subsided he relaxed and lay on her for a few moments before gently rolling away. He lay to her side, leaning on his elbow, and continued to look into her eyes before running his hands through her long brown hair. She thought she recognised him but she surrendered herself to his hand caressing her shoulders and back. Slowly his hand drifted lower over her stomach and his fingers traced light patterns on the inside of her thighs before teasing her with his fingers. At first she sighed gently but as his fingers teased more urgently she gasped and called out in a silent scream of pleasure as the electricity of her orgasm passed through her.

She opened her eyes. She had no idea what time it was but she noticed that it was quieter now and she was only vaguely aware of laughing some distance away. She rolled over and sighed. She was grateful to find herself covered with a sheepskin; despite the onset of summer, there was still a slight chill in the air. She looked up into the cloudless skies and gazed at the stars. They were particularly bright and she marvelled at the grandeur of the night sky designed and built by the goddess Arianrhod herself. She couldn't help smiling broadly at the thought of being Anna and this man, who had held her so tenderly, her Bel. She knew when she awoke later she would realise her folly; after all, she was still a priestess. She sighed, but that was for later. She shuddered slightly, a little embarrassed that she had given into primeval and wonderful urges, a need to be wanted and desired. She reflected that her only discomfiture was she wasn't sure who had seduced her. She shook her head; it must have been Taliesin, and if it was, he certainly exceeded anything she could have hoped for. Perhaps it was some other handsome man? She laughed to herself and then thought of Aedan. He had probably found someone willing and she wouldn't see him again. She chuckled contentedly to herself and fell back into an easy, dreamless sleep.

It was just before the dawn when she became vaguely aware that her Bel was getting to his feet. She felt the weight of a sheepskin being repositioned over her. She sighed before rolling over and clutching the cloak tightly about her. After what might have only been ten minutes, she opened one eye and saw him, seemingly washed and talking to a group of men close by. She couldn't hear what they were saying but she didn't really care that much, but she concluded that her Bel was somebody of stature as the others appeared to be deferring to him.

Consciousness slowly returned to her and she focused much more closely on the man she had lain with. As she focused she felt a rising feeling of apprehension in her stomach. The man's stature, his voice, the way he stood and the clothes he now wore — it certainly wasn't Taliesin, she concluded, almost relieved, but then her throat constricted. No, it couldn't be, by all that was sacred, was it Aedan?

She was now alert and pushed herself up on to her elbow. Yes, she had been attracted to him, who wouldn't be, and flattered by his advances, but she had set herself against any relationship. And yet despite herself she had let her guard down in the reverie that was Beltane. Her fear increased when she absentmindedly started considering at what point of her cycle this had been. "Oh my sweet Ceredwin, oh glorious Arianrhod," she said quietly, "what have I done?" She knew that any woman who became pregnant at Beltane was destined to be blessed by the gods, but if she was pregnant, this didn't feel like a blessing, it was surely a nightmare. Her father would be livid, even murderous.

Laying back on her side, she flushed at the thought and felt the pangs of regret and guilt for Taliesin who she had cruelly betrayed a short few hours before. He had always been kind and attentive toward her and she had come to think that they would consummate their friendship and love for each other, probably here at Beltane. But she had been wrong; the man who she had lain with was none other than Aedan mac Gabrain, the Gorlasser, the Wily. She groaned. Yes, she should have refused him, but in that moment? She wasn't strong enough; she had been carried into the world of spirits and lust; she had been guided in this direction. Was it inevitable that she was always going to lie with Aedan? "Shit," she growled.

Aedan had fooled her; he had drugged her, surely. Her dizziness was not just drink and some hallucinogenic herbs or mushrooms, it was something else. She had been raped. Her stomach twisted. Aedan's reputation for being wily was well known. He had come to that place to have her and he had succeeded. She groaned inwardly; she had been deceived. At that moment Aedan turned to look at her but she shut her eyes and looked away to avoid any eye contact.

When she opened her eyes again she was sure she caught a smile on Aedan's face before he collected his horse and made his way out of the encampment. Crierwy lifted herself onto her elbow again and watched him go. Her certainty of being drugged was confirmed almost instantaneously as her head began to scream and she experienced waves of nausea. How on earth could he get up without any obvious discomfort and ride out as if he'd been out for an evening stroll? She continued to ponder but couldn't help thinking she didn't remember him ever actually drinking anything. *The sneaky bastard*, she thought.

Crierwy dressed in clothing appropriate of a priestess, and with her drum in hand, she walked from the encampment together with many others towards the cliffs to welcome the dawn.

Standing on the top of the cliffs at Tantallon, looking out to sea to watch the sun's rays strike the Bass Rock that May Day morning, Crierwy felt her stomach lurch and she knew at once that a new life quickened inside her. Swallowing hard, she scanned the crowd until she picked out Taliesin who was making his way gingerly towards her. She frowned when she noticed he was nursing a rather nasty looking bump on the head. When he reached her he smiled weakly and duly slumped down on the grass next to her and said nothing.

"Where were you?" she said quietly. "I was waiting for you," she went on.

"Sorry," he said eventually.

"What happened to your head? Did you drink too much?"

Taliesin sighed. "I had an encounter. Aedan's lackeys, I'll wager."

"They hit you?" she exclaimed.

"You could say that." Taliesin rubbed his head. "Let's say we had a disagreement over who I should be spending the celebrations with."

Crierwy felt another wave of nausea flow over her. She stared at him; there was a part of her that wanted to blame Taliesin for her dilemma but she knew she was being foolish and thought better of it.

She said no more. Instead, she stood up and wandered closer to the cliff's edge. She peered down at the rocks below, swallowing hard as she watched the waves crashing against the land far below them. Here was the chance to end this nightmare. She closed her eyes, just one step. Slowly she lifted her foot.

"Crierwy!" Taliesin said, alarmed. "You're too close to the edge."

"Oh, yes," she replied, stepping back from the abyss. "I was… miles away." She looked down again at the rocks and shuddered.

Moving away from the cliff's edge she picked up her drum, turned and moved away from the mass of people. Taliesin called after her but she ignored him and started to walk alone towards the sacred hill. The throbbing in Taliesin's head was too much to contemplate following and his shouts were quickly lost on the breeze. He rubbed his temples and flexed his neck muscles, sighed and lay back down on the grass, choosing to watch the people mill about.

It was a long walk to the sacred hill and the steep incline made her tired and short of breath. She saw a few hardy souls but it was early and most people were either sleeping off the night's rigours or watching the sunrise. At the summit, with her small drum, she sat on the grass and closed her eyes. She started to beat the drum slowly and rhythmically. She calmed her breath and began her journey. As she drifted downwards she called for her spirit allies to give her advice. Her spirit animal guide, a fox, met her and with a warm smile it guided her through thick heather, across seas, and brought her to a lake. It was a lake she had visited before and she recognised it as Llyn Tegid. As she approached the shoreline she saw, waiting for her, was her raven. With the raven she also saw a wolf cub, an eagle and the Salmon of Wisdom. They beckoned her over and she sat with them in comfortable silence looking out at the glass like waters of the lake. The silence stretched but she felt no pressure from her spirit companions. She enjoyed the peace and the serenity of the setting. Eventually she turned to the Raven and asked her question.

The wolf cub wobbled unsteadily over to her. She saw he was newly born and she smiled broadly as the animal stooped and licked her fingers. The wolf raised its head and she was surprised it was the cub and not the raven that responded. "I am familiar of the one you will come to know, the child you are carrying. I can assure you that I will be here, at your side, as your protector and confidant. I will also be here for your son, because that is what you will have at Imbolc, a boy," he said.

The raven nodded. "You will have this boy, dearest Crierwy but no other. He is destined to live long in memory but not in life."

Crierwy's eyes misted. "My only child and he will die young?"

"There is always a choice and nothing is preordained," the raven said, his tone kindly. "If your son chooses the life of priest and peace he will live a long life but will probably be lost to history, but if he chooses the warrior life he will be a hero whose name will echo through the ages, but he will die young."

"But I'll be his mother, can I not influence him?"

"There will be other voices, Crierwy, and they will be greater influences. It is for you to help the boy become a man. This is hard for you to hear, no parent should see their child die, but as you know, in these days this is often the way of things. Do not despair, Crierwy," the raven continued, "your path is written and you will be of great comfort to the child and too many others. The Salmon of Wisdom is with you."

At that the salmon jumped into her. She breathed hard and after recovering, she looked at the other spirit. "And what is this eagle?" she asked.

The eagle cocked its head to one side. "I will be one of your son's spirit guides. He will also have a bear to protect him. I will always be with him from the moment he is born into this world until he draws his last breath. He will always love you, Crierwy, and while he listens to your wise counsel he will overcome any challenge and defeat all before him. But he will be asked a lot of; people will grow to depend on him. You will not always be able to protect him and it will be your fate to outlive him." The eagle took on a serious demeanour. "One day he will look away from you and he will pay the consequences. You can try to dissuade him but be in no doubt he will walk his own path. His fate is his."

"Why me?" she sobbed. "Why should this fall on me and my son?"

"It is fate and only you are strong enough to bear this burden," the Eagle said.

She buried her head in her hands. The raven stepped forward as the other spirits faded from view. "You have asked if this child should be born and you have your answer. Your father will be angry but that anger will subside for he will never have his daughter harmed. You will help him. Choose to be set adrift to satisfy your father's pride. The winds will carry you to sanctuary and you will be safe but the boy must not be born there for events will be triggered that will shape his and your destiny."

"And what of Taliesin?" she asked.

"He will aid you when he is needed. But he has his own path and that path is not and cannot be alongside you. He will be forever remembered as the greatest of bards and poets. He will, I assure you, be content with that."

Crierwy's eyes misted and she fought back the bitter tears of regret and guilt but she couldn't quite hold back a giggle at the Raven's prophecy. The raven appeared to smile. "Dearest Crierwy, do not despair. Your guilt will pass and so will Taliesin's hurt. You are strong and you are a Priestess of the Cauldron, you will be the Lady of the Lake, and in that you will find strength and fulfilment through being chaste. You will be loved and respected; you will teach and bring solace to many as well as to yourself."

Her drumming changed tempo and she knew she had to leave. The raven enveloped her in his wings. He seemed three times bigger than he was just a few moments earlier. "Sleep now, all will be better when you awaken and then go and tell Taliesin."

Gradually she floated away from the lake and returned to her body.

When she returned to the cliffs, she found Taliesin in the same place she had left him. The crowds were thinning and she set herself down next to him and looked out over the sea, enjoying the stiff breeze that blew her long hair out behind her. She looked at him sleeping peacefully; he looked at ease, even happy, although the angry lump on his forehead looked a shade between black and blue. She made no attempt to wake him. She knew what she had to tell him would hurt him and it was possible she would lose him forever. Nonetheless, he was entitled to the truth before it became obvious she was with child. Telling Taliesin would be the hardest things she would ever do, but just as frightening, was her father's volcanic reaction to the news. She shuddered at the thought.

It was then that Taliesin stirred and noticed her return. It was time, she knew; she had to be strong.

Chapter 2

A Father's Wrath

Crierwy chose to stay in the vicinity of Tantallon. Distance, for the moment, was her ally.

The ultimatum from her father was delivered by a messenger but she refused to return to Eidyn despite all kinds of gruesome threats of death. Understandably, the messenger's expression at the thought of having to tell Clydno of his daughter's response was one of undisguised horror. Indeed the man had been close to tears. "But I have a wife and child to consider," he whined. Crierwy was sympathetic but remained committed to her course.

Her father's response was unsurprising but she was distressed nonetheless. Crierwy had hoped her father might be open to gentle persuasion from her mother and brother but being pregnant, she knew, placed her in mortal danger. She had learned from her brother that her father, Clydno Eidyn, in a pique of rage, had threatened to have her killed by having her thrown from the top of Dunpelder, such was his embarrassment at the news of the pregnancy. Her mother had talked Clydno down and sought to find an alternative which meant her husband accept a marriage of Crierwy to Taliesin who could then be passed off as the child's father.

There was also the small matter of Aedan's wife's family. Domelch's brother was Bridei, the King of the Picts, and he had come to hear of Aedan's duplicity and of Crierwy's pregnancy. Clydno's message had painted a pretty dire picture of Bridei's reaction. Crierwy could only conclude that there was a leak in her father's court. As a result of the rumours spreading throughout Lothian, there was mounting panic that Pictish forces were being mustered to attack the settlement if it could be proved that Crierwy was sheltering there.

Within the month, Eidyn's personal guard including her brother, Cynon, arrived at Tantallon. Cynon again urged her to marry Taliesin, but to his irritation, she continued to stubbornly refuse. "You know father cannot allow you to remain without a husband, carrying a child and all," he warned.

"And our mother?"

"She has no say in this, you know that," Cynon protested.

"Really? She introduced the idea of Taliesin marrying me. Anyway, brother, this child," she patted her belly, "was conceived at Beltane and you know what that means," she said pointedly,

"Then marry him, protect yourself and protect the child."

"You fail to understand, Cynon," she said. "I am the Priestess of the Cauldron, I cannot and I will not allow myself to be a mere possession of a man, no matter his status. I am chaste. I have committed myself to this path and marrying to save the embarrassment of others is unacceptable to me."

Cynon sighed and dragged his hand through his long hair. He sat and studied her for a while. He looked tired, Crierwy noticed. But after what seemed like an age Cynon nodded wearily. "You know I will not let anything happen to you both… Father, too, despite his anger, wants no harm to come to you although he feels he must be seen to be making an example of you. So… we must come up with a plan of sorts."

"Set me afloat," Crierwy said evenly.

"Set you afloat?" he replied, his voice climbing a couple of octaves. "The sun has affected you, me thinks, you cannot be thinking straight, sister?"

"Trust me, Cynon," Crierwy said, cutting him off.

Cynon sighed deeply. "I know your power, Crierwy, but do not risk all; there must be another way. Too many people have depended on the gods to protect them and it invariably does not turn out well. The Christian's nailed god can attest to that."

She shrugged. "Just set me off on the morning tide."

"And what then?"

"The tides will take care of that. I will return to the mainland in January to give birth," she said confidently.

Cynon sighed again and shook his head. "You are not sound of mind, I don't like it, there has to be another way. Perhaps I can hide you."

"Hide me," she repeated. "Cynon, do not argue with me on this, please, do as I say."

Cynon stood and kicked the ground in frustration. He looked at the sky as if he was looking for some divine intervention. Eventually, he looked at her. "Fine," he said moodily, "but I do this under protest, your death will not rest easy on me."

Crierwy smiled with relief. "Thank you, brother. And… I must ask you one more favour."

Cynon's eyebrows arched. "What now?" he grunted.

"Find me somewhere where I can find give birth to my son, Cynon?" she asked. "The child must be born on the mainland, it is what I want."

Cynon nodded. "Very well… We do have kinsmen living on Loch Leven," he offered. "I warn you, though, he is a Christian but I am confident he will keep you safe in his community."

"How can you be so sure?"

"They're Christians, it's what they do." He shrugged.

She smirked. "I suppose so. Who is this man, what's his name?" Crierwy asked.

"Serwan, son of Cedig. He is known as Serf. A cousin of sorts."

"If you can get his agreement, so be it." She smiled.

The following morning was bright and seagulls swooped and screamed above them. Cynon said nothing to his sister as she climbed aboard the coracle and she was pushed out into the current by Clydno's retainers. The coracle was caught in a current and she was quickly whisked away. Cynon watched Crierwy being dragged away but showed no outward sign of emotion. He pinched the bridge of his nose and beckoned his men to follow him away from the beach. He looked back briefly but he could no longer see her. Would he ever see her again? Despite Crierwy's confidence of last night he very much doubted it.

Crierwy could feel the panic now as the coracle was whisked along by the tide off the coast of Tantallon and out into open water. Suddenly the shore looked a long way away. Her doubts and fear increased. This was surely a challenge to her faith, would she be another soul lost to the folly of hope over experience? But surely her guides would not put her in harm's way, but her predicament suddenly felt so hopeless and she had to fight to hold back the tears that threatened to overwhelm her.

    She gritted her teeth and prayed to any god that would listen. When she opened her eyes again she could see that the tide was draining out of the river's mouth and began to hope that the coracle might, just might, float towards the Isle of Eilean Mhaigh or the Isle of May as the inhabitants had renamed it. The coracle tossed and spun around in the strong currents. Without anything to paddle the coracle with, she could only rely on the interventions of the gods. She closed her eyes and called on her spirits to help her. Just then, she became aware of a different sound. She looked up and made out the shape of a raven as it flew in a circular motion above the vessel and squawked loudly. It swooped down and landed on the edge of the coracle and looked at her intently. She reached out a hand to it, but it flew away, although it continued to fly close to the tiny craft as if it were keeping her company.

    As she watched the bird climbing and then swooping, Crierwy noticed a number of fishing boats perhaps half a mile away towards the centre of the channel. Despite the rolling of waves she was able to stand up after a fashion and wave to them. The raven, she saw, flew towards the boats and flapped around them, drawing the fishermen's gazes in Crierwy's direction.

    After what felt an eternity, they spotted her and one of the vessels started to tack towards her. She wasn't safe yet and she was conscious that the coracle was inherently unstable in open water. She could feel a sourness rise in her throat as the spinning vessel made her stomach churn.

    The fishing craft tried to pull alongside and a man threw a rope to her which she gathered at the second attempt. "Tie it to something in your craft," the man shouted. The craft closed quickly then and eventually pulled alongside and the man carried her over to his boat.

    "Thank you, thank you," she gasped.

    "What are you doing out here?" a younger man said.

    "She has been set adrift," the older man said.

    "Why would someone do that?

    "It isn't our business, boy."

The young man was ready to protest but Crierwy smiled and admitted to being pregnant. "It's... complicated," she said.

She had been saved. The two men agreed to take her to the isle. The raven continued to squawk overhead in what sounded like triumph.

"What is a raven doing way out here?" the younger fisherman said. "I've never seen that before."

The older man, who Crierwy had concluded was, most probably, an older relative, possibly the father, nodded toward her. "I have a feeling that our raven friend might be something to do with our passenger."

Crierwy smiled and shrugged. "It seems to have brought me luck," she said.

The man then bowed. "It is an honour to meet the Lady Crierwy," he said.

"You know me?" she asked, surprised. "How?"

"Let's say a little bird told me." He smiled. "Your beauty has not been exaggerated, Priestess." Crierwy looked suddenly nervous. "Don't worry, you are among friends here." He smiled.

Crierwy relaxed. "Thank you," she whispered.

"When will the child be born?" he asked.

"Imbolc."

"Ah, a Beltane child."

"Yes," she sighed. "The day my life changed forever."

"So it would seem. I take it that your father took umbrage and the father has escaped all the consequences?"

"We women may have some powers but in these matters, the man holds all the advantages," she snorted.

The man nodded. "I would apologise, Lady, but my apology would be rather hollow."

Crierwy smiled weakly. "It is not for you to apologise for men as a whole."

He shrugged. "So, Lady, you look for sanctuary at the Isle of May?"

"I hope it will provide safety," Crierwy said.

"No one will hear anything from me; my wife would skin me alive if I were to betray you and your child."

Crierwy nodded slowly. "Thank you."

"You should rest, Priestess," he said pointing to land in the near distance. "We should be there within the hour."

Crierwy had no choice but to put faith in the fisherman. She realised that this was a risk, after all she had never met him before, but her instincts told her that this man and his family could be trusted. Once she had been safely deposited on the Isle of May she had asked him to seek out her brother and Taliesin. Cynon, she knew, would have returned to Eidyn. The man was, understandably, sceptical, particularly when Crierwy made clear that he should speak to no one except Cynon. But despite his anxieties, he had accepted gracefully, persuaded no doubt by the likelihood of some sort of reward.

As the summer wore on Crierwy felt more secure. She was treated as a celebrity by all those who lived or sought refuge on May, and to her embarrassment she was not expected to contribute anything to the chores. Nonetheless, she had insisted on contributing to the cooking and the cleaning of eating implements after each meal. She enjoyed the serenity of the place and lived happily and comfortably alongside the women who came and went.

It wasn't until the September with the autumn chill coming that Cynon had arrived on the isle. As it was a women's sanctuary, he had not been allowed to come beyond the shoreline. So, it was there that he warmly hugged his sister in a makeshift hut that was constructed for male relatives. They shared tears and he confided how he thought he would never see her again. He recounted his meeting with Adnan, the fisherman. Crierwy was embarrassed that she didn't know the fisherman's name and she realised she never even thought to ask him. Cynon laughed at her discomfort. As she had hoped, Cynon had rewarded the man generously.

Crierwy shared food with her brother brought to them by the settlement's elders. The senior woman had welcomed Cynon and was delighted by money he had offered the settlement for the upkeep of the isle's homesteads. Crierwy and Cynon spoke at length about plans for the new year and her return to the mainland in January. Cynon had approached

Serf as soon as he had known of her safety and he had been very happy to help in any way that he could.

"What about Mother and Father?" she asked.

"I did confide in Mother," he admitted, "and I left it with her to… choose the right moment to tell Father of your safety. Your whereabouts, I did not share."

She nodded. "It's for the best."

"Have you thought of a name?" Cynon enquired, pointing to her swelling belly."

"No, not yet."

"Pregnancy suits you," he said, smiling, "You're… glowing. Dare I say, you're even more beautiful now than before, if that was possible."

She slapped his knee. "Shut up, you're embarrassing me."

"I'm your brother I can say these things, after all you clearly share my good looks so I also compliment myself,".

"How humble you are, brother," she chided.

As the day was coming to close, Cynon left to ensure he caught the tide to return to Eidyn. He had chosen not to mention that Morcant of Bryneich had sought and had been given refuge after the Angles had defeated the armies of Bryneich and Morcant was exiled. That was for another day.

As Cynon made his way to the water's edge he was greeted by Adnan. Adnan's smile spread across his craggy fence as he waved to Crierwy.

"Adnan!" she cried and ran to him, embracing him tightly. "Have you been waiting here all this time?"

"Yes, but it matters not. I'm not allowed to come beyond the shoreline."

"Thank you," she said, her tears flowing. "I owe you so much," she continued.

"It was my very great honour. Be well, my Lady, that wee baby inside of you will be reward enough."

Chapter 3

The Birth of a Prince

Crierwy was sad to leave. She had been royally looked after by the women of the isle. They had tried to persuade her to stay but her mind was made up. She had been told by the spirits that she had to leave. It was her fate.

In those last few days, Taliesin had, unbidden, joined her on the isle. It needed delicate negotiations for him to remain in the visitors' cottage on the waters' edge. He was also placed under strict instructions not to walk more than twenty paces from the shore and any needs had to be seen to by Crierwy herself. It was not ideal, as the hut faced east and out into the open sea, leaving it open to the weather, but it served.

Crierwy had not seen him since being cast off on that May morning from Tantallon. He had said little and reacted even less after Crierwy had told him of what happened at the Beltane festival. She thought she had seen tears welling in his eyes but he had looked away before she was sure. So she was surprised when she entered his tiny dwelling. She smiled at him and tentatively held out her hands. Her heart almost burst when he held out his hands in response and pulled her towards him. Tears flowed freely from both of them and though she felt the need to explain, and apologise, he simply put a finger to her lips and shook his head.

Crierwy, Taliesin and a young oarsman left the Isle of May in a small coracle barely large enough for its precious cargo. The sun was setting in the west; the tide would be with them. Crierwy, heavy with child, was frozen to the bone. Despite being wrapped in layers of animal skins, she grimaced as she bowed into the stabbing wind sweeping across the river estuary. She felt as if broken glass was raking her face and eyes as she peered into the mid distance. As her misery grew bitter tears fell from her eyes.

Taliesin looked on; it was almost too painful to bear as he watched her struggles. He had learned to accept that his love for her could never be. He fought to overcome his feelings as he leant in closer, pulling her into him and wrapping his arm around her shoulders.

Crierwy looked at him and smiled without any emotion.

"We will be back on land again soon," he said without conviction.

"If we live," she groaned. "If we live."

"Have faith," Taliesin said. "There is a reason for everything and everybody. There is a path laid out for you and the child, although," he looked about him, "the time of year was an unhappy error."

Crierwy shrugged, unconvinced, but deep inside she knew he was right; there was a purpose to all this although, here in the middle of the blackness, it was difficult to see it. She felt miserable and it was freezing, they were surrounded by swirling waters and the world seemed so far away. She wanted to pull away from Taliesin; she was asking too much of him. It wasn't fair; he didn't deserve any of this. But despite herself she remained close to him and shared his body heat. She sighed and tried to let sleep take her but the same question kept percolating into her brain and yet there was still no answer. Why?

Taliesin turned to the oarsman. "What do you think? When will we land?"

The oarsman said nothing for a few moments but then he turned slowly towards him, a look of sympathy spreading across his face. "I can only suggest, sir, that you keep well wrapped up, this will take some time. But if we do maintain this speed, I believe we could… will," he corrected, "land at first light. You both have the ear of the gods so start talking to them. For now let's hope the wind stays in our favour."

"I think I preferred you quiet and moody," Taliesin said, arching an eyebrow.

The oarsman grinned and silently returned to his rowing. "Let's hope Cliodhna, the goddess of the water, is with us this night," he muttered.

The darkness was now impenetrable, and they could see nothing but the water about the coracle. It felt as if they were bobbing in the western oceans rather than tracking across the Forth. Every so often Taliesin thought he could see lights across the estuary but chose to say nothing rather than raising Crierwy's hopes. So they drifted in silence, the sound of oars permeated by the occasional curse as the cold bit.

Crierwy couldn't sleep as a constant fear gripped her. She unconsciously bent down and rubbed her swollen belly, offering words of reassurance to the unborn child inside her. The child would be born in the next couple of weeks and Crierwy was still to name him. And yes it would be a him, she knew it would be, after all it had been foretold, even Taliesin had said so before they set off. Perhaps she should call him Gwyn, Taliesin's childhood name, or after the boy's father, but then again, Aedan or even Uther might draw people's attention to the poor child.

She stared into the nothingness and as her head turned, her gaze fell on the young oarsman. She hadn't paid much attention to him up until now as she was too wrapped up in her own misery. She couldn't help thinking how young he looked to be rowing them through the blackness; he was just a boy. All she could make out was a shock of red hair sticking out from under the boy's hood. How could a boy be tasked with guiding them to the northern shore? Their eyes briefly met, and he looked away, embarrassed. She then glanced at Taliesin hunched to her left, and laughed gently when she realised he had fallen asleep. The boy too, noticing her reaction, chuckled but immediately stopped himself when he realised she had turned her eyes towards him once again.

She smiled at his embarrassment and offered him as reassuring a look as she could. She was certain that if there were any light to see by, she would see his face turning as red as his hair.

"What's your name?" she asked eventually through her shivers.

He looked at her nervously, unable or unwilling to hold her gaze. "Arthmael, Lady," he stuttered.

"Arthmael," she repeated. "Does it mean anything? It is not a name I have heard before."

Arthmael paused a moment before responding. "My mother wanted to name me after a bear and she also wanted me to be a warrior. As you can see, I'm no bear or a warrior, at least, not yet, so I have concluded, Lady, it is more likely that she called me a bear because she always used to say that all babies look like bear cubs."

His face was now a blazing fire and he thought that diving into the frigid waters would be more preferable than having to contend with such embarrassment. He swallowed hard and tried to console himself that she couldn't see him anyway. He hoped that the conversation had come to an end, but his heart sank when Crierwy continued.

"A bear cub," she mused. "Hmm, that's nice. I expect she is very proud of you in anticipation of your promotion to warrior."

"I… I hope so but I still haven't done anything that marks me as a warrior, certainly nothing brave," he stammered.

"And yet here you are, rowing into the blackness. I think that's brave. Aren't you frightened? I certainly am."

"Life is very hard, Lady. There are bigger dangers lurking around every corner I, and my family, have to face than the moods of the river and sea."

She nodded. "I suppose so." She sighed. "Still, I hope that you and your family will prosper, and keep safe," she said in a kindly voice.

"Thank you, Lady. You are very kind."

Arthmael returned to the task of rowing and Crierwy understood the conversation to be at an end.

In the silence her mind wandered back to the Beltane celebrations, the beating drums, the drink, the attention of a man, the sweetness of lovemaking and the anger of betrayal. She sighed, drawing her knees up to her chest and resting her head on them. As she dozed her mind drifted to the time she was cast off at Tantallon. It was something she dreamt about often, the fear she felt followed by the relief that she had survived. She had been warmly welcomed by the women of May and she was taken care of, safe from the ills of the world. And yet here she was, in the middle of a huge blackness, trusting in a man, or more accurately a boy, she had never met, trying to find the shore of the Forth, and by some good luck, if they survived, to be met by Serf, a man she didn't know, and whisked away to an island in the middle of Loch Leven to live among a group of Christians for who knew how long. Christians! And she, a Priestess of the Cauldron.

She blew out her cheeks but for the first time in many hours she genuinely smiled at the irony. At last, she slept.

When Crierwy awoke she could see that the morning light had begun to lift the gloom; she could see the riverbank just some fifty paces away. Taliesin was awake and speaking to Arthmael in hushed tones. She chose to keep herself to herself, preferring not to engage in any conversation. Instead, she silently offered up her thanks to the goddess Cliodhna. They would be safe, for now.

They crossed a very small bay, rounded a promontory and smoothly ran ashore on to a small stony beech, the coracle's bottom scraping loudly against the stony surface. Arthmael bounded from the small craft with unexpected grace and held the coracle still to let his valuable cargo climb out and scramble up the shingle. He secured the craft before unloading a number of personal possessions stowed under skins.

Crierwy sat down on the stones feeling a little unsteady as her body got used to the solidity of the ground. She had decided that after two voyages her sea legs were never going to be good enough to regularly partake in any kind of lake or river trip again. She was not, she reflected, likely to be a lady of any sort of lake.

Taliesin stood some minutes in conversation with Arthmael and there was an exchange of reward and thanks. Arthmael bowed and nodded towards Crierwy and returned to the boat. She smiled and waved, and he acknowledged her with a sheepish grin. He climbed aboard and cast off. She watched him row out into the main flow of the river and gradually pull away towards the opposite shore before navigating eastward. She continued to watch him until he faded from view. "Thank you, young man, and take care," she whispered into the morning mists.

As the morning brightened, the mist thinned and an easterly breeze brought with it a bitterness that cut to the bone. She shivered and pulled the animal skins tightly around herself. Taliesin, meanwhile, was busying himself gathering dry sticks for kindling to light a fire to help keep them warm until Serf arrived to take them to Loch Leven. She smiled at him, realising that he had little idea what he was doing. Nonetheless he was being kind and would do anything for her. She sighed and felt a huge sadness weigh heavy on her and a weariness that felt as if it touched her very soul.

She lay back against a bolder and surveyed her surroundings.

Despite it being a Christian community there were no priests. Serf acted as the community leader and spiritual guide. It occurred to Crierwy that Serf looked rather regal, tall, clean shaven with a dark complexion. Crierwy thought there might be some Roman there but she could also see a passing resemblance to her father. The isle had been named after Serf himself and was quite open to the elements. It must have been about fourteen or fifteen hectares in size and generally flat with a raised area to the south west of the isle where an altar of sorts stood. It was there that the community gathered each day to give praise to the Christian God.

Serf's community consisted of some twenty adults, five older children, two children of two years and two more of a few months. Serf had assured them that at least three of children had been born in the settlement, which reassured Crierwy that there were women on the isle who had experience of birthing.

Crierwy made herself useful and helped with the cooking and cleaning, although she was always ushered away to rest by the other women. Her favourite companion was a woman who Crierwy thought must be in her mid to late forties, known as Aeronwen. The lines on Aeronwen's face and her snow white hair told their own story of struggle. "I never used to be this white you know," she would say. "I saw a ghost! Over there on the mainland by the boats on the shingle."

"Don't listen to her," Serf would say through his laughter.

"I did, I tell you. Completely white. A man standing motionless, staring at me with emotionless eyes, accompanied by an eagle and a bear."

Although Crierwy couldn't help smiling, she was also troubled. Were Aeronwen's ramblings real, had she really seen a vision? Or was she losing her faculties? Nevertheless, she couldn't ignore the reference to the eagle and the bear.

January passed and her belly grew. She felt as if she might explode at any moment. Worse still the baby was lying on a nerve which practically stopped her from walking any distance. The baby constantly kicked and Crierwy stared in wonder at her belly rising and falling, resulting from the constant storms being summoned up by the child within. The other children gathered around her laughing uproariously at the spectacle, which both humoured and annoyed Crierwy. But to Aeronwen's credit she would intervene and shoo them away in a kindly but perfunctory manner.

Crierwy spirits rose when Cynon finally arrived; she had missed him and was relieved that he would be there when her child was born. She was apprehensive but her brother's arrival allowed her to happily retire early to her bed. Aeronwen joined her in amiable company. "The child will come tomorrow, I'm sure," she said cheerfully. "A fine boy I would say."

Crierwy sighed. "Oh I do hope so, I am going to explode if not," she said, gritting her teeth through a contraction.

"You felt a pain?" Aeronwen asked.

"Yes," Crierwy said.

"Have you had other such pains?"

Crierwy nodded.

"And are they coming more often?"

"Definitely," groaned Crierwy.

"Ah ha," Aeronwen said triumphantly. "I will prepare to receive the child. I will heat plenty of water so that the child can be born in water. At this time of year, the waters of the lake are far too cold. I don't know what Christians do, I have never held to their ways."

Crierwy gasped through another contraction. "I thought—"

"No, my lovely." Aeronwen smiled. "They're good people, their beliefs are strong and their hearts are in the right place but they are… just misled. Come, my Lady, let's greet a new hero to our world."

Crierwy could not remember how long it took, it felt like days, but at dawn after a final epic push, the child slipped from her and into the arms of a delighted Aeronwen.

"A boy!" she announced excitedly before resting the screaming child on the mother's belly. She used a damp cloth to wipe the sweat from Crierwy's face and chest and then the blood and gore from the child, finally wrapping them both in sheepskins.

"Aye, he's a healthy looking boy and good lungs on him. Well done, my darling girl."

"Never again," Crierwy groaned.

"We all say that. I did and I have six! It gets easier, you know."

"I'm starting to believe what they say about your sanity," Crierwy groaned

Aeronwen smiled. "The difference between sane and insane is a very fine line."

Crierwy fell silent; she could only look into her son's eyes. He had stopped crying now and stared back at her without blinking.

"Well, well," Aeronwen exclaimed with a huge smile. "Look at that, the little one has gone quiet. I was going to suggest Leolin or Llewellyn for his name. A fine lion's roar and a fine name for a hero."

"Llewellyn," Crierwy repeated.

Crierwy's mind drifted as exhaustion threatened to overcome her. Her mind drifted back to her adventures on the Forth, that bitter night just a week or so ago. She recalled the shy young man, Arthmael. She also recalled other men whose name included Arth, a word for bear, from the stories she had been told from the south of Britannia. As she looked at her son, those grey eyes so large and a stare so intense, she remembered the mixture of bear cub and warrior Arthmael's mother had wished for him. Arthmael might never become a warrior, in fact it seemed remote, but who knew. Nonetheless, he had been kind to her. He may have been silent for the most part, but reassuring nods and smiles coupled with his apparent confidence in their safety had left her feeling stronger.

Surely bravery and kindness would, in this world of struggle, triumph over hate and cruelty. Her son, she was sure, would prove that. Would he be the example people needed to show how hope would ultimately triumph over fear and envy? And yet, she reflected, how could this tiny soul, with a heart of gold and purity, withstand life's setbacks and hurt? Could she protect him? Would his heart, one day, be broken and become cold?

Tears flowed from her eyes and rolled down her cheeks. What would become of this child? Her son, yes, but also the son of a prince who could become a king. Aedan 'Uyther' mac Gabrain always got what he wanted; the child in her arms was an example of that. And one day, he would come calling; he will want her son to be by his side. Despite being a bastard, her son would not remain in the shadows as a page and Aedan would know that. *The father of a son conceived at Beltane, protected by the gods and goddesses — Aedan will understand the importance of this and he will use it to his benefit.* "My poor little boy," she whispered to the child.

She looked up and saw Aeronwen staring at her. "Are you all right, my lovely? You seem too sad for a new mother, the sickness of some women is something I did not expect of you."

Crierwy smiled tightly. "I'm sorry, Aeronwen, I was thinking of what life had in store for this tiny mite. He doesn't deserve to be faced with the pain of living."

Aeronwen smiled and sighed. "None of us know what will come to pass. As his mother all you can do is make your time with him happy. The gods determine the reason why all of us are here and what our role will be. For me, I have my children, I deliver children, and I'm sure, I have or will deliver a child of greatness. Perhaps it is this child who I have brought into this world this very night who will have greatness thrust upon him. He has his purpose and how that will transpire can only be supported by you, never stopped, no matter how powerful you are or will become. Your life's purpose has either already been achieved with this boy or there is much more to come." Aeronwen smiled and continued, "But I suspect there is more to come. You will touch many lives, none more so than this child."

"You speak with great wisdom, Aeronwen." Crierwy smiled sadly.

"We are all more than we seem," she responded with an amused look.

Crierwy was puzzled by her words but let them pass and stretch into the ether. There was a thin frost on the grass and she was becoming cold. Aeronwen taught her to feed the child and guided her to her hut. "You sleep, my lovely," Aeronwen said kindly. "I will look after the little boy."

"No." Crierwy started to protest.

Aeronwen raised her hand. "Sleep, you will need it. This will be the last decent sleep you will have for a while."

"Oh, all right," Crierwy replied reluctantly. She was indeed too tired to argue. "Thank you, you are a very special woman."

"As are you." Aeronwen smiled.

Crierwy stroked the boy's head and retired to her bed and fell into a very deep and dreamless sleep.

Aeronwen sat through the small hours, cooing at the little bundle. "Now, little man, what shall we call you?" she said as she gently touched the end of his nose and stroked his cheek. "Llewellyn is a grand name, or perhaps Arthfael or Bradan or Nuallan; that means noble or famous you know. Your mama likes a name with Arth, me thinks. Do you know that little ones all start out as bears? True or not," she laughed, "the very idea is a fine thing."

It was light when Crierwy groaned sleepily and rolled onto her side and looked out of her doorway. Seeing Aeronwen, she swung her legs off the cot and yawned before calling out, "Good morning and thank you for looking after the baby."

"You can't call him that forever," Aeronwen admonished. "In fact the two of us have been having a long discussion about it."

"I don't doubt it." She grinned. "I'm not completely deaf."

"Earwigging is very rude."

"Hmmm."

"Would you like to hear our list?"

Crierwy stood and bent as she left her lodgings. Straightening, she leant against the stone wall. "Please, no, I'm not sure my sanity will hold that long... Anyway, I know what to call him."

"Really! And?" Aeronwen said impatiently.

"Arthur... He will be called Arthur," Crierwy announced triumphantly. "That will be his name. And I will hide him from the world and he will grow up safe and sound and no one will ever hurt him."

Aeronwen gazed at the younger women and smiled. A mother's love was the strongest and the most certain but her smile faded, as did Crierwy's. "Of course," she said as kindly as she could.

"Let me have this time to dream?" Crierwy said sadly.

"I sense, my lovely, that this idyllic place will not be your haven for long. You will need to be strong, be ready, and pray. I have seen it in my dreams." She turned back to Arthur. "So much will be expected of you, my precious little man."

Chapter 4

The Rise of Morcant Bwlch

Cynon had, with considerable help from his mother, calmed his father. Crierwy was now safe for now. Her mother, Goleudydd, was the sister of Lluan, Aedan's mother and whilst, dynastically, this should have been a favourable coupling, Aedan's wife, Domelch, and the mother of his children, was the sister of Bruide, King the Picts. This was a headache for Clydno but whilst it was discomforting, his own power base was secure because Bruide's eyes were elsewhere. Bruide was concerned with the 'Scorcher', Gabrain mac Domangart, Aedan's father. The Scots were considered a threat and the Picts, in response, had become increasingly aggressive towards them.

Clydno was, however, not complacent. A bigger concern was the growing power of the Angles who had taken control of Bernicia, formerly known to the Britons as Bryneich. Morcant, a prince of Bryneich, had sought and been given sanctuary in Clydno's court having been exiled from Bernicia, but he was far from happy at his lot and constantly called on Clydno to support him in retaking his ancestral lands, but without success. Clydno had no desire to poke the lion that was the Angles. He could, probably, hold them with the support of his powerful neighbour, the Gododdin, but to embark on an offensive campaign was unlikely to succeed.

Morcant, Clydno realised, might become troublesome, but he had chosen to keep him at arm's length, instead ensuring Morcant was made more than comfortable and treated with honour.

Morcant was a man in his early thirties, of dark complexion, well-groomed and bearded as was the custom. He was dower, arrogant and angry. Of average height, there was nothing else to notice about him except for his pale blue eyes that were as cold and soulless as he was. He had clearly benefitted from good living in both Bryneich and now in Lothian and was, as a result, a little thickset. Morcant was a driven man and had little time for his elders and so called wiser counsellors. To his advantage, he could claim familial ties to Coel Hen which gave him an authority that, many would argue, afforded him more respect and stature than he deserved. The Angles, however, were less than complimentary about him.

Cynon, who was some ten years younger, had been tasked by his father with managing Morcant, for managing was the only way it could be described. He had spent hours eating, drinking and hunting for boar with Morcant while constantly and patiently explaining his father's challenges to him. But despite outwardly acknowledging Cynon's words, Morcant remained unmoved; courteous certainly, but unyielding, nonetheless.

Morcant had not come alone to Clydno's court; he had been accompanied by a dozen retainers. It was an open secret that in the dark corners of Clydno's fortress they plotted and dripped poison into the ears of anyone prepared to listen or believed to be sympathetic to the struggles and injustices suffered by Morcant. But as time passed, more and more of Clydno's nobles warmed to Morcant and his cause of winning back Bryneich and evicting the dreaded and hated Angles. Cynon was aware of these feelings and continued to feed information to his father who appeared oblivious to what was, to Cynon's growing alarm, a growing and real threat.

News that Clydno was again to be a grandfather was met by a self-satisfied snort from Morcant when he was told by Cuimin, one of his retainers, in one of many meetings out of sight of prying eyes and ears. "The child will be a bastard then?" Morcant sneered.

"Yes, Lord, that is what's being said. The father's identity is not known but it is said that it might be Aedan mac Gabrain." Cuimin grinned. "Officially, however, I'm told the story being put out for public consumption is that the bard Taliesin is the father, and he will marry the king's daughter."

"But it's a smokescreen?" Morcant put in.

"So it would seem, Lord."

Morcant nodded with satisfaction. "Time to spread the rumours of how disreputable and sleazy the king and his family have become, me thinks. The Pictish King Bruide and his daughter will be most interested in this information." Morcant paused. "Fine, go send word to Bruide. A family rift might be very helpful to us, as will an alliance when the time comes."

As the weeks passed Morcant's mood lifted even more. He was delighted when news arrived that Gabrain had been defeated in battle by Bruide's Picts. It was rumoured that Gabrain had been badly wounded, and his time was short.

"Well, my friends," Morcant grinned, "it would appear the gods are smiling on us."

"What do you have planned, Lord?" Cuimin asked.

"I am told that Cynon will be traveling east to, so I'm led to believe, Loch Leven where his sister and nephew are said to be in hiding." He looked around and paused for effect. "There is enough support now for us to re-establish Bryneich here on the Rock of Eidyn."

"Can we be sure?" Cuimin asked?

"Ruairdri, step forward. Tell Cuimin here what you know," Morcant urged.

"Lord, we can rely on five if not six of the king's battle warriors. They believe that Clydno has become weak out of his love for his daughter. They also believe his head has been turned by this Christ God."

"They will rise with us?" asked Cuimin. "And what of Cynon?"

"I think we can rely on Bruide to deal with the leech Cynon and yes, if the conditions are right."

Cuimin sighed and shrugged. "Conditions?"

"What ails you, Cuimin?" Morcant queried, his anger rising.

"Lord, Clydno has been gracious towards us. Let us call for a round table."

"That time is gone," Morcant snapped. "Your concern is noted, and the conditions will be right." Morcant stared at his man fiercely before saying, "Your doubts trouble me, Cuimin. Can I guarantee your fealty, Cuimin?"

Cumin paused, too long, Morcant thought, but he responded in the affirmative. "Yes of course, Lord, always."

Morcant smiled and nodded to Ruairdri. Before Cuimin could react, he felt a blade slide into the base of his spine. Cumin dropped to his knees, his face contorted with surprise and excruciating agony. Blood dribbled from his mouth. Morcant drew his sword and plunged it deep into Cuimin's chest. Cuimin fell forward and on to his side. Satisfied, Morcant smiled and removed his sword and wiped the blade with the hem of Cuimin's tunic.

There was a stunned silence. Cuimin had friends among the ranks of men and Morcant knew it. He turned and looked at the faces of his retainers and announced, "This is what happens if I am undermined and betrayed. Now... does anyone else doubt me?"

He looked at their faces; some stared at the floor, but no words were uttered. Morcant tapped his sword against a rock that protruded from the ground next to him. This time he said quietly but with cold venom, "I said does anyone else doubt me?" There was a complete and deafening silence, but everyone shook their heads.

"Good."

It was dawn when Cynon mounted his horse and set off from Eidyn to meet up with Crierwy at Serf's Isle on Loch Leven. Winter was still upon the countryside and the trees were still bare. A white blanket of frost covered the rolling hills.

He enjoyed breathing in the cool air and riding alone. The solitude he now enjoyed was a joy. He had felt suffocated and there was always a stench of treachery in his nostrils, so leaving the intrigue at court behind him was a relief. He was particularly pleased, even overjoyed, that his task of managing Morcant could be set aside for a week or two. Nonetheless he could not rid himself of a nagging feeling of foreboding that lingered in his chest.

Yet, despite Morcant's constant malevolent discontent, his father did not appear to feel threatened by him. Cynon had advised his father of his worries, only to be pacified as if he were a child without a favourite toy, and urged to visit his sister. To Cynon's consternation, Clydno had announced that he would, as a sign of confidence, go boar hunting with

Morcant while Cynon was away. "Are you sure that is wise?" Cynon had said.

"You are like your mother," he chided. "You worry too much."

"He's dangerous, Father," Cynon warned.

"He's all mouth, my boy, I will have men around me."

His mother nodded reassuringly and pushed into his baggage a gift of a bonnet for her grandchild. And at that the conversation was terminated. Cynon shrugged at the memory and sighed audibly into the morning mist.

Since Cynon's departure, the weather had been set fair and Clydno was feeling buoyant and excited at the thought of hunting. Morcant appeared less irascible and seemingly more accepting of his exile than at any point since his arrival at court. He remained confident in dismissing his son's words of warning.

At breakfast Morcant had spent a lot of time talking cheerfully to Queen Goleudydd. He recounted, at length, stories of hunting with his father in the lands of Bryneich. Ruairdri, normally a dour presence, was also full of largesse, praising loudly the 'all powerful' Clydno and his bodyguards.

Clydno was very much flattered by the compliments. Everyone knew Clydno's ego was easily boosted, and flattery was the weapon of choice if you wished to get into the king's good books. Yes, Clydno thought, leaning back against his throne, today would be a good and exhilarating day. He was a man at the peak of his powers and he relished it.

Clydno put an arm around Morcant's shoulders before slapping him on the back. "Come, Lord Morcant, let's clear the cobwebs from our heads and enjoy the freshness of the day."

Morcant smiled tightly but maintained his cheery demeanour despite the feelings of rising nausea and sourness in his throat. He nodded and smiled as widely as he could.

Within the hour, a dozen horsemen were mounted and galloping out of the fortress. Clydno led them out with his protector Dara, followed by Morcant, Ruairdri, the retainers of both men and Lord Faolin, one of

Clydno's most senior lords and advisors. As they entered the forest, the hounds were released, and the men sat on their mounts awaiting the sounds of chase.

Morcant sidled up to Faolin. After a pause, Faolin, a gruff and humourless man, nodded a greeting. Morcant gave him a smile. "Lord Faolin, a fine morning. Is your man… with us?" he said.

"Yes, of course," Faolin replied evenly.

"Good, good…" Morcant tailed off. "I believe today will be an excellent day's hunting, don't you agree?"

"Ask me again when the dogs pick up a trail and the business is done," Faolin responded coldly.

"These woods are full of bandits, I hear," Morcant continued.

"Indeed, the king will have to be… careful. But of course, the king will always be impervious to such an attack with Dara at his side."

"Of course!" Morcant said cheerily, looking towards the big man and nodding. "Yes," he continued, "any bandit worth his salt would learn that he would have to deal with Dara first."

Faolin frowned but knew that Morcant would have already considered this. "Failure," he warned, "will mean the end of any stupid attempt and cost many lives."

"I agree." Morcant smiled.

At that moment, the two men swung around on hearing a howl from deep in the forest. "Ah!" Clydno cried out from the front of the group. "Let the hunt begin!"

"Yes, Lord," Morcant and Faolin responded together.

With a whoop of delight, Clydno dug his heels into his horse's ribs and shot off in the direction of the sound. "Lord, wait!' Dara called as he followed in quick pursuit.

Morcant turned to Faolin again, laughing this time. "Mind you, you can never legislate for the recklessness of some."

The twelve men now moved forward in a long line. As they moved the line stretched and no one noticed that their numbers had increased by one. A nondescript hooded man of some six feet had joined the chase. He smoothly overtook the whooping warriors until he drew up alongside Dara, shooting him a toothless grin as he caught his, eye. On impulse Dara grinned back but in a heartbeat he realised that he didn't recognise this man.

The stranger moved ahead and as soon as he was certain Dara could not see his hands, loaded a sling shot.

"Who the fuck are you?" Dara roared, but before he could say anything else the man, Llofan Llaf Difo, also known as Severing-Hand, launched his sling with the small rock hitting its mark right between Dara's eyes. The warrior's world went black and he slumped forward.

Faolin, next in line, saw Dara slump forward and spurred his horse towards the stricken man and nudged Dara's horse off the path and into thick vegetation. The horse reared and bucked as it felt the need to avoid various low branches and thistles. At that, Dara's body fell heavily to the floor. It was Ruairdri who skidded to a stop, jumped down and opened Dara's throat with his long-handled dagger.

Faolin now straddled the path and brought the others to a halt. "Quick," he warned, dismounting and drawing his sword. "Bandits!" Quickly they formed a circle with two of Clydno's retainers being sent out to check the undergrowth. No one noticed the king was missing. Clydno's enthusiasm had carried him a long way in front of his fellow huntsmen, and he eventually pulled his horse up with a sudden realisation that he was alone. He looked around him pondering what to do before he noticed, ahead of him, in the brush, a boar probably some one hundred paces from where he stood. The dogs had ceased their barking and an eerie silence fell on the clearing Clydno was occupying.

A sudden rustling behind him took his attention with a start. He breathed hard; he knew there were bandits and malcontents in these woods, but he was also sure his compatriots were fairly close. He listened carefully then, satisfied that the noise was nothing more than the wind or a small animal, Clydno took the bow from over his shoulder and notched an arrow. The boar would be his and tonight's banquet would celebrate his skills as a great huntsman. He smiled at that with growing satisfaction.

Clydno carefully and slowly dropped from his horse and without any sound, pulled back the bow string and aimed at the boar. He held his aim for a moment and loosed, the arrow finding its mark. Clydno straightened in triumph. He threw back his head, closed his eyes and roared at the sky in triumph. "My kill!"

"No," a quiet voice said dripping with venom, "the kill is mine!"

Clydno opened his eyes in surprise and not a little annoyance at seeing a tall, slim and hooded man in front of him. "Be gone, don't you know who I am?"

"Oh, of course I do, Lord King."

"How dare—"

Clydno never finished his sentence as Llofan slid his blade into the king's belly, the blade grating against his backbone. Blood poured from the surprised king's mouth as he fell forward but not before Llofan had removed the blade. Llofan smiled, knowing he would be a lot richer by the day's end. Clydno, clutching his stomach, looked up in pained surprised but within seconds of choking he let out his last breath.

Llofan reached for the king's hand and removed the jewellery; he may as well make the best of things, he thought. His time was short. The rest of the hunting party would soon realise the king was missing and they would be upon him. He looked down at the king's dead body and smiled. "Hmm," he muttered, "why not?" He pulled the king's arm outward from the body and expertly sliced the hand from the arm. "Severing hand has another trophy," he chuckled, "a king's hand no less."

Llofan cleaned his blade on Clydno's tunic and placed his bounty and the severed hand in a cloth bag. He looked towards the boar. *Too big*, he thought, *shame*. He walked purposefully towards his horse tethered to a tree some fifty paces from the clearing, mounted and without hurry trotted away.

At that same moment Ruaidh, Dara's right hand man, named thus because of his bright red hair, cried, "Wait, where is the king?"

"Shit," Faolin responded. "Did he go on ahead?"

They all looked at each for a moment. Panic rose in Ruaidh's voice. "Come with me, follow the path quick, the king may be in danger."

Ruaidh grabbed his horse and galloped forward, followed by the others. Morcant and his men slowly brought up the rear. As they raced forward the sounds of barking had started again and came nearer. When they reached the clearing, Ruadh jumped from his horse and sprinted to the prone body of the king and squatted next to it. He cradled the king's lolling head for a moment before noticing that king's hand had been removed.

As the others began to gather around him, he looked up, his eyes reddened. "He's dead," he said flatly. He lifted the king's arm and showed everyone the handless arm. "Shit!" he exclaimed. "He's been killed, what the fuck do we do?"

Faolin placed a comforting hand on the man's shoulder before bending down to examine the king's body. He sighed and bowed his head. "Someone will pay for this," he said grimly. "We must take the body back to Eidyn and tell the queen the egregious news that her husband has been murdered." He kneeled on the grass next to the king's body, pinching the bridge of his nose. "Now we must grieve and then we must find a new king for Lothian. We cannot be without leadership in these terrible times."

Morcant strode forward, impressed by Faolin's 'acting'. *He could be a bard*, Morcant thought. "I swear I will avenge him and purge these woods of the scum that has killed him."

"What about Prince Cynon?" Ruadh asked.

"I will ensure a message is sent to him," Faolin put in. "He will be most anxious to return."

"But first," Morcant soothed, "we must return to Eidyn and speak to the queen and make the necessary plans."

With heavy hearts, they wrapped the king in sheepskins, placed over his horses' back, and taken back to the fortress.

Queen Goleudydd was devastated by the news; she retired to her room without a word and refused to come out. Her servants continued to care for her, but she remained silent. Morcant wanted the queen disposed of to ensure there could be no alternative powerbase to his. But his closest allies, including Faolin, persuaded him to let her be.

"Be patient, do not let rumour begin because of your haste."

The disposal of the sister-in-law to King Gabrain, whether he was gravely ill or otherwise, would cause untold damage to his position and would undoubtedly point to his guilt. Morcant would have to bide his time.

Morcant was true to his word. He led Clydno's warriors into the forest and murdered everyone they came across: men, women, children and even the dogs and cattle. Homes were burned to the ground and when the bloodletting was done, he returned to Clydno's court to great acclaim. Support, led by Faolin, for Morcant's accession to the throne increased to such a level that as a descendant of Coel Hen he was unanimously elected to become the new lord. Cynon's name was not even mentioned.

Eidyn and Lothian belonged to Morcant and there was no longer any need to take back Bryneich. He had his kingdom and no one, not even Cynon, if he survived what Morcant had prepared for him, was going to take it back.

Chapter 5

Safety in God's Hands

Cynon had enjoyed being rid of court life and was particularly relieved not having to spend time with, or more accurately molly coddling, the upstart Morcant. He smiled broadly as he rode to Loch Leven, finally reaching Serf's community on an isle just off the south-eastern shore of the loch early in the afternoon.

Sitting now with his sister and nephew gazing out over the loch, he marvelled at its abundance. No longer did he have the smell of human excrement and animal manure under his nose, something he had not really appreciated since enjoying the early spring days. Serf had, with a great flourish, boasted of the volumes of trout and perch to be found which kept the settlement well fed even during the winter months. He spoke, at length, of some Christian tale about five loaves and two fishes, to which both brother and sister dutifully showed the appropriate amazement. As they continued to talk amiably and without care, Crierwy enthusiastically pointed out the flocks of geese, swans and ducks of all kinds and colours. They wondered at the cormorants, pochards, sharders and gadwalls, many of which he had never heard of let alone seen until Crierwy had pointed them out to the gurgling and uncomprehending Arthur.

It was at times like this that he loved being with his sister and he had missed her company. He was still angry that Aedan had yet to make an appearance, but he was also grudgingly conscious of the politics involved. He sighed. Yes, politics, his life had now become so much more complicated and the more he thought about it the more deflated he became. He knew he was a handsome man and his sister ribbed him mercilessly at his conceit. He loved that the girls of Eidyn chased him, but his world had come crashing down when his son was born and his father made him understand that his days of frivolity were at an end. Now, he looked at the people of the community and envied them their simple and uncomplicated lives. Their only responsibility was to each other, and they were accountable to the Christ Jesus. Life was indeed simple, but the people worked hard. Nonetheless, despite all that, they were fed and watered and they cared little for the machinations that swirled around them in the world beyond the isle.

It confused him that this Christ Jesus, a mere man, nailed to a cross in a country thousands of miles from the loch, could be revered by these people. However, he was fascinated by and enjoyed listening to the stories of this man's exploits. He was left dumbfounded by this Jesus bringing a man back to life, turning water into wine — *A clever trick indeed*, he mused — the five loaves and two fishes, of course, or was it the other way around, the story of the Good Samaritan, and his favourite story of all, walking on water. This man, this God or son of God, Cynon did not know which, was indeed powerful.

Crierwy noticed her brother's faraway look and guessed that he probably wasn't listening to her. She paused for a while, staring at him intently for what seemed an age before Cynon turned his head. "Hmm, yes?"

"Hmm yes what?" She grinned as she saw he realised he had been caught out.

"What you just said," he lied.

"I don't know where you were, but it seemed like a place I would very much like to follow you to." She smiled sweetly.

"Trust me, you wouldn't," he said carelessly. He sighed and they sat together in comfortable silence, both knowing that nothing was expected of each other. Eventually, he stretched and said, "How long are you planning to stay here? Father and especially our mother want to see you and this little boy." He pointed at Arthur who was sleeping soundly.

"Will I be safe?" she asked.

"Of course you will be, you have their grandchild, a child of Beltane no less. Anyway, he's come to the conclusion that as you are a priestess you were thus saved by the gods."

She shrugged. "How kind of him."

He smiled. "You know Father, he swings from one extreme to another, but your exile has allowed his temper to cool and Mother, of course, has weaved her magic on him."

"Does Aunt Lluan know?"

"If I know our aunt, she will have given Aedan a telling off even the goddess would have been shocked to hear."

Crierwy snorted. "I will come back if that is what our parents want but it is with heavy heart because this place has become my place of safety and it has helped to ground me. Everyone has been so kind, Cynon, and the woman Aeronwen, a woman of the old ways surprisingly, has filled my world with calm and happiness. There is something serene and magical about this place and to leave will be hard."

"There is something comforting about the stories of the murdered god, Christ Jesus," Cynon said suddenly.

Her eyebrows shot up and knitted together. "I'm not sure you should be saying that to a Priestess of the Cauldron," she teased.

"Well, you can understand the attraction. Look around us, there is strife everywhere. Those bastard Angles, war with the Picts, the Irish, and not to mention that two faced bastard Morcant."

"He wants his kingdom back," she responded lightly.

"Hmm, maybe, but we live a life of constant threat. One day we win, the next we could lose it all. Look at how simple life can be, they don't care what happens beyond this island, they don't need to care. They have everything they need here and in a world like ours, who can blame them for feeling content here."

"Your conclusions are too simplistic, brother," she chided. "Anything that happens on those shores," she pointed to the mainland, "will affect them here. The Picts are just as likely to kill these people as the Angles. Life might seem to be idyllic, but they are part of this world whatever they, or for that matter you, might think. It is too easy, Cynon, to look about you and see how little responsibilities these people might have but you forget how privileged we are."

"I know," he conceded, "but the central part of their belief is love. How can I ever question that?"

"You, dear brother, are becoming swept up by these people. Serf, I have noticed, is exceptionally good at speaking to the people of the settlement and the locals round about promising love and forgiveness. It is very seductive. The promise of plenty of food is enticing too. Fill their bellies and their hearts soon follow." She laughed. "But sometimes you need to look beyond the words."

Crierwy reflected that Cynon had become a strong and ridiculously handsome man with a clean-shaven face and short hair, unusual for a man, but more importantly, he had grown into a good man with strong convictions and he would do the right thing no matter what others might say or the cost to himself. She knew Cynon had fought her corner when Arthur was conceived, and she could only imagine the verbal barrage he would have received in return from their father. She looked at him with loving respect and she could not help smiling at him.

"Cynon," she said quietly, "you will find your own way and if it is with these Christians, then you will do so because it is the right thing for you. But if that is the path you decide to take, I would ask you that you respect my beliefs. It may not be as exciting as this new religion but do not dismiss it."

A few days passed. As usual food was being cooked and all of Serf's community was gathering for the evening meal. Cynon was lending a hand, helping the women carry pots from the stores, when he noticed a small coracle being pushed off from the mainland shore. It only took a matter of minutes for the coracle, with two men aboard, to cross the short distance to the isle where it was greeted by Serf. After clumsily clambering out of the coracle, the bigger of the two men strode over and spoke animatedly to Serf. Cynon could see the concern etched on Serf's face as he turned his face towards the people of his community. Eventually, Serf's eyes settled on Cynon, and he beckoned him over.

"This is Senan, he has news from the outside," Serf announced.

Senan nodded. "Lord."

Before another word was uttered Serf advised that Crierwy should also be summoned. "She needs to hear this news too because danger lurks close at hand and decisions and preparations need to be made."

Cynon frowned and hesitated but in a couple of beats he turned toward the dwellings and set off to seek out his sister. When he returned with Crierwy they were invited to sit by the water's edge. Serf called on Senan to speak.

"Master Serf, Lord and Lady, I have come from Dalriada. I am pained to tell you that the Lord Gabrain has succumbed to his wounds. The Picts, warriors of King Bruide, son of Maelgwyn Hir, have intervened to ensure a new king of their choosing is chosen to replace the 'Scorcher'."

"What of Aedan?" Cynon asked.

"He has chosen to remain in Manau with his wife and children."

"Will he not replace Gabrain?" Cynon queried.

"Definitely not." Senan smiled, "The Gorlassar is not trusted and too clever for Bruide, and Bruide cannot countenance that."

"Bruide is not the cleverest of men, that's for sure." Crierwy smiled.

"Indeed, Lady. I understand the king will be Conall." He shrugged.

"Conall mac Comgall?" Cynon put in.

"Yes, Lord."

Cynon laughed. "Aedan will be beyond furious. There will be consequences, mark my words."

"I think Aedan will bide his time and stay in Manau so as not to provoke any conflict until he feels strong enough to act."

"I have no doubt; my dear cousin is very good at biding his time."

"Indeed, Lord," Senan agreed.

"And what of Clydno Eidyn? Has he sought to intervene?" Cynon asked.

"There has been no word, Lord. Lothian has remained... detached," Senan said carefully.

"Detached," Cynon repeated.

"I assume only," Senan said defensively.

"So," Crierwy interrupted, "why have you come here?"

Senan and Cynon stopped their discussion, and both turned toward Crierwy. "Apologies, my Lady." Senan bowed. "You need to know that Bruide has learned you are here and he has sworn to avenge his sister, the Lady Domelch, for the affront brought upon his family by the child born to you, Lady."

"So, all this is my fault?" Crierwy retorted angrily.

"I fear—"

"No, Senan, do not patronise me; this is the way of this world. Men using women as an excuse to wave their cocks at each other," Crierwy said acidly.

Senan blushed, momentarily surprised by Crierwy's words. "Lady," he stammered "for what it matters, you have many friends, you are a Priestess of the Cauldron and the child you carried has been blessed by the gods. It is foretold he will be a great warrior and that frightens people."

Crierwy sighed deeply. "I am so fed up with hearing that," she said, shaking her head.

"I will always be your servant," Senan continued, "and I promise to protect you."

Crierwy's expression softened, and she nodded slowly. "Thank you, Senan, I mean not to show anger towards you. I am so…" But she stopped, for it was not appropriate to tell people of her exhaustion. Instead, she sighed. "How long do we have before Bruide's men reach this place for I assume they will come?"

"A day at best, Lady."

"A day?" Cynon put in. "You give us a day's notice?" he said angrily.

"It is not always easy to get the information and then escape and evade the Picts, Lord. I came as soon as I could," Senan retorted defensively.

Crierwy interjected. "There is no point arguing now. Let us be grateful that we have had a warning."

"How can you be so tranquil?" Cynon snapped.

"What choice do we have?" she replied soothingly. "Senan here has put himself in great danger to warn us and in these savage days we must give our thanks to the gods." She turned to Senan again. "Thank you, Senan, we will find some way of rewarding you."

Senan was visibly relieved by Crierwy's reaction and nodded. Cynon grimaced but decided not to continue with the argument and grudgingly nodded in turn. He then watched as Senan stood and Serf escorted him back to the coracle. But as Senan stooped, Serf took his arm. "Where are you going and what will you do?" he whispered.

"I was going to travel to Manau and seek out the Prince Aedan."

Serf paused and looked into Senan's eyes. "You say Clydno has not been heard of. Do you not find that strange?"

"Yes, I do, but I didn't feel it my place to say so."

"What is your view?"

"Word is that Morcant has taken control, but the circumstances are unclear. But I am fearful," he said quietly.

"Will you do something for me?" Serf asked.

Senan viewed Serf with suspicion but relented. "What is it you'll have me do?"

Serf smiled at Senan's reticence. "Do not fear, my friend, I simply need your eyes and ears. More specifically, Lord Cynon and Lady Crierwy need them although I am also related to Clydno. Can you travel to Clydno's court and find out what has happened and if the rumours are true?"

"And what about Bruide?" Senan queried.

"If Bruide comes we will arrange for the lord and lady to escape." Serf looked to the south and nodded to the hills that rose from the southern shore. "They will escape with the baby towards Benarty Hill over there and then they can try to return to Eidyn's court. If there is trouble, find them and tell them."

Senan nodded.

"Thank you, Senan." Serf nodded.

Senan clambered aboard the waiting coracle and cast off in the direction of the dock on the south-eastern shore, watched the whole way by Serf. As Senan disappeared into the darkening dusk Serf jogged over to catch up with Cynon and Crierwy as they returned to their lodgings. "My dear cousins, I think it would be best if you prepare to leave us. If the Picts turn up, we have no means of protecting you, even if we had weapons."

They nodded and without complaint or comment set about gathering any belongings they could reasonably carry. Carrying a child and the need to move quickly meant they could only carry a small amount so it was food enough for a couple of days that would have to be prioritised.

Once arrangements were made, the only decision to make was where they should go. Serf promised to discuss plans later that evening, but the nearest and safest, most obvious haven they could travel towards was the fortress at Eidyn and back to the protection of their parents' arms. Cynon was certain that the Picts would shy away from a conflict with Lothian. They would set off early the next day and seek sanctuary with Clydno. But as they prepared to eat their last meal in the settlement, they had no idea they had run out of time.

Chapter 6

A Sanctuary Despoiled

The community had feasted on the day's catch and songs and hymns were being sung. It wasn't lost on Crierwy that it was a year since her life had changed forever. It was the eve of Beltane and whilst this was not officially recognised by the Christians, Serf had always taken a secular view. There was to be no fire jumping or wild reverie, Serf had announced, much to Crierwy's discomfort. Christianity, as preached by Serf's followers, had cleverly subsumed the rituals of the 'old ways', making it a lot easier to convert the locals. Despite herself, Crierwy could not help secretly admiring their stealth.

The moon was near full as the last of the community retired to their beds. Only a couple of retainers were charged with keeping watch for any trouble on the loch's shore. The only obvious access to the island was from the east at the closest point to the mainland. Indeed, nearly all the coracles were moored at that place. It was believed that the proximity of the trees gave the community a semblance of protection in case there was an incursion from 'undesirables', as Serf called them. The distance from the lodgings to where the guards now sat was some two hundred paces, with Serf's own hut the closest to the shore.

As clouds started to drift across the moon, casting shadows, the guards became aware of movement on the far bank. Despite this, both had persuaded themselves that it was simply dancing shadows, although both held the torques that hung around their necks alongside the rudimentary crosses that also hung there. When it came to religion there was nothing wrong, they told themselves, in hedging their bets.

Suddenly a fiery bolt flew high into the sky and landed only a few yards from where the guards sat. Both stood up with a start and drew their swords.

"Who goes there, make yourselves known," one of them shouted into the darkness. Suddenly more flaming arrows hissed through the sky, landing on the dry grass, threatening to catch the scrub alight.

The shouts raised Serf who ran out of his hut, naked except for a pair of trews, in search of the guards. The arrows were falling steadily now, and a shriek of pain rang out as one of the guards was hit by an arrow in his shoulder. The two guards and Serf were forced to retreat and take cover away from the shore. Serf could see there was now a lot of movement on the shore side, and he could make out coracles loaded with men being pushed out into the loch and towards the island. Serf ripped the arrow from the shoulder of the older man, who roared with pain and rage.

"I'm sorry, my friend, better out than in," he proffered. The older man swore through gritted teeth, words Serf thought he should, in the circumstances, ignore. Crossing himself Serf turned to the younger guard. "Find the Lord Cynon now, tell him that he and the Lady Crierwy must fly without delay."

"Yes, master." The guard nodded curtly.

Serf peered at him through the gloom; the guard seemed so young. "In Christ's name, how old are you?" he grunted.

"Thirteen, sir."

Serf grimaced and shrugged. "Go boy, go now!"

Within minutes, the coracles were landing on the isle shore, by which time Cynon was at Serf's side. "At least those arrows have stopped, small mercies," he said breathlessly.

"Anyone hurt?" Cynon asked, drawing his sword.

"Not yet," Serf responded quietly, "except one of the lookouts and judging by his mood he will be okay. And Cynon," he continued, "I want to keep it that way so put the sword away unless you want to fight twenty warriors or more on your own."

"I can fight them."

"Not tonight," Serf answered smoothly.

"But—"

"Don't be a fool, Cynon, just listen to me," Serf interrupted in a voice unrecognisable from the normally calm and overly rational man Cynon had come to know and respect. "Get your sister and your nephew and leave this place. Go into the trees and work your way west around the island until you reach the bay that looks south. There is a coracle there, take it, and row directly south. From there, you will be concealed by thick brush and trees. Wait until things quieten down and you're certain there is no one pursuing you. Is that clear?"

"Crystal clear," Cynon said reluctantly.

"Good. Anyway, as soon as it is safe, climb Benarty Hill and wait there until it is light. From there make your way to the court of your father. I hope there, you will find sanctuary."

"What about you?" Cynon put in.

"Oh, I am going to speak to our visitors and God willing their stay will be short. I do not wish to martyr myself tonight. Now go and good luck to both of you and may God go with you!"

"And with you," Cynon responded.

"Thank you." Serf smiled. "We will make a Christian of you yet. Now go."

Cynon backed away slowly and nodded towards Serf before turning and weaving his way through the gathering settlers towards Crierwy's lodgings. When he arrived, he found she was already prepared to leave and Aeronwen was putting the last touches to the sling that would hold Arthur, who as luck would have it, was sleeping peacefully. Crierwy was pleading with Aeronwen,

"Come with us," she said.

Aeronwen smiled sadly. "Dear Lady, my place is here with these people, anyway I would only hold you up."

"But they might—"

"Kill me?" Aeronwen interrupted. She considered this a moment and shrugging, she went on. "Well, if they do kill me, I am told by the Christians I shall be saved, and better still, live again, whatever that means. As a retired priestess myself, however, I will never die, and I shall live on. My spirit ally is that of a she bear. I will be ferocious in death as I have been in life, despite everyone thinking I am some kind of mad woman to be pitied."

"A priestess?" Crierwy repeated.

"As I say, retired, old and very, very tired." She smiled mischievously. "My fate, Crierwy, was to be here with you and young Arthur. Everything has come to this moment so whatever comes next is written and for a reason."

Crierwy nodded. "You are full of surprises, my dear friend, but I urge you to come with us nonetheless."

"There is nothing more to say, Lady, it's time for you to go."

"I will always remember your kindness, Aeronwen."

"And I will always be there to protect you and that special boy you carry, Priestess of the Cauldron."

"Will we meet again?" she asked

"Not in this life, I fear, Lady, not as I am now."

Crierwy's eyes stung with bitter tears and whilst not wanting to show her sadness, she could not stop tears rolling down her pale cheeks. She flung her arms around the older woman's neck.

"Come now," Aeronwen sighed. Gently easing Crierwy away, she brushed her tears away. "Don't cry for me, I shall be more powerful when I leave this place."

Aeronwen tucked strands of Crierwy's hair behind her ear and stroked her cheek with the palm of her hand. She pondered a moment and continued, "There is one thing you can do for me."

"Anything."

"If you meet my youngest son again, tell him I am very proud of him."

"Again?"

"Yes, again. You will know when you see him."

"Sister we must go!" Cynon interrupted. "If we wait a moment longer, they will catch us."

Crierwy embraced Aeronwen once again. "Go lady, please," Aeronwen implored.

Crierwy and Cynon turned on their heels and fled through the commotion and towards the protection of the trees.

There were some twenty-five warriors standing on the shore next to the fire used by the two guards, both of whom had melted away. "Friends!" Serf opened his arms to greet them. There was no response. Serf studied the warriors painted in their familiar facial tattoos. They looked stern and grim, he reflected, and he wondered whether he would be able to keep control of his bladder as fear threatened to overtake him.

"We are children of the Christ King. This community is a peaceful one, we offer no hostility to you, only welcome and ask you to stay and share what we have," he announced.

"We don't want your food," growled a large muscular warrior who Serf had surmised was the leader of this war band scowled.

"What is your name, stranger, and what can I, we, do for you?"

After a very long pause, the man stepped forward, looking directly into Serf's eyes. "My name is Kaltis. I am here by the orders of the great King Bruide of the Pictish nation."

"I am well aware of King Bruide." Serf smiled.

"And you are the monk, Serf, yes?"

"Yes, my name is Serf. What can I help you with?"

There was another uncomfortable silence. Serf raised a questioning eyebrow. Outwardly Serf was a picture of calm and strength but inside his guts were churning and he was close to vomiting. The question now was how long he would be able to keep these people talking, but just as importantly, if he could keep his community alive.

Kaltis cleared his throat. "We are seeking a priestess, the Lady Crierwy of Eidyn and her child." He smiled venomously.

"A priestess? Why would a priestess reside in a Christian community?"

"To ensure she wouldn't be found," Kaltis shot back.

Serf paused, searching for the right words. "Hmm. Yes, I think I can see that, we do live in strange times, I suppose," he conceded. "We are a sanctuary, we support people who are willing to work and make this place a haven of peace and harmony."

"You do not deny their presence."

Serf sighed. "I do not believe I said that. If they did come here, I would not even know. We do not interrogate people who join us here."

Kaltis eyed Serf suspiciously, his smile turning to a scowl. "You will not be troubled if we search your community?"

"Yes, I would be… troubled," he responded irritably.

"Well, that could be problem." Kaltis sneered.

"As I say, we are a peaceful community, and we deserve respect. This is a place of worship and—"

"Shut up, monk," Kaltis roared. "I do not care about your Christ God. If King Bruide cared, so would I. But he does not care and nor do I. My advice to you is stand aside, and we will make this quick and painless. If you do not, I will not be responsible for what happens next."

"You cast aside responsibility so easily, my friend. But you will be responsible, Kaltis, not to me but to the one God," Serf countered. "Nonetheless," he continued, "if you must search, then do so but please hurt no one."

Suddenly, from behind them and to the north there was a shout of warning. Serf spun round and then looked back at Kaltis. "What is this?"

While Kaltis had been in conversation with Serf, the Picts had divided their force. A number of coracles had rowed around the north of the isle and men were now disembarking on the northern shore and making their way through the trees.

On seeing the coracles, Cynon registered the danger immediately. He could sense movement only a small number of paces away and when a warrior burst into the small clearing, where the fugitives were hiding, he was ready with sword in hand. The warrior's surprise was only compounded by the searing pain in his gut as Cynon's sword slid into his stomach. As he immediately slumped forward, Cynon placed his hand over the man's mouth to muffle any cry. Cynon lowered the man to the floor gently and then dashed towards Crierwy, placing his finger on her lips.

"Shut up," he grunted urgently. "Come on, let's go before they realise there is a man missing and we are discovered."

Crierwy swallowed hard. She closed her eyes and composed herself before nodding and following him.

They kept to the shoreline as instructed by Serf, but they were painfully aware of the commotion close behind them. They stopped at the edge of the wooded area, waiting for the opportunity to dash over the exposed land before the rocks on the shoreline could obscure their presence.

Warriors were now running through the dwellings, pushing their way indoors and setting fire to everything they could find. Aeronwen, in the meantime, had remained in the dwelling where Crierwy had been lodging but she knew that to give Crierwy, Cynon and Arthur any chance to get away she would have to create a distraction. "I am the mad women," she reminded herself. She took a deep breath and stripped off her clothes. She smiled to herself, and picked up a lighted torch and dagger before running outside, screaming at the top of her voice. "The ghosts," she wailed, "they are coming, look can't you see?" She sprinted, surprisingly quickly for someone of her years, swinging the torch in a circular motion at the surprised warriors. The whirling arms inflicted a number of flesh wounds as the chase was joined by the Pictish warriors.

Kaltis shoved Serf aside, the man falling heavily on the rocky ground. This caused angry shouts from people of the community who had by now joined their leader on the loch shore. As Kaltis was joined by his men, they formed a protective ring and a number of residents fell to the ground from sword strokes. Archers also loosed their lethal instruments into the crowd, dispersing them. Suddenly Aeronwen burst through into view and launched herself at Kaltis and his men. "Kill the fucking bitch!" the mortified leader of the war band yelled.

"No," Serf cried. "She is a mad old woman. She is no threat to you, she—"

His words died in his throat as two men stepped forward and dispatched Aeronwen with frightening efficiency and she fell dead at Kaltis' feet. Things had got out of hand, Kaltis knew. There were at least a dozen wounded, and four men lay dead. The killing of the old woman had resulted in a shocked pause to the raging conflict.

Serf had recovered from his fall and had run back towards the fracas, shouting for the fighting to stop. He looked on in horror at Aeronwen's body. The scene stopped him in his tracks. "Oh God, no, what have you done, you animals?" he screamed in anger and shame in equal measure.

"Stop!' Kaltis ordered with a guttural roar. "Lower your weapons." He looked at Serf, pointing his sword toward him. "Tell your people to back away."

"Just stop this destruction," Serf retorted angrily. "This is a place of peace. Have you or your men any decency, any shame? We only wish to live in peace."

Kaltis' eyes were like stalks, and he swore loudly in frustration. He could not apologise, and his pride stopped him from trying to reason with this Serf. He hesitated, suddenly unsure of what to say or do. He held up his hand showing everyone that any further words would not be welcome and allowed his mind to clear. His shoulders slumped as he allowed the tension to flow out of him. He turned to his second. "The burning will stop, but we will continue the search," he instructed. He then turned to Serf. "Tell your people not to hinder us and we will leave when I am satisfied that the priestess and her child are not here. There will be no plundering or further damage." He paused and then continued, "I give you my word."

Serf wanted to argue but discretion now would save further pain and suffering. He nodded his agreement.

"You may treat your injured," Kaltis added quietly.

Serf could only hope that Crierwy and her brother had had enough time to make their escape. He sighed, his emotions bursting forth as he removed his cloak to cover Aeronwen's body. "Why?" he whispered. On his knees, he realised then that her actions had saved the settlement from being torched, as well as Crierwy and the child. "She was a good woman," he said to no one in particular. He looked up at the moon. "And perhaps a little moon touched." He stood and called over a young man who, he realised, had been one of the guards. He placed his hand on the boy's shaking shoulder. "Be strong," he said. "Take her body to the women to prepare for burial. A Christian woman deserves a decent burial and to meet her maker with some dignity."

To Serf's surprise, the boy chuckled. "She was no Christian, and a pyre would be more her suiting."

Somewhere, they could hear a she bear roaring.

Cynon could see that the soldiers had been distracted by trouble in the village. He grabbed Crierwy's arm and dragged her across the large clearing until they reached the rocks on the north-western shore. They could see the coracles moored close by and although he was tempted to grab one, he recognised that to row across the furthest part of the loch at night was dangerous. They would stick to Serf's instructions.

The noise of conflict gradually faded as Crierwy and Cynon picked their way through the rocks and pebbles on the water's edge. Remarkably, and to their relief, Arthur remained asleep throughout the ordeal and Cynon could only wonder at the child's capacity to absorb noise and violence without any apparent distress.

Slowly but surely, they moved around to the south of the island until they reached the small bay described by Serf. And there was the coracle as promised. "Quick, get in." Cynon gestured urgently. Without a word she stepped aboard and settled down. He put his finger to his mouth and listened intently for any signs of danger. He could hear the continuing disturbance to the north of them but there was nothing close enough to be a threat. He paused a little longer and slowly stepped into the coracle and pushed it away from the shore. It was only a short distance to the other shore. The clouds had begun to move in from the west and with the moon hiding behind them, Cynon and Crierwy were mercifully blessed with darkness.

They ran aground on the gravel shore of the mainland, Cynon jumping out and pulling hard on the coracle to secure it. "Wait here," he whispered, and he made his way to the nearest greenery, stopped and listened for any pursuers. Once he was satisfied they were alone he crept back to Crierwy and the child, helping them to unload the small number of belongs they had brought with them, meagre though they were.

He beckoned to Crierwy to follow him, and they moved back to the greenery from which he had just come. There they stayed for what seemed, to Crierwy, an eternity although, in reality, it was only about five minutes until Cynon felt confident enough that they could move in relative safety.

"We will take forever at this rate," she huffed.

Cynon shot her a withering look and Crierwy knew that just perhaps she needed to keep her counsel until they were safe. "Come on," Cynon beckoned, and they moved through some light brush before reaching a small grove of trees. Benarty Hill was straight ahead. Cynon had originally planned to wait as Serf had suggested, but the sudden and unexpected cloud cover offered an opportunity to move further away from the isle and onto higher ground where they would be able to see more clearly once it became light.

"I think we should move on," he said. "Do you want me to carry the boy?" She shook her head and he nodded before taking her hand and guiding her through the trees and on to the slopes of the hill beyond. The hill was bare except for clumps of trees and a little undergrowth so they dashed from one to the next, waiting some minutes in each to check they were not being followed.

Cynon could no longer hear any noises coming from Serf's Isle and he hoped that was a good sign. He glanced at Crierwy, and he saw her gazing in the direction whence they came; she was clearly thinking the same as he was. He squeezed her arm and she smiled weakly at him. He sighed. "Come on, sister, we must make it worth their while and make good our escape." She said nothing in response; instead, she stood in preparation for the next sprint.

At last, they reached the peak, both breathing heavily. Crierwy thought her heart would burst from her chest as she slumped onto the cloak Cynon had spread on the grass for her. The dawn was coming, a finger of light gradually lighting up the eastern sky.

He helped her shed the sling that held Arthur. The baby snuffled but hardly stirred. "Well look at that, I can't believe he slept through that adventure," Cynon marvelled. "He doesn't take after his mother's line," he continued, a smile breaking across his face.

"His father?" She grimaced. "Uther the Wily," she said without emotion.

"Well, if Aedan's anything like this, we'd better keep an eye out for him."

"And that thought frightens me." She smiled coldly.

"Would Aedan hurt you, would he hurt his son?"

"He will do whatever's necessary," she said. "You know this. But he knows that Arthur is a Beltane child and thus blessed by the gods and the divine goddess. And that is more important to him than anything."

Cynon nodded. "He will need that to strengthen his position."

"Aedan will be King of the Scots, of that you can be sure, and Arthur... will be at his side and he will be lost to me anyway. Life or death, the outcome's the same."

They stayed there for some time before Cynon persuaded Crierwy to stay put while he scouted the hill to look for any animal life to sustain them. "Take advantage of the boy's heavy sleep to rest yourself because we have a two day walk to reach Father and safety."

She shuddered at the thought, but without a word she curled herself up and closed her eyes before falling into a fitful sleep.

Meanwhile, Cynon searched the upper reaches of the hill before he dropped back down towards the loch. All was quiet. He skirted the loch and crept as close to the east of the island as he dared. The Pictish warriors were preparing themselves to leave although clearly most of their number were still on the island.

He was satisfied that the Pictish warriors appeared to be in no hurry to search for Crierwy and her son. Indeed, they would be painfully aware that if they tried to follow towards where the fugitives were likely to flee, they would trespass the lands of Lothian. If they did that, it would be tantamount to a declaration of war. The Picts might be full of confidence, following their military successes, but Cynon knew that it would be dangerous to risk another confrontation which might provoke Lothian's allies, the Gododdin. Satisfied, Cynon turned on his heels and made his way back to the top of Benarty Hill where he expected to find Crierwy and Arthur still sleeping. But to his horror they were gone.

Chapter 7

A Saviour Comes

The rising panic twisted his guts. He frantically dashed from one clump of trees to another. "Crierwy!" he called in a loud of whisper. He looked up at the sky; it was probably mid-morning now, could soldiers have rounded the hill and crept behind him? Suddenly he saw a movement from the corner of his eye and drew his sword.

"Stand fast," the man called. "Your sister is safe and so is the child."

"Who are you?" he growled.

The man stepped forward. "It's me, Senan." He smiled broadly.

On recognising the man, Cynon sheathed his sword and rested his hands on his knees as the nausea and relief swept through him and then subsided. "Thank goodness," he breathed.

Senan strode over, offering water, and helped Cynon to stand up straight. Patting him on the shoulder, he said, "Come, we have brought some sustenance to cheer you." The warrior paused. "We also have news that you will need to hear on a full stomach and some rest." He smiled tightly.

"News?" Cynon asked sceptically.

"All in good time. Oh, and your nephew has good lungs on him, he has not stopped crying. I'm surprised you didn't hear him. My head's fit to explode! I do thank any god passing that my children are grown up."

"You'll be a grandfather soon." Cynon grinned, "That will change you."

"I'm too young for that," he grunted. "Come, follow me."

It wasn't a banquet, but Crierwy nonetheless quickly devoured the cheese and bread, much to the amusement of Senan's comrades who had expected her to be more feminine. "I know what you're thinking," she snorted, "but if you are a man, woman, dog or whatever and you're hungry, you do not stand on ceremony. Oh, is that mead? I have not drunk in months." Cynon could only shake his head in amusement.

The food had lightened the mood, and much to everyone's relief, the baby had settled down. The dozen or so warriors gathered around the small campfire, despite all being built like oxen, had taken it in turns to hold and gurgle at little Arthur. Senan appeared to be the most maternal, if indeed that was a good description, Crierwy mused. "Well gentlemen," she said as she stood with an amused grin, "if you are quite finished with my son, I would very much like a cuddle myself." She paused. "With the baby, that is," she corrected quickly.

A snigger rose from the group, but it quickly dissipated when Cynon shot them an irritable glance. He had been quiet throughout the meal, but he had appreciated the sustenance. However, now he wanted the news from Senan.

"Well?" he said irritably.

Senan cleared his throat. "Lord?"

"Your news," Cynon interrupted a little too sharply, something he regretted immediately, acknowledging his rudeness with raised hands.

Senan nodded and continued. "When I left you last night, I had men go before me to get word of the situation in Lothian. The information I have received tells that there has been a," he paused, "purge of the woodland folk by Morcant and his followers."

"Morcant?" Cynon jumped up.

"Yes, Morcant," Senan repeated.

"How so?"

Senan breathed in slowly. "I am told that your father was killed in an ambush while hunting."

Cynon's eyes widened. "What?" he roared incredulously. "Killed?"

"Yes, Lord, I am awaiting confirmation from my men but do not trust to hope. I fear it to be true and it explains why there has been so little news coming from Lothian."

"What of our mother?" Crierwy interjected.

"I do not know." Senan shrugged.

"And Morcant?" Cynon asked.

"I regret to say that he has taken the throne," Senan said carefully.

"Taken the throne?" Cynon roared again. "Impossible, my father's court would never countenance it."

Senan said nothing, and an extremely uncomfortable silence fell upon the group. Cynon threw his bowl to the floor and stomped away. Crierwy was about to follow when Senan gently grabbed her arm and shook his head. "Let him be," he said quietly.

In Cynon's absence, Senan detailed all the information he knew to Crierwy, albeit with the constant proviso that nothing had been confirmed.

"What of Dara and Faolin?" she asked.

"I believe Dara has also been killed but Faolin escaped with Morcant."

"Faolin would never betray our family and allow Morcant to… just take the throne," she spluttered. "He's a cold man but loyal nonetheless."

"That maybe so," Senan responded quietly, "but I think that he may have. I am not from Lothian; I do not know your family or the people around them, Lady. You can only wait for now until we have more information," he repeated.

Crierwy sat in silence trying to process all that she had heard. To her surprise, the death of her father had not upset her as it should. Instead, she gazed at the loch and the isle she had only the previous night been living on. She could see rivulets of smoke rising into the sky, the aftermath of some sort of violence, she assumed, inflicted on innocent people who had been so kind to her and Arthur. Her feelings of guilt were overwhelming; the fault was hers, after all, and she knew it. They had shown her love and respect, something her father demonstrably was unable to do. She shook her head, what could she do? Eventually, turning to Senan, she asked, "Can you find Taliesin?"

"The bard?"

"Yes, he is a dear friend of mine. He will give us the help and the advice we need, and if he can't, he will find someone who can."

"Where will we find him?"

"I'm guessing either Alt Clut or Rheged."

Senan turned to the other warriors. "Tearlach!"

"Yes, sir," the man responded gruffly.

"Take Nessa and Dugald, find the bard Taliesin and bring him to the old Roman Fort at Camlann."

"Yes, sir." Tearlach nodded and summoned the others.

"Why Camlann?" Crierwy asked.

"It is on the route to Eidyn, but it is far enough away from trouble to keep you and the baby safe until we understand the fate of your father and decide what to do next. And," he acknowledged, "it is defensible if it comes to it." He paused a moment before asking, "Do you think we can persuade your brother to come with us?"

She looked over to where Cynon sat on the down slope of the hill looking towards Serf's Isle. "I will speak to him. I think your reasoning will keep him with us for now."

Senan stood and gave Crierwy a slight bow. "I will the make preparations for departure."

Crierwy nodded in response then finally said, "Thank you, Senan, you have been so kind. My son and I owe you a debt."

"You are the Priestess of the Cauldron," he acknowledged. "You have my sword and my loyalty."

With the warmth of the early May sun on their faces and the beauty of countryside with flowers and trees in bud, they made good time, keeping the Forth River to their south until they were able to find a ford near the great rock of a place known as Strevelin. There they stopped for a few days in the hope of more news from Senan's men or even, Crierwy hoped, Taliesin. They were to be disappointed.

They continued, more slowly, towards Camlann, making sure they kept off the paths and moving mostly during the period between dusk and dawn, not only in fear of Morcant but also the Picts. The drizzle that had caught up with them from the west dampened their spirits further.

After another couple of miserable days, they finally arrived at the remains of the Roman fort of Camlann just to the north of the 'lesser' wall of the Emperor Antoninus. For the moment, to everyone's relief, they could camp in relative safety.

The fort was indeed very defensible with much of it still intact. The land sloped down to the south and was broken and stony. At the bottom of the incline a stream snaked its way from west to east. Anyone approaching the fortifications would be certain of a painful day's work. Cynon, at seeing the fort, nodded his approval.

Senan's men continuously patrolled the surrounding areas, but Crierwy was more concerned with Cynon's restlessness. He had become an ever more brooding figure and the others preferred to keep their distance. Despite Crierwy's comforting words, Cynon remained largely quiet. He wandered the old ramparts looking eastwards, always eastwards. Looking after Arthur had been a distraction for her but for Cynon, she knew, there were no such diversions although on the one occasion when Senan was able to persuade him to go hunting, his mood did lighten a bit, albeit temporarily.

Arthur was growing into a bonny little boy and Crierwy amused herself watching big burly warriors cooing and cuddling him. Beneath her cheeriness, her anxiety over the fate of her parents, particularly her mother, tore at her heart. Despite the ruptures over the conception of Arthur her parents did, at least some of the time, offer her sanctuary should her life choices come to nil. But now she felt homeless and isolated, dependent on people she did not know and despite their kindness, still didn't trust completely. She knew, deep down, she was being unfair, and she received much kindness from them. She should be more grateful she reflected. Looking at her gurgling child, she hoped Arthur would not suffer the misfortunes she had experienced and that he would not grow up to be cynical and mistrusting. She held the child closely and sighed. Somehow, she knew he would suffer his own betrayals and the pain that brought.

The following day, the men Senan had sent into Lothian to investigate Clydno's fate returned from the east. As they gathered the men were able to confirm Cynon and Crierwy's worst fears. Clydno had been killed; Goleudydd was living in solitude but was alive, in comfortable lodgings, and was being treated with the respect she deserved as a dowager queen.

Morcant had been proclaimed king and rumours were rife that Clydno and his right-hand man, Dara, had not been killed by woodland bandits but rather through the acts of an assassin hired by either Morcant himself or, more shockingly, Faolin. Faolin had now indeed become Morcant's chief adviser, and it was clear that Cynon would no longer be welcomed home and would only be able to reclaim his birth right through strength of arms.

Cynon was in despair and spent his time in moping melancholy. He knew, like everyone else, that raising a force strong enough to challenge Morcant was unlikely any time soon, if ever. Crierwy tried her best to lift his mood but without a plan, a purpose, there was little or no chance of changing things. They had lost their father and despite the sometimes uncomfortable relationship between them, the thought of being without her father was painful. Where was Taliesin?

Spring turned to summer when it was reported that two riders were seen wandering down past the rock of Strevelin. Both were armed. Senan's men, having picked up their trail, followed from a discreet distance and when they came in sight of the Roman fort, Senan, himself, decided to intercept them.

"Good day, strangers," he said pleasantly, with the confidence half a dozen well-armed horseman at his back gave him.

"We are seeking friends of ours," the smaller man proffered.

"Are you indeed?"

"Yes, a man, someone called Senan, summoned me here."

Senan regarded him with suspicion but having looked at his clothing and in particular his hands, hands not used to conflict, he admitted, "I am Senan."

"Ah, good." The rider slipped off his mount surprisingly smoothly. "I am Taliesin the bard, you will know me by—"

"Reputation?" the other rider put in.

"Well, I suppose, that's true," Taliesin said amiably.

"Ah! So, you are Taliesin," Senan said. "I did expect you to come here in the company of my men, however. No matter, and your friend? If memory serves only you were summoned."

"Oh, Senan." Taliesin sighed. "You would not expect me to ride through these lands on my own? Oh, don't get me wrong, I can wield this thing," he said, pointing to his sword, "but I'm not naïve enough to think I could fight off a troop as your own. Anyway, I should have mentioned, your men will be along soon. We decided to come separately, you never know what is in their hearts."

"That's reassuring. Nonetheless, you can defend yourselves as a couple?" Senan asked, amused.

Taliesin paused for a moment and then a big smile crossed his face. "As this man is Gwallog ap Lleenog, Lord of Lomond and Prince of Elmet, I think I can confidently say yes with two."

"Gwallog ap Lleenog?" Senan nodded his head a fraction. "I meant no offence, Lord. Your reputation precedes you as a great swordsman."

"None taken, Senan, if you had I would have opened your throat."

Gwallog was indeed a man with a reputation for being a ferocious warrior. As a swordsman he was unequalled. A man in his mid-thirties, he was heavily bearded and his features were rugged. He was a tall handsome man with a scar on his right cheek that stretched from below his eye to his beard line. His hair was thick and his expression serious, almost brooding. His eyes were very dark, almost black. He flexed his muscular shoulders and stared at Senan with an intensity that made him shift uncomfortably on his mount.

Senan smiled tightly, the blood rushing into his face. "Yes, Lord. Please, follow and share food with us, you have travelled some distance."

"Thank you," Taliesin chirped. "You must forgive my friend, he gets miserable when he is suffering from one of his headaches."

"Ah, yes of course. I am sure the Lady Crierwy can prepare a tonic that will help," Senan said uncertainly, "I think she uses willow bark extract," he continued.

Gwallog grunted his thanks in response.

As soon as Crierwy saw Taliesin's smiling face, she ran to him and flung her arms about him and allowed him to spin her around. "You are most welcome," she laughed. "It has been too long."

"If you welcome me like that every time you see me, I shall come much more often," he teased.

"Don't make fun of me." She flushed.

"You should allow a little time for me to tease my favourite priestess."

Her smile faded but she had to ask, "Do you forgive me?"

Taliesin laughed and then sighed deeply. "My heart bursts just to see you but our paths, it would seem, were meant to be different. Our spirits demand that we must converge but you are destined to be the Priestess of the Cauldron and I, a famous poet and bard."

"I know your heart and I know you put a brave face on it. I love you but I cannot give my heart to you or indeed any man. I must give my heart and mind to the goddess and there is no room for a man in my affections except my little boy."

Taliesin nodded sadly but gathered himself. "Ah yes, Arthur! I will have my fill of that little fellow. But…" He paused. "I have been remiss. I must present to you the Lord Gwallog ap Lleenog of Lomond," he announced.

Gwallog strode forward and bowed. "Lady."

"Lord Gwallog! I remember my father very much admired your father; he was a fine man." She noticed Gwallog's muscled arms, but his intensity was almost uncomfortable, even threatening.

"You are exceedingly kind, I can only try to step out of his shadow," he said quietly, "but I'm not sure I ever will."

"It is a burden we all bear when we have parents like ours." Crierwy shrugged. "But we have our own place in this world, our own course and we will be remembered for our own actions."

Gwallog bowed slightly and grunted his thanks. "My Lady."

Crierwy studied him for a moment, trying to decide if she liked this man or, more to the point, trusted him. "Come, take sustenance with me and my bodyguard. My brother will join us shortly. I must apologise first; he is a man full of melancholy. These days have been painful for him and he feels angry and lost."

Food was prepared and shared. Crierwy had concocted a tonic for Gwallog which he made clear to anyone who would listen, tasted disgusting. Despite this and much to his surprise and relief, the pain at the back of his head became gradually more manageable. "I would ask you for a whole skin of that, Lady," Gwallog asked. Crierwy was delighted and duly obliged.

Cynon joined them, remaining quiet, but when the effect of the mead began to take its toll, his mood lightened. Crierwy locked on, momentarily happy to see her brother telling embellished stories of their escape from Serf's Isle. While they ate, Arthur was swept from his basket and passed around the warriors again.

As Taliesin promised, Tearlach and his men returned, and they quickly joined in the general merriment. Soon enough Taliesin was being gently pressured into telling a story, although he needed very little persuasion. He stood, pausing for effect, and grandly announced, "My very good friends, both old and new, I would like to give you a rendition of my poem, indeed a song, to mead."

The men roared their appreciation and Crierwy smiled and clapped. Taliesin coughed and cleared his throat. He held a jug of mead above his head, cleared his throat and began:

"So, I will adore the ruler, chief of every place. May Maelgwyn of Mona be affected with mead, and affect us, from the foaming mead-horns, with the choicest pure liquor, which the bees collect, and do not enjoy. Mead distilled sparkling; its praise is everywhere."

"Here, here," they responded.

Taliesin turned to Gwallog, who was smiling now. "You should add the willow tonic to the mead," he announced. Gwallog raised his jug in acknowledgement.

"Where was I?" Taliesin puzzled. "Ah yes... The multitude of creatures," he continued, "which the earth nourishes, for food, for drink, till doom they will continue. I will implore the ruler, sovereign of the country of peace, to liberate Elphin from banishment. The man who gave me wine and ale and mead and the great princely steeds, beautiful their appearance, may he yet give me bounty to the end. By the will of the goddess, she will give in honour, five-hundred festivals in the way of peace. Elphinian knight of mead, late be thy time of rest. And that, my friends, is that," Taliesin announced with exuberant satisfaction.

His audience roared their delight and Taliesin bowed deeply. "A work in progress," he said in mock deprecation.

"You are too modest, Taliesin," Gwallog said quietly with a hint of mockery.

"Well done, Taliesin," the warriors cried.. "To Taliesin," they called, cups raised.

Taliesin bowed again deeply. "Thank you."

"To mead," Cynon called.

"Ah the most important," Taliesin replied. "Yes, to mead."

"To mead!" they saluted as one.

Once the eating and drinking had ended, Crierwy, Cynon and Taliesin sat on the edge of the stream that skirted the hill leading up to the Roman fort. The sun shone on their faces, but it was cool and fresh enough for it to be the perfect antidote to the lingering taste of the mead they had drunk too much of. Taliesin stepped into the shallow stream and splashed water over his legs and torso before bending down to wash his face. It was certainly bracing, and he was instantly refreshed. After some time sitting in amiable silence, it was Cynon who broke the silence. "It's good to see you, my friend."

Taliesin nodded. "I'm sorry it is not in better times."

Cynon gave a tight smile. "I wish it wasn't this way, I wish this pain did not fall to me, I wish—"

"Stop it, brother, you are not the only one in pain. He was my father too, Arthur's grandfather and Mother's husband. When will you acknowledge my responsibility in all this? Don't you think my guilt overflows?"

"I don't hold you responsible," Cynon responded plaintively.

"But you have thought it, brother, I know you too well," she responded, eyeing him closely.

Cynon chose not to respond.

She grunted, "Your silence is deafening. The way I have to see it, otherwise it would eat me up inside, is that if you had not come to find me, you would be dead too. And what then, I would have no father, no brother, and Arthur no grandfather and no uncle."

"Morcant would not have made his move if I had been there," he whispered.

"Maybe. But you cannot know that. And if it wasn't Morcant and it was woodland bandits, what then?" she argued. "I suppose you would have stopped him going hunting?"

"And why not? I would have tried."

She raised an eyebrow. "Yes, of course, Father would have done what you asked of him."

He could not help himself and chuckled at that but fought hard to control himself.

"Cynon," Taliesin interjected, "you cannot escape fate. This was destined to happen. None of us, my friend, choose our fate and there is a reason we find ourselves in such times. We all have a purpose, you have a purpose, Clydno had a purpose, and your sister has a purpose. Fate will pull back its veil and reveal itself in good time."

"Taliesin is right," Crierwy agreed. "I fear this Morcant will always be a figure of divisiveness," she continued. "His part in this tale is far from over and all of us shall pay a price."

As soon as the words were out of her mouth, she immediately regretted them. Cynon did not need to be riled further. The hatred of Morcant was evident and her inflammatory comments were unhelpful at best. She sighed and paused a moment before adding, "This is out of our hands for now. It is our duty to our family and to our followers to show we are still relevant. For the time being let us not think of this; our time will be numbered in years, not days or months."

Cynon shrugged. "My time will come," he whispered under his breath and lay back on the rich grass listening to the trickle of the river. He had been in a kind of purgatory since he had learned the fate of his father. He realised and was beginning to accept, even though he wanted immediate retribution, there was nothing that could be done. Patience was now key, and he would need to find another purpose, a direction, and it would not be in Lothian. For now, he would need to find peace in his heart. At that his eyes closed, and sleep took him.

At the sound of soft snoring, Crierwy looked over at her brother and smiled. She could not remember the last time she had seen such a relaxed expression on her brother's face. It had been too long, it had been so hard for both of them, but life was hard and always full of suffering, she reflected. It was as likely as not that tomorrow might be their last day. Life and death walked the same path too closely. She breathed heavily and cast her eyes across the greenery towards the borders of Lothian and smiled sadly.

Her reverie was disturbed by Taliesin tossing a large stone in the water.

"Where were you, Crierwy? You seem so... distant," he asked.

She shrugged, turning toward him. "More to the point," she said, "where have you been?"

"Where shall I start?" he replied, smiling broadly.

"The short version, please," she begged.

Taliesin feigned hurt. "Are you suggesting I talk too much?"

"Well... it's not a criticism, more of... an observation," she stuttered.

Taliesin harrumphed. "It is my role in life to tell tales and to lift the soul."

"That is as maybe, but this is a hillside by a river, not a great hall. And this is me and not some king or petty warlord."

"All right, I have been travelling. I have seen the lands of Alt Clut, Dalriada, and fleetingly, even Lothian, although the welcome there is rather cold these days. Your father was a much more appreciative audience. Anyway, my last visit was to my uncle's lands, well, his sons to be more accurate."

"Rhun?" she exclaimed.

"Yes, none other than Rhun Hir, brother of Bruide and Domelch."

"It's all a bit incestuous!"

"Aye, it is. Oh, and I have seen Maelgwyn too."

"I remember Maelgwyn. Gwynedd is such a lovely country," she said wistfully

"And you initiated me there." Taliesin smiled,

"Hmmm, I did indeed," she reflected, "and so far away from this place."

They sat in comfortable silence soaking up the warm spring afternoon. The sound of birds and men busying themselves and the occasional snore from Cynon interrupted the peace that enveloped them. But there was one thing that was clearly being unsaid and Crierwy was puzzled that Taliesin hadn't mentioned anything. In the end, curiosity got the best of her.

"Who is this Gwallog and why is he here? More precisely, what is he doing here with you?" she asked.

"Oh, someone I met on the road," he responded carelessly.

"You met on the road," she repeated evenly

"Hmm, yes, I have a magnetism."

"You're lying to me; you are taking me for a fool, my dear friend."

He paused a while ".Well, in a manner of speaking," he responded, trying to remain as detached as he could.

"Don't be irritating, what aren't you telling me?"

Taliesin did not respond but he felt himself shrink as Crierwy shot him a withering look. "I-I—" he stuttered.

"I warn you, little Gwyn, I will turn you into something unnatural if you don't start being honest with me."

"You couldn't," he said flippantly. "You wouldn't," he said, with a little less confidence.

"Shall we find out?" she hissed. "So, I ask again, who is he and why is he here?" Her voice hardened.

He knew his answer would result in a verbal battering. He had given his word that Gwallog's purpose would not be shared, although when he had made his promise, he knew he would never be able to resist Crierwy. Why anyone would think that a man like Gwallog would travel with a bard was, frankly, a naive underestimation. He could not, however, help smiling to himself at the situation he now found himself in. He could, of course just make up another story; after all, he was rather good at that, but judging by Crierwy's face, he was certain he wouldn't get away with it or, at least, not without losing his manhood. No, he would have to tell her and hope he, or worse, Gwallog, would survive the day. Yes, he was stuck between a rock and a hard place.

"All right," he said, holding his hands up in surrender. He paused and took a long breath in. "It was Aedan."

The stream of invective that flowed from Crierwy's mouth was not unexpected but the time it took was quite staggering. He marvelled at her ability to say so much, so loudly and without taking a breath. He also reflected that many of the expletives she had shouted were unknown to him. Heads were turning throughout the encampment and though Cynon remained stubbornly asleep for much of the diatribe, he could not hope to stay in slumber for all of it.

"What's going on?" he asked groggily.

"Oh, shut up," she snapped, "go back to sleep."

"Right," he shrugged, and turned over on to his side, his back to the confrontation.

"Can I do that too?" Taliesin pleaded.

"No, there's more to say." She rounded on him again.

He raised his hands in submission. "What could I do?"

"How about saying no! And if he asked why, you would have said because if I agree she will kill me most horribly," Crierwy spat.

During Crierwy's barrage, Gwallog tentatively made his way over to the group. He didn't want to, but he recognised a comrade in need. He could not help being amused as he noticed Cynon cowering close by and mouthing, "Help me," at the approaching warrior.

"Lady," he announced in his low, gruff voice. "Perhaps I might be able to explain? Our friend the bard appears to have failed to find the words to tell you of my purpose. Surprising as that might seem. I will say that my head throbbed after just a couple of hours of his verbal diarrhoea."

Despite herself, Crierwy could not help but smile at that comment. "Yes well, his voice might be a lot higher by sunset."

Both Gwallog and Taliesin winced, but Gwallog persisted. "Lady, he was not given a lot of choice. Prince Aedan can be very... persuasive, as you know."

Crierwy glowered at him; the potential meaning of his words were not lost on her. "Have a care," she warned. "I hope your words do not have any unwanted meaning." Her eyebrow arched.

"My lady, I meant no insult," Gwallog said quickly, his face flushing.

Crierwy said nothing but a point had been made.

She gathered herself letting the anger subside. She gazed into his eyes. "So, Sir Gwallog ap Lleenog. Why are you here and what is it you ask of me?"

"Lady," he soothed, "Prince Aedan sent me as both your protector and guide. He knew you would be... unwilling to accept his help so he asked me because I am to be betrothed to his daughter, Muirgein, for when she is old enough and he wanted someone he could trust and who would have an interest in your position being resolved."

"My position being resolved?" Crierwy responded incredulously.

"There's that echo again," Taliesin put in.

Both Crierwy and Gwallog shot him a glare and he bowed his head.

"Are those Aedan's words?"

"No, mine, and I apologise again for my poor choice of words." He smiled tightly.

"So, you will be my son's brother-in-law, I suppose?"

"Yes, I suppose so, but we digress."

"We do," she responded abruptly. She sighed and tried to compose herself. "Let us say I accept your help and I am not saying I am. What is your plan?"

"My Lady, Prince Aedan believes that during these times of... uncertainty, you should go south into the land of Dyfed."

"Dyfed," she responded flatly.

"You will be protected by the Lord Conor," he pressed on.

"You mean the father of—"

"Father-in-law," he corrected, "of High King Diarmait of Ireland. Conor has a son of four years, Cai, who would be a companion for Arthur as he grows."

"Conor is a relation of Aedan's?"

"Distant, but yes. There is a Christian settlement there which Aedan thinks will be a safe place for you all, bearing in mind how effective your safety was in Serf's community."

"For a while, I suppose," she acknowledged.

"But you will be far from harm, Lady. The man who is the head monk there is called Dewi. His mother is known to us, and she is sympathetic to the old ways. Once people forget of your existence, or more to the point threat, you can be more secure to travel where you will."

"Forgotten? I very much doubt it," she snorted.

"Crierwy," Taliesin interjected, "you can return to Llyn Tegid."

"Well, that has its attractions but I sense there is something else that remains unsaid," she said suspiciously. "Aedan always has an ulterior motive."

"Yes, Lady, you know him well. When the boy is of age, he wants him to join my lord in Manau."

She sighed audibly, but she knew that Arthur's status as a child of Beltane, blessed by the gods, would be politically advantageous to Aedan's ambitions. She knew too that Arthur would be expendable if his plans did not come to fruition. Aedan was a prince of Manau; his father had been killed and replaced as king by his uncle. Aedan's future appeared bleak. What were the chances of Arthur being recalled? Small? But Aedan was wily, if anyone could go from a man of little hope to a man of power and influence it would be Aedan. Aedan had probably concluded that the final piece of his road to power was Arthur himself. She closed her eyes as her anger began to rise again. Her face reddened and her jaw clenched but she knew it was hopeless trying to fight this battle. She breathed out slowly and stared even deeper into Gwallog's eyes; he physically cringed under her venomous gaze. Eventually she said, "And if I refuse?"

"How can I say this… That option, according to the Prince Aedan, is not available to you."

"You surprise me." She laughed coldly. What choice did she have for now?

"Do you have an answer for me?" Gwallog asked smoothly.

"I suppose I have little choice."

"I suppose not."

"So just you and Taliesin will ride to protect us? Forgive me if I do not feel comforted by that."

"And me," Cynon ventured.

"It will be enough," Gwallog grunted with unnatural confidence.

"And when do we leave?"

"Tomorrow."

"Well then," Taliesin said cheerily, "we should leave on a full stomach and say our farewells to Senan and company,"

"Oh, good grief," Crierwy moaned under her breath.

Chapter 8

Enemies at Every Turn

That night the fires blazed, ale flowed and the food plentiful. "Taliesin," Nessa called, "give us a song."

Taliesin grinned and Crierwy and Gwallog rolled their eyes, a reaction ignored by Taliesin. Instead, he struggled to his feet and stood before the group, a large pot of ale raised above his head. "I have, my friends, as luck would have it, just these last few days composed the very song," he announced.

"Of course you have," Gwallog groaned loudly. "I'm going to have to slit his throat before long," he murmured to Crierwy.

Crierwy chuckled.

Taliesin chose to ignore Gwallog's grumble and cleared his throat. "My worthy warriors," he began, "the qualities shall be extolled of the man who chained the wind. When his powers come, extremely noisy the elements; forever will thy impulse be, thou dost pervade the tide of darkness and day. The day, there will be a shelter to me, the night, it will be rested. Softness is praised. The goddess caused the sun of summer, and its excessive heat; and she caused the abundance of the wood and field. Lie is the powerful cause of the stream, flowing abundantly. It is the powerful cause of every kindness; the goddess redeemed me and before they came, the people of the world to the one hill, they will not be able to do the least, without the power of the king, or queen." He winked. He was in full flow now, gesticulating wildly and pulling exaggerated faces. "Until it shall sprout," he continued, "lie shall steep it another time until it is sodden. Not for a long time will be finished what the elements produce."

He gazed around at the warriors, entranced by his acting and his honeyed voice, and smiled. They were under his spell. "Let his vessels be washed," he continued, "let his wort be clear. And when there shall be an exciter of song, let it be brought from the cell, let it be brought before kings. In splendid festivals will not oppose every two the honey that made it. The provocative of the drunkard is drunkenness. The fishes might show the capacity of the lodgements of the gravel of the salt sea, before it overwhelms the strand, the gravel of the salt sea below the sand."

His audience erupted although Nessa was turning left and right in confusion asking, "I don't know what half of that meant!" Laughter followed, but a couple of his comrades assured him he wasn't alone. The feasting continued and despite his efforts Taliesin was not allowed to continue, much to his obvious annoyance, Crierwy's delight and Gwallog's relief.

As dawn broke, the camp was struck and despite the hangovers afflicting many of the men, Senan, Tearlach, Nessa and Dugald volunteered to accompany Crierwy, and her entourage, until they passed into South Rheged, much to her relief.

Gwallog had planned to keep to the western coast, past the Roman fort of Deva Victrix, through Gwynedd until reaching the settlement of Dewi in the lands of Dyfed, a trip of almost four hundred miles. It would take three weeks of constant daytime traveling.

Crierwy was apprehensive and dreaded the thought of traveling such long distances with an infant, although she had to admit that they were putting a satisfyingly great distance between themselves and the people wanting to manipulate or harm her and little Arthur. She was also depressed at the thought of traveling such distances with her brother, whose brooding over their father's death was hard to watch.

Despite his gruff manner and scary demeanour, Crierwy, with Taliesin's promptings, had concluded Gwallog was probably an honourable man, and despite some initial verbal slips, his increasing openness made her feel safe. His presence also gave her a sense of hope, and to her surprise, she began to have feelings of warmth and affection towards him. Senan, too, had continued to stand by his word and she recognised that he must have given up a lot to continue to accompany her, and she supposed, his comrades Tearlach, Nessa and Dugald must have done likewise. Nonetheless she remained a little uneasy as she knew little of these men, particularly Dugald, whose doubtful behaviour gave her the most concern. She had watched him the previous evening and noticed he drank little and he had disappeared a number of times. He even looked shifty, he wasn't as burly as the other men and there was something haunting about his face which showed no emotion even when his talk and actions warranted it. What worried her, too, was that she couldn't, for the life of her, remember him retiring to sleep. She shrugged and tried to dismiss her concerns; after all, she hadn't stayed awake that late herself.

The train of horses moved out once all was ready and set off in a south easterly direction before turning south. Crierwy saw that Dugald was bringing up the rear just behind Nessa, although within some thirty minutes he disappeared from sight. Ahead of them was a wood and beyond that, she knew, was a narrow burn known locally as the Glen. Despite trying to ignore her rising anxiety she felt lightheaded and her head started to swim. In her stupor she saw men on horseback but she didn't recognise their faces. She also saw Dugald's contorted face, his hateful eyes boring into her. She tried to call out for help when she realised the threat was real but no one appeared to listen. They just talked amongst themselves as if she wasn't there. Dugald strode up to her, drawing his dagger before slashing his blade across her throat. As she choked and her life ebbed away she saw him raise his dagger above Arthur's sleeping body. She tried to scream but no sound came. Instead, she grabbed at the open wound, desperately trying to swallow the blood pulsing from her throat. Slowly, as her life ebbed away, she began to fall forward.

"Lady!" a voice hollered. She could feel herself falling but before she hit the ground two muscular arms were folded around her as she blacked out. She came to with a jolt, her arms flailing and fighting off her imagined assailants. She started to regain her equilibrium and discovered she was lying beneath her horse with Gwallog sprinting over to assist Senan, who had been the man who managed to break her fall whilst also having to fight her off as she tried to defend herself from her imaginary assailants, and laid her gently on the lush grass.

"Lady! Are you ill, are you injured?" Senan repeated urgently.

"Save my boy," she yelled and thrashed. "They're killing him."

Gwallog shook her roughly, until she began to focus and tears began to flow. Together with Senan, they gently removed an uninjured but screaming Arthur from her sling. "Are you all right?" Taliesin asked, concern etched across his face. "Quick," he hollered to Senan, "get her some water."

On Senan's return, Taliesin mopped Crierwy's brow and she gradually gathered herself, drinking deeply from a water bottle. "What happened?" Taliesin asked again. "Can you tell us?"

Crierwy sat up and gulped in the fresh morning air as her panic subsided. "Sorry, I... I must have fainted," she stuttered. Suddenly, she started. "Dugald! Where is he?"

"Dugald?" Senan repeated. "Why I don't know, I thought he was bringing up the rear."

"What about Dugald?" Gwallog asked suspiciously.

"I think I had a dream... a premonition," she whispered.

"About Dugald?" Senan said flatly. "I imagine that's not something he could ever have boasted about before today," he laughed.

"Aye he's a strange one," Nessa put in.

"Is he still with us?" Crierwy asked.

"Nessa?" Senan asked.

"He was behind me," he responded.

Senan glanced at Gwallog. "I'll go with Nessa a hundred or so paces back to see if he's behind us," he said.

Gwallog nodded but before he responded he stopped and looked at Crierwy, his anxiety growing. "Lady? Are we safe?"

Crierwy shrugged, but added, "For the moment, I think."

Gwallog had always been indifferent to the mysteries of the old ways and in most circumstances he would have put the previous few minutes down to an overwrought woman fearful for the safety of her child. Nonetheless, he had a strange feeling about this; a sense of foreboding was growing within him. Crierwy was a Priestess of the Cauldron and he was surprised she had not once made reference to her powers, if that's what they were called. Of course, just because she didn't speak of the old ways and didn't moan about this new religion, Christianity, didn't mean she was a woman who didn't have powers beyond his comprehension. If this woman had had a premonition, or at least had said so, it was probably sensible to take notice of her.

Senan and Nessa trudged away. Gwallog watched the two men push through the bushes to their rear. Trepidation continued to grab his chest, and inevitably, his head began to pound. He stared at Crierwy and then scanned the woods about them. He remained silent and rubbed his bearded chin. "Lady," he said quietly, "what did you see?"

Crierwy explained in detail what she had seen.

"A trap," Gwallog breathed.

"Do you think so?" Crierwy asked nervously.

"It would be the ideal place," he muttered as he continued looking along the path that led towards the burn.

Tearlach approached them. "We should tread carefully. The burn is ahead and it would be ideal place for an ambush," he said as if reading Gwallog's mind.

"I fear you're right," Gwallog said flatly.

Everyone was quiet for a while, no one wanting to believe the vision, but no one could risk not heeding it. Gwallog felt everyone's gaze upon him. Despite his deep seated scepticism, he was worried to the point of nausea. Eventually he said, "Let's wait for Senan and Nessa," then added quietly, almost to himself, "I don't like this, I don't like it at all."

It seemed an age before Senan and Nessa returned. "There's no sign of him. No horse, no personal items, nothing," Senan said.

"No sign of any fight," Nessa added.

"We can't just plough on," Taliesin said. "If Crierwy has seen something we shouldn't ignore it." He looked at Cynon. "You know this."

Gwallog shrugged, taking a sip of the draft Crierwy had made for him to help soothe his head. He stood up, and standing motionless for moment, he thought through their options. "I agree we should not ignore what the Lady has seen," he said eventually. He looked about him again. "They could take us in here in the trees," he offered, "but it would be chaotic and there is a chance of escape." He looked to his front again. "If they attack us between the tree line and the burn, Tearlach is right, they could trap us." He looked over to Senan. "We need to know what we're up against."

"They wouldn't want to take any risks. They will know we are armed and that Gwallog is with us so I suspect we will be heavily outnumbered." Senan shrugged.

"Yes, they wouldn't risk attacking us unless they have two or even three times our number," Gwallog snorted, "so we need to know where they will fall upon us." He sighed loudly. "So," he continued, "Senan, how are Nessa and Tearlach at tracking?"

Senan grinned. "You won't find better."

"And you?"

"You won't find better, except me!" He grinned.

"Why aren't I surprised," Gwallog grunted, remembering how easily he and Taliesin had lost them on their journey to the fort of Camlann. "All right," he said, straightening, "you three scout the trees and then identify where our friends are concealing themselves and when you return we'll make a plan of action."

"We'll be quick before they suspect something," Senan called over his shoulder and disappeared into the undergrowth with Nessa and Tearlach in hot pursuit.

Gwallog, Taliesin, Cynon, Crierwy and Arthur found a hiding place around a large oak and waited for the others to return. They sat in silence, the tension palpable. Gwallog took a stone from the earth and used it to start sharpening his sword, the noise grating against their nerves. Time passed slowly, any noises of twigs snapping or trees rustling keeping them on edge. Taliesin was certain that warriors would burst through the trees and kill them before they were able to prepare their weapons. But Gwallog, on the other hand, looked completely calm keeping his eyes on the trail. But when he stopped mid scrape, any comfort anyone was taking from his calm demeanour was quickly extinguished.

Cynon drew his sword first followed, reluctantly, by Taliesin. Silently they formed a semi-circle in front of Crierwy and waited. They could all hear the rustling coming in their direction until a warrior burst into the clearing. Gwallog strode forward to strike but stopped as Senan lifted his arms in submission.

There was a collective groan, a mixture of relief and pent up emotion. "By all the gods, Gwallog." Senan's panicked voice came out in a squeal that sounded more childlike than he intended. His mood didn't improve much when he heard sniggering from behind him. He spun round and gave his comrades an angry scowl which stopped the merriment quickly, although the smiles still remained. "I'll be having words with you bastards later," Senan growled.

"I had to be... cautious." Gwallog smiled.

"Quite," Senan sighed.

"Your hair has turned white, Senan," Taliesin goaded.

"You'll have no head for your white hair to grow on if you say another fucking word," Senan warned testily.

"Do you need some time to... compose yourself, Senan?" Nessa asked.

"Fuck off."

"That is fine language to say in front of a lady," Cynon taunted.

Senan coloured. "I-I... am sorry, Lady," he stuttered, mortified.

Crierwy arched her eyebrows, nodded and bowed to him. "Apology accepted."

"I think you might learn a whole new vocabulary from the Lady Crierwy," Taliesin chimed in.

"You're still in my bad books, little Gwyn," Crierwy retorted. "Ribbit." She imitated a frog.

Taliesin's smile faded immediately.

"Now," Gwallog said gruffly, "can we focus on the problem in hand?"

"Of course," Senan said, his breathing less heavy.

Senan rooted around for a stick and created a canvas in the earth with his foot. He began drawing a rudimentary map starting with the tree line, the land from the trees down to the burn and a number of steps the other side. To cross the burn they would have to turn left immediately after they left the tree line and walk between fifty and hundred steps until they reached the ford where they could cross the burn before turning south eastward and then westward. The distance from the trees to the burn was no more than twenty steps; there were even a couple of trees on the burn's bank offering some cover, but also narrowing the distance between the wood and the burn.

Senan explained that about five or six soldiers were to the right of the exit so they would be behind them as they came into the open. Another half a dozen were just beyond the ford and another four men hidden on the other side.

"Like rats in a trap," Taliesin muttered.

"Not necessarily," Gwallog responded, "but we do need to even the odds."

"What do you propose?" Cynon said.

"Look at the map, assuming it's accurate." He arched an eyebrow, glancing at Senan.

Senan's mouth twitched. "do I sense distrust in my abilities?"

"Should I?"

"For goodness sake," Crierwy interrupted, "are we planning to escape or do we plan to build a fort and hope for the best that old age overtakes us?"

Taliesin burst out laughing. "I don't know who I should be afraid of, you or the lady?" He chuckled.

There was silence for a moment before there was an eruption of laughter from all of them before Crierwy rolled her eyes and uttered expletives unbecoming of a priestess. "How can you be so... childish at a time like this?"

Gwallog smiled grimly. "Men do strange things when there is a strong possibility they're about to die," he said quietly.

He returned to the map, and pointed out that the riverbank was slightly curved and there were over a hundred yards or so between the two groups of horsemen, so it would be highly unlikely they would be able to see each other. Furthermore, the five warriors on the other bank of the burn had a blind spot which meant that they too could not see the horseman who would be at their back as they came out of the trees.

The distance from the tree line to the steep banks of the river were only about five horses wide with the terrain making it nearly impossible for them to be outflanked. So their adversaries could only corral them towards the other horseman who, in all probability, didn't expect Crierwy's party to put up a fight until it was too late, by which time they would be done for.

It was agreed after some discussion that Senan would take Tearlach and Cynon, and move around behind the horseman to the west of their position and jump them. Once that was done they would drop down the bank and follow the water's edge to set up an ambush point at the spot where the rest of them would become visible to the other horseman. The biggest problem they faced was the four horsemen across the river, so speed was imperative before they concentrated their efforts on the remaining horsemen.

Gwallog, searched everyone's faces for their reactions and when nothing more was said he took everyone over the plan again twice more. He was only left satisfied when Taliesin yawned mockingly. "Good," he said. "We have now been here for a lot longer than they expected. So…" he breathed, "they will be wondering if their trap is going to be sprung."

Cynon shot him a worried look. "Will they come searching for us?"

"I doubt it," Gwallog replied, "but they will, by now, start to think that we won't be coming out of the wood so, with luck, they'll start to lose focus and we can strike whilst they are distracted. Remember to screech like an owl when the first phase is complete," he pressed. "Oh, and I must stress to you all, that we cannot allow any of these men to leave this place. Whoever is behind this cannot know how much of a head start we have or in which direction we are travelling once we leave here. We must trust that anything our friend Dugald knows has only been shared with his new friends. "

Everyone nodded grimly; the plan was in play.

Crierwy brought up the rear but she had unsheathed her dagger from its scabbard inside her tunic. She would play her part if she had to. She was no shrinking violet; she was a Priestess of the Cauldron and those willing to kill a sacred woman would die and deserve it.

Senan, Tearlach and Cynon set off through the trees armed with swords and hunting bows. Much of the wood was free from thick undergrowth and allowed them to travel without hindrance, but at the same time they were still able to benefit from the little undergrowth there was so they could hide behind it if needed. Having made good time, they moved to the point chosen at the rear of the unsuspecting horsemen. As expected, the horsemen swirled around, clearly discussing how much longer they should stay and whether they should enter the woods which might leave them open to ambush themselves.

After some fifteen minutes, Gwallog led the rest of them along the path and towards the tree line. When they reached the edge of the wood, they crouched and waited for the signal for the action to begin. Meanwhile,

Senan motioned to the others to work their way around the horseman so that they formed a semi-circle.

Senan, Cynon and Tearlach took bows from over their shoulders and notched arrows. They marked their targets and drew back the strings. At Senan's signal they loosed their arrows and three of the men pitched forward. None of the fallen knew what was happening as their world went black. Before the remaining three had time to react they were set upon. Tearlach and Senan were ruthlessly efficient, but Cynon was initially forced away and kicked in the rib area, winding him, as the target man's horse spun around. Taking his sword from its scabbard to strike at Cynon, the horseman continued to spin before Tearlach notched another arrow, his shot taking the man in the throat. He spluttered and choked and his expression turned from one of evil intent to one of complete surprise and then of horrified realisation. Slowly he slipped off his horse and Senan sprinted across the ground and dispatched him.

Cynon coughed and fingered his ribs, struggling for air. He rolled into a foetal position, moaning. At that Senan strolled up to him and checked him over. "You're only winded, my friend."

"Oh that's good," he gasped. "Does getting killed hurt more?"

"You have to be alive to feel pain," Tearlach muttered.

"Come on, sit up, catch your breath and compose yourself, the fun has just begun." Senan smiled.

Senan wrapped his arms under Cynon's armpits and pulled him up. Cynon groaned at the exertion and grimaced as a fresh wave of pain shot across his ribs, making him bend over, and struggle for air again.

"All right?"

"I will be," he gasped.

"Come on, down the bank into the burn. I will send the signal for phase two."

They scrambled down and Senan let out the screech of an owl. Moments later there came the response.

Now it was Gwallog's turn to run the gauntlet, a time to show his mettle. He slowly unfolded himself and stood. His swords were strapped to his back; he fingered them and released them a few inches to ensure they could be drawn quickly and smoothly. He looked around at the others and nodded. Nessa beckoned Taliesin who, in turn, held out his hand for

Crierwy to take. He gazed into her eyes for a moment and looked away. Gwallog rolled his shoulders, took a breath and closed his eyes, offering up a prayer to the Morrigan. He might be sceptical about the gods but there was no harm in hedging his bets. He stepped into the clearing and with an unpleasant grin, whispered, "Let's go."

They left the safety of the tree line and made their way towards the other horsemen on their side of the bank. They turned slightly left, bringing them face to face with their foe. What met them stopped their hearts; the horsemen on the opposite bank had crossed over and they were now facing ten warriors.

"Oh shit!" Taliesin groaned.

Gwallog stopped and drew his swords. Weighing up the situation quickly, he turned his head and whistled. Immediately, Senan popped his head over the bank and quickly gestured to the others. They clambered up and ran over to Gwallog's side. "Shields," he roared and they immediately formed a shield wall with Taliesin standing behind with Crierwy.

They recognised Dugald immediately. He smiled viciously, raising a horn to his lips, ready to call the others who were to Gwallog's rear. Gwallog lowered his shield a fraction. "Don't waste your breath, you're going to need it for the fight ahead." He grinned.

"You think?" Dugald laughed.

"Let's see. Who wants to count?"

Time passed slowly and as it did, Dugald's smile began to fade. The horsemen were looking at each other in confusion. "Come on, you little shit stain, ten versus five, a bard and a woman. Those odds not good enough for you? Come and earn your pay," Gwallog taunted.

"Charge!" the man at Dugald's shoulder screamed and the horses leapt forward as all the horsemen dug their heels into their horses' ribs.

The bristling shield wall made the horses veer left and right, but it still forced the small group into a tighter circle around Crierwy. Spears were thrown and arrows loosed but the lack of a firm base resulted in those arrows skittering high and wide. The horsemen came again with swords drawn and axes swinging, bringing them down with jarring clangs on the shields. Nessa lost his footing as he stepped in a rabbit hole, momentarily separating himself from his companions. He was quickly dispatched by a triumphant bearded and thickset man whose grin was all too visible. As the assailant swung his horse away from the defensive wall, Taliesin hurled a dagger which pierced the warrior's shoulder blades. The man grunted and tried frantically to pull out the deadly blade, before slipping off the horse and falling face first into the mud.

Tearlach, too, had dropped to one knee as the horsemen attacked again. The anticipated finishing blow was, however, parried by Gwallog's lightning fast reflexes, much to the horseman's surprise. As Gwallog sprang at the man, Cynon plugged the gap and fought off another sword thrust. Meanwhile Senan had killed or wounded three others and had wounded the horse Dugald had been riding. The horse reared and screamed in pain.

Gwallog dispatched two others in whirl of arms, but as he made his way back to their ever diminishing skirmish line, he saw that Tearlach had succumbed and now rolled over with arrows in his chest. Senan, seeing his comrade fall, lost control. He roared like a wounded mountain lion, and in his grief, struck out from the group and attacked a couple of the horsemen milling around close to the melee. But despite his frenzied swings he left himself open from attack to his rear. Despite the shouts of warning a sword was driven into his back, severing his spine. He dropped to his knees and slumped to his side. Death was immediately upon him.

They were now four against five horsemen. But despite the number advantage, the horsemen began to waver, their losses unexpected. They had lost eleven men. How could this be worth it? Then Dugald called out, "More gold for us, fucking kill them!" Reluctantly, the horsemen rallied again and charged. Gwallog took advantage at the slight pause in the skirmish and had repositioned himself and the others near the steep bank that fell away into the river, using the small number of young trees to make the horses veer away once again.

Crierwy had backed down the bank, finding a little bushy clearing to place Arthur in what was the only safe place she could think of. She scrambled up one of the trees and when she reached a head high branch she used it to leap, dagger raised, onto Dugald's horse, plunging the blade deep into his chest. Gwallog and Cynon took Crierwy's cue and rushed at the remaining horsemen as they tried to turn their horses to face the fray. The riders fell and Gwallog threw one of his swords with unerring accuracy and speed into the face of another rider.

The last horsemen alive swung his horse away as though to flee the scene but as he galloped towards the tree line, both Cynon and Taliesin notched arrows and let fly. Their aim was true; both arrows caught the man between the shoulders. He went rigid and let out a strangled yelp before toppling off his horse.

Gwallog ran to the horseman but he was already dead. Gwallog slumped to one knee, using his sword as a crutch, his breathing heavy from the exertion of the fight. Eventually he raised his head and surveyed the scene. The riderless horses wandered around aimlessly. At least they still had transportation for the journey ahead, he thought.

He noticed Crierwy and Taliesin walking towards him whilst Cynon had taken on the responsibility for rounding up the horses. They looked at him with considerable concern. Initially he was puzzled by their expressions but once he looked at himself, he realised his arms, his legs and his tunic were covered in blood and gore.

"Are you all right? Are you hurt?" Taliesin asked.

Gwallog shook his head. "It's not all my blood."

Crierwy sighed with relief. "You look awful." She grinned.

"Thank you."

"I think a wash in the river might make you more palatable, should we meet people on the road," she said.

"He'll scare them half to death," Taliesin agreed.

"We must leave this place," Gwallog grunted, holding his arm as rivulets of blood streamed down its length and around his fingers.

"We can't just leave them here," Crierwy said disbelievingly. "They should be given dignity in death."

Cynon nodded as he approached. "At least Senan and his comrades deserve it for saving us. We owe them respect in death even more than in life."

Gwallog sighed heavily. He didn't want to stay in this place of carnage and danger but he could find no good argument against them. He pondered a heartbeat and nodded. "So be it."

"And you will wash too?" Crierwy nagged.

"I will."

"We'll make a decent soul of you yet, Sir Gwallog."

Gwallog shrugged and rolled his eyes.

Senan, Tearlach and Nessa were buried in separate graves whilst the others were buried, at Gwallog's insistence, in a single grave. By the time the bodies were buried and funeral incantations sung by both Crierwy and Taliesin, the sun had begun to set over the trees. The onset of night, a weary Gwallog knew, would give them some protection and as long as they got an early start they should remain safe from here on in. The road would be long but each step would take them further from harm.

As he had promised, Gwallog took himself away from the others and scrambled down to the river where he washed away the grubbiness of soil, sweat and blood. The water was cold but refreshing and he was soon joined by the others, except for Crierwy who claimed her own spot fifty yards downstream.

Once they were clean and presentable, Gwallog beckoned them over. "Let us go back into the woods, to where the clearing is and sleep… There must be no fire so no cooked foods. It would appear, from the rich pickings of our friends and fallen comrades, we now have ample provisions," he said matter of factly.

There was no dissent and they did as he instructed although Gwallog stayed behind and gazed over the scene which was eerily quiet now, except for the sounds of the nearby burn. He breathed heavily and turned, almost bumping into Cynon.

"Who was it, who sent them here?" Cynon questioned.

"I don't know, but if I had to guess I would say it's our friend Morcant," Gwallog said wearily.

"That bastard," Cynon growled. "I will have my revenge."

Gwallog grabbed his shoulder. "One day, my friend, when the time is right, one day. And when that day comes," he continued, "I vow to be at your side."

Cynon nodded and grasped Gwallog's arm. "Thank you!"

Chapter 9

Out of Sight, Out of Mind

The trip had been a long one and everyone's rear was red raw as they passed out of Midlothian, travelled through the lands of Segovia, North and South Rheged, skirted the Roman legionary town of Deva Victrix, into the lands of the Welsh lords, before striking south towards the coast overlooking the Irish Sea. Reaching the sea near Dinas Maelor and the River Ystwyth, they stopped and rested for almost a week. The weather had become hot, their only solace being the breezes that wafted in from the sea.

From Dinas Maelor, they followed the coast until they reached Dewi's settlement which overlooked a huge bay that had been named after an Irish nun, St. Bride. Cynon reflected how ironic that a Christian nun, Irish to boot, should have somewhere named after her in a place often overrun by Irish invaders. He shrugged. This new religion was taking hold and people like his sister would only be able to hold it back for so long. Christianity was just like the tides of the Irish Sea, unstoppable. The days of the old ways were numbered, he realised, and there was no prospect of compromise, something he deeply regretted.

Gwallog became ever more separated from his fellow travellers, often riding ahead to scout out the route or, sometimes, he rode off to the rear to investigate the possibility of being followed. Sometimes he did not appear for two or three days at a time and whilst this was a little disconcerting to start with, they soon became used to it. To Crierwy's disappointment the conversations they had, which until now had always been open and friendly, became more awkward and Gwallog became ever more distant from her and less willing to engage. Much to her surprise, she missed him during his absences more and more, a folly in the making, she knew.

They had been travelling for almost a month. Crierwy had been annoyed that the sun had reddened her skin and her freckles stood out. She had never considered herself overly sensitive about her looks but somehow it seemed to matter at this moment, travelling with this group. Cynon had been the first to notice her discomfort.

"Perhaps you are too aware of the Lord Gwallog," he had said, trying to sound innocent. She became ever snappier; Cynon's words had touched a nerve. She tried to ignore her feelings, but she could not help wondering why Gwallog had become so detached. He was a strange, silent, and solitary man, who judging by his demeanour, had seen too much disappointment for someone of his age, although being one of Aedan's acolytes was probably a reason for it.

The fire had almost gone out and Cynon and Taliesin had already settled into an easy slumber. Crierwy and Gwallog sat in awkward silence until Crierwy cleared her throat. Gwallog quickly looked up at her. "Do you require anything, Lady?' he asked, with exaggerated deference.

"I'm puzzled," she mused. "After the fight at the river you were attentive, even effusive which, I suspect, is unusual for you. I enjoyed your company but you have become more and more... distant," she said picking her words carefully. "Have we, or maybe have I offended you in any way?"

"Of course not," he grunted defensively.

"Then what is it?" she pressed.

Gwallog paused a moment. "I have a task to carry out," he said eventually.

"Why do you think Aedan entrusted you with this... task?" she continued.

"He trusts me," he muttered without conviction.

"You must be one of a very small number. And what will your reward be, Gwallog?"

"I am to be his son-in-law, what more of honour can a man ask?"

"And how old is this woman?"

"Muirgein," he interrupted.

"How old is Muirgein?" she probed.

"Eleven, but when she is of age," he said.

"Tell me, Lord Gwallog, are you here to keep Arthur safe?"

"Both of you, of course, but that always depends on the Prince Aedan," Gwallog responded carelessly. "Now if you will forgive me, I have to check the terrain for our travels tomorrow."

"You're running off again?"

"It's best for all of us," Gwallog grumbled. "Trust me on this."

Crierwy looked away and said nothing.

Gwallog strode away and refused to look back until he mounted his horse and rode silently away. He had dreaded any conversation with the Lady Crierwy. Despite his loyalty to Prince Aedan and his eleven-year-old daughter, he found himself attracted to Crierwy and was fearful of his feelings. She was beautiful, more beautiful than he had been told, and he envied Aedan for having her, but he also despised him for his actions. It offended his notion of honour and that troubled him.

He had just lied to her and he hated himself for it. Yes, he was tasked with watching over her, but not the child. His task was, simply put, to judge whether she might pose a threat to Aedan. She was clearly unlikely to threaten Aedan so he could rest easy. But to his surprise he had become committed to protecting her and the child. He had never intended to travel beyond Deva Victrix and yet here he was. He wanted to be *her* man, not Aedan's. It was a dangerous path to tread and a potential romantic liaison, even if she entertained it, would be foolhardy and a probable death sentence. Aedan would certainly regard any relationship as a betrayal as well as a potentially alternative power base. Reluctantly he had to keep her at arm's length, no matter how painful that was. Nothing was ever simple.

News had filtered through of the strife experienced at Loch Leven and she suspected that a story of the possessed wild woman killed by the Picts might probably have been Aeronwen. Crierwy hoped not but the tale filled her with a sense of foreboding.

Gwallog had returned to the borders of Elmet and South Rheged, much to Crierwy's disappointment, choosing to stay there rather than returning to Lomond where his father Lleenog resided. From there, he was within easy distance of Crierwy should the occasion arise, but far enough away to avoid temptation.

Despite continuing disappointments and sadness, life in South Wales had been good to and for Crierwy. She had spent almost seven years in and around Dewi's Settlement. The winters were less harsh than in Lothian, the summers less fresh. Her skin had become healthier looking and her freckles bothered her less. Growing maturity and confidence in herself had indeed been the greatest thing to have happened to her.

She had been taken in and looked after by Dewi's mother, Non, a kindly woman who treated Crierwy as if she were a fine piece of pottery. Despite herself, she had allowed Arthur, once he turned five years, to be fostered by the Lord Conor at the Red Fort. She reasoned that he needed male influences in his life and with Cynon vacant, bodily and mentally, and Gwallog sadly returned home, Conor was the perfect choice.

The separation from Arthur was painful but Crierwy made sure she visited him, regularly spending hours together wandering the hills and gazing out across the sea. Conor had a son, Cai, with whom Arthur had made a grudging friendship. But the family also included Arthur's cousin Drystan and a serious boy called Bedwyr. Crierwy particularly liked Bedwyr and she would often take him with them on their walks. Bedwyr was a shy boy, the same age as Arthur, but he was always loyal to and kind toward Arthur.

Cynon had happily settled into Dewi's settlement. He seemed content labouring in the community, although the other inhabitants looked upon him with some suspicion, not least because he was royalty first and a follower second. Nonetheless, his devotion to Crierwy, albeit fleetingly, was complete despite their spiritual differences.

Crierwy half hoped that Taliesin might stay to mentor Arthur but he appeared to be relieved when Conor had offered to foster the boy. His lack of moral courage, as she saw it, annoyed Crierwy, but she realised she was in no position to complain. She was sad that fate had dealt a poisonous hand but railing against it was of no use to anyone. But Taliesin, Crierwy knew, still had feelings for her and though nothing was ever said, a tension remained. She knew he could not stay and was unsurprised when he had decided his fate lay elsewhere.

As soon as he had rested, he wanted to travel. Much to everyone's surprise, he did not choose to return to Alt Clut; instead he decided on travelling to the court of King Urien in Rheged. Urien was a relatively young king who was building a reputation for his military prowess. As it turned out, Taliesin was very much welcomed, not least because he had a knack for smoothing Urien's ego. Taliesin had concluded that this was a man worth following. Before departing, he chattered enthusiastically, saying that Urien would inevitably be the next Pendragon.

As time moved on, Crierwy became more and more uneasy. She was not fulfilling her role as a priestess. She had come to the conclusion that she could no longer impose on the Christian community that had openly welcomed her. She had been surprised at how friendly and respectful they had been even though they knew what she represented. It was time to move on. She longed to return to Llyn Tegid in the lands of Gwynedd where she had once practiced her craft and had initiated, amongst others, Taliesin. But it wasn't her responsibilities as a priestess that were being neglected, but also being the mother she wanted to be to Arthur. She could not stay hidden from the world forever. Her followers needed guidance, Christianity was spreading quickly and the old ways needed defending. It was time to resume her duties as the Priestess of the Cauldron.

She was flattered that even the man Dewi had told her she could stay, but the experience of Serf's community and the sacrifices they had made for her and Arthur could not be ignored. She would not countenance the risk of that happening again.

These were good people but she also recognised that the nature of Christianity was changing. They were more aggressive in spreading their message and less respect was being shown to so called pagans. She had heard of the arrival of Crimthann, the self-styled Dove of God, Columba, from Ireland. Columba had been part of the royal family, and as the youngest, decided he would be more influential as a Christian monk. Crierwy considered him to be another showman seeking fame.

What had surprised her, and indeed many throughout the lands of Dalriada, was King Conall's desire to gift Iona to Columba. The final decision had not yet been taken but Conall clearly believed the gift would give him more options should Christianity take hold, and strengthen his position as king of Dalriada.

She wondered what Aedan would think of that. Any rebellion would undoubtedly suit him, but she doubted that he would openly support overthrowing his cousin. He was too canny to be so overt. If Aedan was prepared to wait for Arthur to come of age, he was clearly prepared to play the long game. Despite herself she found she was smiling at the thought and found herself beginning to admire this man. Catching herself, she shook her head in annoyance and pushed the thoughts aside.

The machinations of these men were not anything she could influence; her prime concern was for the safety of her child. At least the distance between her and the Picts, who were more interested in their own internal politics, was enough so she could discount any threat. The Christians and those who did their bidding were unlikely to threaten her; after all, there would always be enough doubt amongst Christian followers of the power of the old ways. There were, she mused, a large number of people who followed both religions, just in case.

She was pragmatic enough to understand that one day, people of her beliefs would be overwhelmed by either this Christian God or even the gods of the Angles or Saxons. It was easy to reflect on the machinations of the Britons, Scots and Picts but the invaders from the lands of the Saxons, Angles, Friesians, Franks and Jutes were powerful and their forces were near at hand. The news was that the Saxons had conquered the lands east of the great river Hafren and that they had triumphed at a great battle known as Deorham. It had been a catastrophic reverse and all the gains secured by the great war leader Emrys at Baden had been swept way.

Her trip northwards would be without incident. The protection of twenty warriors of Conor's personal bodyguard made sure of that. The column included many of Arthur's friends as well as an older child called Collen, a distant relative to the great Cunedda. The education and initiation of Cai and the other children into Druidry and the Cauldron Cult was to be her payment for Conor's protection.

Cai was a constant irritant. He was fully aware that the patronage offered by his father very much protected him from any rebuke, although Crierwy would not allow that to cow her. Cai constantly bullied little Arthur and she dealt with it, as often as she could, but Arthur continually refused to ever tell on his foster brother. When she was alone, she wept for her child, but she respected how Arthur continued to show a level of confidence and tenacity far beyond his years. Nonetheless, she could not fail to see the hurt in his eyes.

She had fond memories of Llyn Tegid; it was there where the carefree young woman she had once been had initiated little Gwyn into the cult. Little Gwyn, born of royalty, the nephew of Maelgwyn, but gifted with words, had become Taliesin. Life had been so simple. She and Taliesin were happy together, safe under Maelgwyn's protection but all that certainty had changed almost overnight when the Pendragon had died.

As they progressed, following the coastal paths, the terrain became more mountainous. They reached an old fort where legend said the giant Maelor Gawr had lived. She was surprised that his name was still revered by the locals and smiled as her escort bowed, out of reverence, as they passed by the ancient remains. Legend was indeed important.

On the seventh day they caught sight of the southern shore of the lake that would be their home for the foreseeable future. Crierwy breathed in the sweet air. She was pulled from her reverie when she saw Arthur suddenly tear free from his friends and sprint down the incline and jump, headfirst, into what must have been the frigid water. After her shock, she flung back her head and laughed aloud. It had been the first time for many months that she had laughed so. Her companions stared at her with expressions that said,

'Shouldn't you be stopping him?' Instead, she slid from her horse and ran after him to the lake, and joined her squealing child, followed by Arthur's raucous friends.

Crierwy was unable to stay in the water for long as she was overwhelmed by her students' exuberance. She stepped out of the water and smiled as she cast her eyes over the lake, a place she knew so well, a place of happy memories. She sighed. She was safe for now, but her heart continued to be full of sadness because beyond this haven the world had become bleak and she despaired for her followers.

She found herself watching Arthur swimming with his friends, wondering what the future held. Their hearts were still pure but for how much longer? She began to fear that the pieces were beginning to fall into place and her beautiful boy would soon be wrenched away from her. Aedan would soon come.

Chapter 10

Lailoken

Crierwy and her community had spent their first winter on Lake Tegid. It had been cold, certainly, but her new found security had given her an opportunity to repair her mind and body. Following months of rain, snow and wind, it was a relief to see the onset of spring, flowers blooming, trees in bud and warmth on her face. Life was indeed a miracle. Spring also meant something else to Crierwy. The Beltane celebrations were approaching once again and for Crierwy this was a time of introspection. The memories of when Arthur was conceived were still painfully vivid and would forever be etched into her whole being. A child she loved with a passion was a joy to her, but Aedan's act of deception left her melancholy and yearning for a different life, a less complicated life. Looking out over the lake, she struggled to dismiss the desire that the difficulties she would soon face were not hers.

She had packed the boys off to forage around the lake shore and had busied herself with various tasks, not least putting the small altar back together after the boys had thoroughly examined every wand and crystal that had been placed upon it. Whilst it was irritating that the boys were being less than reverential, she reflected with a feeling of satisfaction that they were still excited by the thought of training, despite having to live such a frugal existence over the winter months.

She was also enormously proud of how Arthur had warmed to his new environment. His confidence, too, appeared to be increasing every day and she noticed he was beginning to show himself as a fledgling leader of the little group. Crierwy was particularly surprised that Arthur had started to wrest influence away from Cai, who was still overbearing and a bully. But Cai's bullying had now stopped after Arthur had given the older, bigger boy a heavy kick in the groin. Cai's goading continued but the impact of his words on Arthur had noticeably diminished.

Of the boys, her favourite, Bedwyr, was the most attentive toward her and toward Arthur. Arthur and Bedwyr had forged a strong bond and it was interesting that when there was any dispute, Bedwyr was always there at Arthur's side. Of the other boys, Collen was the odd one out. He was a loner and the least interested in the activities Crierwy set for the boys. She had tried to speak to the boy at length, fearing his isolation from everyone in the sanctuary. He was always polite but there was something unsettling about his demeanour. Once Crierwy was done speaking with the boy, she could not help casting her mind back to Dugald. She knew it was stupid — he was just a young boy — nonetheless, she was beginning to suspect that this Collen would have some part to play in the coming years. It was ridiculous, she knew, but it was a feeling she could not shake.

She breathed deeply and tried to push the feelings to the back of her mind. She had nobody to confide in except perhaps Taliesin or Cynon on one of their ever-diminishing visits to her settlement. She could not help feeling sad about her brother's growing estrangement, but she knew with complete certainty that she could always turn to him if she ever needed it. Cynon may have become distant but the essence of the man she knew would never change and that thought comforted her.

She walked down to the lake's edge and dipped her hands into the cold water. Thankfully the water was certainly more bearable than the dip she had taken with Arthur on their arrival. She looked about her and when she was satisfied of her solitude, she shed her clothes and dived in. The feeling of the water caressing her skin was both sensuous and invigorating. She swam out further and dipped below the water, swimming to the bottom then pushing her way back to the surface, bursting forth like a salmon.

She rubbed her eyes until they were focused. Then, to her shock and embarrassment, she spotted a man on a grey horse watching her. Instinctively she sank back into the water so that only her neck and head were visible. Reluctantly, she paddled closer so that she could, at least, make out more clearly the man's facial features. When she got closer she called, "And who might you be? Do you enjoy watching naked women bathing?" She immediately regretted her words. There was nothing more stupid than asking a man whether he enjoyed watching a woman bathing naked.

The man must have been her age, mid-thirties she guessed, his hair short on top but long at the back. Not the most attractive hairstyle, she reflected, but the man was clearly quite well to do. He was tall with a beard that was long at the chin but tightly tied like a rat's tail which dangled down to his stomach and was decorated with beads.

"You must the Priestess Crierwy of the Cauldron?" the man responded in a singsong voice.

"And who wants to know?" she responded, more abruptly than she intended.

"My name? My name is Lailoken but some call me Myrddin. I answer to all. I am brother to the Lady Langoureth, and I am the chief adviser to Prince Rhydderch," he announced.

"Am I supposed to impressed?" she responded with mock amusement.

"Some are." He shrugged.

She snorted. "I have heard of you. I am honoured that a man of your stature should visit me. I know your sister, and I must say, there is striking resemblance."

"We are twins, Lady."

"That makes sense, your bonds must be strong."

"They are."

There was an awkward pause as the two eyed each other across the water. Lailoken eventually broke the silence. "Lady, I wish to speak to you. The distance between us makes that rather difficult."

"Do you think I am simply going to walk up to you naked and have a cosy chat?" she said with an air of mockery.

"I can think of worse things," he murmured under his breath, but then spoke loud and clearly. "No, that is a fair point." His face began to burn under her gaze, and he hoped she wouldn't notice.

Crierwy might be older than he was, but she was still a very beautiful woman, and it was widely acknowledged that she was probably the most beautiful woman in the Northern Kingdoms. He breathed in heavily and retreated some twenty steps or so from the shore and dismounted. He turned again just as she stepped out of the water. Her pale glistening body was enveloped in the glow of sun's glare across the lake.

She stopped, her hands on her slim hips, her head slightly tilted. "Well?" she said, twirling her finger in the air, gesturing that Lailoken should turn around. To her amusement he dithered for a moment then turned, spluttering some words that were inaudible, but the meaning was clear.

When she called to him again, she was clothed and her wet hair clung to her head and shoulders. She reached for a woollen cloth and rubbed her head vigorously whilst she bent her head forward, sending droplets of water in every direction.

Lailoken stood rigid not wanting to point out the obvious smattering of water on his tunic. "Oh, please forgive me," she said in mock shock.

"That's quite all right," he responded stiffly.

She laughed. "Well then, you have something to say so shall we warm you up with a glass of mead?"

"I would like that, thank you, Lady," he responded happily.

"Come on, follow me," she said happily. "And oh," she continued, "do your three companions need sustenance?"

"Companions?" he said innocently.

"Yes, the three up on the hill there." She pointed.

"Your eyesight is quite extraordinary!"

"Eyesight, feelings and experience, Lailoken." She smiled warmly. "People of your importance never ride alone."

"Quite so." He nodded "I will call them down, but I wish to talk to you privately first."

She beckoned him over to a stool and poured honeyed mead into a clay jar. He picked it up and drank deeply and the two talked about the evil of the worlds. Crierwy enjoyed talking to someone of such knowledge and interest. After some time Crierwy finally interjected, "You want to ask me something?"

"I'm sorry," he said. "Yes of course. I digress. I want to be initiated into the Cauldron."

She studied him for a few beats then asked, "Why? You speak of your sister, but you don't speak of your own fame. People say you are a wizard, a Druid, but you hide the fact because you are in the pay of Prince Rhydderch who leans towards the Christians."

"It is more the influence of my sister that keeps me... safe."

"I can see that. So, again, why?"

"If I am honest, I must re-find my faith. Christianity has knocked my beliefs and that has left me bereft. I have drifted too far from the goddess. I need to be nourished. She needs to be nourished and that can only happen by recommitting to the old ways."

Crierwy nodded. "It appears to me that you would like to have a foot in, how should I say this without giving offence, both camps?"

"You think me weak and in love with my position."

"Aren't you?'

He sighed. "Lady, you are perhaps too close to the truth for comfort. But the journey I must undertake is one that releases me from the world of power, I need to learn how to serve rather than be served."

"So you have no designs on this settlement?"

"Absolutely not, I can assure you that I have no designs on this settlement. You are a Priestess of the Cauldron and because of that you will never have to fear me."

"Fear? That's a loaded word. I wasn't fearful until then."

"It's just a word."

"Words are important, Lailoken, and have an effect whether you wish them to or not."

He nodded. "I want to return to the true path. My time with Rhydderch is ending and war will be upon us soon. Religion and belief will be the cause, or should I say the excuse. I am a descendant of Coel Hen and so is the man who stands for the old way."

"Gwenddoleu the aspiring Pendragon?" she chimed in.

"Yes. Urien and Rhydderch will soon find a reason to march on him. So far, he has resisted the... provocations, but pressure will surely be brought to bear."

"But Urien," she remembered as Taliesin's protector, "is not Christian. Why should he have anything to do with this?"

"As you have accused me, he is someone who has a foot in both camps, and he will make sure he is on the right side. And then of course there is the troublesome Columba."

She groaned at the name. "I'll wager he has meddled in this."

Lailoken welcomed his jug being refilled. "So, Lady, will you initiate me? If you do, I will use it to strengthen the old ways and I will be at

Gwenddoleu's side when the great battle comes. I will send forth the fog of battle and Gwenddoleu will be triumphant. The bane of Christianity will be snuffed out forever."

"I admire your optimism," Crierwy said cynically.

Despite some misgivings, Crierwy believed Lailoken was earnest. She was wary of his power, and in truth, his motives were almost too good to be true. She continued to question him until she could find no reason to refuse him. She recognised that Lailoken's presence in the settlement could be a significant draw for new initiates but it might also bring its threats. Would she then attract unwanted notice?

"Let me consider what you have said, Lailoken," she said, standing. "Invite your guard and share our food while I walk awhile."

"Shall I accompany you?" Lailoken said enthusiastically.

"No, no, I need time to consider," she soothed. "I will give you my answer shortly."

"And I will make a contribution to your community," he offered.

"I am grateful for the offer but it will make no difference to me in my decision. The mark will be whether a contribution is made if I accept you or not." She grinned mischievously.

As Crierwy wandered, she recognised there was something, or at least, someone who had not been mentioned in their discussions, Aedan. She knew that any side he allied with would mean, sooner or later, that Arthur would be obliged to follow. Surely, as Aedan was, himself, a follower of the old ways he was bound to side with the new Pendragon. She also recognised that Aedan did not operate on the basis of right or wrong; he was more concerned with what benefitted him the most. Of course, Aedan was still answerable to his cousin, but everyone knew who really had the influence. If Aedan sided with the Pendragon there was a good chance that Gwenddoleu would have a chance of success but if he did not, she could only see calamity. For now, she, and the world, would have to wait and see. Aedan was clever and he was unlikely to share his plans with anyone.

After what felt like age, Crierwy returned and informed him, to his delight, that he could stay. She also reminded him of his promise to contribute towards the upkeep of her community. "You said it didn't matter," Lailoken chided.

"Did I?" she responded innocently. "I hate being too obvious."

It wasn't long after Lailoken's men departed for the lands of Alt Clut that the boys returned. She introduced Lailoken to those gathered around the roaring fire. The boys had all heard of him, and they were all, particularly Arthur, in awe. It wasn't long before the two were deep in conversation. Crierwy had never seen Arthur so animated. He gesticulated wildly and Lailoken laughed freely at what he was being told. He often placed his hand on Arthur's shoulder which appeared to quiet him immediately as he listened in total rapture.

Crierwy smiled. It was perhaps the father figure Arthur needed. She sighed at length while gazing across the still waters of the lake. Yes, sadly, boys of Arthur's age needed a father figure, she conceded. Arthur had responded positively to Cynon, Conor — Cai's father — and now Lailoken? She considered finding a man as a romantic partner, Gwallog possibly, even Lailoken but quickly banished that stupidity from her consciousness. She didn't need a man, she was above that, she was a priestess, and was determined not to show the world she was weak and in need of protection. She had survived thus far, had made a reputation for herself, and she had a growing number of followers. Nonetheless, she could only imagine Arthur's reaction when his father, a prince, possibly even a king by then, came striding into the camp and announced his parentage. Even if there was a man in their lives, what chance would he ever have against that sort of competition.

She shook her head and tried to dismiss the thoughts that continually weighed heavily on her mind. The best thing, she concluded, was to intensify the education and training, but she could use Lailoken to help support her as well as her initiating him.

As Lailoken was now a member of the community, it seemed appropriate for the children to start, from tomorrow, to learn the Shamanic practice of journeying and meeting their spirit allies. The truth of it would be shown to all.

Chapter 11

Initiation

Despite her reservations, Crierwy was persuaded that the younger students should not be taken through the cult initiation but that they should undertake the training. Lailoken felt certain that children, more likely to enjoy play battles, would be put off the idea of living a pious, spiritual life that teaches the complete opposite to childish play.

During the first week of training, Crierwy challenged the initiates to consider their lives, the people they lived with, and the demands placed upon them by their leaders and peers. Arthur found this particularly easy because he had never really spent any time in one place and certainly, he did not identify with any kingdom. Instead, he studied Cai, whose father's kingdom was his only point of reference. This was followed by the initiates, and the boys, being instructed to dig their own graves. She told them that once their training was complete, they would spend a night in their grave. To help them with the feelings of solitude they would surely feel, they were to also spend the night alone on the lake in a Coracle. Arthur, and indeed probably everyone else, wondered if this was all worth it.

All the initiates felt a rising anxiety of being buried alive as the time of their ordeal drew nearer. The sense of being in a confined space underground was a terrifying prospect, particularly for the younger ones, although Crierwy, after some prevarication, decided that the youngsters were not obliged to take part.

Arthur was surprised and even bewildered that Lailoken appeared to be looking forward it. He finished his grave quicker and more enthusiastically than everyone else and then happily, and a little morbidly, reflected Arthur, helped the others dig theirs. Bedwyr, too, seemed surprisingly sanguine but Cai, after his initial bravado, had become fearful and chose to withdraw. Arthur had already concluded that the luxury of pulling out of the burial was out of the question because of his mother but now he had an incentive to complete the task to prove he was braver than Cai.

Before the burial, a night of solitude on the lake had turned out to be a joyous experience for Arthur. It had been a clear night and he wiled away his waking hours staring at the stars. Armed only with a drum, Arthur had drifted on the quiet waters, drumming gently, trying to journey. Despite his best intentions, he could not stop his mind drifting. Instead, he dreamed about what it would be like to be a warrior before the gently rocking movement of the coracle lured him into sleep. When he was dragged back to shore at first light, he felt upbeat and well rested. To him it was all too easy.

Digging his own grave had been strangely cathartic. Despite it being a hard physical process, he began to form a relationship with Mother Earth. As his mother would explain, it was an incredible privilege to be held and healed by Mother Earth.

Later when Lailoken asked what he had learned during his education, he was surprised Arthur announced that it was so much easier to take his shame to one person and deal with it in secret, but what affected him would also affect others in his community. "That," he announced to Lailoken, "was the most important thing."

Lailoken smiled indulgently. "Your insight, Arthur, is remarkable for one so young. To realise things that affect others in your community will touch and affect you, enables us to heal each other. That is something people never fully understand. And yet you already understand it. Remarkable! You have the talent to become a great Druid if you are allowed."

"Allowed?" Arthur questioned.

Lailoken realised he had said too much and tried to backtrack quickly for it was not his place to say such things. "What I mean is," he stuttered, "life has an unfortunate habit of getting in the way of what we want or need."

Arthur shrugged, and to Lailoken's relief chose to say no more.

The following morning, he stood in the circle and vowed, "I will always work in service to the community." He looked at his mother, smiling. "Because," he continued, "in community, together, and brave, I and we can achieve wonderful things together."

Lailoken turned to Crierwy. "Your boy is only eight and yet he speaks like a man. You have unleashed something quite extraordinary on this world. He will be spoken of through the ages. That I can promise you."

"He is extraordinary," she agreed, "and that's what frightens me."

"How so?"

"A child speaking like this, is a child who will not stay in the shadows for long. He is too young, Lailoken, and he will be used by people who care too little for him and care too much for themselves."

"That doesn't necessarily follow," Lailoken said reassuringly.

Crierwy looked at him quizzically. "You are being naïve."

Lailoken shrugged. "I am just saying that fate isn't written in stone. There are always options."

"Options," she snorted. "There can only be options if you know the outcome."

"It's what we grown-ups are here for," he smiled, "to guide."

"Depends on the biggest voice." She grimaced. "Can you guarantee who that will be?"

Crierwy stood and looked sadly down at Lailoken. Sighing, she walked away.

The sun was beginning to set in the west and there was an air of tension as the time for Mother Earth's embrace and the Druids' rebirth rapidly approached. All the graves were neatly spaced into a semi-circle. At the centre Crierwy would sit, drum in hand, to ensure the initiates remained awake throughout their rebirth, or ordeal as many of the initiates considered it to be. All the youngsters except for Arthur had chosen not to take part. Arthur also wanted to pull out because, as far as he was concerned, he understood his lesson. He wanted to play with the other children, he wanted to be a warrior, screaming at the top of his voice whilst running among the trees. All this Druidry was for his mother and he felt stifled. It was not lost on him that being buried in a hole was as stifling as his mother's expectations of him. It wasn't fair.

Despite his unhappiness, Arthur had become surprisingly attached to his grave. His young mind couldn't understand that there was a relationship being built during the digging process and he began to feel somehow protective towards this space. By the time they all gathered around the fire, he had become genuinely intrigued to see how this would turn out. Looking around him, Arthur could see the faces of the initiates that ranged from panic to a sad but grudging acceptance. He smiled to himself; he somehow felt liberated from the claustrophobia of the past, hiding from others, hiding under bushes, hiding in the airless dark as Cai would chase and yes, deal out a beating.

He was the first to volunteer to slide into his grave space, abandoning most of what he might need, snuggling down into the warmth of his new home. The last handhold of his mother as he found the most comfortable position felt so important; she smiled at him at that moment and his heart was filled with love for her. The whole act of ceremony, honour and connection flooded through him. A strong bond of trust with and unconditional love of his mother had always been a safety blanket and saved him from the outside world but as he gazed up at her he could not help feeling that this could no longer be. He nodded to confirm that the planks of wood, animal skins and earth could be placed on top of him with just a gap for a reed to be fed through the layers of earth so he could breathe. Once he was subsumed by the darkness he felt genuinely at peace. Fiery torches flashed as the other initiates slid into their womb-spaces too. Some were whimpering, but with his mother's reassurance they had all gradually surrendered.

He lay there allowing the noises all around him to settle down. He found himself enjoying the feeling of being deeply held. He didn't feel alone as he knew the other initiates were all around him in their joint endeavour merely feet away. He felt content and at peace as he absorbed the sounds of drumming and harmonious singing drifting down into his earth space.

As the outside world quieted, Arthur knew he had to begin to examine who he was in order to enable his rebirth. He began to consider how to begin telling his life story to the earth. He was stuck on how to begin which was unexpected, clearly confused about what he did not know rather than what he had experienced. There had been no one else to talk to besides his mother, and more recently Lailoken, but there was always something missing, he realised. Something was being kept from him and even though he was expected to start life anew he vowed that he had to know.

He closed his eyes and took himself back, right back to the beginning. He tried to imagine what it was like before his birth. For the first time, he examined his relationship with his mother, his uncle, his foster parents and what their lives were like before he had arrived in this world. He felt himself plunging into deep feelings of pain and grief. He felt the pain of the burden he had unknowingly carried all his life. There were so many questions, too many, but most importantly was who was his father and was being a Druid his fate? He didn't believe so.

As the night drew on he began to wonder about his purpose and how he would learn about living in the outside world. He could offer love freely, and in that way, he reasoned, people might also want to share or return love in his direction; others may not but he must not take that personally. In the end, he concluded, he must rely on himself to generate all that he needed otherwise he would become weak and dependent and always having to seek the approval of others. Any signs of weakness would be because of the need to please. "When I please others for me, they will not be pleased and then I am rejected and bruised," he whispered.

He lost all sense of time; he heard nothing but the drumming from above. He sang quietly to himself, he journeyed. But then he realised that he hadn't asked any questions. He wanted to know his fate. And so he asked. He saw his eagle setting him free to glide above the forests and glens; the bear cub played. He was amazed by how easy it was to journey whilst being held within the earth. It was then that he saw the raven. It stretched out its wings and laced them around his shoulders. "Arthur," it said, its voice kindly, "you are near the end of your rebirth, and I am here to give you a warning your mother wishes you to know."

"My mother?"

"Do not rush your life, Arthur. You will be faced with choices soon enough. Enjoy your time for it will be shorter here than you imagine. You will be faced with being either being a priest of substance but lost to history or a great warrior, remembered for all time but destined to die young and with a broken heart."

"When will I have to choose?" Arthur replied.

"Soon enough," the raven answered, before fading away.

Before he knew it, it was dawn. He wasn't sure if he had slept or not. He inwardly shrugged and an unbidden giggle came from him. *Who knows?* he thought. *Perhaps only Mother Earth herself knows what really happened in those hours.* The first bird sang; light began to creep into his space. He knew he had been through something significant, something profound, an experience which meant there was nothing more to do, despite an overwhelming desire to do something. He surrendered, woken by his mother gently asking if he was ready to come out.

She reached in and took his hand. "Well done," she whispered, studying him very closely. "You have done well, Arthur. You are no longer a little boy, I fear."

Arthur noticed her sad smile and flung his arms around her. "I will always be your little boy, even when I'm older," he lied. She nodded and hugged him tightly. She felt tears rolling down her cheeks; she held him and never wanted to let him go.

Arthur felt very vulnerable out in the light. The glare of the sun hurt his eyes; he kept them tightly shut until he was able to open them and focus. Sitting around the fire, he was grateful that nobody else seemed to want to talk, except, unsurprisingly, Lailoken. Arthur wanted to preserve that feeling of being 'held, safe and supported' he had experienced for those hours.

Following the silent breakfast, the initiates broke up into smaller groups. Arthur made his apologies and wandered over to a grassy verge at the edge of the nearby woods. He lay himself down and looked up at the morning sky. He sighed to himself and closed his eyes. Despite himself he fell into a deep and dreamless sleep. And there he lay until dusk.

Chapter 12

A Prince in Waiting

Arthur flourished with his mother as his teacher. Besides the Druidic training she also educated the younger boys more widely. Lessons included a history of the British peoples, and they became acquainted with the royal families of the Britons. They learned how there was an interconnectedness between the kings and queens. This, Crierwy knew, would place her in difficulties when the link between herself and Aedan became apparent. She chose instead to concentrate on earlier generations, a subject that both fascinated and intrigued her young students.

She told them of Brychan of Brecon and how he used his family and allies to build networks that maintained the peace whilst enhancing his own personal power and prestige. Crierwy was Brychan's great granddaughter, and she tracked her family tree, and of course Arthur's, through Brychan of Manau, the son of Brychan of Brecon, to her mother Goleudydd. Arthur learned that his grandparents were indeed cousins with his great grandfather Dyfnwal Hen of Alt Clut. A great pedigree indeed and Arthur became more excited that he was of royal blood.

As the year drew on and the summer heat began to cool, Crierwy continued to struggle with how she should tell Arthur about his connection to Aedan's family, beyond that they were distant cousins. At least Drystan was also in the dark, so she didn't have to be too wary of trying to control family secrets. She was not sure whether it was a good thing or not that he showed a lot of interest in his Irish roots.

Cynon came to visit Drystan and as they all gathered around the fire the boys were excited to hear the stories shared which added to and indeed embellished what they had learned. They also spoke at length of the Shamanic journeying they had undertaken. Arthur, despite his tender years, had assumed the air of an adult and remained apart from the other boys. Bedwyr, however, was never too far away and Cai continued to needle him at every opportunity but with less and less intensity. But Arthur remained aloof and spent many hours talking with Lailoken as well as walking and running alone around the shores of the lake. He was becoming leaner, but he was also becoming stronger. He was growing quickly and was already the same height as the others who were a couple of years his senior.

With the evening coming to an end and everyone retiring to their dwellings, Crierwy, Cynon and Lailoken sat alone together.

"Drystan is enjoying his time here," Cynon said lightly.

"Yes, he is very talented," Crierwy acknowledged, barely above a whisper

Cynon studied her closely. He knew Crierwy well enough to recognise she was worried. "What troubles you, sister?" he nudged.

Cynon and Lailoken both looked intently at her. Crierwy was very much aware of their eyes upon her, and she so wanted to unload this burden hanging over her. She stared into the flames and poked the fire with a stick before throwing it onto the fire. She sighed deeply then raised her eyes. "What do I tell him?' she breathed.

"What do you mean?" Lailoken asked, a little puzzled.

Cynon stared at his sister for a few beats. "You mean Arthur and his father?"

She nodded but said nothing.

"You have to tell him," Cynon said softly.

"Yes," Lailoken agreed, "he has a right to know."

"It'll change everything," she groaned.

"Not necessarily," Cynon said softly.

She shrugged. The pause that followed was uncomfortable. Eventually she said, "He will no longer be mine."

Cynon stretched his hand over and rested it on Crierwy's knee. "That is, of course, possible but he is so connected to you, you won't lose him."

"I will. All boys need a male figure and when he realises he has a father, an infamous one at that, he will want to see him, be with him, be like him."

"You exaggerate, sister," Cynon soothed. "Yes, he will be interested, and in time he will want to meet his father. But wouldn't it be better if you tell him on your terms rather than Aedan just turning up and announcing himself?"

"For the love of the goddess, do you think he will just turn up? That would be horrific." She felt her insides twist, so it pained her.

"You know he will."

"I have to agree with Cynon again," Lailoken said kindly. "Perhaps I might make a suggestion?"

"A suggestion?" she repeated.

"Let me talk to the boy. I have spent many hours talking him through the initiation and what that will mean for when he is older. He has changed so much; he may have the body and the appearance of a little boy, but he has developed an inner strength and he will take the news much better than you fear, I'm sure. I believe he feels he is different to the other boys. He inspires devotion and envy in equal proportions. If you want him to be a balanced young man you will have to be honest to him… If you are honest with him, he may be angry to begin with, but he will recover. He will always love and most importantly respect you if he knows his mother respects and trusts him."

"I'm sorry, Crierwy, Lailoken is right," Cynon said, "and you know it."

Crierwy nodded, stood up and touched both men on the shoulder. "You both speak true, I know it, but let me think on it," and she started towards the lake.

"I've heard that before," Lailoken laughed.

"Indeed," she said without expression, "but I made the right decision last time, did I not?"

"How can I argue with that?" Lailoken shrugged.

When she was out of sight of them, she stripped off her clothes and dived into the cool water. The lake was her solace, a place she could cleanse herself of the pains of existence. By the time she had swum to the bottom of the lake and then burst out of the glass like surface, she knew what she must do.

A few days passed before the initiates were brought together. Crierwy stood before them, firstly addressing the older initiates. "Your journey is now at an end," she announced. "You are now Priests of the Cauldron. How you use your learnings is for your conscience, but I hope that the revelations you have found here in this community will enable you to travel through our beautiful but dangerous world. I hope you will spread our message of enlightenment and our connection to Mother Earth to all those you meet. Teach people to treat, with respect, the trees, the rivers, the seas and other people both in life and in death. And if you choose not to follow the Cauldron, live its values. Never judge and never fall foul of temptation, to anger, to jealousy and most of all hatred. Hatred will destroy you. Arawn already has too many followers."

She then turned to her younger students. "You boys have sampled what it takes to be a Druid. You now have an opportunity to consider if you wish to join the rest of us. This is for you and your parents to decide. All I will say is I am here to guide you if you wish. So," she paused, "I urge you to journey regularly, meet with your spirit allies, speak with them, ask for their advice, share with them, listen to their wisdom. They will always be there for you; do not forget them and do not neglect them. Like people they need nourishment."

Crierwy nodded to each person in turn, "you who are now initiates of the Cauldron Cult will have your head emblazoned with the tattoos to announce that you are Salmons of Wisdom. You will be awarded a gift of an animal familiar. Some of you will already know them, others will not." She again turned to each initiate and one by one gifted them a spirit ally. When she reached Lailoken she announced that his animal spirit guide was a wolf cub. "I have journeyed, and I have been told that you should be Myrddin. You must go forth and show your power but beware, you will have great questions to answer, and you will suffer as a result. I have seen this, Myrddin, but do not despair because if you do, you will lose your mind. You might not understand my words today but one day you will and when you do you will be saved."

Lastly, she turned to Arthur. "Your spirit guide is the eagle," she smiled, "but you knew that already, didn't you?" Arthur smiled and nodded but said nothing. Instead, he looked, almost, expectantly at his mother. Crierwy knew that the time had come. "I fear, my beautiful son, that your life experiences will test you to the limit," she said sadly. "Do not lose sight of your friends, listen, be humble, never be petty and do not succumb to anger." She continued, "You will have a choice to make but only you can make it." She saw Arthur's confusion and reached out and stroked his face. She sighed and glanced around at Myrddin.

"I'll be waiting by the coracle," he said reassuringly.

"Can I have some time with him first, Myrddin?" Crierwy interjected. "If you don't mind?"

"Yes, of course," Myrddin nodded. He turned toward Arthur. "Arthur, my boy, join me, we can talk about the world once you finish with your mother. I thought I might tell you of my plans once I leave this place and how you might be of some assistance to me."

Arthur looked puzzled but nodded a little reluctantly.

Myrddin smiled and wandered away. Crierwy could only wonder at the poverty of Myrddin's acting; if that was not a hint that she was going to say something quite momentous she did not know what was. She almost laughed aloud; instead she snorted and covered her mouth. At that she glanced at Arthur who had crossed his arms with one eyebrow arched. He might be eight years old, but he was already a man in his mannerisms. She coloured slightly before composing herself.

She beckoned him to follow her along the lake shore. They walked together in comfortable silence until they were well away from anyone else. "You are almost a man; you may have the body of an eight-year-old but there is no denying that the little boy who came here last year is no longer that same boy. So… I must tell you something," she breathed, her nerves rising.

Arthur could see that his mother was struggling and reached for her hand. The laughing had stopped all too quickly and he realised this was serious, but he knew what she was going to say. "Are you going to tell me who my father is?"

"Yes," she whispered. "But before I do," she straightened, "it is important to explain why I have taken until now to tell you. I hope you understand what I am going to tell you, and if you do not, I hope you find it within yourself to suspend your judgement of me."

They continued to walk awhile longer. Arthur waited patiently but his excitement was beginning to overtake him. Eventually, he nudged her. "You were saying, Mother?"

"Sorry… this… this is hard and I'm embarrassed," she stuttered. She swallowed hard. "I was celebrating the Beltane festival when I was approached by your father. He was covered in ashes from the fires, and I thought he was someone else."

"You were fooled?" Arthur interjected

"Yes, I was, but what is more important is why I have not told you before now," Crierwy began. She explained the importance of children being conceived at Beltane. She described their escape from those who wanted them controlled or killed. She also explained that Arthur's father would, eventually come to claim him and take him from her. Something, she explained, frightened her and she was fearful that she would lose him forever. "I hope, sincerely, that you can forgive me, Arthur. I was being selfish, and I had no right to keep this from you. I am sorry, Arthur."

Arthur remained silent for what seemed an age.

"Well?" Crierwy asked.

"Mother," he started, "you should never have kept this from me."

"Arthur."

"Mother!" Arthur said sharply. "We can talk about this… For now let me think about things. That is why Lailoken or Myrddin is waiting to take me out on the lake?"

"Yes I… I thought…it would help."

"And my father is?" Arthur continued, trying his best to stifle a laugh.

Crierwy flushed. "Oh I am so sorry… I…" She took a deep breath. "All right. You must know that your father is Aedan of Manau."

Arthur's eyes widened. "Aedan mac Gabrain? Son of the Scorcher! King of the Scots."

"Yes," she nodded.

"Gabrain was my grandfather? I am of the line of Fergus Mor?"

"Yes, you are. You are of the line of Fergus and of Dyfnwal Hen and of Brychan."

"All those people you taught us about? I am related to all of them?" he squealed in excitement.

"Yes," she confirmed again.

"Do I have siblings?"

"Your father is married to Domelch, the daughter of Maelgwyn Hir. I am aware of a sister, Muirgein, who is a priestess in her own right, and Gartnait, both older than you. There might be others."

"Why hasn't he come for me?"

"You are a threat, Arthur. And your father is not strong enough to admit you."

"But he will come?" Arthur almost pleaded.

"Yes, I believe he will," she said sadly.

"When?"

She did not respond for a few beats but then she admitted, "I don't know, Arthur."

"But he will come," he continued, "and I will be a knight?"

"Yes, I suppose so if that is what you want. But it isn't inevitable," she said with a hint of resignation in her voice. "Arthur, do not get over excited, there are good reasons why he hasn't come, and we cannot know if those reasons still or will continue to stand."

"You mean he doesn't want me," Arthur responded, his heart suddenly frozen.

"Arthur, I don't know. We are here because I, and yes, you, were a… problem." She regretted immediately her words even though they were true.

Arthur looked crestfallen and Crierwy's heart broke. She reflected that despite appearances, Arthur was still a child. She had been surprised how he had reacted, not in the way of a teenager might but in the way an eight-year-old would. Her relief over his lack of obvious anger toward her was almost overwhelming but she also realised that time would pass extremely slowly for a child who clearly was now determined to be a warrior. That, she knew, would be a source of frustration for him and for them. For now, she was resigned to having to wait for the day her son would be called to arms. She reached for him, but he backed away because she could not guarantee his father would come for him any time soon. She sighed and watched Arthur run towards the lake's edge to join Myrddin.

Arthur reached the place where Myrddin had placed himself and flung himself at Myrddin's coracle, practically turning it over with Myrddin scrabbling with moderate success to keep it upright.

"Whoa, young Arthur, steady there. Why you could have… drowned me."

"Drowned you? Pah!"

"Hmmm, you seem a little excited?"

"Lailoken… whatever your name is now."

"Myrddin, my boy,"

"Yes, yes… whatever."

"Whatever?" Myrddin laughed. "Your mother told you something?"

"Myrddin! I am Arthur mac Aedan… a… a… a prince. I am a *prince*."

"Ah, so your mother has told you then?"

"You knew?" Arthur said, almost bursting.

"Come on, young prince," Myrddin soothed, "let's row out into the lake where we can talk and you can be… contained."

They cast off across the flat water and after some ten minutes of rowing, Myrddin pulled in his oars and allowed the coracle to drift until it stopped. He held up his hand to stop the oncoming of Arthur's tirade and placed his hands behind his head, before tilting it back and looking into the cloudless sky.

Myrddin sat there, like that, for an age. Arthur was gradually reaching bursting point before Myrddin leant forward with the widest grin imaginable. "So, young Arthur. Take a very deep breath, we have plenty of time. Enjoy the day, get sun burned. Your life will fly quickly enough in the years to come."

"What do you mean?" Arthur asked, feeling confused. "Will my father come? My mother claims not to know but that means she doesn't want him to come. But he must come."

"She is managing your expectations, Arthur. We can never know the reasons why things do or do not happen until after the event."

"But he will come," Arthur persisted.

Myrddin shrugged. "Don't get ahead of yourself. You have a lot to look forward to, some good, but I'm afraid with all good things there will always come bad. Don't rush fate, boy, it will come for you in good time."

"I don't understand," Arthur admitted.

"You will soon enough. It's what frightens your mother more than anything. If your father doesn't come to claim you or she could hide you, you will live a quiet life, you will grow old, and have children of your own. You will be a great father, a great Druid, people will probably know you in years to come even after you're dead and gone."

"And if he does come for me?"

"Have you forgotten what you have learned during the initiation?"

Arthur paused. He remembered the raven, but it was a dream, wasn't it?"

"I have triggered a memory, I see," Myrddin said.

"Maybe," Arthur admitted, "but you said he will come?" he continued, the excitement rising once again. "We must make it easy for him."

"Oh, I suspect he knows where you are."

"And when he does come, what will become of me?" Arthur said breathlessly.

"When... if he does you could well see glory, known throughout the ages. A great warrior, possibly a Pendragon."

Arthur clapped his hands excitedly. "And? And?"

Myrddin groaned.

"A king?" Arthur asked.

"I do not know, my boy, but you will know betrayal, envy, jealousy and pain before the end..."

"What pain?" Arthur said doubtfully.

"All I will say is, do not trust anyone except your mother."

"And you?"

"Not even me, my boy. None of us can know what choices we are forced to make and how those decisions will determine our actions. No, lad, I wish you no evil, I love you like a father loves a son, but all of us are weak and thus we cannot be trusted."

"But what about giving love and receiving it back?"

"That, my boy, is admirable and will always make you a man to follow and admire. But Arthur, what you have learned here is truly how life should be lived but what happens is dependent on the decisions of those less... enlightened. For all those men, and yes, women who will follow and revere you, there will be people who will mistrust and fear you. And frightened men are a stain on this world, it is why there is always war."

"That is horrible," Arthur responded with sadness.

"Yes, it is, but if you choose a warrior's life, how does that fit the teachings of Druidry? A soldier kills and not always for the right reasons. You might think you're fighting for a noble cause, but your opponent will not necessarily share your righteousness. It cuts both ways."

Myrddin's words had shocked him; thoughts of glory were cut to shreds by this man's words. Tears stung his eyes. How could so much hope turn to hurt and pain? Why would people turn against him? Surely everything he did would be for good. How could that be thought of as threatening and yet... He considered his friends and peers. Surely Bedwyr was to be trusted, and Cai, well maybe, and there was Collen who he had always felt uncomfortable with. He reflected too on the people who had protected his mother, not least Gwallog, the man Senan who was killed, the woman Aeronwen, Taliesin, Uncle Cynon, Serf and his foster family. Without them, he would be dead and so would his mother. Myrddin had to be wrong, he concluded. And yet...

He thought more on it and realised that there were others like the man Dugald who had apparently claimed to protect his mother and had turned against her. His grandfather who, he now realised from his history lessons, had condemned his mother to death because of his own conception by a stranger and then cast his mother out. So, what would he do? The answer, to him, was obvious to an eight-year-old: he would make people love him. And if he were to die in battle it would be in a noble cause and yes, he would be revered for being a great and powerful man. A man who dispensed right and justice. Myrddin was only trying to put him off, make him stay with his mother. And yet...

Myrddin gazed at Arthur, knowing full well what the boy was processing. He smiled sadly. This boy would have to learn the hard way. He only hoped it would not be too painful. He knew the ways of men like Arthur's father; they cared little for anything but their power and influence and he would discard Arthur if the boy did not live up to what was expected. He patted Arthur's leg and gazed out into the lake.

They spent the rest of the day bobbing in the clear waters, Myrddin telling Arthur of the ways of the world, the crises in the north, of Gwenddoleu and Rhydderch, of Urien, Lleenog, the father of Gwallog, and the lords of Ebruac, Eliffer and his young sons, Peredur and Gwrgi. But Arthur was most interested in his own family and the rumours of Morcant's treachery, his new family, his grandfather Gabrain and the new king of Dalriada, Conall mac Comgall, his father's cousin, as well as that snake, Columba.

Myrddin knew then he had failed.

Within the week, Myrddin gathered his belongings and said his farewells to those fellow initiates who had decided to remain with Crierwy. Crierwy held him tightly and though she had tried to persuade him to stay, she knew that Myrddin's path was his own and he must follow it. He had come to regain his faith in the old ways and the initiation into the Cauldron had renewed his commitment and reinvigorated him. He realised that his path would result in losing the friendship of a prince and his wife, Myrddin's sister, and gain the friendship of a king. The future of the old way would rest with Gwenddoleu the Pendragon, and he would prevail despite the day of reckoning being close at hand. Crierwy let go of her friend with sorrow, not only for herself but for Arthur who was losing yet another male figure.

She let Myrddin say his goodbyes to Arthur in private and much to Myrddin's surprise the boy wept. Their bond was strong. Arthur walked with Myrddin for a couple of miles, but they said little to each other. They had spent a lot of time together in comfortable silence, fishing in the lake. No words were needed. When Myrddin stopped at a spot which overlooked the lake in all its grandeur, he bent down and put his hands on the boy's shoulders. "Your mother needs you. Do not waste time wishing for things to happen. You cannot make things happen any quicker than they are fated to. Take good care of her and yourself. Do not make rash decisions. Always carefully consider your motives and the motives of others."

"Are you telling me not to trust people again?" Arthur said grumpily.

"I have said what I needed to say. You can accept that or not. Remember, people are essentially fearful and will act upon that fear in ways we cannot always anticipate. Do not be surprised by their actions."

"I will try," Arthur said quietly.

"Promise me, Arthur. I do not want to leave this place knowing you misunderstand the world in which we live."

"Yes," the boy responded irritably, stepping back out of reach, "I said I will try."

"I'm sorry, my boy," Myrddin said. "I didn't mean to upset you, I just want you to be safe."

Arthur said nothing. His initial baleful look dissipated into sadness as Myrddin climbed onto his horse. Tears stung Arthur's eyes as Myrddin waved his staff in farewell. "We shall meet again, Arthur, of that you can be certain."

At that, he rode away at a canter.

The time Arthur would spend at the lake with his mother, the Priestess of the Cauldron, the Lady of the Lake, would feel never ending. His hope that Aedan would soon come to claim him felt increasingly forlorn and Arthur would often drift into melancholy as he dwelt on his life, or lack of it as he saw it, and that he would never be fulfilled. Yes, he remembered all the warnings, but his overriding ambition was not to become an ageing Druid as Myrddin described or his mother wanted, wandering the land telling stories, being welcomed because he was his mother's son.

The company of Bedwyr and Drystan was a welcome relief, and the boys spent many hours fishing and hunting boar near the lake. Inevitably the boys would play war games against imaginary foes, Arthur was very much the horseman, springing traps that Drystan and Bedwyr dutifully walked into. For Arthur this was a distraction from the continuing work as a trainee druid. He, without complaint, continued his Shamanic practices but as time went on, they became nothing but a perfunctory chore that had to be completed to keep the peace with his mother.

Regularly, Arthur rode up the paths away from the lake and gazed out towards the northeast to where Manau lay in the hope of catching sight of his father. But he never came.

Little did he know that his father would not turn up for another five years, by which time Arthur had all but given up any hope. And little did he realise when he awoke on the Feast of Imbolc, his thirteenth birthday, how much his life would change.

Chapter 13

Aedan the Uther

News of the coming of armed men escorting an important dignitary spread quickly through the lands of Gwynedd and ultimately through the forests surrounding Llyn Tegid.

With the spread of Christianity, the community of Llyn Tegid always felt under threat, despite the claimed protection of local lords. They had devised a number of strategies to conceal themselves using specially dug pits and holes where people of the community could hide in relative safety for long enough to out wait any dangerous interlopers.

Crierwy stole herself for this new threat, comforted in the knowledge that Arthur would be safe in the care of Bedwyr and Drystan. She brushed herself down and placed herself at the entrance to the lodges of the community. She breathed deeply and slowly, calming her nerves, trying to find her equilibrium, and perfecting the look of indifference that, she knew, was likely to feel disconcerting to any soldier.

As the line of riders came into view, she strained her eyes to catch a sight of the stranger leading them. There was something vaguely familiar in his demeanour but as they drew closer, the leader's ready smile made both her heart flip and bile rise in her throat. To her utter despair she realised it was Aedan mac Gabrain, King of Manau, Prince of Lothian and Arthur's father. The Uther! The wily. At his side rode someone much more familiar and reassuring, Gwallog.

Her eyes widened as Aedan came ever closer. She tried to imagine what Arthur was thinking, seeing all this from his hiding place. Could he guess? She found herself crossing her arms, swallowing the sourness in her throat and forcing herself to go back to smoothing her tunic and resuming her breathing exercises.

When Aedan came to within twenty paces of where Crierwy stood, he languidly slid off this horse, beckoning Gwallog to follow, and strode purposefully to where she was standing. Taking off his gloves, he bowed deeply. "Lady."

"Lord Aedan," she responded tightly, "what a pleasant surprise to have someone of your stature visit us." She turned to Gwallog, her smile becoming warmer. "And the Lord Gwallog, our greatest friend. It has been far too long, Lord. But you are always most welcome."

The obvious slight to Aedan was noted and uncomfortably sharp but he said nothing, instead exaggerating his smile. Aedan was everything she remembered except, of course, he was fourteen years older. She guessed he was in his early forties, by now, tall, thin but well built. His upper arms, she noticed, were well formed and there was obvious power there. He was well tanned with penetrating dark eyes. He was heavily bearded, but it was not overly bushy. Aedan was a man who clearly had looked after himself. His hair, she noticed, was still dark but he now sported slightly greying sideburns. Aedan had an intelligent face; his eyes seemed to dance, and she was sure he was taking in her every feature. Aedan's reputation of being quick witted, clever, and wily was very well deserved. But what was certain was his ambition, his hunger for power. These were dangerous attributes and thus Aedan was very dangerous. Despite herself, however, she had to admit, he was still an incredibly attractive man and she felt dismay that she still found herself attracted to him.

"It has been too long," Aedan said carelessly.

"It has… Fourteen years if memory permits?" she interrupted.

Aedan smiled tightly and his jaw clenched but he breathed in and resumed his ready smile. "Yes, Lady, far too long."

"So why are you here now?" she said coldly.

"It's time to meet my son." He shrugged.

"On the day of his thirteenth birthday? Is it really so far from Manau that it's taken you so many years to come and find him," she sneered.

Aedan sighed. "You speak truly, Lady," he replied differentially, "and yes, I have no excuses. He is of age and… let's say… it has been politically difficult to present myself," he said carefully.

"Your wife, you mean."

"Yes, partly," Aedan responded quietly

"And her family?" she continued

"And her family," he confirmed, his jaw twitching.

Aedan paused for a few beats before eventually straightening and rolling his shoulders. "I know it has been too long and I know that you have had your… challenges." She arched her eyebrows at that, but Aedan pressed on. "Gwallog has supported you, yes? He came under my instructions." He paused, expecting an appreciative response but when none came, he pressed on. "Yes, my wife and her family were angry with your pregnancy and yes, perhaps I should have helped personally but my situation, particularly after the death of my father, meant my hands were tied, particularly when I was overlooked as king."

Crierwy rolled her eyes. "Do your wife and her brother know you are here?"

"No."

"So, what's changed, my Lord?"

"Me?"

"You?"

"The Picts are less aggressive since my power base has been made stronger and Domelch is less attached to her brethren. I am now able to stand up and announce my son and announce that he will be at my side."

"This has nothing to do with his Beltane connections?"

"Beltane? I know not what you mean." Aedan shrugged.

"Don't take me for a fool," she snapped. "That may have happened once but don't think you can do that again."

Aedan's lips curled. "You're a clever woman."

"No, but I'm no longer stupid! And what about Arthur?" she retorted.

"What about Arthur?"

"Will he be your son or a symbol? What of his feelings?"

"Have you told him about me?" He cut across her.

"He knows. And he has waited for you to come."

"And is he here?"

"He is, but what guarantees can you give that he will be treated as your son and not just a trophy or someone to boast about? He deserves the love of a father, Aedan, and I will not allow you to take advantage of him. I know you, or more to the point, of your reputation. You cast people aside if they are of no advantage to you. Will this be Arthur's fate?"

"I assure you, Crierwy, I am honourable in this. Yes, he does symbolise something special, but he is my son. And as my son I have a responsibility to him."

"Responsibility?" Crierwy erupted venomously. "It has taken you until now to come here and claim that? You do take me for a fool, Aedan, don't you?"

"You cannot speak to me like that," Aedan snapped, suddenly angry.

"You have no power here, my Prince' she said sarcastically.

"My Lord," Gwallog interrupted, "perhaps—"

"Silence, Gwallog," Aedan retorted. "Do not push me, Crierwy," he continued.

She held her hand up and stopped him. "Hmm, you show your true colours, will you have me whipped, my Prince? Perhaps that will be a fine sight for Arthur to witness."

Aedan held up his hands in surrender. "I—"

"Before you say any more," Crierwy interrupted, "I want your word, Aedan, because without it you can turn around and take your men with you. I do not think you want to threaten the Priestess of the Cauldron for I will curse you and your descendants for all time and any benefit you think you might have, I can and will ensure it is countervailed. Please just try me if you do not think I will. I want your word that you will treat Arthur as your son and with the respect he deserves."

Aedan's angry smile disappeared, and he blinked hard. He may well have a large body of men behind him, but Crierwy represented a powerful foe, a foe many of his men would not be prepared to overcome. They knew what she represented and the powers with which she was blessed. Aedan also knew that Crierwy's followers were hidden all around them and potentially ready to attack. There were too many risks; he would be foolish to be imprudent.

He knew too that Crierwy's instinct about his motives was uncomfortably close to the mark; he was ambivalent, at best, about his children, a result of having children at such a young age. He was a politician and decisions were made for pragmatic reasons and for gain. Yes, Arthur was blessed as a Beltane child, but he was also the son of the Priestess of the Cauldron.

Arthur was now thirteen and ready for military training. Reports from Gwallog held much hope. This young man had a maturity beyond his years, a young man of intelligence, personal bravery who had already attracted loyalty and jealousy in equal part. Aedan smiled inwardly at that; the boy was in his father's mould, and he realised that Arthur would be vital to his aspirations. Aedan felt sure that he could turn Arthur's head; his knowledge of the boy pointed towards a desperate need to be a warrior. But he now realised that Arthur would not be the only one who needed persuading. His mother could represent a significant problem and he would need to be at his political best to win her over. He must proceed slowly and patiently, although he was aware that his presence in the land of Gwynedd could provoke anger, so time was of the essence.

"Can I meet Arthur?" he asked quietly. "Please."

"Do I have your word?" she repeated.

"Yes, you have my word." He paused. "Just let me talk to the boy."

She stared at him with an intensity that made Aedan shift his feet. She sighed deeply. "You are his father."

He smiled. "Yes indeed."

"And I do not have the right to stop you despite my feelings about your motives. Without you he could become a great Druid. With you he will always have to watch his back and probably get himself killed in some meaningless battle to deliver the crown to you."

"You don't know any of that," he snapped.

She ignored his response and pressed on. "Let him ask you questions. Give him true answers," she said coldly.

"Yes, I can do that."

"Really?"

"Really, I promise you."

"Do not do that, Aedan, because I don't trust you, Uther. I know you will try to turn his head but beware, I will always be there, feeding him the truth at every step."

Aedan nodded.

Only after accepting Aedan's assurances did Crierwy signal for her followers to come out of hiding. Aedan was shocked at their ability to hide so close to his soldiers. He chuckled and shook his head. "I await Arthur's company," he said happily and at that returned to his soldiers, directing them to set up camp by the lake shore at a respectful distance. Crierwy agreed to organise some food and drink in exchange for Aedan's guarantee that none of the soldiers entered the settlement for any reason except Gwallog.

Crierwy would talk to Arthur first before introducing him to his father. She felt sick at the thought, but she could not prevent it. Arthur wanted, so much, to meet his father. The thought of being a prince was bound to turn his head but whilst she knew how manipulative Aedan could be, she also tried to assure herself that Arthur was mature and intelligent enough not to get carried away. Her stomach churned and sourness again rose in her throat.

When Arthur finally joined his mother at her lodgings her hands were shaking, and she felt physically sick. Arthur noticed her discomfort and sat close to her before stretching over to hold her hand. They sat in silence for many minutes. Arthur was desperate to know who these strangers were, but he chose to keep his counsel and concentrated on trying to control his breathing.

Eventually, having mastered her own emotions as best she could, Crierwy turned to Arthur. "I know what you want to know, Arthur. Yes, those soldiers belong to your father."

Arthur's eyes widened. "Have they come for me?"

"Arthur, your father is with them, and he wants to meet with you."

"When? Now?" Arthur asked, his voice rising with excitement.

"Shortly," she soothed.

"When?"

"Arthur!" Crierwy spoke sternly. She closed her eyes and held out her hands in a sign of calm, and took his hands. "Sorry, I know your excitement, Arthur."

Arthur went quiet, surprised and hurt by his mother's tone. "Forgive me, Mother."

"No..." She hugged him tightly. "Don't apologise. I know your heart has always desired this... I am happy for you but I fear too."

"Why?"

"It doesn't matter," she sighed. "This is your life, and your decisions are now for you to make."

Arthur frowned. "My decision?" he asked, confused. "Does he want to take me from you?"

"I believe he does." She nodded. "If my guess is right he will want you to join his horsemen of Manau."

"Really?"

She paused, looking for the words to warn him but also trying to avoid appearing vindictive towards Aedan. "Listen to how he answers but I warn you to beware. Your father is a wily operator and cannot be completely trusted. All that glitters is not gold, my son."

"I will do as you ask, Mother," he said quietly, "but I must know that you will accept my decision when I make it."

She smiled. "That sounds as if you've made up your mind."

"No, of course not."

She ignored his assurances. "It doesn't matter, Arthur, just remember I am always here for you. Go now." She smiled weakly. "Go meet your father," she said quietly, pointing at a man sitting on some rocks between the settlement and the soldiers' camp. He nodded and kissed her on her forehead. As he turned to walk away, he was sure he could hear his mother sob, but he walked on, choosing not to look back.

Outside his mother's hut, he found Gwallog. He put his arm on Arthur's shoulder. "I will take you to Aedan." Arthur puffed out his chest; it was time to be a man.

As he approached the man who he knew to be his father, Aedan stood and opened his arms in greeting. Gwallog ushered Arthur forward. "Good luck, my boy," he said before turning towards Crierwy who had followed at a respectful distance. She stopped as Gwallog made to walk towards her. He was surprised when she put her arms around him but said nothing, allowing her to hold him tightly. He could feel her sobbing against chest.

"It'll be all right," he soothed, stroking the back of her head.

"You don't know that," she sobbed

"I suppose not, but it is the destiny of a prince to be a warrior in these days.

"It's not true, he could be a Druid."

"He is a prince, Crierwy, he could never be a Druid, whether he or you willed it. You know this."

She released herself and stood back, glaring at him. "You are in thrall to him, you would say that. You're Aedan's man, his whelp!"

"I'm sorry you think so poorly of me," Gwallog said sadly and turned to walk away.

"Stop," Crierwy called urgently. "I didn't mean that. You deserve better than that from me. You saved us and I should not treat you badly."

"It's all right, I understand," he grunted. "I am uncomfortable around women and I should have been more sensitive."

"You are married now, are you not? To Aedan's daughter?" Crierwy said trying to change and lighten the conversation.

"Muirgein? No, Aedan gave her to Urien of Rheged."

"Urien? But I thought—,"

"You really are cut off from the world in this place Crierwy. You have obviously not heard."

"Clearly."

"He is the coming man. I should not have expected any different. They are clearly well matched because they have children too."

"I'm sorry," she said reaching for his hand, "and yet you are still Aedan's man?"

"My father desires it. We all have our duty, Lady."

She looked towards Arthur and his father who were deep in conversation and invited Gwallog to walk with her. "Are you sure?" he asked.

"It's been a long time since we last met although you have visited, I understand."

"And how did you know that?"

"Arthur is my son, and he tells me everything, at least up until now."

Gwallog grunted. "I hoped you wouldn't know. I came to check on your safety."

"Under Aedan's instruction, I suppose."

"Sometimes, yes, but not always."

They walked along the lake's edge reminiscing. Gwallog so much wanted to share his feelings for her, but he knew he could not. He suspected she knew but if she did, she was choosing to keep silent. The Priestess of the Cauldron was in no position to share her calling with a man. He sighed inwardly.

As they returned to the lodgings she asked, "Will you continue to look after Arthur?"

"Look after?" he repeated. "I never looked after him."

"You know what I mean."

"I imagine I will come into contact with the boy,"

"I must ask a favour of you."

"I will do whatever I can," he said sceptically.

"I cannot ask for anything more than that, I suppose." She paused. "But can you keep him safe?"

Gwallog studied her. "I don't—"

She placed a finger on his lips. "I'm not asking you to act as a bodyguard, just to… counsel him. He will listen to you, he is honour bound for what you did for us."

"He will be a prince, he cannot be honour bound," Gwallog said quietly.

"Please, Gwallog, I will do anything."

Gwallog swallowed hard. He knew what he wanted but the consequences would be too high a cost. He was not ready to look after someone, but he felt unable to turn Crierwy down. It was possible, he reflected, to stay close enough to check on Arthur as well as being a probable spy for Aedan. *Playing both sides again*, he thought with a sinking feeling. Eventually, he turned to Crierwy and nodded his agreement. "I ask nothing but your friendship, my Lady."

A smile spread across Crierwy's furrowed brow. For the first time, she thought that her son might be safe, at least for now.

Aedan smiled at the boy and offered him a seat next to him. He sensed the boy was nervous, but he was also surprised that he felt nervous too.

"You're a fine young man," Aedan began.

"Thank you, Lord," Arthur said quietly.

"I am your father and when we are together like this you can call me that," Aedan responded, patting Arthur's knee.

"Of course, sir."

"Quite," Aedan laughed. "Your mother," he nodded his head towards her, "has asked me to answer any questions you might have for me. And of course, I will, but I must also warn you that the answers I give may not be what you want to hear. The things we do as young men and the price we all pay for doing the wrong things are sometimes too high, not just for ourselves but our children too."

Arthur said nothing.

"Your mother has a fondness for the Lord Gwallog I see," Aedan said casually, trying to lighten the mood.

"He has been a support to us, Father," Arthur responded, "but, we see him little."

"Does your mother have feelings for him?" Aedan probed.

"If she does, she hasn't said."

Aedan grunted and decided there was nothing more he could glean from further questioning. He was not even sure why he was so curious, but he couldn't deny that he felt a pang of envy even jealousy towards Gwallog. Did he still have feelings for Crierwy? She was still a beautiful woman and he thought of her regularly. He was annoyed with himself for such feelings and chose to press on with what he intended to say. "I digress," he said nonchalantly. "So when I was young, my father married me to Domelch. I was too young, and we had children, your brothers, and sisters. But as a man of royal heritage, too many temptations are thrust upon me. I was tempted by other women, and I took advantage of that. The only woman to refuse me was your mother and that enraged me, so I used subterfuge."

"That is hardly honourable, Father," Arthur offered.

Aedan's jaw clenched but he let the comment pass. "Perhaps," he said carelessly, "but I got what I wanted, and in this day and age that is all that counts. You have been sheltered from the world out there." He waved his arms at nowhere in particular. "It is a dangerous place, and you must be bold when necessary but also careful. Politics is what has kept me from you, but things change and that is no longer the case. I am sorry, it must be hard to accept, but you are now of an age which demands your recognition. Someone who will ride at my side because the time nears, Arthur, when we need to be bold. Join me, my boy, and we will do remarkable things together. Fame is but a sword's length away," Aedan finished triumphantly.

"Yes, I will!" Arthur almost shouted.

No questions were needed; Arthur was convinced. He was shocked by some of his father's words but the thought of becoming a famous man riding at his father's side was too much of a temptation. Any fears or doubts over the consequences of his decision were cast aside.

As Aedan watched Arthur return to the settlement, he smiled to himself.

Chapter 14

The Horsemen of Manau

Before his training began, Arthur spent many hours listening to the stories about the horsemen of Manau. They were an army of expert horsemen developed by the great Cunedda and were the descendants of the legendary Roman Sarmatians. They had a reputation for supernatural ferocity and were feared by their adversaries. So effective had this force been that they had become mercenaries and sought after by all the neighbouring kingdoms. Lot, the previous Lord of the Gododdin, had helped fund the force and Aedan had used this to his advantage since becoming the King of Manau and the Prince of Forth.

The status and multi-national make-up of the horsemen of Manau meant that its recruits included all the princes of the neighbouring kingdoms. Arthur had thus been accompanied by Drystan, much to Cynon's pride, and Bedwyr. They were also joined by Cai, now known as the Tall, for reasons that were clear to all, and most surprisingly, Collen, who had appeared less than enthusiastic but then suddenly became energetically supportive of the enterprise. Arthur had been puzzled by such a turnaround and slightly suspicious, but he reasoned that pressure had been brought to bear by his father.

Cai had sprung up in size and his physical presence fed into his growing confidence, and he would claim, assertiveness. Most of the other new recruits believed his boasts and air of self-importance bordered on arrogance and malevolence. The current warriors were simply wary of him. Despite this there was a grudging respect for Cai's prowess in the use of weapons and physical activity.

To Arthur's surprise, a trainee was expected to master more than just riding and using weapons. The new recruits were introduced to a training programme known as the 'Four and Twenty Games'. The depth and breadth of the training felt both puzzling and overwhelming to him, as it was for most recruits. But once he had established himself within the group of trainees and showed off his intelligence and positivity, he grew into the challenges he was required to confront. The training was multi-layered and enabled would-be warriors to operate in all sorts of combat situations.

The training included the six 'feats of activity'. The six elements included improving personal fitness; weapons training; survival skills; cultural skills including, to the horror of the new recruits, dance; diplomacy; and board games including Drafts and Brandah, designed to develop strategic thinking. If these activities weren't challenging enough, there were additional exercises including sword juggling, spear vaulting, high jump from a standing position, tossing the caber and voice training. The young men also played a game called Shinty whilst riding horses to replicate the fast moving melees of the battlefield. Arthur didn't initially pretend to understand why the training covered such a multitude of skills but he found it rewarding, even enjoyable.

The trainees were being moulded into a band of brothers; they lived, they would fight and they would die together. Death, Arthur knew, would be his inevitable fate, but he and his warrior friends would be heroes of their age, bound by a strict code of honour. He cared little for his own safety, a trait that discomforted his trainers.

Arthur thrived at most of the activities where intelligence and speed were required. His leadership qualities had also come to the fore, with him frequently guiding his peers through exercises that promoted the skills of others as well as himself. His skills had been noted by his mentors, Fergus and Gwalhafed. They frequently reported to Aedan's agent, Gwallog, who, when he could, ventured from his kingdom of Elmet to check on Arthur's progress.

Arthur was always pleased to see Gwallog but he could not help wondering why the constant checks were needed. He concluded that his father was showing a paternal interest but he also suspected, although Gwallog never admitted it, that his mother was at centre of it.

It felt like an ordinary day. As day broke Arthur went out with Bedwyr and Drystan for a run towards the great rock. He was lean and muscular and he left them in his wake within a short space of time. An hour later he sprinted back into the camp before jumping fully clothed into the small stream that circled the enclosure.

He stepped out, bending over with his hands on his knees. As his breath slowed he noticed Cai coming towards him holding two wooden swords. Arthur straightened and stretched his back.

"Arthur!" Cai called. "Let's play!"

"No, Cai, I'm fine," Arthur gasped.

"Come on, are you afraid of me?" Cai chided.

Arthur laughed. "Maybe once, my dear foster brother."

Cai threw the sword at Arthur's feet. "Come on, my over rated friend," he said, quickly closing the gap between them.

"Have you been drinking, Cai?" Arthur queried. "It's a bit early, don't you think?"

Without warning, Cai swept his wooden sword across Arthur's thighs, delivering a stinging blow. "Come on, Arthur, or do I need to hit you again?" He laughed. "It'll be just like old times."

Arthur rubbed his legs, trying to numb the searing pain, responding only with a pained growl.

Cai suddenly closed the gap again, this time slapping Arthur's torso with his sword. He jumped back, laughing. "You think you will lead these men? I am the better man. I know it, you know it, everyone knows it," he taunted.

"I think not," a puffing Bedwyr said as he ran up to join them. "Don't you think it's a bit early for this, Cai?"

"You talk rubbish, my star struck friend, men follow the brave."

"They do," Arthur put in, "but not the bully."

"Have a care, Arthur," Cai spat.

"Me have a care? You are a sad husk of a man. Take your wooden sword and go back to playing soldiers with the children."

At that Cai snapped. "You bastard, we'll see about that. Let's see what happens to little pointless shits like you." At that he stormed off.

Arthur looked at Bedwyr and the newly arrived, red faced, Drystan and shrugged. Arthur turned back to the stream and washed off any remaining sweat and rubbed softly at his reddened limbs and upper arm.

"What the hell was that about?' Bedwyr said.

"Your guess is as good as mine," Arthur responded bemused.

"He was probably turned down by the local whore," Drystan laughed.

"Good grief." Bedwyr sniggered.

Suddenly a warning from Drystan attracted Arthur's attention as Cai strode purposefully out of his lodgings holding a real sword. "I am going to show you what it's like to be the bastard you are."

Drystan tried to block Cai's path. "What are doing Cai? What the fuck is wrong with you."

"Fuck off," Cai retorted and pushed Drystan aside.

Arthur spun around looking for anything to defend himself. All he could find was the wooden weapon Cai had previously thrown at his feet and a worn shield. Still, what choice did he have? Arthur braced himself for the attack that was surely going to come.

Cai was quick but he was all arms and legs and was slightly ungainly, as he swung the sword in a wide arc. But Cai was too slow and Arthur had plenty of time to sidestep to his left and away from the slashing sword. Cai turned and Arthur resumed a defensive position. Cai again stepped in, this time slashing backhanded towards Arthur's midriff, but again Arthur sprang backwards and waited for the follow up arcing slash which duly arrived, grazing his upper arm, immediately opening a gash. Arthur felt the connection and the sting made his body scream with pain.

Cai let out an evil laugh. "Bleed, you bastard."

Bedwyr and Drystan continued to plead with Cai to stop but he ignored them. Bedwyr, realising there was no reasoning with the inebriated assailant, shouted for Drystan to get help. "Go quickly, my friend."

Arthur was able to remain out of reach despite two further swings of the sword. By now a small group of men and boys began to gather, some protesting at the unfair fight whilst others chanted for their favourites. Cai swung again. Arthur partly parried the blow on his shield which fell uselessly to the floor, but he was still able to land a hefty blow on the side of Cai's head. Cai grunted, shook his head and came forward again, although a little unbalanced.

From his right, Arthur recognised Bedwyr's voice. He glanced over to see a sword flying through the air towards him. He grabbed at the hilt and spun round in one movement, and faced Cai with the blade at the ready. Momentarily Cai hesitated, suddenly realising the danger. But that hesitation was all Arthur needed. He stepped forward, his sword striking Cai's sword hand which made him drop the blade and with one liquid movement he spun around and brought the wooden sword hard down on nape of Cai's neck, throwing him forward on to the ground with a heavy thud. The wind had been forced out of him but the speed of Arthur's swordsmanship had him feeling the point of Arthur blade piercing his neck.

"Have you quite finished?" came a voice Arthur recognised.

"I have," Arthur said with a cold calmness that sent a silence across those present. "How about you, Cai? Are you finished?"

Gwallog strode over, bent down and dropped to his knees so he could look into Cai's eyes. "So, what about you?"

Cai nodded. "Yes," he snarled.

"We will deal with you later. Unprovoked attacks on others is not what we would expect from a trainee warrior."

"You can't tell me what to do," Cai snarled again. "My father is a king."

"Oh, I see," Gwallog grunted knowingly. "I'll tell you what." He stood up and then bent over and picked up Cai's sword and laid it next to him. "All right, Prince Cai," he said, drawing his own sword. "Stand up."

A panic flashed across Cai's face. "Why?" His words now were more panicked and less confrontational.

"Stand up, Prince. You and me, let's settle this. Let's see who prevails, you, the arrogant son of a king, or me. Get up."

"I-I-I can't match you," Cai stammered.

"And yet you are prepared to fight someone using a wooden sword. You are a little turd and now it's time to learn your lesson."

"No, please no," Cai begged. "I'm sorry."

"So what happens now, Cai? I step away and as soon as my back is turned you'll stab me from behind? Is that it, Cai?"

"No, of course not. No!"

"How can I — how can anyone," Gwallog swept his arm around the crowd, "trust you?"

Cai looked down at his feet, humiliated and shamefaced.

Gwallog sighed and shook his head. "Cai, you are an idiot. Get out of my sight. You will stay out of my sight until I call for you, do you hear me?" He studied Cai closely. "Is your brain beginning to work now? You are a fool, boy, an embarrassment to your family and a danger to our unit. Now fuck off."

Cai nodded, stood gingerly, bowed slightly and dragged himself away.

Gwallog rolled his shoulders and then rolled his eyes. He put his hands on his hips and breathed deeply and then called Gwalhafed over to him. "Get someone to look at his wounds," he said with a tone of almost resignation. He breathed hard and looked at the crowd and at Arthur. "All of you, go and do something else, there is nothing more to see." He saw, out of the corner of his eye, Arthur turn. "Not you, young man," he warned.

"But Lord Gwallog, it wasn't—"Bedwyr started.

"Shut up," Gwallog interrupted. "This is not your affair. Leave us!"

Bedwyr wanted to protest but Gwallog's expression warned him off that course of action and he gave a perfunctory nod. "Yes, sir." He turned and walked away, shrugging towards Arthur as he went.

Gwallog turned to Arthur who was trying to stop himself smiling. "You, young man, come with me, we need to talk."

Arthur and Gwallog walked awhile in silence until they came to a spot out of the earshot of everyone and sat, cross legged, across from each other. Arthur considered how he might answer the questions Gwallog was going to ask following the morning's melee. There was a large part of him that wanted Cai kicked out of the unit; after all he had terrorised him and his peers for months. And for Arthur, it had been years. Nonetheless, Arthur was painfully aware of Myrddin's words about the jealousy of others and whether dispensing with Cai would, at some stage in the future, come back to haunt him. Surely, he reasoned, keeping Cai close would be better for all. Cai would be a great warrior and he didn't believe that he had the propensity for undermining people, he wasn't that clever. The anger he had shown had clearly dimmed his reason, that and the alcohol, and Arthur had been able to take advantage of that. But after all was said and done, Cai was his foster brother and he didn't want to upset his father who had been so kind to him and his mother.

Gwallog disturbed Arthur's thoughts. "Well?" he said gruffly.

"Well what? I don't understand," he said unconvincingly.

"Hmmm," Gwallog grunted. "Your fight with Cai?"

"It was nothing," Arthur responded lightly, waving his hand nonchalantly.

Gwallog felt a surge of irritation. "Don't be cocky with me, boy. He had a sword!"

"We were training," Arthur countered.

"That is total bullshit and you know it," Gwallog retorted irritably. "Drystan would not come running for help if you were... training."

Arthur breathed in slowly, trying to calm his rising nervousness. "We... we just had a... disagreement," he stuttered.

"A disagreement," Gwallog repeated, his frustration and anger barely concealed. "That idiot had a sword and judging by his curses and look of sheer evil he was going to use it!" Gwallog closed his eyes and rolled his shoulders, calming himself. "He broke the code, he used a lethal weapon against a peer. The boy will be whipped and if he survives he will be sent home in disgrace."

"No, wait," Arthur pleaded.

"Wait? Why? We both know Cai is an out of control bully, an unstable loose cannon who would see his friends die if it means advancement and glory. He is a liability who will be the death of anyone unfortunate enough to fight alongside him."

"That may be true," Arthur conceded, "but he has the ability to be a good if not great warrior."

Gwallog harrumphed, "Bullshit." He leant forward, a look of suspicion etched across his face. "I'm going to regret this aren't I? Why are you setting yourself against my judgement?"

"Lord," he started.

"I really am going to regret this. Cut out the bullshit. Calling me lord is not going to make any difference," Gwallog grunted.

Arthur tried to stifle a smile. "Fair enough." He paused a few beats and decided to press on. "Myrddin spoke to me a few years ago and one thing he told me was that I would always inspire many emotions, both good and bad. I recognise I can inspire loyalty but Cai has shown me I can inspire jealousy, hatred and even… fear."

"So?"

Look, I know Cai is a bully, and yes he is a complete shit but he will be a great warrior."

"And your point is?"

"If I am seen to want him to go home in disgrace, some people would accept it but others will resent me and will want me to find another way."

"That's the way of the world," Gwallog said quietly

"Cai is someone who will not take humiliation and he cannot allow himself to be seen as an idiot. He will always hold it against me. Whatever I or you think of him, we need him with us; we need his father with us too."

"His father?"

"Yes, I owe him a debt of gratitude."

"The diplomacy lessons have been well taught I see," Gwallog grinned, "but there is a problem, isn't there?"

"What?"

"Cai, will he or, can he, work with you? Can you work with him? A wounded animal is difficult to tame. I don't think he can be tamed, he will more than likely stab you in the back than he will accept your authority."

"The enemy of my enemy?" Arthur countered.

Gwallog thought for a moment and shook his head. He didn't agree with Arthur but he realised and admitted that there was, perhaps, some truth in what he said. He wasn't a great believer in the likes of Myrddin, although Crierwy had given him pause for thought. That fight, all those years ago, at the river had been successful, if losing such good men was a success. But his survival, along with Cynon and Taliesin, was down to Crierwy's premonition and he couldn't forget that.

Gwallog knew how men operated. How fear could sway them to extraordinary actions that no one could fathom. Myrddin was right, jealousy of Arthur would probably be his undoing like it had been for so many leaders and heroes. He remembered stories of Caradoc, the leader of the Catuvellauni and his betrayal by Cartimandua. Oh yes there were many, too many.

"All right, speak to him and you decide," Gwallog said with an air of resignation.

"Thank you," Arthur responded with relief. "I will speak to him... If there is no likelihood that I can work with him, I will accept your decision and he goes."

Gwallog smiled. "Fine but I will give you some cover."

"Some cover?" he repeated.

"If you fail, I will tell Cai and everyone else that you argued for his retention. Maybe, just maybe, he will not hold it against you. It might also help you to make a more reasoned decision."

"Thank you."

"Hmm. Fuck off and don't make me regret it," Gwallog grunted.

"I won't."

"Yeah, we'll see." Gwallog smiled.

Some hours passed. Arthur approached the hut Cai had been secured in. Two men were at the entrance but they moved aside as Arthur approached them. They both nodded toward him but before Arthur entered he stopped and picked up the sword he surmised had been used against him earlier that day. For a moment, Arthur lifted the sword, studying it against the last rays of light of the day. He slapped the blade against the palm of his hand and closed his fingers around it. He smiled as he realised the blade was dull. Perhaps he wouldn't have been badly injured if he was struck, although the injury he did receive still stung and it gave him pause for thought.

The guards eyed him as he stooped and entered the space. It was dark inside and it took him a moment for his eyes to adjust to what light there was. He looked around and saw Cai lying on a cot barely long enough to take the length of his body.

He poured a cup of water and sat down next to the cot, grunting as he folded himself on to the stool. He waited a moment or two until Cai shifted his weight to face him. Arthur saw Cai's face was heavily bruised, the result, he guessed, of rough handling from his guards. Cai groaned and Arthur offered him the cup which he took without hesitation, drinking greedily.

Cai raked his hand through his long hair but froze the moment he met Arthur's eyes. He then noticed the sword in Arthur's hand and smiled grimly. "Come to finish me off, Arthur?" he asked with an air of resignation.

Arthur said nothing, keeping all emotion from his face. After a pause he tilted his head and handed the sword, hilt first, to Cai. "No."

Cai eyed him suspiciously but then shifted himself so that he could lever himself up to a sitting position. Arthur offered his hand and to his surprise Cai took it. "You look dreadful," Arthur said with an amused look.

"You should have seen the other guy." Cai smiled ruefully.

"Aye, I bet he would still be better looking than you even if he were busted up," Arthur chided.

"Bastard! I let him win," Cai said. "The little shit needed a boost."

A silence followed and Arthur found himself feeling warmth for the young man facing him. Despite their differences there was always an unspoken bond between them. Yes, Cai had beaten him black and blue on far too many occasions, but he had always looked out for him and accepted Arthur into his home when he and his mother had nowhere else to go. He couldn't ignore that but he also could not let what had happened go and he certainly could not allow Cai to terrorise him and his friends any more, no matter how much bigger, and yes, stronger he was. Nonetheless, Arthur had proven to Cai, and more importantly, to himself that he was the superior warrior, more controlled, faster and more agile.

He straightened and sighed deeply, looking intently into Cai's face. "Why, Cai, what did I do to deserve your trying to kill me?"

Cai said nothing, instead looking at the floor.

"Why, Cai?" Arthur said louder. "What was it you wanted to achieve?"

Cai looked tired, his head was throbbing and he ached all over. He gratefully took another drink of water and tipped the rest into his cupped hand and splashed his face, "You know what, I don't know, Arthur. I suppose I wanted to show everyone I was better than you. I wanted to be the leader of these horsemen. I wanted... I needed to show everyone that despite you being a golden boy I was the coming man."

Arthur shook his head. He understood ambition but to kill or maim for power was alien to him. Was this what Myrddin alluded to? "What have I ever done to you?" he persisted. "What have Bedwyr and Drystan done to you?"

Cai leant back against the wall. "I wanted to be the best and I thought I was, but it was you, always you, they wanted to follow. They kept away from me."

"They were scared of you, for fucks sake," Arthur interrupted. "You are aggressive, you scare people, Cai. Yes, I suppose you could force them to follow you through fear and intimidation but they will never be with you. Why would men give their lives to a man who thinks only of his own destiny, his own advancement without a care for them?"

Cai's jaw tightened and Arthur could see his anger rising.

"You're getting angry, Cai, why? Is it because I'm questioning you? When you fought me today you lost because of your anger, you weren't thinking, you were slashing at me, completely blind to what I was doing. And where is your anger getting you? Where is your bullying getting you? We are here tonight because you want to be in charge? You were prepared to risk being kicked out, beaten up, possibly even beaten to death, because you want to be in charge?"

Arthur could see tears filling Cai's eyes. He knew how Cai's father pushed him, had high hopes of him and expected him to be a great warrior. But Cai's father was never one to show Cai any affection; he never praised him despite his clear abilities. Arthur leant forward and put his hand on Cai's shoulder. "You have nothing to prove, brother. Everyone knows your calibre, but you have to earn respect from others. Surely the Druidic training we went through helped you understand that. Look, I know we've all let our education slip but those foundations should still be there."

Cai used the back of his hand to wipe his nose. "It's too late, Arthur. I'm done," he said gloomily.

"Maybe, but I know I am stronger, the horsemen of Manau are stronger with you among us. Brother, I can't do this without you, at your best you are the very best of us. If they give you the chance, take it. Please."

"You forgive me!" Cai gaped.

"Maybe not completely." Arthur grinned. "Surely you can't expect that after you tried to kill me, you bastard. You beating me black and blue is one thing but killing me is a whole new low for you."

Arthur held out his arm and Cai grasped him at the elbow. "I'm sorry, brother," Cai said.

Arthur held his gaze for a while, searching for something in Cai's expression, some reassurance that Cai really was sorry. Perhaps he might never know for certain, Arthur reflected, but he was desperate for it to be true. He puffed up his cheeks and eventually nodded and stood, clapping Cai on the shoulder. He was satisfied that everything that needed to be said had been said. "Let's see what tomorrow brings. Sleep well." Arthur smiled as he walked to the door, stooped and exited into the evening sunshine.

Chapter 15

A Call to Arms

Aedan rode into the camp with some two hundred warriors at his back. He was accompanied, Arthur noted, by Gwallog and a woman he reckoned was in her mid-twenties. She looked very similar to Aedan and he guessed that she might well be related. He felt a warm glow at the thought. He thought he caught her eye and he was sure she smiled at him. Perhaps, he thought, it was wishful thinking; she was beautiful, after all.

Gwalhafed, the head trainer, strode forward to meet Aedan, bowing deeply as he reached for the horse's reins. Aedan slid elegantly from his mount, followed closely by Gwallog and the young woman. He said something to Gwalhafed who nodded and guided Aedan to the large roundhouse. Arthur saw Gwalhafed looking around until the man's eye settled on him. As he strode over he called on Arthur and beckoned Bedwyr, Cai, Collen and Drystan to join him. "You are all summoned," he growled. "Come with me, Aedan awaits your presence."

They walked to the large roundhouse and were joined by another five warriors who entered just ahead of them. Arthur felt exhilarated; something important was in the offing. He stooped to enter and noticed that everyone had settled on benches set out in a rough circle. There were thirteen of them including the woman.

Aedan signalled to everyone to sit and water was passed around. Aedan leant forward, his elbows resting on his knees. "Gentleman," he said clearly and confidently, "we have a problem to solve and preparations to make." His eyes wandered around the room and he nodded as his eyes met Arthur. He had the room's attention and he knew it. He smiled. "First I will introduce you and you can make small talk afterwards if you choose." He waved carelessly. "From my right is Gwallog, Gwalhafed, Bedwyr, Cai,

Blane, Fergus, Collen, my son Arthur, Bran, Huail, Nascien and Drystan. Next to me is Muirgein, my daughter and the soon to be Priestess of Iona which my cousin, apparently, seems bent on giving to this self-styled Dove of God, Columba the Christian turd." He smiled then and begged forgiveness for his irritable outburst. "The damn Christian," he corrected.

Everyone in attendance laughed.

"I am here to appraise you of troubles to the west of us. You will be acquainted with Gwenddoleu ap Ceidio and the escalating tensions between him and the Lord Rhydderch of Alt Clut. We know that forces are on the move and Gwenddoleu's borders are under threat. Needless to say, Gwenddoleu has appealed to Conall and me for help and this becomes particularly urgent as it would appear King Urien has allied himself to Rhydderch. I don't need to remind you that Urien is a coming man."

"Myrddin is going to be compromised," Cai put in.

"Yes, he will be," Aedan said, "and so are all of us."

"How so?" Arthur asked. "Gwenddoleu follows the old ways as do we."

"So we ally with him," Gwallog said flatly, shrugging.

"Yes, we should," Aedan said smoothly, "but he will lose and thus so will we." There was silence until Aedan continued. "We cannot afford to be on the wrong side, my friends. I know Conall has chosen to be neutral, the gutless water snake that he is." There was laughter from all those present; they all knew Aedan's thoughts on his cousin.

"What are you proposing?" Bran asked.

"We throw our lot in with Rhydderch but we will avoid direct involvement in any major engagement." He glanced around him. "We will stay on the sidelines and choose our side when the time is right."

"Father?" Muirgein chimed in. "We can't betray fellow believers, the gods will never forgive us."

"The gods cannot determine a battle if the numbers are overwhelming, daughter. Anyway religion has nothing to do with this. It is power and land and anyone who tells you differently wants more than we can afford."

"Surely it's better to do the right thing," Collen said. "At least our consciences will be clear."

Aedan glowered at the young man. "You believe dying for a principle is doing the right thing, young man? A worthy sentiment, perhaps, but a complete waste of life. War is coming, my friend, not just with Gwenddoleu but the Angles too. Do you believe they will just stand by and let us rebuild ourselves? Or, as I believe, will they attack when we are at our weakest and without allies such as Rhydderch and Urien? And what about you, Gwallog, and the territory of Elmet, the Angles to the east of you and Rheged to the north? Who will protect you? The sons of Eliffer? They will come north to help Gwenddoleu certainly, but they can just as easily retreat to Ebruac. We may be fools, but you can guarantee they won't be?"

Arthur raised his hand to speak. He was uneasy with his father's reasoning but despite that he could see why he argued for supporting Alt Clut. Arthur knew that Aedan was also keen to gather allies around him for his inevitable assault on Conall to usurp the crown of Dalriada and to sideline the Irish Dalriadans who might just side with a pliant Conall. Arthur also thought that Aedan could keep Columba on his side, or at least, he might prevent Columba from challenging his authority. The cunning bastard. His mother was right, Aedan was wily.

Aedan nodded at him.

"Lord Aedan," he began, "I know this must be difficult for you and I'm sure you can see it is difficult for us. You are our lord and you understand the bigger picture." He looked around him. "Brothers, Aedan is our lord, he is asking us to support him. He believes that he can secure the security we need in these difficult days. Christianity, treacherous neighbours and the Angles are sat on our borders. What an opportunity we have to be the strong arm of all the kingdoms north of the great wall. We should trust him. I, for one, will follow him."

Aedan's grin widened. "Thank you, Arthur."

Cai stood then. "I too support Lord Aedan."

"As do I," Bedwyr called out.

"And I," Drystan said.

When everyone had had their say, Aedan rose from his seat. "My Lords, I thank you for your support. Tonight let us feast."

That night the feast was both hearty and raucous. By the time Aedan had risen to his feet, the stew had been devoured and the drink was flowing. Arthur had been placed to Aedan's right although there had been little discussion, Aedan choosing largesse with his men arranged to his left. Arthur found these occasions tiresome although he recognised that anything that gave men a sense of bravery was something that shouldn't be ignored. He watched his father seemingly enjoying the whole process of being the great leader and centre of attention. He noticed how his men revered his father and accepted without question his strategic cunning. Arthur realised that if he were in Aedan's position, he too would have to do this. Did his father really enjoy this show or was it something he simply had to go through? Arthur suspected that it was all a performance. His father was wily for sure and to succeed he had a lot to learn.

His mother, he knew, would be unhappy that he was even thinking this way but the world was complicated and to survive, strength was in both your sword arm and with your mind. Did he want this? Could he do it? Could he play the game his father was so good at? He smiled to himself, yes he could and he would.

Aedan clapped his son on the back as he stood holding his hands wide. Gwallog banged the bench with his cup and the room gradually became quiet. "Gentlemen, let us have a refill." He beckoned to the men and women serving and stood there very still, patiently waiting for everyone to have their cups filled.

When everything was done Aedan gestured to his man servant, a man known as Cormons, a dark, big, heavily set man. Clearly a man not to tangle with, Arthur considered. Arthur looked at the man eying him up and down. He sighed and shrugged, mildly amused at this brooding presence. He looked forward, catching the eye of his friends, Bedwyr, Drystan and the greatly changed Cai. He smiled at them and they lifted their cups to him. Oh, how he wished he were sat with them. He would, one day, he was sure of it.

Despite everyone having their cups full and quiet restored to the room once again, Aedan stood there silent, face now impassive surveying his audience. His hands were on his hips and his chest puffed out. Finally he nodded and looked to the back. "Gentlemen, I hope you enjoyed your food and you've had your fill of mead and beer." He stopped to allow the audience to roar their appreciation and smiled. "And there is more to come. Tomorrow we rest, for the next day we ride. We ride to war," he bellowed.

The hall erupted. The drink had done its job, Arthur reflected.

"Where are we going?" someone called from the left of the top table.

"We ride south to the borders of Alt Clut and the lands of Gwenddoleu," he shouted again.

There was an inevitable roar. Aedan, this time, beckoned for silence and continued in a more sober way. "War, my friends, is full of glory, and that glory will be yours when it comes. Your names will be long remembered, not just in the hearts of your comrades here but by people throughout the ages. Many of us will not return." He paused. "War is unforgiving. War is pain. Taking another man's life should not be a cause for celebration. But respect of our enemies does not blunt us, it makes us fight harder, better and the credit each of us gains with each victory is a sacred thing. It makes us feared and our road to glory is assured. Friends," he raised his cup, *"to glory!"*

The answering roar was deafening. And Aedan stood there fist raised taking the acclaim but without any emotion on his face. Arthur stood there, glass raised, watching him, completely captivated by his father's performance. And yes, it was a performance, words balancing success and loss, somehow making this a sacred act despite the war being between natural allies and for reasons that were evidently not an immediate danger for Manau. It was a means to an end, Arthur knew. The question was, how far was Aedan prepared to go. King of Dalriada definitely, King of the Scots very possibly. And what would Arthur's role be? He had a feeling he would know soon enough.

"Friends, friends. To finish. You will know that I found, after far too long, my son Arthur. He has proven to be a man of talent. His work here has been exemplary and his skills will have made our Sarmatian forebears very proud. He has proven himself worthy of leadership. The horsemen of Manau need someone to lead them into battle. I am proud to," he paused, "announce that my son, Prince Arthur, will be our battle leader in the conflicts ahead." The warriors cheered as Aedan reached back for a cloak held by Cormons. He took it and stepped forward holding the cloak towards

Arthur, a big smile plastered across his face. "Arthur," he announced, "in recognition of your elevation, I hereby award you with the Cloak of Padarn. Congratulations, my boy!"

Cries of, "Arthur, Arthur, Arthur," rang out around the hall as Arthur took the deep red cloak from his father. He held it close to his chest, not knowing what to say. He was so young, barely fourteen years, and he would command the legendary cavalry of Manau, the greatest cavalry in Britain.

Aedan smiled broadly and ruffled Arthur's hair, something he had not done before. He took the cloak from Arthur's hands and swung it around his son's shoulders, clasping it below Arthur's chin before adjusting it. "Well done, Arthur, my son."

"Thank you, I'm speechless."

"Be the man I know you are, my boy."

"Thank you... Father."

Aedan clapped Arthur on the shoulder and lifted his arm.

Inevitably, the following day was a rather quiet one as Arthur set off for his morning run. He looked about him and there was no one, no warriors, guards or servants. As he moved through the camp he reflected, with a mixture of dismay and amusement, that an opposing force could quite easily overrun their camp and they would all be slaughtered in their cots and never know what had happened.

To his surprise, Aedan had not summoned Arthur or his senior men together to discuss the plans for the upcoming campaign. Arthur surmised that the reasons were probably drink related and some sort of meeting would be held later in the morning. He was still disappointed, however, that his father had not seen fit to prioritise war planning. He shook his head and tried to banish the incredulity of it all from his mind.

He jogged out of the camp dreaming of last night and the cloak he was presented with. He would now lead his cavalry alongside his friends just like the Great Alexander and his companion cavalry all those centuries ago. Yes, Arthur smiled to himself, he would be another Alexander and with Bedwyr and Drystan at his shoulder and Cai his lieutenant, he would destroy all their foes. He smiled at that, playing out scenarios in his head of how he would vanquish all and sundry. The Angles and Picts would rue the day they came up against him.

Without realising it, he had broken into a sprint as he tore through the undergrowth skirting the camp, finally bursting through the trees and pulling up short of the stream. He stopped, his hands on his knees, breathing heavily. He slumped down and dipped his head into the water and splashed his face with the invigorating water, cupping it and drinking deeply. Satisfied, he rolled onto his side and then onto his back, gazing up into the sunny sky. He closed his eyes and breathed deeply, enjoying the time on his own; the silence was blissful. He sighed contentedly.

He must have dozed for what could only have been a few beats when he became aware of a shadow standing over him. He opened his eyes with a jolt, scrabbling for something to protect himself from this perceived threat. "Stop," the person standing above him said with a vaguely familiar voice. He looked up and when his eyes adjusted, he could make out the shape of a young woman. It was Muirgein, his half-sister.

"I'm not an assassin, brother, take a breath," she laughed.

Muirgein was tall and slender, her hair rich red. She was elegant and graceful; her hair was in ringlets and flowed down her slim shoulders. Urien was a lucky man to have married her but he was perplexed why she was here with her father rather than at home with her husband. He shrugged inwardly, but for the first time in his life, he felt a surge in his groin. He swallowed hard, trying to compose himself. *Arthur*, he thought, *you have to focus*.

"Sorry... I..." he stammered.

"No, no, my fault, I shouldn't have surprised you. I should be more careful approaching a man of your... importance," she said with an amused look.

He laughed. "I thought everyone was asleep and nursing their hangovers."

"We don't all need to drink ourselves into oblivion to find courage or indeed to enjoy ourselves. But you obviously know that."

"I don't like the feeling of being out of control."

"You're our father's son."

"I doubt it, he drank more than anyone."

Muirgein arched her eyebrows. "Did you see him drink or perhaps I should say what he drank?" She laughed. "Everything he drank was watered down, Arthur. Cormons sees to that. You will learn, soon enough, that he is not what you think."

Arthur laughed. "He seemed full of alcoholic openheartedness."

"Openheartedness?" She grinned. "Our father is anything but that, dear brother. Calculation maybe, openness no."

"So where is he?" Arthur questioned.

"He's gone, he left at dawn."

"Gone?"

"Indeed. People to meet, places to go, plans to be made. I imagine Gwallog will pass on the details to you."

"Your love of our father is not without question," Arthur chided.

"Oh, of course I love our father, he is my father after all." She paused. "But even though I love him, I don't like him and I don't trust him and nor should you," she warned.

"You sound like my mother," he groaned.

"I will take that as a compliment, to be compared to the Priestess Crierwy is a rare thing."

"Not necessarily," Arthur retorted.

Muirgein grinned. "I think that is the way of things, mothers prefer their boys and love them without question, boys love their mother but hate to admit it, fathers worship their daughters and girls enjoy that although they are stifled and used as trophies. The problem is, the line is often far too thin. Our father has to be in control and will do what it takes to keep it. He will expect your obedience to the familial cause, to be in his mould, an extension of his power, but he will set you loose, if you do not succeed."

"I don't understand what you're saying?" he responded, puzzled.

She sighed deeply. "Aedan," she said patiently, "will show love until and if you fulfil his expectations. But make no mistake, he will drop you if you fail him."

"For our first conversation, you are not exactly spreading sisterly love," Arthur grumbled.

Muirgein laughed. "Forgive me, brother, you're quite right."

Arthur found himself smiling. He was fascinated by this woman, his sister. She wasn't like anyone he had ever met before. Her loved her friendliness and yes, even her cynicism. He was, it was starting to dawn on him, beginning to feel an aching desire for her.

Muirgein stared at him, her head tilted to one side, almost amused. "I'm sorry, you are so young and I fear for you. I have brothers but expectations of them are so much less than for you. And now that I have met you I begin to understand why. I didn't want to like you because your existence has hurt my mother greatly. But your heart is pure which, as the son of Crierwy, is to be expected."

"Should I be flattered?" he said.

"You can feel as you wish. But now that I have met you, I am sure that we have a connection and I want you to know that I am here for you if you need the advice of someone who has seen too many political manipulations and too much violence and pain."

"That sounds very personal," Arthur offered.

"More than you think," she snorted.

Arthur didn't really know what to think but he realised a hand of friendship was being offered to him, but at the same time, he couldn't shake from his mind Myrddin's warning about trusting others. Was this too easy? Muirgein, he knew, was a priestess of the old way, but he had just thrown in his lot with his father apparently joining a Christian alliance against a king of the old ways, a Pendragon no less. He felt torn and wished Myrddin had never uttered those words.

He knew doubting the motives of others could cause him indecision and it greatly troubled him. He again remembered how his mother was betrayed, how his father never came for him, how his grandfather had been deposed, how Cai had turned on him. He swallowed hard and his head began to swim.

Sensing his doubts and confusion, Muirgein leaned forward and took Arthur's chin in her palm and stared into his eyes. "I see your confusion, brother. It pains me to see it but it does not surprise me. You don't know me and I have cast doubts. Only you can determine your actions and I strongly believe that you will be a man to fear. I only ask you to keep a clear mind and to understand what and why people want from you. Only you can decide who you can trust but I sense Bedwyr, Drystan and Cai are three you can be confident of, and Gwallog too."

Arthur flinched at her comment about trust. Had she read his mind? She was powerful, he knew. She was a priestess. "I am sorry for my… hesitance, Muirgein, my experiences have been too many," he responded.

"And there will be a lot more experiences, Arthur," she interrupted. "That will be your fate."

"My fate?"

Muirgein smiled thinly said no more. She nodded and stood up. "Beautiful day," she said, stretching. "Enjoy your day, Arthur and enjoy the glassy eyed looks of your men. Today, I regret to inform you, is the last day of your youth. Gwallog will, no doubt, find you shortly."

"I would like to spend time with you," Arthur mumbled, "honestly I would."

"That's good," she responded, gently ruffling his hair, and strolled away.

"I am a grownup," he called after her.

"Of course you are," she called back, waving without turning.

Arthur watched her disappear from view. This was madness, was he smitten by his sister? And why on earth had he said that he was a grownup. He groaned. Had he had fallen in love for the first time with his sister? By all the gods, his mother would strangle him if she knew. He ran his fingers through his hair, trying and failing to ignore his feelings and stop his imagination running away as he imagined clandestine meetings with the beautiful Muirgein. He sat down with a grunt, his back against a tree. "Shit!" he exclaimed.

Gradually the camp awakened around. He rubbed his eyes and concluded he needed a clear mind. He was determined not to let his personal feelings get in the way. He stood up, rolled his shoulders, stretched his limbs, and set off for his second run that morning. Tomorrow he would lead the horsemen of Manau and ride into history.

Chapter 16

A Mentor's Plea

The news that the horsemen of Manau were riding to war brought locals and well-wishers from all of the villages near to the camp to the gates of the camp. As was the custom, the soldiers war their battle dress and acknowledged the cheers. Each wore knee length tunics, long trousers tied at the waist and ankles, with cloaks held by a clasp-brooch.

The people gazed upon the new leader wrapped in his red cloak around his neck held with a bear clasp as protection from the cool morning air.

Arthur and Gwallog led two hundred men out of the camp and travelled south towards Gwenddoleu's fort which sat by the confluence of the River Esk and the Lid Water. Under Arthur's instructions, a hundred horsemen were left to protect the camp and its surrounding area. Arthur's inclination towards distrust of people led him to conclude that it was too much of a risk to leave Manau unguarded. He was sure Morcant of Eidyn would be watching for any weakness and he would offer no incentive to attack Manau. Morcant was a coward, he concluded; it was unlikely he would take such action but a coward could never be relied upon.

Aedan had left instructions to make sure that Gwenddoleu must not receive reinforcements from King Eliffer of Elbruac led by his sons, Peredur and Gwrgi. Without any guidance, Arthur had identified the River Glein as a place to cut off any support. The plan Arthur had devised had surprised Gwallog, who was sure his charge was too inexperienced to come up with such a strategy. Arthur had called it the hammer and anvil. Men with local knowledge had spoken of a crossing on the river easy for soldiers and horsemen to cross. In front of the river, coming up from the south was a break in the trees where the land dropped to the bank. Arthur decided that he would split his force, placing Cai in that gap so he would be clearly visible to Peredur and Gwrgi and be few enough in number to make them a tempting target. Cai would hold their opponents for as long as he could and then conduct a fighting retreat across the river, drawing their opponents across the river until the majority of the force were on the northern bank. Arthur would station his cavalry in the trees off to the west of the battlefield and charge to cut their opponents forces in two. Arthur believed that the shock of that attack would break their opponents and cut off Gwenddoleu's forces.

They planned to be there within three days, traveling around Selgovian territory, and remain out of sight for as long as possible. Surprise was all.

Once the men were out of sight of their encampment, they removed their battle dress and moved on in more relaxed dress. As hoped, their journey had been without incident but the pace Arthur set was tough. Despite pleas to rest, Arthur was determined to get to his position quickly to ensure maximum time would be available to prepare for the conflict ahead.

On the last day of marching, Arthur instructed his horsemen to dress for battle. Besides their familiar clothing, the men now also wore a further knee length tunic made of leather with a coat of chainmail belted at the waist. Long cutting swords similar to the Roman spada hung from their waists, oval wooden shields slung on their backs along with a wooden shaft spear, a diamond shaped head axe, a dagger and sling. To add to the mounting discomfort the heat of the day brought, they also wore a leather cap covered in a metal helmet with neck and ear guards and flexible cheek pieces.

Arthur reflected that any engagement would need to be quick because, otherwise, he and the rest of his men would die of heat exhaustion. Thank goodness, he was fit and he now realised why strength and fitness was believed to be such a key element of their training. It would always give them an advantage over infantry.

He patted his horse. He had only made its acquaintance on the day they left their camp. Like the other horses he was small, only twelve to fifteen hands, but very sturdy. Arthur thought he looked very smart with its decoration of pendants and discs. He had been awarded an elegant four horned saddle which thankfully held Arthur in place. The man riding just behind him and Gwallog carried a bear standard, another, known as the Draconarius carried the brightly coloured Draco, something carried by the Sarmatians after the Romano Dacian wars. The horsemen trotted forward looking neither left or right; no words were exchanged, they just looked forward and headed with grim determination to their chosen site of battle.

Myrddin was agitated. There had been no response from Aedan. He had sent messages, numerous messages, messages to Gwallog and even to Muirgein. Aedan supported the old ways; how could he not support Gwenddoleu Pendragon in the fight against the Christian loving Rhydderch, the husband of his sister no less. And what of Arthur? Did he have the influence to coax his father to the battlefield?

Gwenddoleu regarded him with some amusement. He knew Myrddin's concerns, after all he had voiced them often enough. Gwenddoleu shared those concerns but he had become sanguine. He no longer believed that Aedan would come to his aid but there were other options. Messages had gone out to Eliffer, one of his kin, asking for help. They would come, he knew, his army only had to hold their ground, war would be on the land of his choosing. Rhydderch and Urien would pay a high price for their greed and he would delight in dealing with Aeden and Conall in his own good time if their support was not forthcoming. Doubts over his ultimate success were extinguished when Myrddin joined him. It must have been hard to betray Rhydderch and his sister to join Gwenddoleu's righteous crusade, a fight, Gwenddoleu knew, would end the spread of this hideous Christianity nonsense. Myrddin was a Druid reborn and powerful, he would release the fire that would break his enemies. Gwenddoleu grinned at the thought.

"Lord?" Myrddin said.

"Yes, Myrddin," Gwenddoleu sighed, "what ails you?"

"You know what ails me, Lord," Myrddin responded, frustrated. "Why hasn't Aedan responded?"

Gwenddoleu scratched his head and pinched the bridge of his nose. He sighed again, "Aedan?" he questioned. "He's not coming, my dear Myrddin, Aedan puts politics above right."

Myrddin looked confused. "But—"

Gwenddoleu cut him off, "Aedan is treacherous, he won't come unless he believes we are winning."

"How can you be sure? Our beliefs will always be more important than mere politics," he spat.

Gwenddoleu grunted. "I never had you down as naïve, Myrddin. Aedan does not think as you or I, my friend. Anyway, scouts have told me that a force of Aedan's men is somewhere to the east of us, some twenty miles. He'll wait to see what happens."

"You make conclusions on that alone, Lord?"

"That and the fact this boy Prince Arthur recently left Manau a couple of days ago with a couple of hundred cavalry men heading to the south of us."

"Perhaps they plan to surround our enemies?"

Gwenddoleu smirked. "No, my friend, they seek to cut off the army of Elbruac. But they won't succeed. Arthur is just a whelp, an untried insignificance."

"Lord, this is dangerous," Myrddin warned. "Arthur has been chosen for greatness, I have seen it."

Gwenddoleu raised an eyebrow. "He is fourteen years old." He paused a moment, a sudden unpleasant feeling of doubt running through him. Dispelling that he continued. "Well, we'll have to ensure he is not involved in the fight. The battle, when it comes, will be a ferocious thing and it will live long in the memory. Arthur will be of no consequence. That I assure you. And when he fails, Aedan will dispense with him. The bubble will be burst and Arthur will disappear back into the fog of history he came from."

"I shall try to speak to him," Myrddin said. "I was his mentor. I might be able to persuade him to back away. At least then we can make it into a fair fight."

Gwenddoleu scratched his chin and considered Myrddin's proposition. It was something to try, he thought. What was there to lose? "All right, Myrddin," Gwenddoleu said eventually, "go and seek out the whelp and find out his dispositions in the event that he refuses you."

At that Gwenddoleu beckoned over a man servant and whispered in his ear. It was time to use cunning as well as force. Eliffer's men, he knew, would probably need some help. He would send word to Eliffer's sons as soon as Myrddin returned with the information they would need to escape Arthur's clutches.

Gwenddoleu stretched and yawned. He turned back to Myrddin and smiled, suddenly feeling very tired. "Go now, I need to rest. Come back quickly and we will, old friend, plan our defence."

Myrddin nodded. "Your will, my Lord," he said quietly.

"Oh, and Myrddin," called Gwenddoleu, "I want you to consider what you can do with your... magic. Set your fire against them and we will prevail and the Christians will be forever be ejected from our world."

Arthur arrived at the designated place late in the afternoon. He was pleasantly surprised at the accuracy of the scout's report; it was as if he had already been there and walked the ground. He smiled with satisfaction.

They crossed the Glein and made their way up the north bank and continued until they found the reverse slopes. The camp was set up bordering a wood. Arthur beckoned Gwallog, Cai, Bedwyr and Drystan to him and invited them to ride over the ground with him.

They could see the natural gap leading from the south. It looked like a bay with the open sea beyond. Arthur pointed Cai towards the opening. "How many men will you need to hold that gap?'

Cai pondered. "Three lines of fifty perhaps?"

"One hundred and fifty men," he clarified, "which leaves me fifty... Hmm." He turned around and looked back at the river. The ground, he noted, was narrow which meant Cai could not be turned. "Hmm," he repeated. The trees were not thick and he decided that it was unlikely he could hide any more than fifty men. If anything he thought that he might have to split his force further so that his horsemen could attack both flanks. He sucked his teeth and stroked the growth at his chin. He needed more men.

"Come on, Cai," Drystan chimed in, "you can do with a little less, can't you?"

Drystan's confidence had grown during their training. He had developed a keen ability to spot the weakness in plans and ideas and wasn't backwards in pointing out any obvious flaws. Nonetheless, Drystan was not someone who preached caution and his over enthusiasm and willingness to take risks made him potentially reckless. An interesting dichotomy, Arthur thought, but he supposed there was nothing wrong with that if some control could be exerted on him.

"I was already getting a sinking feeling," Cai said quietly.

"Can you?" Arthur asked.

"What do you need, Arthur?" Cai grunted.

Arthur rolled his shoulders and pondered his response. He took a moment to marshal his thoughts. "So, we want to tempt their men in but we don't want them to be put off by the size of our contingent. If they are put off they will try to march around us, probably to the east. The cavalry can attack when you have retreated but there remains the fear of encirclement so additional cavalry holding your left flank would be significantly more effective."

"I see the problem," Cai breathed. "You will need, what, forty horsemen on each flank? I think too, Arthur, that you will need men in reserve to plug gaps."

"Not enough," he sighed.

"No."

"Our options are reducing by the minute," Arthur reflected. "Can you hold on with one hundred men, fifty in reserve and twenty five horsemen on each flank?"

"They'll think it's Yuletide!" Bedwyr said.

"It fucking will be," Cai agreed, "which means they won't be able to resist." He grinned.

"I think we have a plan, gentlemen," Arthur concluded slowly. "Any further thoughts?"

Everyone shook their heads.

"Good, let's get some food into us, the next few days will be... interesting."

As they turned to return to camp, Arthur beckoned to Drystan and Bedwyr to follow him back across the river and then move off to the east to scout the terrain on the off chance that their enemies chose to avoid them and move to the east.

Cai and Gwallog returned to the camp in silence until they reached the camp guards. "What do you think?" Gwallog said.

"I'm thinking I don't know Arthur any more."

"Your meaning?"

"He's different, he's grown up and he is thinking like someone twice his age. Frankly? He scares me and I have no doubt he is going scare an awful lot more people before this battle has ended."

Gwallog nodded. He hadn't said a word when they checked out the terrain. Arthur was clearly their leader. He knew how he wanted to act and he had already changed his approach when faced with new information. There was a maturity there that left him slightly in awe. "Yes, he is absolutely in control of his mind and his strategy, whilst risky, is clever, flexible and I believe he'll win the day."

"One thing I can promise you, I will give those bastards the kind hammering they'll never forget."

Gwallog clapped him on the shoulder. "I think you will, Cai. I owe you an apology, my young friend."

"Oh?" Cai responded.

"After the fight with Arthur, I thought you were a weight we couldn't afford to carry. But I was wrong, you are a fine warrior and I am proud to fight at your side."

"I'm grateful," Cai responded. His eyes were filled with tears.

"Come on," Gwallog interrupted. "Let's go eat before you make me blubber as well!"

Arthur sat alone under a large oak. Bedwyr made sure no one approached him. Arthur, he could see, was in one of his reflective moods. *He spends far too much time in his own head*, he thought. Bedwyr had taken responsibility for Arthur's wellbeing. He was slightly older with a similar physique to his friend. Bearded as was the way, his eyes were grey and he seemed to have a permanent scowl on his face. Around Arthur he was calm and authoritative, someone Arthur would listen to, but with the others, especially Cai, he was less confident. It was something Arthur continually chided him for but before any decision was made, Arthur always felt better passing it by his best friend and ally.

Bedwyr stood up and stretched his limbs. He had spent some time digging at his finger nails, meticulously winkling out the muck with a small knife he had secreted under his tunic. Out of the corner of his eye, Bedwyr caught sight of one of the camp guards trotting over towards Arthur. He swiftly strode over to intervene, challenging the man. Bedwyr leant close to the man, allowing him to speak quietly in his ear. Bedwyr nodded and told the man to stand fast.

Bedwyr walked over to Arthur whose eyes were shut, but he wasn't asleep. "Lord?"

"If that's you, Bedwyr, calling me lord, you can fuck off."

Bedwyr sighed. "Arthur?"

"It's not hard is it?" Arthur grunted.

"I'm sorry, Arthur. It's not seemly calling you by name when you are a Prince of Manau."

"Seemly? You can be a prudish shit sometimes, my friend. You are nobility yourself," Arthur said evenly. "Anyway," Arthur sighed, "what is it, Bedwyr?"

"The man Myrddin is here to speak to you."

"Myrddin, here?"

"At the outer markers, beyond the hills."

"Out of site of the camp?" he asked anxiously.

"As you instructed, Arthur."

Arthur visibly relaxed. "Is he alone?"

"Yes, Arthur."

"All right, I'll meet with him."

Bedwyr called the guard to them and he led Arthur away alone, despite Bedwyr's protestations. The guard took Arthur to a clearing where Myrddin waited. He climbed down from his mount and strode quickly to his mentor. They embraced warmly. "My goodness, Arthur, you have turned into a fine young man," Myrddin effused.

They sat there in amiable companionship for some time until Arthur finally asked, "Myrddin, why are you here?"

"You have learned to be direct." Myrddin sighed. "I have come to ask you to walk away,"

"Walk away?" Arthur repeated.

"You can't fight Gwenddoleu. He is of the old way. Rhydderch and Urien are on the side of the Christians."

"I'm not fighting for the Christians," Arthur responded coldly.

Myrddin sighed. "Well who are you here to fight for, Arthur?"

"I'm here to fight for my father."

"I didn't mean that."

"It's the only answer I can give. If I'm not mistaken, you are asking me to betray my father? He is determined to remain neutral like his kin, Conall."

"Really? With his army waiting to come in on the winner's side?"

"I do not know what my father's intentions are," Arthur said evasively.

"So why are you here? You are keeping me from joining you for drink at your fireside."

Arthur smiled. "So you can see our dispositions? I am young, yes, but I am not foolish."

"You don't trust me," Myrddin commented petulantly.

"You forget what you once said, Myrddin," Arthur said sadly.

Myrddin nodded. "Nonetheless, you cannot fight Gwenddoleu, he is your friend and ally. Surely we are on the same side," Myrddin implored.

Arthur shrugged. "It is my hope," he said carefully, "that my duties here are purely defensive and no more. If I can avoid a fight I will. You cannot ask any more of me."

"Your decision will tarnish you, you will never be forgiven," Myrddin retorted.

"You may well be right, my friend, but it is not my decision to make."

"Be your own man—"

Arthur held his hand up. "Don't think for one moment, Myrddin, that you can pretend to tell me my duty. I wish with all my heart that I can see things as clearly as you. I have learned it is not a case of light or darkness, there are all sorts of light in between. And from what I have seen, life is a lot more complicated than I ever thought. What if I asked you to leave, betray the Pendragon?"

"I would never do so, anyway it is not the same thing."

"Really?" Arthur stood quickly. "Myrddin, I cannot do as you ask. I am sorry. More than you will ever know. Perhaps one day we will be reconciled." He turned and strode away. Myrddin sat there for a while as tears welled up in his eyes. They were doomed, he was sure.

Chapter 17

The Battle of Arderydd

The forces of Rhydderch and Urien approached Caer Gwenddoleu from the west. They had camped a couple of miles from the place of battle to the west of the Esk. Rhydderch had hoped Gwenddoleu would come out from behind his wooden walls and face his forces in the open. That would have suited Rhydderch, Gwenddoleu reflected, but because of the size of his force, he had decided to fight a defensive battle.

The land approaching the fort was generally flat but the terrain did not allow for any flanking attack. A full frontal assault was the only option open to the men of Alt Clut and Rheged. The numbers spread out in front of Gwenddoleu's forces were in the region of four thousand men against the one thousand five hundred men he had. He knew the challenge before him was great but with his allies coming from the south he would have to play for time.

He had received Myrddin's report with an air of resignation. The lack of information on Arthur's dispositions was also disappointing. This Arthur was no fool, despite his young age, Gwenddoleu reflected. He was nothing but pragmatic; he was neither one step forward nor one step back from what he knew some twenty-four hours before. Messengers had been sent warning the men Ebruac that there were forces ranged against them to the south of their destination.

Gwenddoleu had expected some attempt to negotiate terms, something that would delay any action and improve the chances of his allies reaching the battlefield but he was to be disappointed. Rhydderch wanted Segovia and Gwenddoleu's wellbeing was not among his priorities. This was, Gwenddoleu knew, a fight of annihilation and if he lost this would be his last day on this earth. He sighed deeply. *Well, so be it*, he thought. He gazed up at the sky; it was overcast. Rain would help, he thought. He smiled at his forlorn hope and shook the thought from his head.

He stood straighter and puffed out his chest. He needed to show confidence for his men. Whether he was afraid of death or not, he knew his men's confidence hung by a thread. He saw the looks on their faces as they surveyed the manoeuvring of their enemies before them. "They wander around like lost sheep and Rhydderch is the dog!" he roared to a round of laughter.

Hardly had the many chiefs had time to dress their lines before their warriors were charging across the open ground and storming the walls. The fighting was ferocious and reckless across the whole length of the wooden palisades as the attackers tried to scramble up the walls. Men fell on both sides in dreadful slaughter. As the clash of armies continued, the carnage was terrible, shields were shattered and swords bloodied, the ground slicked with blood and gore. Gwenddoleu found himself admiring his enemies' bravery, throwing themselves as they did at the walls and at his soldiers. It was almost as if the wall wasn't there. He roared encouragement and urged his men to keep their discipline but the blood lust of battle rendered his instructions pointless. He sighed deeply, but against all the odds, his men held them off. He noticed one of his warriors, a man he knew as Maelgwn, a young, able and brave warrior, launch himself into the fray, his comrades acclaiming him with a great roar. Their intensity became even stronger than anyone could have foreseen.

As the walls were gradually breached, the pressure of numbers increased, the Segovians fell back into the court yard. Shouts of shield wall were screamed by the many lieutenants. Shields were frantically locked and further attacks somehow absorbed. Myrddin ran into the human maelstrom and pushed himself into the shield wall. The buffeting felt as if they were being charged at by a herd of cows escaping the Beltane fires. Again and again the throng of enemy soldiers were repelled. Time and again the men of Alt Clut came on with increasing ferocity and savagery. It was unceasing in its intensity and sheer violence. The lines moved apart and rushed together like the tides of the Forth. Blood was flowing in streams on the slick grass, and warriors fell in droves on both sides. Maelgwn led charge after charge against the enemy and gradually, against all mad hope, the enemy was being pushed back step by step out of the fort and back into the land outside.

With Gwenddoleu's forces holding their own and perhaps in the ascendency, it was time for the Druid's mist. Gwenddoleu pushed his way through to the front line and stood beside his brothers, every one of them grinning with bloodlust. He turned to Myrddin. "I think it's time for your mist, my friend, and we shall prevail, allies or not," he shouted triumphantly.

Myrddin, laughing maniacally, turned, called over a handful of men and ran to the bundles of rowan branches at the back of the fort. *The gods are with us he*, thought, how could he have doubted them and the great Gwenddoleu? He was exultant.

Arthur's men gathered at their designated places, and waited.

Arthur knew, from the constant stream of messengers and scouts, that a confrontation had started to the north. The temptation to ride towards battle was strong but his instructions were clear; he must keep the men of Ebruac away. He felt twitchy, his stomach ever more knotted, the muscles in his chest and upper arms so tight they stung. He rolled his shoulders to find some sort of relief. Swallowing hard, Arthur looked down at his hands and he saw they were shaking. He closed his eyes and tried to regulate his breathing whilst clenching his fists. He realised then he was frightened; his mouth was dry and sour. He could drink a river, he thought.

Bedwyr sat silently next to Arthur, watching the other man. He could see the nerves and leant towards him. "Arthur," he whispered, "try chewing this." He held out some leaves.

"What is it?" Arthur grumbled

"Betony. It's good for nerves."

"Nerves, what makes you think—"

"Because I'm frightened to death too."

"Bastard." Arthur chuckled, taking the offered herbs.

"The taste is surprisingly pleasant too." Bedwyr shrugged.

Arthur placed the herbs in his mouth and began to chew the minty flavoured leaves. He turned towards Bedwyr and nodded.

As Arthur scoured the horizon one of his scouts rode up. He recognised Collen just behind. "What news?"

"The men of Ebruac, my Lord, are approaching from than south."

"How many?"

"At least a thousand."

"How far away?"

"Thirty minutes at most."

"What are their dispositions?"

"They are stretched out," the scout confirmed.

Arthur sighed deeply. "Well we can be grateful for that." He shrugged.

Arthur turned to Collen. "Old friend, let Cai know, if you please." He turned then to the scout. "What's your name?"

"Arthmael, Lord."

"Hmm, I know that name." Arthmael said nothing. "Still," Arthur continued, "thank you for your service, friend. Please let Drystan know and tell him the plan remains."

Arthmael nodded, swung his mount around and galloped away. Collen too raced off towards where Cai was standing.

It wasn't long before Arthur could see the approaching army coming directly toward them. Cai had seen them too and had sent a messenger to confirm. It was up to Cai to attract their attention. Arthur watched closely as Cai's men began moving forward some one hundred paces, beating their swords against their shields. He could see right away that the tactic appeared to have succeeded. It was not long before he could see that Cai had given the order to slowly retreat back towards his original position.

Arthur noticed horsemen of the Ebraucan army break off the front, some one hundred riders, with at least two hundred warriors on foot in pursuit. They had recognised the likelihood of an easy victory and came on quickly. Cai ordered a shield wall into the shape of a spear point and continued to retreat step by step until their adversaries had begun to enter the flat area leading towards the river. Spear and sword crashed into the shields. The initial clash drove Cai's men backwards but the shock was gradually absorbed and the line steadied. Arthur could see Cai at the point of the spear. He was swinging his sword in huge arcs, slashing at the oncoming soldiers. Arthur couldn't help but laugh at his recklessness. He turned to Bedwyr, grinning. "He doesn't learn, does he?"

"Looks effective though."

"It does indeed."

"I wouldn't want to be amongst the men attacking that formation," Bedwyr continued.

Cai gave the order to retreat more quickly. The quicker they retreated, the more of the enemy joined the fray. But despite the mismatch in numbers, they were keeping their formation and the enemy were being led closer and closer to the banks of the river.

Arthur turned to Bedwyr. "Tell the men to ready themselves." He closed his eyes and sent his prayers to his spirit allies, to his eagle and to his bear. "Keep me safe, give me strength, and give me courage," he whispered.

Gwallog rode forward and clapped Arthur on the shoulder. "Let's do this." He grinned.

"Wait," Bedwyr called and he pointed at a horseman galloping across from Drystan's position, waving frantically towards the warriors of Ebruac and pointing towards Arthur's position.

As Cai's men disengaged to cross the river, the enemy faltered and stopped. Cai halted his men and they formed a shield wall that stretched along the bank. Cai looked over his shoulder towards Arthur's position and then moved his men forward again in formation towards the men of Ebruac. Cai, sensing his foes were faltering, decided that his men should take the initiative and surged forward.

Arthur called forward Bedwyr. "Get down there and make sure Cai doesn't go too far or he'll get himself flanked," he shouted.

"Yes, Lord."

As the man galloped away, Arthur called Bedwyr forward. "Something's amiss here," he grunted. He then called forward another of his messengers. "Ride, friend, to Drystan and tell him of the situation and advise him to prepare for the back-up plan."

The man nodded and left.

Arthur lifted his sword, the fear suddenly gone, and led his men from the trees slowly whilst carefully watching the scene before him. He could see that the men of Ebruac had begun to manoeuvre to the east as Arthur had anticipated might happen. He looked at the sky. "Betrayed, I am betrayed," he shouted in frustration. As he looked towards Drystan's men he saw the man he sent, Arthmael riding towards him. *Well, it wasn't Arthmael*, he thought in relief.

"Yes, Arthmael," he said.

"Lord, the Lord Drystan is taking his men east and invites you to follow."

"Good, we will shadow them."

Gwallog pointed south and noted that the army before them was taking a long time to concentrate and were still stretched out. Arthur looked over and saw Gwallog was right. He turned to Arthmael. "Go back to Drystan and tell him to continue as planned and I will attack their lines here." He turned to Gwallog. "My Lord Gwallog," he continued, "please ride down to Cai and get him to disengage and attack their rear."

Both Gwallog and Arthmael nodded and rode off.

Arthur looked down at his hands; they no longer shook. He started to feel an inner calm, a feeling that felt like joy. Everything was crystal clear in his mind. He looked around him and it felt as if time had slowed to a crawl as he led his cavalry down the slope and across the river. He was furious, he was livid and now he would get his revenge.

He lowered his spear and charged forward as everyone around him followed his lead. He heard roars from every direction. As he reached the enemy lines he burst into maniacal laughter as he saw the panicked men before him trying to form a defensive line. The crash of metal on metal was ear splitting. Men fell as spear, swords and axes fell upon them. Arthur swung his horse around, raining blows on men's skulls and slicing through limbs. The screams of killing and the screams of being killed were nightmarish but bloodlust had taken him over. The shock of the attack broke the line and men turned to run. Arthur looked both left and right and could see that Cai was taking casualties.

Meanwhile Drystan had swung his forces in a large arc and attacked the head of the enemy's column in a series of hit and run attacks. His casualties were also mounting but those of his enemy were far more severe and it wasn't too long before the general retreat was signalled by their leader, the Prince Peredur.

Myrddin, with the help of his chosen men, placed the wood bundles and lit them. The thick acrid smoke rose immediately and Gwenddoleu ordered his forces to retreat behind it to wait for the cover they needed to attack their blinded enemies.

Myrddin stood straight and proud, folding his arms in triumph. He was sure now that they would triumph after all. He raised his arms to the sky and exulted the old gods to do his bidding. But almost immediately, his smile faded and turned to concern. He looked around and then up at the trees. Was the wind turning? "No, no, no," he screamed. Yes, the wind was turning, the wind had switched around and the Druid's mist was now being blown back towards Gwenddoleu's own ranks.

An ear-splitting roar rose from their opponents as their sight was restored. Gwenddoleu immediately saw that his men were suddenly isolated and worse still, could not see their foes. "Myrddin!" he roared. "What the fuck, have you done?"

Myrddin looked on in horror as everything began to fall apart in front of him. Gwenddoleu found himself completely surrounded by smoke and adversaries. He gathered what little forces he had left around him. He roared, beckoning his men to his voice. Having successfully formed a wedge, they charged forward. With his brothers they rushed almost recklessly through the crowded ranks before them. But it was to no avail, their recklessness was to be their undoing. The attack faltered and Gwenddoleu's brothers, chiefs in their own right, men who had followed him through his wars, loyally always fighting his foes, were mercilessly cut down and their battle lines broken.

Seeing his dead brothers lying next to him, their lifeless eyes staring at the smoked filled skies, he snapped and screamed a challenge to all and sundry, swinging his sword wildly until he felt a searing pain in his gut. His shield dropped to the ground and he felt for his wound. His hand fell to the shaft of wood he knew was embedded in his stomach. He dropped to his knees and looked to the heavens for one last time. He sighed and smiled momentarily as an axe was brought down on his neck. Everything went black.

Myrddin's mouth fell open when he saw them all fall. The battle, he knew, was over. He slumped to his knees and gave out such a cry of grief that anyone who heard could not help being moved to tears themselves.

With Gwenddoleu's death, his men lost heart and the remains of the army finally broke. The bloodshed that followed was brutal and men fleeing were cut down without mercy. Pleas of surrender were ignored. Suddenly a host of spears arched high into the sky and dropped in amongst anyone who still stood. This was followed by an attack from all quarters of the field by the men of Alt Clut and their allies.

Myrddin suddenly snapped out of his reverie, turned and ran. He ran and ran, his chest, his legs were screaming from the exertion. He could feel the horsemen at his back but he didn't look back. Instead he screamed and screamed and kept running across rivers, over the hills, and through the trees of the south western part of the Caledonian Wood. At the same time the scattered remnants of Gwenddoleu's army kept up a running fight until there was no one left to stand. Only a handful of Myrddin's fellow escapees found safety in the Caledonian Wood. Segovia was no more.

Like a wild animal, he hid in the darkest parts of the woods, his mind broken. He would not be seen for another seven years.

Arthur sent out messengers to tell both Cai and Drystan not to pursue, only to sting. His instructions were to hold the line and stop Gwenddoleu from getting any reinforcements. Instead of driving home his advantage, Arthur decided to retreat to the tree line but continued to send out horsemen on hit and run attacks to harass the enemy. As time passed and the day grew late, the forces of Ebruac were no longer concerned with the battle to their north. Instead they looked to their protection and drew back to a defendable low hill and set up camp.

At last a messenger from Caer Gwenddoleu arrived to announce that the battle had been won. Gwenddoleu had been killed and so had his brothers. Rhydderch had claimed Segovia for Alt Clut.

"What of Myrddin?" Arthur asked with concern.

"Myrddin?"

"Lailoken, he might have been called."

"I know of him, Lord, but I have no idea. Very few people survived and those who did will have escaped into the Caledonia Wood."

"Thank you," Arthur said, sighing deeply. "If you find his body, please let me know. He is... important to me," he stuttered.

The man nodded and Arthur dismissed him. He turned to Bedwyr. "Come on, let's go talk to the Princes Peredur and Gwrgi and end this."

They mounted their horses and rode from the trees and headed towards the enemy camp. Messengers were sent ahead as Arthur and Bedwyr, along with some twenty horsemen, made their way to the enemy camp. When they reached the outskirts of the camp Arthur and Bedwyr dismounted and were escorted alone to the largest of the tents where Peredur and Gwrgi were talking animatedly.

Peredur elbowed his brother and they stood as Arthur approached. He rode forward and grasped Arthur's elbow, a friendly gesture which surprised Arthur but he accepted the gesture with disguised pleasure. "You must be the Lord Arthur," Peredur said respectfully.

"Prince Peredur," Arthur responded, nodding with equal respect.

"It would appear the day is yours."

"You are gracious."

"Well, it's the truth and even though I hate to say it, you won all too easily,"

"You flatter me, my Lord Prince."

Peredur smiled at that. "Sadly it is the truth."

Peredur presented Arthur to his brother, a man shorter and stockier than Peredur but who resembled him closely. Gwrgi was much more withdrawn than his brother and was clearly quite devoid of any warmth.

"Please forgive my brother, he hates to lose," Peredur said smoothly.

Gwrgi rolled his eyes. "Everyone hates losing, brother," he grunted.

Arthur smiled. "Quite so."

"So," Peredur said, "can I ask, Arthur, what is your intention?"

"My intention? My hope is that this conflict is ended. No one else has to die."

"Admirable, but I am honour bound to join the Pendragon, you must understand that. If I don't you couldn't call me honourable."

Arthur nodded. "You obviously haven't heard, Lord, of Gwenddoleu's demise. The king has been defeated and his army killed to a man."

"And the king?" he managed ask through his obvious shock.

"I am told that he has been slain, as have all his brothers. Rhydderch sleeps in Caer Gwenddoleu this night. I know this must be a bitter blow for you both and for that you have my sympathy,"

A silence fell over the group until Peredur whispered into the ear of his brother, who uttered an expletive Arthur had never heard before. Following a further exchange, Peredur stood straighter. He was clearly a very proud man, Arthur reflected.

"We appreciate your intention and we will, by your leave, accept that our purpose here appears to be no longer needed. You will understand that we will want conformation of what you say."

"Of course, I understand. My second here will accompany your man through our lines."

"Subject to my satisfaction, we will return to Ebruac first thing."

Arthur nodded. "I hope we will meet again, Prince Peredur, in better times."

"Yes, hopefully on the same side." Peredur smiled. "With those Angles on both our borders, we will need each other before long, I suspect."

Arthur nodded, held out his arm, bowed and walked away.

Chapter 18

Aedan's Gambit

The rain had come too late in the day to save Gwenddoleu. But now the clouds had cleared and it was a perfect night to rest and savour victory.

Rhydderch, Urien and Aedan met amidst the celebrations of victory. Arthur sat in a nearby glade watching them shaking hands and clapping each other on the back. He admired that Aedan could keep this company when he had contributed next to nothing in the battle except, of course, Arthur's contribution.

To Arthur, it seemed sickening following the deaths of so many good men including Gwenddoleu who had, by all accounts, died a hero's death. He pondered how life could be snuffed out in a single moment. The warriors of the old way believed in life and death being a single continuum. It made them less fearful in the knowledge that the mortal world ran parallel to an immortal world. After all, death simply meant crossing over. He wondered what or how Christians viewed death. Did they go to the same place as believers of the old way? He had heard from Cynon that Christians, when they died, went to a place called paradise. Perhaps they weren't so different after all.

He had personally spent some hours searching for news of Myrddin. Rhydderch had, he knew, sent out men in search of the Druid so, Arthur concluded, he was probably still alive. Rhydderch's wife was Myrddin's twin sister so if the Druid was found he would surely be spared. Arthur hoped so.

He leant back against a yew. His battle had been against a man he trusted and loved as a father, the man who had advised him to trust no one, not even him. And yet fate had brought them here on opposite sides, Myrddin holding true to his beliefs and Arthur ignoring his for political reasons. It had been far too easy to ignore his values and his beliefs when commanded to. He remembered overhearing his mother saying that Aedan had values but he had other values if required. Perhaps Arthur was the same?

He shook his head as he sat quietly chewing on the remainder of the betony leaves Bedwyr had given him. Were these thoughts and feelings what men experienced once the bloodlust had subsided? He hated that so many men had been killed this day. They would have had mothers, wives and children who would now be alone in this cruel world. It made him weep.

There had been some repercussions over Arthur's decision to allow Peredur and Gwrgi to leave with their men. Rhydderch had been particularly critical but Arthur, with Bedwyr at his side, had stood their ground, much to Urien's amusement. Arthur's final word before being sent from Rhydderch and Urien's presence was that they would need each other when the Angles came. Everyone knew he was probably right but no one was ready to listen quite yet.

The revelry whirled around him but he blocked it out, preferring to remain in his own world. He spent his time journeying to the lower world where he sought sanctuary and answers from his spirit allies. Welcomed by a hare, he was taken through pathways surrounded by trees and then mountains. He was joined by a wolf, a bear and his eagle. "Where is Myrddin?" he asked. He could only see woods and he could only feel panic, guilt and pain. He felt overwhelming sadness. *Poor Myrddin*, he thought. *I hope he finds redemption and solace.* The eagle then turned to him and told him that Myrddin would return, seven years hence. It told him that his own guilt would not last and he would return to the right path but he was warned, *beware of the Dove.*

As Arthur journeyed, Bedwyr stood at a respectful distance from his friend. Any reveller approaching too close was kindly but firmly turned away. He was only in the sixteenth summer, but over the previous five years he had developed a strong bond with Arthur, becoming Arthur's confidant and advisor. He had come to recognise Arthur's trust issues and that his friendship was unique. It most certainly meant that he probably would have to work very hard to maintain that trust. The line was an exceptionally thin one.

He smiled to himself as he thought of Arthur's annoyance at being called lord. Arthur considered titles superfluous and that he and his 'knights', as he had begun to refer to them, were equals. All councils were held in a circle but everyone knew that to assert any influence they needed Bedwyr's support. Arthur had, after a very short space of time, gained a level of authority seldom seen.

Bedwyr was well respected for his calmness and light-heartedness at times of stress. His stature helped; he was almost six foot but not as tall as Cai who was keen to remind him of this at every opportunity. His easy going demeanour, his intelligence and bravery gave him a level of gravitas that made men follow him so his position as a conduit to Arthur was not questioned. Nonetheless, although outwardly confident, it belied a streak of self-doubt resulting from overthinking things and he was too sensitive to criticism. His brown eyes and hair gave him a slightly southern European look. It was his father, Pedr of Dyfed, who had persuaded Crierwy to take Bedwyr under her wing and he loved her like a mother and she, in turn, loved him like a son.

It was some thirty minutes before Arthur returned to reality. He opened his eyes and peered into the firelight that seemed to flare in front of him. He rubbed his eyes, allowing them to focus gradually. He dragged his hand through his tangled hair and stretched his back. A smile widened across his face as he saw Bedwyr coming toward him carrying a pot of mead.

"I thought you might want this," Bedwyr said.

"Thank you, old friend," Arthur responded, stretching out his arm to accept the liquid. He drank deeply, savouring the taste.

"Do you want another?" Bedwyr laughed.

"No, no. That will do me. I have to stay focused."

"What for?"

"Well… who knows what lurks in the shadows."

Bedwyr raised his eyebrows. "Fuck me," he exclaimed.

Arthur smiled. "You should moderate your language, old friend."

"And you, Arthur, should stop moderating your drinking, particularly when there are things to celebrate."

Arthur grunted, "I hate the feeling the morning after. Besides, you are vulnerable when you're drunk or when you're hungover."

Bedwyr sighed. "You are surrounded by friends here, Arthur. There is nothing to fear."

"I'm sure you're right," Arthur said almost in disdain. "But just in case, eh."

Arthur's gaze shifted to where Aedan and the other kings had been. The meeting had finished, he noticed. He surmised Aedan would, in all probability, seek him out to warn him not to repeat his act of mercy should the occasion arise again. Should Arthur feel at risk from Rhydderch and Urien, or even his father? He shrugged, almost resigned to his fate. It would surely be a short-lived but successful career. He would find out soon enough.

As long as it was mutually beneficial, this alliance would prosper, but he couldn't help thinking that it would not last. All the leaders had their own ambitions. Rhydderch in particular had further designs which must unnerve Urien and Aedan. They knew Alt Clut was too big to invade but not to deter. Urien, however, was the better warrior and capable of anything. Arthur liked him and saw him as a possible friend in the political upheavals that would surely permeate the lands north of the Great Wall. And of course there were also Muirgein and Taliesin in Urien's Court; that must count for something?

And there was Conall, of course, the King of Dalriada, the throne his father desired. What price would he pay or, more likely, what price would he expect others to pay to fulfil his ambition? Would his father go after Rhydderch, and if he did, then what?

He wandered aimlessly around the camp watching the celebrations until, finally, things began to calm down as drink finally defeated the undefeated. He suddenly realised he was alone, having been completely wrapped up in his own thoughts. Bedwyr had drifted off. He chuckled to himself and found his way back to his yew tree and settled himself down in the increasing silence. Shifting his position until he found some comfort, he closed his eyes until sleep took him.

In the morning, Caer Gwenddoleu was eerily quiet. Warriors were lying in and around the tree lines, choosing to sleep well away from the place of death. Arthur washed in the river, sinking into a deep section right up to his chin before ducking his head under the water. He climbed the nearest bank and set off on his morning run. The sun was out but the morning was fresh. He was glad to put distance between himself and the place of bitter spirits.

As he ran, he heard the sounds of hooves cantering up behind him. He felt anxiety rise within him and he veered off the path into a patch of trees and dived into the undergrowth. When he finished rolling he glanced back to see his father grinning at him. "Impressive, young man."

Arthur pursed his lips and scrambled out of the undergrowth. He brushed himself down, feeling rather stupid at his actions.

"Have you hurt yourself?" Aedan chuckled.

"Just my pride, Lord," Arthur said grumpily.

Aedan slid off his horse and placed his arm around his son's shoulders. "Come, let's walk awhile, there is a lot to discuss and plan."

Arthur eyed him warily. "I thought you were doing that last night?"

Aedan's jaw tightened, his smile briefly vanishing before composing himself. "You are very observant, Arthur, did you feel… left out?"

It was Arthur's turn to grit his teeth, realising Aedan had struck a nerve. "Possibly," he said carelessly.

"Victors have a need to self-congratulate, do they not? Anyway, the issue of what comes next is important to all of us. I don't think Rhydderch is very happy with me and with you for that matter."

"You surprise me." Arthur grimaced.

"He did give you a dressing down," Aedan laughed.

"I'm still alive despite the tongue lashing." He shrugged.

Aedan threw his head back and laughed harder.

It took a while for Aedan to bring himself back under control and he had to wipe his eyes before resuming their conversation. "So… why did you let them ride away, Arthur?"

"We are going to need them soon."

"Meaning?"

"The Angles have Bernicia."

"Bryneich," Aedan corrected.

"You can call it whatever you want, Father, but the Angles now own it and Peredur and Gwrgi both have an incentive to see the Angles... contained."

"Hmmm," Aedan pondered, "looks like you have my instincts."

"Time will tell, I suppose." Arthur tried to change the conversation back to Aedan. "Do you know what Rhydderch's intentions are?" he asked

"Besides the very obvious, that is making sure he follows his father to the throne of Alt Clut, I'm not completely sure. I would guess he wants a super kingdom with Alt Clut at its centre."

"I'm sure all the leaders of these lands would like that, which is probably why it doesn't happen."

"You are shrewd, my boy. Would you be distrusting of him?"

"I think he is a man on a mission. Triumph can put fire into the blood," Arthur admitted.

"Yes it can, which is why we must be on our guard. He won't antagonise Urien because he is far too strong. We, on the other hand, are fair game."

"What of Urien? What will he do if Rhydderch turns on us?"

Aedan shrugged. "I don't know but if he doesn't mean to support us, we need him to stand aside and stay neutral. I think he will stay out of it unless there are advantages for him to join in."

"So?"

"So we don't want too much time to pass."

Arthur was puzzled. "What are your intentions, Father?"

Aedan smiled. "To claim what is rightly mine and will be yours, my boy,"

Arthur grunted, "And my siblings?"

"They are not your equal, Arthur. It is the way of the world that the strongest prevails. I'm sure your brothers will recognise that."

Arthur shrugged. He wasn't sure what Aedan meant and how things would turn out. He decided to say nothing more. They sat together in awkward silence. Arthur wondered if that was all Aedan was going to say. Once again Aedan had given him an insight but nothing concrete. He concluded that Aedan would, once again, say nothing of substance until he was ready. Until then, he would be closed out. He looked over to study his father who had leant against a tree. He tried to read him; he tried to trust him; he desperately wanted to trust him. After a few moments Aedan caught his eye. He smiled a little awkwardly but held Arthur's stare.

Aedan cleared his throat and sat forward. Sighing, he picked up a stone and threw it some distance into the nearby meadow. "Arthur," he said at last, "you understand that this is just the beginning. War will be a constant theme in your life."

Arthur nodded.

"You are central to my success... our success, that is."

Arthur smiled.

"You wanted to know my intentions. They are three fold, first to protect Manau, Lothian and the Forth, second to becomes the King of the Scots and being free of our Irish brethren, and lastly to protect ourselves from the Angles and the Picts."

"War is the only way to achieve these aims?" Arthur asked.

"Mostly, my boy. Imagine, you and me fighting shoulder to shoulder. Taking on and defeating all before us."

"I'm honoured, Father, but," he couldn't hold back any longer, "what about Rhydderch? You said we can't let time drag on. What does that even mean?"

"Straight to the point, my boy, I like that." Aedan smiled. "We need to strike quickly, Arthur. Rhydderch is moving his forces back to the great Rock of Alt Clut, Dun Breatainn. He will split his forces for the end of the campaigning season. We will take our forces there and bring him to battle."

"You want to provoke a war? But that will force us to fight too many battles. They outnumber us, they will flank us, surround and destroy us."

"We don't need to defeat them in a war. They need to know that we are not a pushover. But what's more important is that we bring them to the negotiating table."

"Negotiating table?" Arthur repeated.

"If you grab a man by the balls, his heart and mind will surely follow. We take advantage of the absence of Rhydderch and his army."

Arthur nodded although he was still unsure of the game Aedan was playing. "When do we leave?"

"Soon."

Aedan stood, stretched his back and mounted his horse. "I hope you enjoy the rest of your run, Arthur." He turned the horse and cantered away.

Arthur stayed there for a while. So there it was, Aedan wanted to be king and needed him, Arthur, to make it happen. He breathed in deeply and dragged his hand through this hair. He should be proud, of course, but he couldn't help thinking that his reward would be to be the fool who would be used as collateral damage.

He got to his feet and started to jog. He had to admire his father's ambition, and he couldn't fault his strategic acumen. So now he would follow him to the Dun Breatainn. At least it seemed that Aedan would be with him this time. He was annoyed that Aedan had left him to it at the Glein and he was angered that his father had not tried to intervene on his behalf with Rhydderch. In fact, Arthur reflected, his father had not even congratulated him on his victory. It probably made little difference to the outcome of the main battle but he had played his part, under resourced and with no support.

He stopped at another stream and cupped some water and threw it in his face. But what if he was wrong, what if his father couldn't intervene, after all that was the plan wasn't it? He was Aedan the 'Wily', and there was a good reason for that. He shook his head and ran on.

Chapter 19

The Game Begins

When Rhydderch awoke from a restless sleep, he was surprised to see his wife, Langoreth, sitting next to his cot. He could see she had been crying, mourning her son. He sat up and groaned and pulled his wife to him.

"I'm so sorry," he whispered.

Langoreth whimpered quietly and his heart broke. She had lost a son and probably a brother.

They held each other like that for some minutes and when she finally pulled away, she gave her husband an unhappy smile. "What now?" she said sadly.

"We go home." He shrugged. "The campaigning season is done and we must prepare for winter and for next year."

"More fighting?" she sighed.

"You know that is the way of things. We must be ever watchful of Aedan, he is too clever by half and he can't be trusted. He is also of the old way and my father will want him out of the picture."

"But you too are of the old way?" she questioned.

"Yes, but this Christianity is what everyone is talking about, not least my father. I cannot be seen to be overtly against him if I am to succeed him."

"You know that's difficult for me what with my brother—"

"You will, one day, be Queen of Alt Clut, there is too much at stake to risk all. Hold your counsel and do not give anyone a chance to doubt you."

"Hold my counsel." Langoreth snorted derisively.

"Take time to grieve. We are in no position to challenge the fates. Patience is our only weapon for now," he replied smoothly.

She nodded. She was not persuaded by the sermons given by the likes of Mungo and Columba. Mungo had acted like a thug and had fallen out with all and sundry, hardly a man to look up to and revere. Even her father-in-law had had enough and sent him to Wales where he had even fallen out with the endlessly patient Dewi. She smiled at the thought. There was no certainty that her husband would become the King of Alt Clut, so any victories would be well received when it was time to select a replacement for the ailing Tutgal. Her husband was right, she would have to keep her counsel, and whilst it was not how she wanted things to be, the death of her dear son would allow her to take a lower profile role during a period of grieving. The thought made her sick to the stomach. These then were the consequences of power and the search for it. She cringed.

But there was something that worried her too. Aedan, she knew, was not a man to be underestimated. She had heard from her brother Lailoken, or was it Myrddin now, that Aedan's son, no older than her own son, was a man to be reckoned with, a man destined for great deeds. Would facing Aedan in battle be a risk too far? Gwenddoleu had been old and ailing, the numbers against him too great. But despite the advantage of numbers too many men were lost. She pondered if she should voice her concerns. She shouldn't have worried, her mind was made up for her.

"What are you thinking, my love?" Rhydderch said quietly.

"Too many things," she sighed shaking her head.

He looked at her intently. "You've never been a good liar," he laughed. "Is it our boy?"

"Of course," she said grimly, "but that is not all husband."

"Oh?"

"It was something Myrddin warned me about..."

"That traitor?" he snapped.

She breathed deeply. "Yes," she said patiently, "I know your heart and those are words of pain not truth."

He snorted.

"No, he warned me about Aedan's son."

"I suppose you mean this Arthur," he conceded. "Naive fool."

"Aedan and Arthur will be formidable in the spring. Destiny is on that boy's side and what with his father's... political skills, don't think all your allies are going to come running to your side if you take him on. And let's not forget his Irish brethren."

Rhydderch laughed. "They'll side with Conall and he's in our pocket."

"Are you certain?"

"Of course."

"Fine, but beware, trusting the other Britons is a hazardous pastime."

She said no more but the seed was sown.

Aedan had hoped to strike at Alt Clut quickly but he felt unprepared. Instead he led his forces back towards Manau, much to Arthur's relief, but if he thought that Aedan would completely change his strategy he would be disappointed.

The decision to hunker down for the winter proved to be inspired. The snows had come early and lay thick upon the ground. Sub-zero temperatures drove the population indoors. The silence that followed the frequent snowstorms was almost painful for Arthur who was left for too long with his own thoughts. Bedwyr had returned home for the winter so, essentially, he was alone and he hated it.

The bitter winter claimed Domelch, Aedan's wife. She had come down with a chill which was followed by a fever. As the days passed Domelch had passed into delirium. Aedan had invited soothsayers, Druids and Shamans but nothing could be done. The weather had been too inclement to call for assistance over long distances so local 'experts', had to be relied upon. As the new year passed, Domelch died. She was a mere skeleton, the vibrant woman that Aedan had known since they were barely adults so diminished, he barely recognised her on her death bed.

He was sad, of course, but since his seduction of Crierwy, even before then he had grown tired of her and it was rumoured they had been estranged. Aedan had had to suffer constant criticisms and threats from her father, Bruide of the Picts, but they came to nothing because it was considered politically ruinous to pick a fight with a kingdom, no matter how small, that could pack a military punch like Manau.

So it was to everyone's surprise that Aedan had called on his men to gather to him at Imbolc. Snow was still lying on the ground and it was cold. Arthur could only groan when he was told.

Within days, Aedan had led his forces west from Manannon towards the great river and Dun Breatainn. Arthur rode with the cavalry of Manau at the rear of the army. His position in line, far from his father, puzzled him, but upon learning of Domelch's death he understood it. Perhaps, Arthur concluded, Aedan thought he might gloat at Aedan's misfortune. It was a thought that saddened him. Arthur knew he wasn't like that but the tragedy was that Aedan didn't know him well enough to know that.

Arthur rode alongside Bedwyr. He was happy to be alongside his friend again. He enjoyed Bedwyr's stories of home and their Yuletide festivities. Cai and Drystan followed, poking fun at the tireless Bedwyr as he tore back and forth passing on messages and reporting back to Arthur any information brought back by the scouts. Each ride by was interspersed with verbal expletives and physical hand gestures. Arthur could hear the frivolity behind him and smiled broadly at no one in particular. When Bedwyr settled himself next to Arthur, he playfully slapped him on the back.

The pace was hard and relentless. Aedan was keen to choose his ground and he knew Rhydderch's men would be unprepared after their winter hibernation, and Alt Clut did not have a standing army of any note as Aedan did. Aedan had also learned from his spies in Rhydderch's camp that Rhydderch's son, a boy of Arthur's age, had died at Arderydd and that he and his wife were greatly grieved by it. Aedan concluded that Rhydderch would be dispirited and would not have the heart to engage in strife and his thinking would be blunted. This would mean he would be prone to error.

He knew, too, that Rhydderch's father, a cantankerous and ailing man, would take a while to decide on a course of action. So Aedan would seek a quick engagement, sue for peace and secure an alliance for when he turned his gaze on his cousin Conall.

Aedan too, was anxious to sever ties with the Irish Dalriadans and with Rhydderch and his father, Tutgal, on his side, or at least remaining neutral, he would have the muscle and influence to persuade Aed, the Irish leader, to give the Scottish Dalriadans independence. Aedan had other ambitions, chiefly to rein in Columba-Crimthann's influence and allow the old ways to continue without threat or fear. That would placate Muirgein and he would hopefully keep Columba in his sphere of influence to cement his power.

As he approached the great rock Aedan received word that, for the most part, Dun Breatainn, was poorly protected as he had anticipated. The court of Tutgal was wintering in the estates of Pertneck some twelve miles to the south east. If he could draw the defenders out he could score a quick victory and bargain from a position of strength. He could not afford a long drawn out conflict and if his bluff was called he would probably have to withdraw. The risk he was taking was close to recklessness but he knew that sooner or later, if he was to take the crown, a risk of this magnitude had to be taken.

Aedan sent Gwallog back down the line to call Arthur forward for a planning meeting. The army was moved to areas of woodland and scouts were sent widely to check on the enemy's dispositions. They agreed that Cai would take a detachment of horsemen to block off the road to Pertneck in case Rhydderch and the men of Alt Clut came out to aid Dun Breatainn. Aedan would approach Dun Breatainn head on and draw out the defenders. Arthur and Drystan would place their cavalry out of sight of the defenders on either flank to envelop their prey to press home their advantage when the time came.

Aedan sent forward skirmishers to alert the fort to their presence and scatter the peoples who lived outside the defensive barricades. Aedan knew this would cause enough disturbance for some of the fort's guards to sally out. Aedan, after some minutes, seeing alarm ahead of him, brought forward his hundred or so men. They were the minimum he could risk. As he walked forward at a comfortable pace, he could only hope that he could hold on until Arthur and Drystan arrived.

As Aedan came on he could see horsemen ahead skitter and swing round. He smiled; they were beckoning out others. Aedan turned to Gwallog and instructed him to quicken the pace. "Not too fast," he called. "Give them time to come out." Gwallog nodded and urged the men forward.

Aedan could see their opponents forming into a shield wall but they were still too close to the fort. Aedan raised his arm and called a halt. The time of hurling insults and obscenities had arrived, an art form his men had perfected. Archers, too, were called forward and sent a couple of volleys into the rear of the enemy.

Aedan's shield wall edged forward. Men ran ahead and dropped their trousers, revealing their pock marked backsides. One man even defecated on the field which brought a cheer and disgusted groans in equal measure.

"Spears," Aedan called and they were levelled at their foe. They were close enough now to make out their enemy's faces. But just when Aedan had resigned himself to having to take the fight to his enemy, they charged. Screams of hatred and anger spewed forth as the enemy sprinted forward. "Steady," Aedan called calmly, hiding his feelings of fear and exhilaration.

Within moments, the two front lines crashed together with a fearful crunching of metal that sounded like thunder. Many a man felt an extraordinary vibration shock through his arms. The shield wall was not for the faint hearted although the number of deaths were small while the process of pushing and shoving played out. Grunting and cursing permeated by the odd scream reverberated around the battlefield.

Arthur sat impassively on his mount, sometimes playing with his horse's ears, patting its neck and stroking its mane. No one, not even Bedwyr, said a word to him. Arthur, Bedwyr knew, was waiting to move, his concentration fully on events before him. Arthur could see that more and more men were becoming involved in the fight below them. Soldiers were still coming from the gates of the fort although it had become more of a trickle. He smiled as he saw Aedan's forces were beginning to fall back under the pressure coming from the much larger force.

Arthur nodded with satisfaction and took in a deep breath. He turned to Bedwyr, and rolling his shoulders, he drew his sword and held it above his head. His men quietly followed his action and Arthur led them slowly forward.

Across the valley, Drystan, who had not taken his eyes off Arthur, also now lifted his sword and moved his men forward.

Arthur signalled the charge and the horsemen swarmed down the slope into the flank of the men of Alt Clut. Shouts of warning spread across the field as the horsemen came on. Those at the rear turned to face the danger but the attack was too fierce and too quick. The shield wall immediately broke as Aedan's men reasserted themselves on their retreating foe. Men right and left dropped their swords and tried to surrender as the slaughter began. On seeing this, Aedan and Arthur had horns sounded to stop the engagement. For a time it was pointless as many of their men, blinded by bloodlust, landed killer blows on their adversaries. Slowly but surely the pressure lessened and the soldiers separated.

Aedan stepped forward. "Surrender, my friends, no one else needs to die, drop your weapons and no one else on this field and within the walls will be harmed," he called.

"You speak true?" a voice came.

"Yes."

"We will surrender, Gorlassar."

"Good, what do I call you, friend?"

"They call me Galahad."

"Are you in charge here?"

Galahad looked around. "I believe so."

Aedan nodded to the man and beckoned him to walk with him. They were joined by Arthur and Bedwyr and the four of them walked from the battlefield and towards the gates of Dun Breatainn. As they approached, Galahad signalled for the gates to remain open and they passed under the arch and made for the nearest tavern. The people watched them warily and stepped to one side to let them pass. Aedan's soldiers funnelled in gradually carrying the wounded from both sides. Women wailed as their husbands were counted as missing or dead. "Even a battle won is distressing," Bedwyr grumbled.

"Yes it is," Galahad returned sadly.

Drinks were served to the men and Arthur had to stifle a laugh because he couldn't help thinking how surreal all this was. They had just fought an engagement and despite the hatred and death, here they were sitting and drinking comfortably together as if nothing had happened.

"What is it you want of me, Lord Aedan?" Galahad started.

Aedan smiled warmly. "Thank you for agreeing to surrender, my friend. As I informed you, I have no wish to punish or inflict any further pain or indignity to the people of Dunn Breatainn or indeed Alt Clut."

"I'm grateful. But Lord… you were our allies just last year at Arderydd, what brings you against us now?"

Aedan smiled again. "That will all become apparent soon enough."

It was Galahad's turn to smile. "Of course, Lord, forgive me."

Aedan chose to ignore the smirk and carried on smoothly. "All I want is to meet with your king or the Lord Rhydderch here at this place. And I want you, my new friend, Galahad, to deliver that message.

Within the hour Arthur rode with Galahad until they met Cai on the road to Pertneck. The ride had been pleasant enough and surprisingly good humoured. Galahad had spoken at length of his cousin, the fair Lady Gwenhwyfar. It seemed she was slightly younger than Arthur but Galahad's outpouring of enthusiasm for beauty and character had piqued Arthur's interest. As a consequence he found himself asking more questions of her, and in no time at all, he was keen to make plans to meet up with the lady as soon as possible.

"I have piqued your interest, young prince." Galahad grinned.

"Maybe," Arthur replied evasively.

Arthur couldn't be sure if he was being lured into some sort trap but he comforted himself in the knowledge that while his loins might be getting the better of him there would be little or no opportunity of a meeting until the conquest of Dalriada. As they separated, Galahad offered to stay in touch and with that, a rather nervous Galahad, continued towards his destination.

As Galahad trotted slowly towards Pertneck, he considered what awaited him. It seemed strange to him that he felt more fear relaying the message than standing in a shield wall. He was acutely aware that messengers were often unfairly dealt with. After all, they were merely conveying a message. Frustration was always a misplaced and ill directed emotion and did nothing to help sound decision making. Galahad knew the king was cantankerous, temperamental and subject to ill-considered bouts of anger. Rhydderch, on the other hand, was at least fair and thoughtful despite his clear desire to replace his father as king when the time came. Surely that wouldn't be long. Nonetheless, the upstart Prince of Lothian and Manau had brazenly crossed uninvited into Alt Clut and taken a major fortress. If anything was going to rile Rhydderch it was that, in which case he ought to enjoy the horse ride because it could conceivably be his last one. He shuddered at the thought.

What Galahad couldn't understand was that Aedan had not sought to massacre everyone at Dun Breatainn and then move on to Pertneck. Surely he had the advantage of surprise, but it was dawning on Galahad that there was something else at play here. A war with Alt Clut would surely badly damage one or both sides. Aedan must know that the Angles of Bernicia and Deira were looking on in delight as the Britons waged war with each over. The Gododdin were still a buffer but they could be bypassed and with the right incentive may be willing to stand aside. The bloody Britons were their own worst enemies, he mused, but could a man like Aedan, a man known for his political prowess and deviousness, be the man who would bring the Britons together as allies strong enough to repel the Angle threat. Who knew? But what about this Arthur? Oh yes, he was young, that was for sure, but his military acumen had been proven and further successes would undoubtedly strengthen his reputation. He liked Arthur, and with a fair wind there might be an opportunity for Galahad to ally him with the help of his cousin. That was if, of course, he survived the next hour or so.

He was disturbed from his thoughts when a voice rang out from above him. "You, stranger, what is your business?"

Galahad quickly recovered his composure and glanced up at where the voice had come from. "My name is Galahad," he started. "I come from Dun Breatainn with an urgent message for," he paused, "for... the Lord Rhydderch. Can you or one of your men take me to him directly?"

The guard stood watching him for some time, obviously considering what he should do. Galahad couldn't help smile at this man who, like all the other guards he could see, was big and hairy. He waited patiently for the response.

"Wait there."

A few moments later two heavily armed men approached him. He was told he had to give up his sword and he was guided through a number of dwellings towards the hall where Alt Clut royalty resided. It was dark as they entered and he was beckoned to wait in a small room where benches had been set up for visitors. One of the soldiers disappeared for a few moments and Galahad sat in uneasy silence next to the other man. Galahad noticed the man had no front teeth and his nose was crooked. Clearly he had had quite a pummelling at some stage. The other man noticed Galahad's stare and grinned. "I was pretty once." Galahad doubted that but found himself chuckling.

The first man returned with, Galahad guessed, a man servant. He was a slight and fastidious a man, the polar opposite to the guards Galahad had encountered. He couldn't helped laughing at this little man as he shooed these man mountains, which earned him a withering look from both of them. He was beckoned briskly into a large hall and over to the only person sitting in one corner.

At a bench, in the shadows, Galahad could make out a man he recognised to be Rhydderch. The prince who Galahad knew to be about the same age as himself, sat with his head nestled in the palm of his hand looking down at a parchment on the table before him. Even when Galahad was announced Rhydderch did not look up. Instead he sighed and waved Galahad towards a seat in front of him.

For what seemed an age, Galahad sat before the prince in silence waiting for any sign from Rhydderch to deliver his message. Still Rhydderch didn't look up, but Galahad was struck by the amount of grey flecks in the man's hair. He looked a lot older than he remembered just a few short months before.

"Well, what is it?" Rhydderch said tersely without lifting his head.

Galahad's temper flared at what he felt was a total lack of respect this man was showing him. Instead he took a sharp breath and tried to remind himself that Rhydderch was of royal blood and could do or say anything he wanted. "My Lord," he said tentatively, "please accept my apologies for… disturbing you."

Rhydderch finally looked up, sighed and leaned back. "Well, what do you have to say?"

"My name is Galahad, I bring a message from Aedan at Dun Breatainn."

Rhydderch frowned. He considered the name and he couldn't, for the life of him, recall an Aedan. He looked at Galahad, puzzlement spreading across his face. "Aedan?"

"Aedan mac Gabrain, Lord."

"Aedan mac Gabrain? Are you deluded, man? Aedan is a couple of hundred miles away. Have you been drinking, man? You had better leave before I have your balls cut off," Rhydderch said, his anger rising.

"I wish I had been drinking, Lord, but Aedan has captured the fort. He now sits at Dun Breatainn, Lord, and he wants to meet with you."

Rhydderch mouth opened and closed but no words came out. He sighed deeply. "Are you telling me he has taken the fort by force?"

"I'm afraid so and he has sent me to—"

"Yes, I heard, he wants to meet me. All right, Galahad," Rhydderch said, pinching his nose, "you'd better explain, I'm too tired." Rhydderch pointed to a jug and invited Galahad to drink. "It's only water but it might revive you. Indulge me... Why is Aedan at Dun Breatainn?"

Galahad swallowed hard. "There was an engagement before the walls with Aedan's army,"

Rhydderch's eyes widened. "A military engagement?"

"Yes, Lord."

"Outside the walls? You fought an engagement with Aedan outside the walls?" His voice rose in incredulity. "What possessed you to fight on open ground?"

Galahad tried to calmly describe the attack, how the defenders of Dun Breatainn had been tricked into believing that it was a small number of soldiers threatening them, and how they had been surprised by horsemen who had cut off their retreat. Rhydderch closed his eyes and leaned forward onto his elbows before steepling his fingers, resting his head in his thumbs. He suddenly felt very weary and he blew out his cheeks.

As Galahad waited he became aware of another presence behind his right shoulder. He tensed but the figure moved away and walked around the table. He saw that it was a woman. She stooped and put her mouth close to Rhydderch's ear, whispering something to him, words which Galahad could not hear. He stood for a moment in this woman's presence, not absolutely sure who she was.

The woman smiled weakly and waved at him to retake his seat. "I am the Lady Langoreth, the prince is my husband."

"My lady," he said, bowing. "Please accept my apologies for I did not recognise you."

"No matter," she responded carelessly. "You are a descendant of Cunedda, are you not?"

"Yes, Lady, you are well informed.

"It pays to be informed, Galahad, for we live in troubled times. But the news you have brought is... troubling. Did Aedan say what his intentions are? He isn't intending to invade us, is he?"

"I believe not, my Lady."

"Hmmm, one thing is for sure, what that man shows is not always what he intends. Did he ask you to seek out the Lord Rhydderch?"

"Not exactly but I'm pretty certain he expected this message to be delivered to your husband."

"You did well, Galahad." She turned and patted Rhydderch on the shoulder. "He wants something from us and I'm pretty certain I know what."

Rhydderch looked up. "The bastard is after Dalriada and he wants our neutrality. The cunning little shit."

Langoreth smiled. "How many men did we lose?"

"Less than a hundred and he promised not to harm the women and children."

"The fortress is undamaged?" Rhydderch chimed in.

"Completely."

Rhydderch was now sitting up. The glassy look of a few minutes earlier had disappeared. He stole a glance at Langoreth. "So," he announced, "we have a chance to save face and keep the king from—"

He never finished the sentence, he didn't have to.

Chapter 20

An Understanding of Equals

The morning was bright and fresh. Rhydderch led his men out of Pertneck in silence and deep in thought. He had been instructed to bring no more than ten men to the meeting with Aedan. As he rode towards Dun Breatainn, he struggled to keep his anger in check. Aedan had not been provoked and yet here he was in Alt Clut. The insolence of a small kingdom inflicting an embarrassing defeat on the most powerful kingdom north of the wall was almost too much to bear. And here he was being summoned. The consequences of other kingdoms knowing of this embarrassment were not lost on him. Worse still, if his father became aware, the fault would be heaped on Rhydderch and his ambitions to lead Alt Clut would be at an end. He knew he would have to play this very carefully.

He was struck by the numbers of Aedan's men that lined the approaches to Dun Breatainn. He was at a disadvantage but he also knew that demands made could not be sustained as Alt Clut was simply too big. Aedan wanted something and that meant weakness of sorts, something that could be manipulated in a way that was not one sided, and just maybe, could result in benefits for both men.

They entered the fort unchallenged until Gwallog stepped forward to grasp the reins of Rhydderch's horse. Rhydderch's expression hardened at this action but then changed as a look of recognition crossed his face. "Gwallog ap Lleenog, if I'm not mistaken?"

"Yes, Lord Rhydderch," he replied flatly

"It's a shame we meet in these," he paused, "circumstances."

"Yes it is, Lord," he replied with just a hint of embarrassment.

"I am here at Lord Aedan's request," he continued smoothly. "Is he available?"

"Of course, Lord. You should follow me."

Galahad's heart sank, damn vain hope, he thought. He had been enjoying himself with his newly found importance as he saw it.

"You too," Gwallog called, disturbing Galahad from his thoughts.

"Me?" He pointed to himself.

"It appears so." Rhydderch smiled. "It seems that you have become a player too, my friend."

Climbing down from their horses, they started to follow Gwallog. Rhydderch's men were invited to remain with their horses although they were ever watchful for any signs of betrayal. Gwallog, seeing their reticence, turned and called for refreshments to be brought. "Lord Rhydderch, please accept my assurances that your men won't be harmed and nor will you be. You must realise there is no benefit in that."

Rhydderch nodded and then signalled to his men to stand down.

"Please, gentlemen." Gwallog beckoned them to follow him.

They reached the fort commander's quarters where they found Aedan, Arthur and Bedwyr sitting at benches formed into circle. Aedan rose to greet the prince, opening his arms in a warm embrace. Rhydderch fought back a strong desire to resist this intrusion of his space but accepted the hug, albeit rather awkwardly.

"Welcome, Lord Rhydderch, my friend," Aedan began expansively.

"I will admit, my dear Aedan, that I am surprised to meet you, at your request, at my fort," he responded.

"Understandable."

"Hmm, I'll probably regret asking this but what are you planning? I suspect you aren't going to invade Alt Clut because I know as well as you, you're unlikely to succeed."

"But I'm here," he interrupted.

"You're here," Rhydderch repeated. "And so? There is always a reason for all your actions, Aedan, and I suspect, if you invited me here, there is something you want."

Aedan showed no reaction but he regarded the other man with new interest. Rhydderch was not to be underestimated, he realised. "Yes, you are right, my friend. I need your neutrality,"

"Straight to the point. So my guess would be that you want Alt Clut to step aside to allow you to attack Conall, I suppose."

Aedan smiled. "Yes indeed."

"You could have just asked me rather than invade my territory."

"You would have said no and I wanted to get your attention."

Rhydderch snorted. "So what's in it for me?"

"You get your fort back and you don't lose face, of course. You wouldn't want your father to think you took your eye off things?"

Rhydderch's jaw tightened and Aedan, seeing him discomforted, continued. "I have no desire to embarrass you, I don't want you turning on me next to court your Christian friends. I know you hold to the old ways, your wife is evidence of that. I know, too, that we will need each other in the years to come."

"You mean against the Picts and the Angles?"

"Quite, we need to be independently and collectively strong."

"An Alba?"

"I doubt that. But a force that will protect ourselves, a strong Dalriada, Alt Clut and Rheged."

"Urien is supportive?"

"He sees the advantages."

"And what of your Irish counterparts? They are always hovering like unwanted guests at a celebration."

"If you support me, Rhydderch, I will deal with the Irish but that can only happen if I am king. Alliance with Alt Clut will give me some clout when I speak to the Lord Aed. I will support you too when the time comes."

Rhydderch sat back in his chair and contemplated Aedan's words. He realised that he wouldn't lose anything by accepting Aedan's offer but he had to cover himself and also had to find a way that would keep his father on board.

All eyes, he noticed, were on him with an air of expectation. He smiled to himself and decided to draw things out. He looked at the circle of benches before him, "I've heard of your circle."

"Round table," Arthur put in.

"Of course." Rhydderch regarded the young man. "Prince Arthur," he continued jovially, "I think we will hearing about your achievements for many years to come. I have come to realise that your decisions at the Glein may have had their merits." He looked at Aedan but his words were for Arthur. "You will be a worthy successor to your father," he said mischievously.

"Yes he will," Aedan interjected, "all in good time and there are other, older sons."

"And yet they're not here," Rhydderch observed.

"Someone has to look after affairs at home," Aedan advised.

"And what of the Lady Muirgein, I am told that she and King Urien have parted ways."

Aedan coloured. He knew that Rhydderch was testing the strength of Aedan's friendship with the King of Rheged. Keeping his calm he waved the comment away. "Urien wants a younger woman and Muirgein's fate is as a priestess. We have an understanding."

"Yes, of course, still you can't have been overly happy with that," Rhydderch pressed.

"Our daughters are… political tools, there is no room for animosity, it is a business transaction," Aedan replied pompously.

Rhydderch smiled and nodded. "As you wish. Still," he continued, this time to Arthur, "you are the coming man?"

Arthur tried to stifle an embarrassed smile but nodded his acknowledgment.

"Tell me, Prince Arthur, why do you sit in a circle?"

"Lord Rhydderch," Arthur said stiffly, "we sit in a circle when we discuss plans of importance. It signifies to all who sit here that they have an equal say."

Rhydderch nodded and turned towards Aedan, I suppose you are a first man amongst equals," he mused.

The comment irritated Aedan but his scowl softened. "I am the leader, my dear Rhydderch, yes, I command. Additionally it appears I don't do the job too badly. I'm sure you'll agree. After all I am here." He paused. "You might want to belittle what we do here but from small acorns great oak trees grow. I have some excellent leaders in my ranks and they have much to say about how we attain our goals. This table enables all of us to have our say."

"There is no weakness, Lord Rhydderch, in consultation," Arthur replied. "We are stronger together. I… we appreciate the opportunity to have our say but the Lord Aedan is our leader and we will, I assure you, do everything necessary to do his will."

Rhydderch shrugged. "I meant no offence, young Prince. You speak well." He stayed quiet for a while, again eying the men before him. His eyes constantly stopped at Arthur who held his stare on each occasion. Sighing, Rhydderch finally turned to Aedan. "Your position is not as strong as you believe but I can see benefits in your suggestion. I have one problem that needs to be overcome."

"And what's that?" Aedan responded.

"My father will need something that explains my agreement here."

"Oh?"

"If you want me to persuade my father to ignore our friend Conall and let you walk your army across our lands, because you will have to, he will want something in return."

"And what, Lord Rhydderch, do you have in mind?"

"Well, if we are talking an alliance with our nations working together to take on the Picts and the Angles, we need a gesture of goodwill."

Aedan looked sceptical and sensed a trap. He had become increasingly rigid. Rhydderch sensed this and stretched forward, patting Aedan's knee. "Lord Aedan, besides some reparation for the damage you have caused here and a guarantee of your silence, I merely wanted to suggest a marriage alliance. The Lady Domelch, I am told, has passed, for which I offer you my deepest condolences, but life must go on and you will need a queen for your new domain."

Aedan's raised his eyebrows. "A marriage?"

"Yes."

"Who?"

"My cousin, Igraine."

"The Lady of Strathclyde? You are a canny negotiator, Lord Rhydderch, your cousin's position will allow you some influence in Dalriada?"

"I need to be canny when dealing with you, Aedan. A marital bond will simply ensure that you will not turn against me without me having some advance notice. And vice a versa, of course."

Aedan smiled. "All right, when you return to us with your agreement, we will leave here and advance to Kintyre."

Rhydderch stood to leave. Aedan offered his hand and Rhydderch grasped it. They had an agreement and Galahad would act as their ambassador, remaining with Aedan's army once the agreement was fully adhered to.

Aedan walked with Rhydderch back to where his men were being entertained. Before Rhydderch mounted his horse he leant close to Aedan's ear. "Have a care, Aedan. We have had a friendly discussion and we have made an agreement but do not fool yourself that your being on my land without provocation isn't somehow an affront and I will not forget or forgive. If you even think about doing something like this again, I promise Alt Clut will obliterate you and your people from the map and no one will ever know that Aedan existed. I trust I make myself plain?"

"You do, sir," Aedan replied flatly and without expression.

"Good," Rhydderch said cheerfully, straightening himself to his full height.

Arthur watched Rhydderch and his guard leave the fortress. He pondered the initial exchanges. Muirgein was no longer Urien's wife? That was news to him and he was excited by the prospect of his sister being free from her husband. There was, of course, Gwallog, but surely that ship had long since sailed. Yes, he was well pleased.

As he stared at their disappearing backs he couldn't help wondering who had actually got the better of that exchange. Aedan certainly did not have it all his own way and Rhydderch had unsettled him. Arthur felt he was being used as a political pawn, Rhydderch had clearly sought to cause disunity and Arthur, on reflection, was not overly happy with Aedan's responses. His feelings for his father remained confused and uncertain. Aedan had secured everything he wanted so the meeting had been a success and yet Rhydderch had left with his own position apparently undiminished, and if anything, enhanced. He smiled; he had a lot to learn; it wasn't only skill on the battlefield that made you famous.

Arthur shook the thoughts from his head. Instead he hoped that the man Galahad would soon return; his interest in the Lady Gwenhwyfar was piqued. His manhood stirred and he blushed outwardly. Growing up was exciting, he mused. He only wished he were older.

He stood there until Rhydderch's men had ridden out of sight. Sighing outwardly he idly kicked a stone before turning and walking back inside to where Bedwyr was waiting. "That was interesting. Aedan is clearly extremely clever but Rhydderch was no fool."

"It was quite a dual; I must admit I was glad I was only a witness and not a protagonist. My head aches at the complexity of it all."

"Come on," Bedwyr said, "let's have a… small drink."

Arthur nodded. "Yes, why not, I think I need one."

"At least we can stop you thinking for a few hours," Bedwyr laughed.

"It's worth a try," Arthur admitted.

Chapter 21

Invasion

Once confirmation had been received from Galahad that the King of Alt Clut had accepted the movement of Aedan's men across his land, the camp at Dun Breatainn was struck and the army set off westward along the north bank of the River Clut.

Aedan had decided that he did not want to pass by Dunadd and risk a long drawn out siege or worse, be faced by an army ready to receive him. Instead he would march to the mouth of the sea loch, Loch Gare, whereupon he would use boats to transfer his army to the Kyles and then from the westward coast cross over to Kintyre and approach Dunadd from the south. Surely, he believed, he would have the advantage of surprise. Yes, it was a long way, but geography would surely be on his side.

Arthur commanded the cavalry and set a net around the marching men. It was probably not needed, certainly at the beginning of the march, but there was widespread gratitude from the men who knew they would either be protected or given plenty of time to prepare against any attack. Arthur's reputation as a military commander was growing despite his tender years.

Arthur's self-esteem was rising by the moment and he was particularly pleased at the affection shown him by his father despite the presence of Aedan's second eldest son, Eochaid, who was some five year's Arthur's senior. The initial meeting was strained and awkward, but Eochaid had settled into the role of subordinate without any apparent rancour. Arthur suspected he had been managed by Bedwyr and Drystan and he was happy that Eochaid accepted Arthur's position was earned, not gifted.

They reached a shallow dock near the Rhu Narrows. Transports had been requisitioned by Gwallog with Galahad's help and were moored and made ready. It was decided to wait for the weather to settle as unseasonal winds had made the crossing treacherous. The men too, were deeply apprehensive and the thought of choppy waters and the inevitable sea sickness that would afflict large numbers was enough to err on the cautious side. Arthur noted Aedan's irritation but he gradually calmed, instead wandering around the encampment making fun of some of the more squeamish veterans.

On the third day the winds began to calm and on the day of the planned crossing the army was greeted by a fine sunny morning with little or no cloud. There was relief all round as the swarms of gnats that gathered around the encampment had driven some of the men to distraction. It was not unheard of that men would run cursing through the camp before diving into the frigid waters of the Clut.

The camp was struck and the men were corralled onto the flotilla of water transports and the crossing to the claw shaped Cowal Peninsula began. From there they marched swiftly to the other side of the Cowal. They walked around Loch Striven, down the east coast of the Kyles facing Bute and across to the western shore.

On the fourth afternoon they reached the coast overlooking Kintyre. For Arthur this was the first time he had seen this place. He stood overlooking the sea letting the sun settle on his face. Breathing in slowly and deeply, he enjoyed the sea air. Kintyre and the Kingdom of Dalriada would surely be his future. That land across the waters was green if a little barren.

He reflected on the past twelve months, a year that had changed his life forever. He hadn't picked up sword before eighteen months ago and here he was, second in command, in charge of the cavalry and apparently well regarded and trusted by his father, and more importantly, his men. He turned and saw his horseman milling about with Drystan eagerly making arrangements for men to rest and settle down. Arthur's smiled at his cousin's enthusiasm. He had changed from the quiet introverted youth into a bouncing, almost annoying, man. He was five years older than Arthur, a very good looking man, Arthur reflected, and a man who turned women's heads. It was inevitable that Drystan would, at some stage, annoy some husband or father.

Arthur shrugged. Fate would show its hand sooner or later. His attention was drawn to Bedwyr's approach at a canter as he slid off his saddle. Arthur had to admit that he didn't understand how Bedwyr managed that without injuring himself. Arthur found himself cringing but straightened as Bedwyr jogged towards him.

"Lord!" he called breathlessly.

"Don't call me lord, how many more times."

"Good grief," Bedwyr responded, slightly exasperated.

"Perhaps we could settle for some middle ground?"

Bedwyr stopped open mouthed and then burst into laughter. "Arthur."

"There you have it, my friend." He grinned. "When I was educated next to you I was your friend. I am still your friend and there are very few people I trust more in this world."

"You're a prince now, things change, Arthur."

Arthur sighed. "Please, Bedwyr, let's not have this discussion. I don't want it and I don't need it. I have no wish to fall out with you."

"Nor I with you."

"Good, that's settled, now let's speak no more of this. What do you want of me?"

Bedwyr nodded. "I almost forgot. Lord Aedan wants to invite you to a meeting of the Round Table at dusk."

"To discuss what?" he groaned.

"Our plans for the invasion of Dalriada, of course." Bedwyr smiled broadly. "It would appear that the Lord Aedan has decided to share with us what he intends."

Arthur rolled his eyes. "That's nice of him."

"It's the way, my dear friend."

"Isn't it just," Arthur replied flatly.

In the tent erected especially for Aedan and his commanders, benches of a kind were set out in a circle. Aedan sat with his back to the rear of the tent; Arthur was sitting opposite him with his back to the entrance which made him feel slightly vulnerable. It was probably, he suspected, done purposely. With them sat Gwallog to Aedan's right and Eochaid to his left. Cai,

Drystan, Galahad and Bedwyr filled the spaces either side of Arthur with Bedwyr sitting on his right side.

Mead, bread, some meat and cheese was laid out before them and there was general conversation as they waited for Aedan to start the meeting. Arthur remained silent and ate nothing. Instead he stared at his father. As he did so, he thought of his mother who he hadn't seen for over eighteen months and whilst he recognised that a warrior should not harbour such thoughts, he missed her. Perhaps once this war was over she could come back north and be closer to him. Perhaps Loch Leven, but Loch Lomond was also an option. It was land owned by Gwallog's family and he knew Gwallog felt well inclined towards his mother.

He reflected that the company of men could be positively tedious. He liked, even loved, his comrades. He and Bedwyr were inseparable and to his surprise he and Cai had become close friends and allies. The drinking and whoring of the others was something he hadn't wanted to indulge in but it seemed to Arthur that he would probably have to live with it unless he could escape once in a while. He fervently hoped so. But he very much missed his mother.

Eventually Aedan banged his bench and brought Arthur out of his thoughts. Aedan, for effect as always, looked silently around the benches. It was a trick, Arthur realised, that made everyone hang on his every word. Arthur smiled inwardly. *Clever*, he thought.

"Friends," Aedan began, "I wanted to bring you together to discuss why we are here and what my intentions are." He paused again before continuing, "Tomorrow we will sail to Kintyre and the heart of Dalriada, after which we will march towards Dunadd. I expect that somewhere south of Dunadd we will be confronted by Conall and his sons."

There was silence until Drystan asked, "Why didn't we sail directly to Kintyre rather than marching across the Cowal? Surely it would have been quicker."

"Indeed," Aedan responded, "the reason is simple, my young Prince. Surprise!"

"Surprise?" Cai interrupted.

"Yes, Lord Cai. Let's not be naïve, gentlemen, Conall will have spies everywhere. He is bound to know we are coming. He will undoubtedly have spies in the camp as we do in his." He grinned.

"How do you know this?" Drystan asked.

"Oh we have had some success in rooting them out but we are still looking. But to return to your question, young Drystan, I wanted to keep the enemy guessing. So far we have shown we might be attacking from two different directions and I am assured that Conall's army has busily moved from one area to the next in anticipation. They will be stretched and I want to choose where we give battle."

"Where do you have in mind?" Arthur asked.

"My preference is where the sea loch almost cuts the land in two at An Tairbeart. We will be certain to have no one at our backs and we can control the shipping lanes."

"So we land there?" Arthur asked flatly.

"The land to the east of the sea loch is flat but there are also good slopes that will give us the advantage of the high ground."

Arthur nodded. "And what numbers are we likely to face, Lord?"

Aedan smiled. "I am guessing we will be outnumbered two to one at least, Arthur. Are the odds good enough for you?"

"As long as they don't have horsemen?" Arthur responded grimly.

"They will have some, I'm sure, but nowhere near as many as us. Or as effective."

"Then I say, they are at a disadvantage," Arthur responded with a grin. "But they will know, surely, that we are strong and will not necessarily give battle. So..."

"So," Aedan said, "we must make them think we do not have that much cavalry,"

"How so?" Gwallog grunted.

"At the Glein our tactic, perfectly executed by Arthur," Aedan said, nodding to Arthur in acknowledgement, "was to lure the enemy in and then flank them. So something similar might well work here."

"I agree," Arthur put in. "Can I make a suggestion?"

"The floor is yours, my boy," Aedan replied.

"Are the heights wooded?"

"They are."

"Well, in view of the terrain you speak of, I suggest we split our forces in three."

"Divide our force against superior numbers?" Cai asked.

"Yes, I know it's a risk but there are wooded heights, cavalry can be hidden from view."

"Are you thinking of suggesting, Arthur," Bedwyr said, "that we use soldiers on foot to fight a fighting retreat and then deploy the cavalry and envelop them?"

"Precisely."

"But if they have spies?"

"There's not enough time for them to react," Arthur said patiently. "We land our forces the furthest north and the cavalry shall follow some five miles to the rear. We can bring them up without being seen and after they commit their forces that are bound to concentrate before the slopes."

"Like the boar hunt," Cai smirked, "we tempt in the boar then, as hunters, snap the trap shut."

Gwallog turned to Aedan. "What do you think, Lord Aedan? The plan is sound, I believe."

Aedan sat quietly for some moments and slowly nodded his assent. "So be it," he said. "I, Cai and Gwallog will lead the men on foot, that'll undoubtedly tempt them in. There is no doubt that they will come for me, they will believe that killing me will end our cause. All right, Arthur, we will hold a line in front of the slopes and you with Drystan will hide yourselves in the trees on the reverse slopes. We will hold as long as we dare and gradually drop back until we call you in."

"I think," Gwallog said, "that if we can set down earthworks and stakes it will help to break up their formations."

Again Aedan nodded. "We break camp at first light, the ships from our Ulster brethren will be ready to transport us. No one is to be told of our plans until we are ready to deploy. Am I clear?."

Aedan's scowl when delivering the last message was both sinister and threatening. Everyone around that table was left in no doubt that the consequences of blurting out anything would be severe. Then Aedan stood, the meeting was at an end; the others stood and waited for Aedan to leave. As Aedan departed, he glanced at Arthur. "Well done, my boy. Another chance to show your quality."

Everyone was ushered out the tent but there was no talk. Everyone knew what was expected; the next few days would either make or break them.

The next morning was grey and murky but there was precious little breeze, much to the relief of the whole army, when they were told to strike camp just before the dawn. As agreed the previous evening, the foot soldiers sailed separately from the horsemen. With the foot soldiers casting off first, it was almost an hour before the cavalrymen were embarked and sailed to a point some ten miles south of Aedan and the footmen.

As anticipated they encountered no resistance on landing with only curious locals watching on, and more than likely, feeling rather anxious at the sight of an army tramping up the beaches.

It took over half the morning for all the men and horses to be disembarked before Arthur led them northwards. Drystan followed with his men at a mile distant. Galahad was sent forward to catch up with Aedan to check on the army's dispositions. On his return Arthur was advised that the army had taken up positions below the hills identified the previous evening. Aedan, Galahad advised, had sent out scouts towards the north and west of their position.

Arthur decided to make camp and await further instructions. Drystan was directed to follow suit whilst maintaining the gap between the cavalry units.

It was a number of days before news was brought to Arthur by Galahad that Conall's army were approaching Aedan's position. Foraging was becoming a problem and food provisions were beginning to dwindle. Arthur breathed a sigh of relief as he struck camp again and travelled north using the hills to screen his movements. When the horsemen had arrived Arthur placed them on the reverse slopes, and with Bedwyr, scrambled to the top of the hill so that he could see across the whole of the intended battlefield.

He could see Aedan's encampment below him, rivulets of smoke spiralling up into the evening sky. He looked across the flat plain to see Conall's army around half a mile away. Arthur could see the skirmishers bating each other. He was especially amused at one of his men dropping his trousers. Bedwyr laughed. "I'm sure I've seen that hairy arse around the camp," he said.

"I can't say I've noticed." Arthur grinned.

"This is not good terrain," Bedwyr snorted.

"Hmm, we will probably have to move further north to find better terrain for our horses. Perhaps we will have to come around the hill and trees."

"There's a risk they'll see us early enough and manoeuvre to meet us," Bedwyr countered. "Plus it's going to be difficult to coordinate with Drystan," he continued.

"Can't be helped," Arthur said sharply. "The whole thing will need careful timing. My concern, Bedwyr, my friend, is that Aedan and Cai may have to hold on longer than perhaps they would want."

Bedwyr's eyebrows arched. "If this goes wrong, Aedan will rip your balls off."

"I suppose so." Arthur smiled. "Probably best to avoid that, eh?"

Bedwyr nodded, amused.

Arthur continued to stare towards the enemy and the over the terrain leading down the inclines. Once he was satisfied he nodded and turned to Bedwyr. "Right, my friend, we move to the right as far as we dare. I need you to find Galahad and get him to ride over to Drystan and call him here to talk tactics."

"Why not tell Aedan?" Bedwyr asked.

"Spies, my friend. If there is a spy, we cannot alert him to our position."

"They must know we are in the area," Bedwyr countered.

"I'm sure they do, I'm counting on it," Arthur responded patiently.

"Really?"

"They will be unable to commit all their forces because they will be worried about us."

"Perhaps we need to heighten their worries."

"What are you thinking, Bedwyr?"

"A diversion?"

"Hmmm, an interesting idea. What do you think will be needed? Forty men?"

"I'm not sure we can spare too many."

"Let it be so. We'll speak to Drystan and get Galahad to lead the decoy horsemen. They mustn't engage though. We just want them to make as much noise as possible."

"Yes, Lord."

Arthur scowled. "What?"

"Yes, Arthur."

"If this goes wrong, I'll be blaming you," Arthur joked.

"Naturally,"

Arthur stayed on the crest of the hill a little while longer gazing across the valley. Drizzle had rolled in again as it had done this past week. He felt wet through and wondered why his family had crossed from Ireland and headed north. Some sort of sick joke, he mused. Nonetheless, this apparently miserable, midge infected place could be his destiny. He smiled but a sense of foreboding rose through his body. He had little doubt that tomorrow and indeed many more tomorrows would see him sweep all before him but would he become king? The trouble was, he just couldn't see it. He shook himself from the thoughts and tried to ignore the doubt and the melancholy that came with them.

He stood and breathed in very slowly, swiping his hand across his face to flick away a tell-tale buzzing noise near his nose. *One day at a time, one battle at a time, one traitor at a time*, he thought. Who was this spy, he wondered, was he among the horsemen standing with Arthur or Drystan or perhaps he was standing next to his father, or to Gwallog, or to Cai. He gritted his teeth and hissed.

He turned and made his way to his horse and walked down the reverse slopes. Tomorrow destiny awaited.

Chapter 22

Delgon

Agreement with Drystan secured, Arthur waved Galahad off. The sun was setting and thankfully the mizzle had cleared.

Arthur returned to his men as darkness fell and he moved them further around the hills. The men had been dressed in their battle dress for almost twenty-four hours and they moaned as they were ushered, in almost complete silence, to a new position. Arthur and Bedwyr sat on their mounts to one side, Bedwyr smiling at the discontent and chiding those he recognised and knew well. Arthur, however, looked stern and those who caught his eye were careful enough to quieten and look down at their feet.

Bedwyr noticed Arthur's aloofness and decided he should nudge his friend to be a lot more supportive to his men. "Come on, Arthur, they're tired, wet and rightly miserable," Bedwyr breathed. "Be more... kindly," he said, pausing.

Arthur was quiet for a moment. He knew Bedwyr was right and he should be more sympathetic and urge the men on himself, but this was surely too important for pettiness. He looked at Bedwyr and shrugged. "Yes I suppose you're right... it must be... nerves."

Bedwyr nodded. "Tomorrow will be different."

"It will be."

The morning was, almost inevitably, grey and miserable. The same drizzle as yesterday added to the feelings of dampness that seemed to spread through Arthur's body. He looked about him and saw his men stretched out in various stages of misery. He knew he was too hard on them the night before. He now felt as they did and he didn't like it one bit. "It was clearing up last night," he moaned to no one in particular.

He shook himself back into focus and called in the scouts and guards. On their arrival they huddled together. There were no fires to keep their presence hidden so any proximity gave them a little cheer.

Arthur was advised that Galahad was enjoying some success and that their foes were distracted. Whether it was enough would be shown to Arthur soon enough. It was clear that Aedan was outnumbered some three to one and his soldiers were going to endure a heavy attack until they were relieved. Arthur sucked his teeth; he knew that the distance that his men had to cover would delay his arrival. He breathed deeply, and stared up at the enormous sky. Closing his eyes, he offered up a silent prayer to the goddess Morrigan for guidance and the gift of timing.

He was deep in thought when Bedwyr's voice disturbed him. "I have had the ground checked around the hills and it is soft but not muddy," Bedwyr said.

"The horses will not be slowed?"

"Maybe a little but I don't think it will greatly change what we need to do."

"And Drystan?"

"I'm told the same."

"Good." He turned to a dour man, sitting next to Bedwyr. "You there."

"Lord?"

"Your name?"

"Bors, Lord."

"I know of you I think, Bors. You, I'm told, scouted the position and battle readiness of Conall's forces?"

"Yes, Lord."

"And?"

"Lord. The camp was awake early. As you have been told, Galahad's horsemen have caused some disquiet."

Arthur smiled at that. "Go on."

"They intend to fight. They are confident, Lord, but Conall is ailing, they are saying, and his son Dunchaid is commanding the army,"

"Really? Is Conall in the host?"

"No, Lord, he has retired to Dunadd to convalesce."

"Does Aedan know about this?"

"I do not know but I'm sure he does."

Arthur rubbed his chin and smiled. "I imagine you're right, Bors."

Arthur pondered the information a while and then looked at the others about him. "Does anyone know of this Dunchaid?"

"Only by reputation," Bors replied

"Reputation?"

"Yes, Lord, entitled and aggressive. He wants to be king."

"I'm sure he does." Arthur smiled tightly. "He'll want to win too much, prove his mettle and annihilate us all, I imagine."

"Yes, Lord."

"Hmm... that's good."

As the morning progressed the armies began to form up across the plain in front of Aedan's force. As planned, Aedan had ordered his forces some one hundred paces forward so that the opposing shield walls could quite clearly make out each other's faces. The clouds of midges were a constant irritation, with men regularly using their shields and swords to swipe the irritating insects away.

Arthur had found an excellent vantage point where he could see the deployments of both armies. He noted how useful it might be to have a constant stream of information from someone within Aedan's forces but that that was impossible. It was a disadvantage but it had to be overcome and it would be.

Arthur noted a man walking in front of the Dalriadan forces berating his men. *That must be Dunchaid,* he thought. The man gesticulated towards Aedan's men. Arthur guessed he would be using words such as usurper and traitor. *No truer word said*, he thought, and smiled grimly. The hypocrisy wasn't lost on him but he would probably do the same. Meanwhile Aedan was standing in the centre of his frontline. No cajoling, just grim determination. Arthur realised that Aedan commanded respect and the reverence his men felt for him was powerful enough. The difference was plain for all to see.

With the preamble over, Dunchaid joined the ranks in the centre of his men's lines and a great roar rose from the host as they began to move forward in a single block. Arthur saw the space between the two armies close quickly. He was mesmerised as these men prepared to clash. He was in awe at the bravery of the men at the centre of such savagery, the anticipation of killing other men for someone they would never probably meet, the jarring through their bodies as the shield walls crashed together. Even from where he was watching he heard the two armies come together like a clap of thunder. His father and many of his friends would be fighting for their lives. He shook his head then. "Life is cheap," he whispered to himself.

He scrambled to his feet, looked down at the throng one more time, turned and scrambled down the reverse slopes and back to his mount. Bedwyr nodded towards him and Arthur smiled grimly. "It has begun," he said simply.

The front ranks of Aedan's force locked shields and braced themselves, grimly looking to their front.

"Steady!" Gwallog called.

"Stand with your king," Cai called.

"Spears!" Aedan roared.

There was a clatter along the line as spears were thrust forward as Conall's Dalriadans marched at a slow stride with insults and threats being screamed at their foes. The space closed quickly before a sudden surge brought the front lines together. The grunts of men charging forward and holding their ground were blocked out by the crash of steel on steel. The pushing and shoving began.

The front rows held their ground as the men behind them brought their spears to bear, stabbing at the men over their shields. Men screamed. Some found it difficult to keep their balance on the bloody grass and were trampled underfoot. Other men, incapacitated by swords and axes, were held up by the sheer weight being brought to bear from both sides.

It wasn't long, however, before the pressure of superior numbers began to tell. Aedan was well aware that the longer Dalriadan lines meant he would be flanked. To counter this Aedan's flanks were at angles but those flanks were coming under severe pressure and the left wing was beginning to buckle. Aedan's men were gradually being redeployed to shore up the line but as the centre was being weakened the front line was becoming more unstable. Soon Aedan gave the order to pull back towards the slope. The ground was treacherous; it was broken and stony. It inhibited the defenders but it was proving far more difficult for Dunchaid's men.

Breeches along the length of the shield wall had resulted in increasing numbers of men falling; if they weren't killed outright they were being trampled underfoot and skewered by the following lines. The stench of men opening their bowels was almost overwhelming and the gore made the grass and gorse treacherously slippery. The cries of dying men were pitiful, Gwallog swallowed hard as the man next to him fell, calling out for his mother. But Aedan's line continued to hold as it slowly fell back.

The trenches dug by Aedan's men came into play as the army retreated. Inevitably gaps opened up but the sudden roar of the Dalriadans as they saw an opportunity to push through turned to shouts of warning as the traps swallowed men screaming by the dozen.

If it were possible, the fighting became more intense. Both Gwallog and Cai fought ferociously as Aedan's arm weakened through fatigue, slashing down on now unprotected throats and shoulders. "Lord!" Cai screamed, "we cannot hold them for much longer."

The lines were indeed thinning as men perished without a care for themselves. The slaughter made Aedan feel sick to the stomach as he slipped on a man's entrails. His chest was heaving at the effort he was making but still he refused to call for assistance. "Just a while longer," he shouted.

"We don't fucking have a little while longer," Cai retorted. "Sound the fucking horn!"

Aedan swung around at his subordinate's words. "How dare you!" he screamed.

But Cai held his stare. "Have me run through if it makes you feel better, Lord, but for now, blow the fucking horn."

Gwallog again swung his sword with lightning speed and killed another foe. He looked at Aedan and nodded. "Lord King, we are almost done. Cai is right, you must call for help."

"Sound the horn," Aedan said reluctantly to a man just behind him. "I'll deal with you later, Sir Cai."

"If I live, my Lord," Cai responded, laughing.

Aedan grunted and drove his sword into the belly of a man who had

broken through a newly formed shield wall.

Arthur heard the horn sound from the other side of the hill and raised his sword. "Today we show the world that we are the true heirs of the Sarmatian knights. On me, my friends, come with me. To the king!"

There was a roar from his men. Bedwyr smiled grimly as Arthur started at a canter and then broke into a gallop. The horsemen initially rode in two columns to avoid the broken ground that stretched out either side of them. As they broke from the trees they found no one to challenge them. Arthur again raised his sword and this time the horsemen spread out in a long line either side of him.

It was over five minutes before they came into view of the battle raging beneath the hills. The delay had resulted in Aedan's forces being almost broken but each man lost had sold their life dearly. The slaughter was immense.

The Dalriadans were within moments of victory when shouts from their flanks stalled their advance. A bloodied Dunchaid stared in horrified disbelief as first cavalry came from their left flank and then from their right. Quickly the Dalriadans tried to form up to accept the charge but it was too late. First Arthur and then Drystan crashed through the defenders, slaying men as they went. The panic spread through the ranks of soldiers and the pressure on Aedan's men suddenly eased, and after a strange confused lull, Aedan shouted for his men to charge. He had lost more than half his men but with their bloodlust up, they charged blindly into the confused hordes before them.

Arthur stood at the centre of the melee directing his men and despite many attempts to unseat him, he stood supreme and untouchable. Swinging his sword right and left, he cut down countless foes. Bedwyr stared in awe, unable to comprehend the sheer magnificence of Arthur's sword play. It wasn't long before the Dalriadans could no longer bear the slaughter within their ranks and they broke. The men, trapped on all sides, dropped their weapons and waved their arms in submission. The fear in their eyes was palpable as they expected to be slain where they stood. Those who could escape did so, throwing their weapons and shields to the ground in their haste. They didn't get far as horsemen chased them down.

Arthur looked on in horror. He galloped across the field to where Aedan stood. "Lord, we are doing murder. You must stop it now."

"Stop? Why, we have them?"

"They are Dalriadans. Your new subjects!"

"You're soft boy," Aedan said scornfully.

"They will respect you if you show mercy," Arthur responded, unfazed by his father's ridicule.

Aedan looked at Arthur considering his options. Finally, he said, "Yes, you're right." He turned to his horn blower and signalled the recall.

Arthur breathed a sigh of relief as he noted the horsemen reining in their mounts and turning back. He knew there would be some filled with bloodlust who would continue the pursuit slaughter. That was, after all, the nature of horsemen, he reflected.

Much to Arthur's satisfaction and relief, the men who had surrendered were being spared, with only the most arrogant being cuffed for their insolence. Arthur surveyed the field of carnage and wondered what had become of Dunchaid. He saw Bedwyr speaking to Bors and trotted over to them. On seeing Arthur, Bors bowed deeply. "Lord."

Arthur nodded in return and turned to Bedwyr. "What news of Dunchaid?"

"We have no news, Arthur. We know his brother Conrad has been killed but there is no sign of Eoganan and Dunchaid. Bors here knows them both by sight and I have asked him to search those living and dead."

"All three sons were here?"

"Yes, Arthur, they were clearly desperate."

"Too desperate." Arthur sighed deeply. "Lord Aedan will see them all dead," he noted quietly.

"There is no choice, Arthur," Bedwyr soothed. "So many more people will die if Dunchaid and Eoganan are free to raise a rebellion, you know this."

Arthur nodded. "Let me know if you find anything." He turned to Bors. "Thank you, my friend, you have been of great service to us today,"

"The pleasure, my Lord, is mine."

Arthur beckoned Bedwyr to follow him, and they trotted together in silence.

"Are you hungry?" Bedwyr asked eventually.

"No, but I could drink a river, my friend."

They slid off their horses some way from the horror, Arthur sitting with his back to the carnage. The sight of massacre made him want to wretch. Bedwyr found provisions as an exhausted Arthur dozed in the midday sun.

It could have only been a few minutes when Bedwyr shook him awake. "You've been summoned to the Round Table."

Arthur groaned. "Shit, already?"

"I don't think Aedan is too happy at the... tardiness of our arrival."

Arthur sighed deeply. "I can't blame him, I suppose."

"I'm sure he'll understand," Bedwyr said hopefully.

"Well, there's two ways this might go. He'll understand, as you say, or he'll think I did all this in the hope that he perishes and I become king."

"Surely not."

"I don't think we can ever be sure of my father's motives or thoughts. He's not known as wily for nothing. Don't forget we are expendable, my friend. What troubles me is that our future or should I say, my future., will be dependent on how many foes there are still to slay. Don't tell me otherwise, my friend, because you know I speak true."

Bedwyr rubbed his face and grunted. "Where has your youthful exuberance gone, Arthur?"

Arthur pointed with his thumb over his shoulder. "The moment my eyes saw this," he breathed.

The two men walked towards where the meeting was to be held. Arthur felt numb inside and was rather surprised at himself for feeling no nerves or fear of what might lie ahead. Bors had reported that Dunchaid's body had been found with his retainers around him but Eoganan could not be found. Dunchaid's last stand, if that's what it could be described as, had doubtless been heroic and he certainly ensured that many a brave warrior would accompany him to the spirit world. Arthur could almost feel the presence of the man walking alongside him. They had been cousins, Arthur reflected, and yet the pursuit of power had come to this.

Arthur and Bedwyr were last to arrive and Arthur was relieved to see that everyone was there. Cai looked battered and bruised and both Gwallog and Aedan had cuts across their arms. Galahad was also there, although he looked completely unscathed from his exploits. Arthur grinned at the man. "You look well, Galahad."

"Aye, Lord," Galahad spat through his clenched teeth.

Others laughed and Galahad noticeably relaxed. "Aye, Lord."

Aedan looked grim and stared at Arthur who stared back, holding his gaze. The tension could be cut with a knife but finally Aedan looked away and his eyes swept around the gathering. "Gentlemen," he began, "I am pleased to see you well. We have prevailed although I must confess it was a close run thing. Our horsemen were late, much later than I would have liked."

Bedwyr glanced at Arthur whose face was completely impassive. Indeed Arthur, despite tension rising in his chest, was able to remain calm.

"Well, boy?" Aedan growled. "Is it your intention to sit here?" He pointed to his own seat. "Was that your plan? Five more minutes and we were all—"

Arthur, to everyone's surprise, held up his hand, cutting Aedan dead. "I have no desire to be sat in your place. If I did I wouldn't have come at all. Furthermore," he continued, ignoring Aedan's attempt to remonstrate, "if I had intervened earlier, we would have been seen as we charged down a hill where the terrain was too steep and too muddy. You admitted, Lord, that there was a spy in the camp and so I couldn't send a message. I knew the enemy would know a horse contingent was close so I sent Galahad out to create a diversion."

Aedan spluttered but then turned his ire on Cai. "And you ignored my orders. How dare you defy me."

Cai's face reddened. "Lord," he straightened and swallowed his anger, "if I didn't push you to sound that horn, Arthur would be sat in your seat and he would need replacements for Gwallog and me."

Silence fell upon the group, everyone focusing on the fire that had been lit before them. Arthur gazed at the glowing embers that flickered restlessly when the breeze picked up.

Aedan stared balefully around him but realised that his subordinates had spoken with reason. He sighed deeply; he had been affronted and he allowed paranoia to overcome him. He had pursued a familial dispute and had assumed that others would have the same motives. He was also going to unleash his anger over sparing the enemy survivors but as he had been so firmly put in his place by both Arthur and Cai, he chose discretion rather than confrontation.

Gwallog eventually raised his hand. "Lord," he said "we have prevailed, we have shown resilience, we have shown battlefield acumen. You should be proud of what has been achieved. The road to Dunadd is open, Dalriada is yours."

"Yes, of course," Aedan agreed. "Thank you all, please accept my... apologies." He nodded to Arthur and Cai. "You did well."

"Thank you, Lord," Arthur said quietly through gritted teeth.

"Thank you," Cai hissed.

Arthur shot Cai a warning and Cai nodded his acknowledgement.

"So, Lord Aedan," Gwallog said, "what plans have you?"

Aedan looked up, relieved at the opportunity to move on. "Gentlemen, I have sent scouts towards Dunadd to check on any potential resistance before we move forward. I anticipate we will stay here for a further two days before we move north."

"Would it not be prudent, Lord, to move now before any resistance can be mounted," Arthur suggested.

Aedan nodded. "A fair point." He turned to Drystan. "Take your men and ride to Dunadd at first light."

"Why not me?" Arthur puzzled.

"I need you with me," Aedan said bluntly.

"Yes, Lord," Arthur, replied biting back his frustration.

"There will be time enough, young prince," Aedan said, trying and failing to smile warmly.

"What about, erm, what's his name now? Dove of something or other," Gwallog said.

"Crimthann or Columba, as he likes to be called," Aedan corrected.

"He doesn't like you," Galahad said.

"The feeling is entirely mutual." Aedan grimaced.

"Why don't you just have him killed?" Drystan suggested.

Aedan smiled mirthlessly. "You can't kill a tonsured prick."

"Keeping your options open?" Eochaid grinned.

Aedan shot him a glance but Gwallog burst out laughing. "A chip off the old block, Lord."

"So it would seem," Aedan said doubtfully. "Nonetheless, this Columba has turned many heads. They say he is powerful, some say even more powerful than our own Druids."

"Even Crierwy or the mad man Myrddin?" Bedwyr said.

"It's what they say," Aedan responded. "A man like that can be troublesome to us so we must keep him close. He's threatened not to crown me but he's no fool. Conall's finished and he'll try and keep up some pretence that he has the whip hand but he will change his mind, probably using his God as an excuse."

Arthur smiled. "You know, how these people think, Lord."

"Arthur my boy," his voice was softer now, "people the whole world over are the same. We are all characters in a play. There has to be good, there has to be evil, the hero, the just, the cunning and the realist. But in the end, there are the powerful and the powerless. The powerful want to keep their power, the powerless want power. The people who don't have power will always be destined to be ruled by those who do. It doesn't matter if they follow the old way or this Christianity. It's all the same."

"That's depressing, Lord," Galahad interrupted. "Surely we can be better than them?"

"No, Galahad, my pure and pious friend. We all do the same thing; we just use different excuses to do it. Columba will need his sense of self-importance stroked. I will make him feel that his words mean something." He nodded grimly. "Because, my friends, this world is changing and his kind will prevail in the end but not quite yet."

Chapter 23

Columba's Acceptance

It was a bright sunny day. By mid-morning Aedan had led his men off towards Dunadd. There had been reports from Drystan's scouts that the road ahead was empty and all opposition fighters had melted away. It seemed the vanquished had satisfied themselves that the change of leadership would not make much difference to their world. One Scots King was as good as another but the difference was the mercy shown to the defeated army. Yes, of course, there was no quarter given or taken and the slaughter was merciless but when the time came, mercy was dispensed. That news had spread throughout the kingdom of Dalriada and Aedan's arrival would not be signalling any detrimental change.

Aedan's forces moved slowly north, there was no hurry now. When the army camped for the night they were just five miles south of Dunadd. Drystan's men were a further four miles north and they kept a watchful eye on the comings and goings at Dunadd. Drystan had observed frantic comings and goings but chose to remain a decent distance so as not to provoke any unnecessary conflicts and once everything appeared to calm down he rode south to meet with Aedan.

It was a harrowing approach to Aedan's camp, security was still foremost in Aedan's plans it would seem reflected Drystan when he was challenged for a third time. He was becoming ever more exasperated until he met the familiar face of Bors.

Arthur watched Aedan's men march away. His irritation at being, as he saw it, side-lined bubbled close to the surface. His now famous calm exterior was beginning to crack but his now notorious tetchiness was growing stronger. Bedwyr spent much of his time keeping the more mundane issues as far from Arthur as was humanly possible although the men were grateful for an alternative route to getting the instructions they needed. Bedwyr was respected, even liked, although his closeness to Arthur roused some suspicion. Despite this, however, Bedwyr was still considered a "decent and fair man," to deal with.

Arthur had been tasked with clearing the battlefield and ensure the proper rights of the dead on both sides were observed. It had been Arthur and Bedwyr's idea but Arthur had been surprised and disgruntled when Aedan agreed and given the task to Arthur to carry out.

He now sat on his mount overlooking the carnage that had, just a few hours before, raged across this field of death. He felt an almost overwhelming sense of guilt at the needless deaths. The spirits of the men who had passed over were, he could feel, streaming all about him. He could feel they're enmity but also their fear and respect towards a young man who had vanquished them. He also knew that there were men around him who perhaps would not have died if Arthur had come sooner. When he closed his eyes, he could see their faces, he could see the expressions of extreme sadness. These men were fathers, brothers and sons and they would never see their loved ones again. He would join them soon enough but death, he knew, would not be the end of his journey, but he hoped that it would be the end of pain. He sighed deeply, "we will meet again one day my brothers," he breathed, and they would share ale and break bread together and celebrate their lives and their accomplishments in this mortal life.

He was distracted from his thoughts by the sound of approaching horse hooves. His head jolted up and when his eyes focused he recognised a grim looking Gwallog coming toward him.

"Gwallog," Arthur called out flatly.

"Lord Arthur," Gwallog growled.

"And what are you doing here? I thought you would be away, wallowing in the glory of the approach to Dunadd."

"Rather than wallowing like you in misery," Gwallog retorted

Arthur's lips twitched and he grunted, "So, why has the gracious and magnanimous Lord given me this task to complete? I am… I was to be his second and yet… …."

Gwallog sighed, "I think our Lord wants to ensure you know your place."

"I know my place," Arthur grunted.

"That's for your father to determine."

"As is my safety I suppose."

"As long as you keep winning my friend you will be safe enough," Gwallog smiled.

"And if I don't?"

"That might be a problem but you are his son after all and you are a child of Beltane. Aedan is many things but he isn't someone who likes to tempt fate. He's a pragmatic man."

"So what do I do?"

"Absolutely nothing. Despite your doubts, you will be the second when Aedan is crowned. War will be upon us whether Aedan is crowned or not. If it isn't the Picts, it will be the Angles. You are needed my friend because without you Dalriada could well disappear into the mists of time."

"And what will your role be Gwallog?"

"I have a feeling it will be entangled with you."

"And my sister?"

"A fiction, it would seem. I was and indeed am expendable. It kept me close," he shrugged.

"And now?"

"I will stay with the man who best represents my family's…interests," Gwallog said sadly

"I'm sorry," Arthur replied.

"Don't be, I am better off than most."

Arthur looked at the man who had become yet another surrogate father to him. Part of him thought that Gwallog would have jumped at the opportunity to be with his mother. How religion and war tarnished so many lives. He could see the greying hair and the increasing lines on the man's face. He knew Gwallog was a great and loyal warrior, the speed of his swordsmanship was legendary but equally his parentage was noble. He was son of Lleenog of Lomond; he was of noble stock and he deserved better Arthur knew.

Arthur clasped his shoulder but said no more. Gwallog nodded and rode away towards Dunadd, his sadness clear to see.

Drystan and Bors spent a couple of hours in good natured company, drinking and eating before finally arriving at Aedan's tent. There they were joined by Gwallog who had just returned from the battlefield where he had left Arthur to prepare the dead for their journey into the immortal realm.

Gwallog welcomed the other two and they waited to be given access to Aedan's tent. Their wait was a long one but they spent the time regaling tales of bravery as well as discussions on the fate of King Conall and whether support for him was likely to come from the Picts although everyone was aware of the familial ties between Aedan and the Pictish royal house. "How is Arthur? Is he enjoying his job of field cleanser?" said Drystan to general laughter.

"Don't say that to him," grinned Gwallog, "judging by his mood when I left he might whip off your manhood with that sword of his."

"Ah, not happy then," said Bors.

"You are a man of understatement dear Bors."

Eventually Eochaid, the King's son, ventured out of the tent. "Gentlemen," he said quietly, my father, the Lord Aedan, will see you shortly. He is awaiting one other person, a person shall we say of interest and probably importance to what might come next in our adventure." The last few words were said with an amused glint in his eyes.

"And who might that be?" grunted Gwallog

"The dove of the church of course," smiled Eochaid.

"Crimthann?" Drystan said

"Well... Columba as he is known now," continued Eochaid.

"There's a surprise as I live and breathe," grimaced Bors.

"He plays his cards early, this dove of the church," grumbled Gwallog, "what's his game?"

At that Aedan appeared at the entrance of the tent. "His game?" he snorted. "We are about to start the game of power my friends. As I've said, he'll want to increase his influence, he'll want to keep Iona, and he will want to impress on me the importance of his mission and the power that he could wield on behalf of his God."

"The man's a fool," said Bors.

Aedan stared at Bors for a moment and chuckled. "My dear Bors, he is no fool, he is clever and devious, and as such, very dangerous. He's not like other priests of this Christian God. He combines their ways with ours. He adapts the old way and makes it… attractive to our people. He threatens all sorts of heinous things upon his enemies, and so some say, strange things have happened and his prophesies have come to pass," he shrugged.

Gwallog smirked, this he knew was superstitious nonsense, no one had powers like that but even he had to admit that it would be imprudent to mock or dismiss such things.

"He's no madman like Mungo Kentigern," continued Aedan, "and he is no pious prick like many of the Christians although, as you will see he does the pious prick thing extremely well. My friends, not only is he a holy man but a devious politician to boot."

"Let me slit the prick's throat," growled Bors.

Aedan laughed, "it may come to that my friend but an act of that magnitude could, and probably would, undermine everything we try to do here." Aedan clapped Bors on the shoulder.

Turning to the others, Aedan asked for reports about the safety of Dunadd and the surrounding areas. Drystan was convinced that all was subdued and there was no obvious underlying current of discontent from the locals he and is scouts had encountered.

No one knew the fate of Conall but the news was that the King had been moved from Dunadd before Aedan's forces could surround the fortress. "In all likelihood Lord," Drystan said "he has either been evacuated or his body has given out and he is dead. He was reportedly gravely ill after all."

Aedan nodded at this information and considered his next steps. "Drystan," he said after some moments, "take half of your men and make your way into Dunadd and if it seems safe make arrangements for me to ride in the day after tomorrow. Find out about Conall and report back. Take Bors with you and... ... ... oh, stop him from killing any priests will you?"

Bors' face coloured and Drystan laughed. "I will try to keep him calm Lord."

They bowed curtly, turned on their heels and strode away with Drystan's hand in the nape of Bors' back.

Once out of earshot Aedan beckoned Gwallog to follow him into the tent. Eochaid made to follow but Aedan shook his head and the disappointed prince dropped back, unsure what to do for the moment, and then decided to head off towards one of the camps' entrances in anticipation of Columba's arrival.

Inside the tent, Aedan sat on a rudimentary stool and offered Gwallog an opportunity to sit near him. Both men gave an audible grunt as they squatted down and both of them burst into laughter as they caught each other's eye. "The pains of age my dear friend," Aedan said.

"It'll be worse when we stand back up Lord," grunted Gwallog.

"Sad but true I'm very much afraid to say,"

Aedan offered Gwallog some ale and they sat together in amiable company for some time before Gwallog proffered, "Lord, may I speak freely?"

"That sounds ominous," said Aedan. "Do I need to watch my words as I will when our friend Crimthann joins me?"

"I sincerely hope not," Gwallog responded.

"So be it. What will you ask of me Gwallog?"

"It's about Arthur."

Aedan eyebrows arched slightly but there didn't appear to be any friction so Gwallog continued, "the boy speaks to me but to my sadness he is becoming more cynical and less inclined."

"And?"

"Well he doesn't understand why you have treated him as you have."

"And how is that?"

"He wants to share in your glory. He wants you to acknowledge him and his... abilities. The boy needs you to compliment him, he's not as old as he seems. You are his father and you mean everything to him."

Aedan sighed, "his actions at Delgon could have lost us the battle."

"But they didn't, he explained why he did what he did and you cannot criticise him for that. What he said and what he did was sound. You know this."

"And there was his allowing of Conall's men to escape."

"You're looking for a reason Lord. He's been proven right about that as well."

"And that's the fucking problem!" Aedan responded irritably.

They sat in silence for a while, Gwallog waiting for the tension to subside. He knew he had touched a nerve and Gwallog now realised, as if he didn't already know, that Aedan was feeling threatened by his young prodigy. Of course no one should be surprised, after all Arthur was now in the position Aedan had held and who was going to wager that history wouldn't repeat itself. Aedan slowly lifted his head and held Gwallog's gaze. "Why are you interested old friend?" he said coolly.

Gwallog detected a moment of danger and he considered whether he should rise to the bait. Aedan's question was provocative and he felt as if someone had slapped him across the face. He had been loyal to this man despite the constant breaking of promises. He swallowed hard and struggled to control his escalating anger. He grunted and allowed a smile to spread across his lips, "your sense of humour Lord, I find hard to understand even after all these years… In my experience, a man's reaction to threat is to do everything he can to make sure his worst fears come to pass. Why am I interested? Because I think we could all do with avoiding that."

Aedan nodded, "Yes that was uncalled for."

"Your son is not your enemy. And even if he were you should always keep friends close and your enemies closer."

Aedan's mouth twitched, "You're a wise man." Aedan sighed as the face of a guard poked his head into the tent, "Lord!"

"Yes?"

"The Monk has arrived."

"Thank you. Make sure he is given refreshment while I finish here with the Lord Gwallog."

The Guard nodded and his face disappeared.

"Lord Gwallog, we must bring this discussion to an end."

"Lord," Gwallog nodded

"Oh Gwallog, I almost forgot. I wanted to ask your opinion although, I must say, I think you have answered already."

"Lord?"

"Arthur's ability to be the second, of course. It looks like you might agree." Aedan said breezily, a broad smile spreading across his face. "Perhaps you can find our new friend Galahad to ride to Arthur and ask him to meet me in Dunadd in two days to meet the Dove and make arrangements for my coronation and his drawing the sword from the stone."

"I think," Gwallog responded with a smile "that would be an excellent idea."

Aedan nodded and Gwallog took his leave. Gwallog had walked in to act as Arthurs advocate but wasn't sure what, if anything, he had achieved. At least Arthur's position would be secured for now and that would please the Lady Crierwy. This family were a nest of vipers and he was playing with fire! He shook his head sadly. The workings of Aedan's mind left him…speechless. Yes speechless.

Raking his hand through his hair he glanced around the immediate area hoping to catch a sight of this Dove. Eventually, his eye alighted on a group of Christian priests, probably half a dozen of them, all tonsured and generally looking dishevelled even grubby. He stared a while until one of the Priests caught his eye and acknowledged him by bowing in his direction. Gwallog initial reaction was to ignore the man but good grace and the feeling that this person was, more than likely, the man Crimthann chose to acknowledge him with a nod. He turned away, called for his mount and walked off in search of refreshment and Galahad. He needed company he could rely on, his encounter with Aedan had left him unsettled and with a rather uncomfortable pain behind his eyes. He would have to dig out his tincture to settle the pain before it took hold. Even so, the thought of being a fly on the wall in a discussion between Aedan and Crimthann, the arch politicians, flooded Gwallog with feelings of rising nausea.

Arthur and Bedwyr arrived at Aedan's camp late in the evening. They were met by Drystan and Cai and ushered to a campfire where meat was being roasted and ale served from a large pottery jug. As usual Arthur drank little but for the first time in many weeks he felt the responsibilities of battle and pastoral duties of leadership slip from him. Even Cai was allowed to mercilessly rib him about his tardiness at Delgon. He tried his best to maintain a straight face but eventually dissolved into a fit of giggles that reminded all around him of how old he really was.

Arthur was painfully aware he had grown up far too fast, all those years under the protection of his mother when he so desperately wanted to be a warrior, seemed so long ago. The excitement of learning who his father was, then meeting his father and being warned by Muirgein of Aedan's motives, and of course, Myrddin's warning about all and sundry. What on earth happened? Where did that time go?

Bedwyr noticed Arthur's dip in mood and nudged him back into the here and now, "keep up," he quipped. Arthur smiled a response and leaned forward toward the centre of the circle. The discussion had moved onto politics and particularly the arrival of Columba in the camp and how long he had spent with Aedan. Eochaid who had quietly joined the circle was questioned at length but he, as well as Bors, had been kept away from the discussions and Gwallog, it was understood, had been seen leaving Aedan's tent before the "tonsured terror," had entered.

Cai turned towards Arthur and shouted from the far side of the fire, "what do you think young Prince?"

Arthur looked up and shrugged. He wasn't going to say any more but he could see all faces turned towards him and he realised that he had to proffer something. He grimaced but following an epic sigh he began, "well I suspect Columba would have played hard to get, trying to persuade Aedan of his usefulness to him. I imagine he will have told Aedan he could not countenance supporting him."

"And Aedan?" asked Bedwyr

"Will probably have reminded Columba that he doesn't have a choice. They will have haggled, Iona would have been discussed, Aedan may even have offered Columba an opportunity to be a chief advisor and a trip to Drumceatt. Of course Columba would say he is being bribed and it is all below him. All of it, posturing shit."

The circle had grown quiet, "I'm not sure we wanted to know that much," grinned Cai.

"Sorry I find it difficult to keep up with all this positioning and grasping for power," groaned Arthur.

"You're probably right," said Cai but will he acknowledge Aedan as King?"

Arthur laughed, "I should think so. Give it a couple of days and you'll find the Dove standing there and crowning our new King."

"You're becoming cynical cousin," said Drystan

"Maybe," Arthur responded flatly

"I just want to be out in the field giving the Picts a good thrashing," Drystan interrupted enthusiastically.

"And the Angles," rejoined Cai

"Definitely," smiled Drystan

"I'll drink to that," called Bors.

"Yeah," roared everyone.

"To Arthur's army!" called Bedwyr.

"To Arthur's army," they saluted

They all raised their cups and saluted the young man, "Thank you," he voiced soundlessly, his cheeks flushed with embarrassment but his chest swelled with pride although he felt strangely unenthusiastic. He had found the battle exhilarating but when he had seen the slaughter and was left to clear the battlefield, he felt sick to the stomach. Battle was like drinking too much ale, but the aftermath felt like the worst hangover imaginable. He suddenly wanted to be with his mother, foraging in the woods, helping to cook the food, enjoying the beauty and running around the lake. Would he ever have the opportunity to go back, he suspected not.

Three days had passed and Columba had visited Aedan every day. It was well known that Columba did not favour Aedan becoming King believing that Conall was the rightful ruler, vanquished, dead or otherwise but a story had spread through the camp that Columba had received dreams telling him that he should crown Aedan. Aedan wasn't sure if the stories were true but if they were it was probably, considered Aedan, a ruse dreamt up by Columba to justify agreeing to Aedan's accession to the crown. To add to the effect Aedan ensured the stories were embellished so that his men and camp followers were convinced that it was the work of Shamans or even this Christian God to influence the Dove! Of course, Aedan had also hired himself a Shaman to help him, just in case. You can't take risks with these things after all he reflected.

It was becoming clear now that Conall, if he was even alive, had departed Dunadd and had, it was rumoured, entered a Monastery. Aedan doubted that but he was, however, amused, even impressed at Columba's ingenuity.

The camp was struck, later than planned while Columba prevaricated, and the army meandered its way to the great Fortress of Dunadd. As they approached Aedan looked up at what was to be his new home and couldn't help be impressed at the strength of its walls and the vista's across the valleys stretching off in all directions.

The people were out in force to welcome the victorious army and Arthur could see his father relishing the adulation he was receiving. Aedan waved this way and that. The crowds became thicker the closer they came to the centre of the complex. After a final short sharp climb Aedan and Arthur found themselves face to face with the Dove himself.

"Lord Aedan," Columba bowed deeply. I am pleased to welcome you to your new capital.

"I'm grateful Lord Priest," Aedan acknowledged.

Columba blushed at the title and deference he was being shown although Arthur suspected it was all an elaborate act. He hated it but he shrugged his acceptance. It was as it was he supposed.

"Ah, and you must be the famous Prince Arthur," Columba oiled.

"Yes Lord Priest, it is a pleasure to make your acquaintance. I have heard so much about your work with the people of Dalriada."

"Creep," muttered Bedwyr

Columba shot Bedwyr a sharp glare but said nothing. "Why thank you," said Columba, "I'm sure your father is very proud of you. To be so successful whilst so young. I'm sure we'll hear a lot about you over the months and years. I fear there will be much to do."

"So it would seem," Arthur nodded.

Columba grunted, "There are a lot of preparations to be made for your Father's coronation. And it is God's Will that I will be there to guide your father to become a brave, wise and just king. And of course, to help guide you Lord Prince."

"I'm sure he will appreciate your guidance." smiled Arthur.

"Anyway," interrupted Aedan, "Lord Priest, I am anxious to discuss arrangements to make the ceremony successful for all my subjects. I know your interest is for my Christian subjects but my… subjects of the old way cannot be ignored. I'm sure you agree?"

Columba's jaw tightened but he stopped himself from protesting, "God, I hope, will give me the wisdom to love all of his people, believers and non-believers."

"I'm sure," smiled Aedan broadly.

"When shall we begin?" asked Columba

"No time like the present I say," said Aedan whilst sliding off his mount. "Gwallog and Galahad will accompany me. Step forward gentlemen," he continued. "Oh and I would be grateful if my men are fed?"

"Of course my Lord, my brothers are at your service."

Chapter 24

Gwenhwyfar

Aedan decreed that Arthur was to be made second before his own coronation. Walking to the summit of Dunadd he would be invited to place his foot in the foot step cut into the sacred stone and be offered the sword of Celeborn which rested on the sacred stone as a sign of his willingness to serve the new king, and as his deputy, to protect the people.

Aedan had made it clear that Arthur's ceremony should be low key which disappointed Arthur particularly when he learned more of the preparations for Aedan's coronation. Everyone, who was anyone, had been invited even Aed had been invited and accepted. Urien, Rhydderch and even Morcant were in attendance. To Arthur's delight, his mother Crierwy was invited. Arthur suspected that Aedan's motives had been political rather than anything fatherly. Crierwy's appearance was the perfect slight to Columba but dressed up in familial relations.

Gwallog had arranged for Arthur's mother to travel from Lyn Tegid to live on the shores of Loch Lomond now that her safety could now be guaranteed he had counselled against Cynon attending because of any potential confrontation with Morcant. Additionally, Urien had brought with him Taliesin.

But despite Arthur's disappointment, his chest still swelled with pride. In just two years he had been a servant of Crierwy's community, started his military training, successfully fought two engagements, made his reputation, and he was now someone to be feared. Also, despite misgivings on both sides, Aedan had made Arthur his second in command at the age of fifteen years.

He rested his eyes on his men who all bowed solemnly to him. With them stood Muirgein who nodded toward him with an enigmatic smile.

Next to her was his mother. His sister was attracting much attention, her beauty was unquestioned but her powers as a Priestess attracted, Arthur saw, men of influence. His jealousy rose as Morcant addressed her at length. She demurred and nodded sweetly.

Gwallog, noticing Arthur's sharp change of mood slid quietly up to him. "Arthur," he whispered, "your thoughts betray you and will betray you. That, my friend, is your sister. She is not someone to be besotted by although that is something she has an extraordinary talent for."

"I have no idea of what you speak," Arthur responded defensively.

"Of course you don't," smiled Gwallog,

"Why is she is no longer married?" Arthur deflected

He laughed, "not being Christian made things… complicated for Urien, not that he cares much. A means to an end and that is all."

"And you?"

"My friend, women like your sister are the pawns of power. My family were once considered useful allies and as such our relationship was thought to be advantageous but things change!"

"And what of your heart Gwallog?"

"I make do. But do not lose your heart to her, it is folly and she won't allow it. The pain of lost love even the love of that which is unnatural will be worst if it is allowed to fester. You will not like what I say, but my experiences should not be ignored."

"So what do I do? Arthur said carelessly

"Find a servant girl. One who is older than you. Someone who can teach you."

"I don't need teaching," Arthur retorted

"I'm sure you don't," he smiled, "but it does save embarrassment when the time comes."

It was Taliesin who called Arthur forward finishing a conversation that was becoming more and more awkward. Arthur straightened and stepped forward with huge relief. He was surprised that Colomba was not in attendance but he realised it was well known that he disapproved that someone of the old way was to inaugurate the prince. Not only that, but there were priestesses who also looked on and Colomba was certainly not willing to stand against them.

Arthur placed his foot in the foot print which was a good deal smaller than his foot and took the oath to serve the King, his knights, and his people. Taliesin anointed Arthur from the bowl and invited Arthur to pick up the sword. Arthur bent over and picked up Celiborn. He was surprised by its weight and he held it up to the light of the sun studying its blade and the intricate markings that adorned the top half of the blade. Slowly he lifted the sword and swung it above his head. His bond with his people was now complete.

He stared skyward and watched the flashing blade. All around him warriors and people roared their approval and Aedan strode forward, clapping Arthur on the shoulder before hugging him warmly. "Congratulations my boy."

"Thank you my Lord."

After extracting himself from Aedan he hurried over to his mother and hugged her warmly. He could feel her tears against his cheek and despite himself he couldn't help sob in return.

"I've missed you Mama."

"And I you. You're not my little boy any more," she said sadly.

"I will always be your little boy," he whispered.

She said nothing, instead she held him more tightly.

Aedan walked over to mother and son and bowed. "Lady Crierwy," he said with almost too much reverence.

"My Lord Aedan," Crierwy responded curtly. "I understand that you have a new wife."

Aedan's jaw clenched, "Not quite yet."

Crierwy nodded. "May I be the first to congratulate you?"

"You mock me Madame," Aedan responded

"You have become cynical my Lord," smiled Crierwy, "to what end?"

Aedan lips curled, "It's a question I'm already wrestling myself with."

Crierwy merely nodded, "I ask one thing Aedan."

"And that is?"

"You will treat our son as he deserves. He is a Prince after all and he is someone who ties our families together. He is no threat to you although how he has been treated thus far, you should count yourself lucky."

"And what do know of my treatment of him?"

"I'll always know more than you think," she responded flatly.

Aedan sighed. "You have asked this of me before and yet here we are and you feel you have to ask me again. Do you not think that our son is my world. And so would you have been Lady if you wished it."

Crierwy raised her eyebrow, "you may want to change history but it doesn't mean that it is so. Let's speak no more of this for it is but a fancy."

Crierwy turned away and beckoned Taliesin towards her. Taliesin bowed to Aedan and walked away from the top of the citadel and toward the feasting hall.

Two days hence the sun rose over the great Fort of Dunadd. Many hundreds

gathered along the route as Aedan climbed to the place of the stone and the footprint of fealty. He felt his age as he struggled to climb the steeper parts of the passage, as he breathed heavily under the weight of his garments.

The place was full of dignitaries. All those who had attended Arthur's ceremony were still there, joined this time by their consorts. Arthur's eye strayed across the crowds and he recognised the faces of great warriors and Kings. Two new people took Arthur's eye. A beautiful women stood alongside Rhydderch and his wife. Was this Igraine? He also noted Galahad standing next to a young woman who must have been Arthur's age. Could this be the cousin Galahad had spoken about. The woman or the girl was pretty, tall and graceful. Her simple gown fell from her shoulders as a waterfall. He detected the faint curve of her breasts. Arthur felt a rush in his groin.

He stared at the girl for some time until their eyes met. She flushed and dropped her eyes. She must have said something to Galahad because he looked up and glanced in Arthur's direction. He nodded briefly and clearly whispered something in return. She looked up again and this time nodded in his direction and smiled.

Arthur breathed deeply in quiet satisfaction but then looked ahead and this time caught Muirgein's gaze who was looking at him with mock amusement. She had seen him and it felt like he had somehow betrayed her. His heart pounded and his confusion grew.

He looked up at her again and Muirgein nodded her head towards Galahad's guest. Raising her eyebrows she seemed to be urging him on. He felt himself colouring and his face felt like fire and the only thing he could think of doing was shrug. He felt a tug to his arm and he spun round to find his mother's eyes staring at him. "Your sister's very attractive," she mused.

"Hmm, beautiful," said Arthur thoughtlessly.

"Beautiful," she repeated, "Yes, a sister of beauty needs to be protected by her brother and not fawned over."

Arthur froze, this was becoming a hugely embarrassing experience and all he could offer was, "I don't know what you're taking about."

"Indeed," his mother responded flatly.

Crierwy tucked her arm through Arthur's and she guided him towards where Muirgein stood. "Lady Muirgein," Crierwy began.

"Lady Crierwy," Muirgein responded, "it is a pleasure to meet with you."

Crierwy looked sceptical.

Muirgein laughed softly, "Lady Crierwy, you have nothing to fear or doubt about me. I hold no animosity towards you. I know how men treat women. My father is not or has not always been as honourable as he should have been, my mother would attest to that if she were still here. You are Arthur's mother and you are a Priestess of the Cauldron. We have much in common."

"I am sorry for your loss."

"Thank you."

"Arthur seems taken by you," Crierwy said bluntly.

Muirgein smiled, "I suppose I should be flattered if I were not his sister. I am twelve years older than him and he is an adolescent in need of becoming a man. That lass, over there might be someone he might practice on."

"I am his mother and don't need or want to hear of such things."

"Please accept my apologies I meant no offence."

"None taken," Crierwy laughed mischievously.

Standing beside them Arthur was mortified. His mouth opened and shut without any sounds coming forth. This was beyond embarrassing and even though he tried on a couple occasions to edge away, his mother was having nothing of it. If he had a sword or dagger he would happily have dispatched himself to the other world.

"Can I be plain with you?" Crierwy asked bluntly.

"Of course, I think," Muirgein responded sceptically.

"My Arthur is clearly infatuated with you," she continued

"Mother!" Arthur interjected with rising panic.

"He is?" Muirgein responded.

"Yes and you know it. Your ego must be well stroked."

"He's just a boy."

"Sister!" Arthur croaked.

"And he's your brother."

"And he's my brother," Muirgein repeated

" It's not unheard of," argued Crierwy

"No," Muirgein acknowledged tentatively "but I can assure you."

"So, can we agree, Arthur and you will not have any friendship beyond what is considered appropriate."

Muirgein flushed, "you have nothing to fear from me. But if I might say, shouldn't you be talking to him?"

"I fully intend to."

Muirgein had been shaken by this surprising turn of events but was now beginning to pull herself together and feeling more in control of her senses. She looked at and studied Arthur before teasing him with a "good luck."

Crierwy gave Muirgein a withering look but by now Arthur had placed his head in his hands. "Have you quite finished, perhaps you could just kill me next time."

After what felt like an eternity, Crierwy gently cupped Arthur's chin and lifted it up until his eyes met hers. I'm sorry Arthur, you've had precious time to grow up and your body is growing faster than your brain."

"As all men," chirped in Muirgein.

Crierwy ignored that although she knew it to be true, "your desires cannot be directed towards your sister no matter how beautiful, how mysterious or, indeed, powerful she is."

It was Muirgein's turn to be embarrassed and feel flattered. "Thank you," she muttered.

"Muirgein is a grown woman who can guide you but not lead you. So stop your silliness and find someone more your age and who is of noble birth, someone to explore love and sexual experiences together."

Arthur could only stare at his mother, his jaw dropping alarmingly. His world was spinning, his mouth dry. He felt as if he had been stripped bare in front of everyone and paraded through the streets. As he stood there dumbstruck tears began to prick his eyes. Suddenly the arms of both women were around him.

Eventually Arthur could hear Bedwyr's muffled voice as he gradually surfaced from the many arms that stifled his very breathing. Bedwyr cleared his throat and asked if Arthur might be escorted to join the coronation procession. With relief Arthur almost sprinted away from his mother and sister who simply glanced at each other and strode away arm in arm.

"What was that about?" questioned Bedwyr

"I'd rather not say but please never leave me alone with older women," Arthur grunted.

"As you wish."

"I do wish it, I really do."

They gathered in the small courtyard area where the ceremony would take place. Both Columba and Taliesin stood together, the tension between them was palpable. Everyone knew Aedan was of the old way and Columba hated him for it and he certainly mistrusted this usurper as Columba considered him. But Columba was no fool and as he stood there covered in an old cloak that covered his tonsure he realised that being there to officiate even with a heathen like Taliesin was a major success for him. What gnawed at him was whether he got what he wanted or whether it was Aedan who had got what he wanted, acceptance of the Church.

The ceremony took the same format as that of Arthur's. Aedan waived his sword towards the north, east, south and west over the marshy land that surrounded the Fort of Dunadd. Aedan looked out at the River Add stretching out on two sides. He could see the sea on the horizon, the sea he would cross shortly to finish the job he had started, to be the King of an independent Scottish Dalriada.

As Aedan received the adulation of the crowds and the respects of his fellow kings he eventually felt the hand of Columba slip into his. Aedan's belief in prophesy and his uncertainty of the power of the Christian God prompted him to ask about his fate and that of his children.

"Make no mistake, Aedan," said Columba quietly, "but believe that, until you commit some act of treason against me or my successors, none of your enemies will be able to oppose you. For this reason you must alert your sons, as they must pass on the warning to their sons and grandsons and descendants, so that they do not follow evil counsel. For whenever it should happen that they do wrong to me or to my kindred in Ireland, the scourge that I have suffered from the angel for your sake will be turned by the hand of God to deliver a heavy punishment on them. Men's heart will be taken from them; their enemies will draw strength mightily against them."

"Your threats stand for nothing priest," a rattled Aedan responded fiercely. "Don't take me to be a man wracked by fear and superstition."

"Are you willing to risk it." smirked Columba.

Aedan hissed dangerously but Columba held his ground. "I tell you now your sons will not follow you on this throne. They will die in battle and your glories will have to be won alone."

Aedan snorted and stalked off, his face was like thunder. Both Arthur and Bedwyr witnessed the confrontation but neither had heard anything. Arthur was troubled but his senses were still well and truly scrambled from what had happened barely an hour earlier. Bedwyr turned to his friend, "come on let's feast, the night is young and there is fair game to be had."

"Fair game? Not you as well."

"What?" shrugged Bedwyr in obvious confusion.

The Feasting Hall was a heaving mass. At the top table a grim faced Aedan sat next to his new wife to be, Igraine. Arthur was sat with his family from both of his mother's and father's side. To Arthur's left was Muirgein and to his right Galahad and his guest and then a man he knew well, Collen who was supposedly the girl's foster father.

"Are you talking to me?" chided Muirgein.

"After what was said before? I never want to speak to you again."

Muirgein laughed, "go on with you, your mother cares for you and your virtue."

"You make fun of me despite how I feel."

There was a long pause, "I am your sister, if I weren't, that might change things but I am. I am a fancy, I am not what you think and I could never make you happy. For what it matters, I'm a free spirit, I will never be caged and I would hurt you time and again."

"I don't think that's true."

"No Arthur, I am your sister and you will never lay with me," she said assertively. "Can we please perhaps enjoy the evening and move on?"

Muirgein waited several moments before Arthur grudgingly nodded. "Good, that's a welcome relief. Now…" she grinned, "let's see what we can do to help you with your adolescent needs."

"Galahad's cousin seems very…nice."

"Nice," she repeated, "goodness you have a long road ahead of you."

"What?"

"Never mind," Muirgein groaned, "have you introduced yourself yet? she enquired.

"Well, um, ah no," he stuttered.

"Well then little brother, time to grow up and be brave."

"I am brave," Arthur protested.

"That may be true but you're not going to skewer her, well not like that anyway,"

"That's awful, you can't say that," he protested.

"Don't be such a prude," she laughed. "To approach a girl is an art that precious few men are able to do. Now, just talk to her."

"About what?" his voicing rising in panic.

Muirgein ran her hand down her face, "just introduce yourself, ask her who she is, ask her how old she is, how did come to be here? You know, small talk?"

Arthur looked at her blankly and Muirgein let out a huge sigh. "All right," she said suddenly and stood up.

"What are you doing?" he said sharply.

"Helping you."

"You're what? No absolutely not," he protested.

"You'll thank me later Brother, she's a pretty thing."

With that she pulled herself away from Arthur's grasping hands and sidled up between Galahad and the girl. She had met Galahad before and was in conversation with him immediately. Arthur could see that Muirgein was being introduced to the girl and they started with easy conversation. Then, to Arthur's horror, he could see his sister pointing at him. The girl, he saw, flushed a little. He swallowed hard glancing around him in search of help but none was forthcoming.

After a moment there was a scraping of chairs and Arthur found himself sitting between Galahad and the girl. Muirgein shuffled to the other side of Galahad. Galahad grinned at Arthur, "ah, Arthur, I don't know if you remember me mentioning my cousin Gwenhwyfar?"

"Yes I do," he tried to say nonchalantly.

"Well then, this, Lord, is my cousin, the Lady Gwenhwyfar."

Before Arthur could say anything, even if he were able, Gwenhwyfar offered her delicate hand and quietly said, "I am so very honoured to meet you Lord Arthur, I have heard so much about your military exploits. I should be so grateful if you could tell me about them." Gwenhwyfar leant in conspiratorially, "It's because I'm a girl that no one tells me anything. I can shoot a bow and arrow better than you, I'll wager."

"My...my sister gave me a list of questions I should ask," he stammered.

Gwenhwyfar laughed, "Let me guess, I am Arthur and you are, and how old are you?"

"Small talk?"

"Well I'm old enough and my name is Gwenhwyfar but you can call me Gwen. My great grandfather was Cunedda which makes me royalty too."

Arthur laughed, this Gwen had completely disarmed him. With some semblance of confidence returning he straightened and he flexed his neck muscles. "So you like to talk about battles and wars. Is there anything a little more trivial we can discuss?"

"Do you have a wife or are you to be betrothed?"

"Not yet, I don't think so. I mean, should I?"

"It's a simple question."

"Then, no," he said guardedly.

"Good," she smiled, "we don't need to rush or be expected to rush."

"No, I suppose not. I'm tempted to ask why you might even ask that?"

"Because you're attracted to me!"

"I am? Sorry, what I meant to say, how do you know?"

"Well you are aren't you?" she asked without expression.

"Any man would..."

"And you?"

Arthur could feel the blood rushing to his face, "Yes, of course. Yes."

"Good we've got that out of the way. Let's enjoy the evening.

The two youngsters fell into companionable conversation. Despite feeling uncomfortable talking about killing and battle tactics, Arthur started rearranging cups and plates to describe the engagements he had been involved with. Gwenhwyfar maintained a look of deep concentration and not a bit of boredom although she made absolutely sure that he kept to the point and didn't disappear into fancy.

She then enquired after his mother and sister and didn't appear to realise that Muirgein and Arthur were half siblings. She wanted to be a priestess of the cauldron and she made it quite clear she was determined to speak to both Crierwy and Muirgein before she left for home in Gwynedd.

Arthur described, at length, his induction into the Cauldron Cult and his being buried alive along with the great Myrddin. Arthur felt very much at ease with this Gwen and whilst he still felt strong urges towards Muirgein this girl he thought guiltily was her equal in many ways, not least they were very similar in personality.

When Gwenhwyfar started to talk of herself Arthur's eye was drawn to her figure and how her clothes clung to her. Yes she was young but Gwen was clearly already a woman and as he looked at his sister for a comparison and to the other woman in that hall he could see that she was beautiful with high cheek bones, a shapely mouth with full lips and a chin which showed a little puppy fat, and she was tall and her figure was that of a woman. Her face was a picture of calm but her demeanour cool. Nonetheless, her smile was quick and her voice quiet and sweet.

His attention was drawn back to her suddenly. She was staring deeply into his eyes. Her eyes were an emerald green and they sparkled from the light of the fires. He realised that she looked amused.

"What?" he said

"You were gone there. May I ask where you went and whether it was because I was boring?"

"No, absolutely not, something... ... caught my eye."

"Really?"

"It's... embarrassing," he admitted, "I was just looking at other..."

"Women?"

"Yes, I mean no. Not like that."

"Were you comparing me?"

"No, no of course not, well not that way,"

She ran her tongue over her bottom teeth and then smirked, "I suppose it's an age thing. Do I match up?"

"You're good at embarrassing me," he sighed.

"Good," she grinned.

Before they could continue, Aedan had raised himself from his seat. As always, Arthur noticed, he looked remarkably sober compared with the others on the top table. As Aedan stood, an immediate silence fell across the hall. When he spoke, Aedan described the campaign he had waged and he lauded all those who had stood by him. He saluted the dead and those who still lived. He made a special acknowledgment to Gwallog and for Cai's valour at Delgon. He moved on to his wife to be and praised her great beauty and then onto Arthur.

Arthur caught Gwenhwyfar's glance and smiled at her. To his delight she smiled back. He then caught Muirgein smiling at him. He nodded at her and looked away, his embarrassment complete. Gwenhwyfar whispered to him, "you love your sister perhaps more than you should."

He grunted, "maybe… once," he admitted, "the silly feelings of a boy but things have changed now." He looked at her steadily, "now I have feelings for another."

She smiled, "all in good time my Prince, I am not a deer to rut."

At that Arthur's jaw dropped and Gwenhwyfar eyes dropped to the floor and she stared at her feet,

"Stand up my boy," boomed Aedan's voice.

Arthur did so in almost relief and bowed to the audience. He nodded his thanks to his father who moved on to other matters.

It was a good twenty minutes when Aedan announced that he was to travel to Irish Dalriada to discuss his relationship with his Irish brethren, and to almost everyone's surprise he announced that Columba would accompany him. He added too that Columba would become one of Aedan's advisors to support the Christians in his country. Clever bastard, Arthur thought.

As the night drew to a close, Galahad and Collen decided to withdraw which meant Gwenhwyfar was compelled to leave too.

"Don't go," pleaded Arthur.

"I must," she said, "we are here for the week."

"We will meet each other again?"

"Yes, that would be… lovely. Promise me something," she said, more seriously, "don't beg anything of me, you are a warrior. I want you to be a man, not a boy. I'll search you out."

"If that is your will," he said with a tinge of disappointment.

She smiled, "you have nothing to worry about my Lord. I promise."

Arthur nodded and bowed. He took her hand and kissed it, "thank you for your company Lady."

"And yours," she responded.

Arthur noticed Muirgein and Galahad sharing a knowing glance although Collen seemed less happy. He shrugged inwardly, said goodnight to all of them and turned back towards his friends.

"About bloody time," said Cai and offered Arthur a drink.

Chapter 25

Greedy Eyes Look West

King Aethelric had drunk far too much ale, his hall was filled with song and stories of great exploits, Beowulf included. His storytellers were wondrously clever at capturing his men's imagination. The excitement came to a crescendo as Grendel was laid low by the muscled and clever warrior. There had been the odd dispute, a handful of fist fights but despite that the evening had been very good natured.

The food had been plentiful, the roasting meat had made the mouths of his warriors water and they had devoured the food with vigour. The beards of his followers dripped with fat and ale.

Aethelric, a portly, slightly rotund man, belched happily and slumped back into his high backed chair. His elbow rested on his knee whilst his thumb supported his chin and his index finger rested at the corner of his eye.

The island named by the Angles as Lindisfarena was a spectacular backdrop to the Angle camp. King Aethelric, in his mind's eye surveyed his lands. At last the kingdom of Northumberland was becoming a reality under his Kingship. Bernicia and Deira were in Angle control and it would only be a matter of time before the work of his predecessor, Ida, would be realised. It would be Aethelric who received the adulation of his people and he smiled in anticipation of his name forever revered throughout the history of this land. The idea of a single Germanic land that stretched from the lands settled by Hengist to the lands bordering those of the Picts, perhaps even farther north, would soon be a reality. A land so bountiful compared to the grimness of the Germanic plains that his people had settled for centuries would be his and his Saxon cousins for all time.

He gazed at the great fires in the centre of his hall and the smoke that rose like rope up through the hole in the thatched roof. It was a good start, yes, but there was much more to do. The Britons in the south had been pushed to the margins of Cornwall and the kingdoms of the Welsc. These Britons were now merely outsiders, he mused. The old peoples were defeated. He smiled at how easy it had been. Oh yes battles had been lost but invasion was always inevitable, after all they were the stronger, more superior people, even the women were too tough for these weaklings.

Now it was time to finish the work Ida had started and invade the puny peoples of the north, the Britons of Rheged and Alt Clut, the Scots of Dalriada and Lothian. They would be too powerful together so he would have to divide and conquer. It was a tactic that had already paid dividends. Yes, he thought, one at a time. The Britons were forever fighting among themselves and while they did so, he, King Aethelric would take full advantage. He would ensure that any potential alliance would be undermined. So circumstances dictated that the first moves were his to make.

"Cuffa? Hussa?" he called out into the darkness.

Two men stepped forward, "Yes Lord."

"Sit with me."

He waved to one of the serving girls and held out his drinking horn for her to fill. He beckoned his men over and invited them to hold out their cups. The two men shuffled over to him and readily accepted the ale before settling down to the side and slightly behind the King's throne.

Aethelric regarded the two younger men evenly, Cuffa was a bearded man with large muscled arms, a renowned warrior and feared by everyone who knew him. He was the man who stood tall and stoically at the centre of the Angle shield wall. His arms were heavily scarred his were his legs. A craggy face that had seen too many battles and a broken, slightly twisted nose that must have received a massive blow with either a shield boss or the butt of a sword. Cuffa had lost his front teeth many years past and his smile made him look almost maniacal. He had been told to keep his mouth shut so as to not frighten the children and the livestock. As a result he tended to mumble his words much to Aethelric's annoyance.

Hussa, on the other hand, was wiry, short blond hair and piercing blue eyes. His face was chiselled and he hardly any facial hair. Hussa always presented himself immaculately and… clean!

"Lord, how may we be of service?" asked Hussa

"What news from our scouts and that idiot cockroach Morcant?"

"Of course Lord, this is what we know," Hussa began "since Gwenddoleu's defeat at Arderydd, Aedan mac Gabran, Morcant's overlord, has defeated Conall and his sons in Dalriada and will be crowned any day if he hasn't already been so. It would seem that Rhydderch of Alt Clut, who we believe, will be the next King of Alt Clut, has come to some sort of arrangement with Aedan, and Urien is likely to follow."

"Urien is married to Aedan's daughter is he not?"

"No longer," mumbled Cuffa.

"Really? How interesting. Nonetheless," slurred Aethelric "they are beginning to come together then. How inconvenient." His insides twisted, had he missed his chance?

"I wouldn't be so sure, Hussa added, "Aedan is not trusted and the Picts are becoming aggressive since the death of Domelch, Aedan's wife. They are suspicious too that Alt Clut have imposed a new wife on Aedan."

"We must move soon," said Cuffa.

"Yes but when the time is right," Aethelric muttered grimly. "What of Morcant?"

"Nothing Lord."

"Little shit." Aethelric groaned as he stood up, belched loudly, much to the delight of those in earshot. "I'm stuffed and pissed," he announced, "I'm going to lie down on a bed rather than sleep here. I couldn't walk for a week last time." He turned to Hussa and Cuffa, "we will talk further in the morning, no make that afternoon, and start making the necessary plans so we can move quickly when we have to. Perhaps that toad Morcant will bring us news."

The following evening Aethelric called for a map produced by both Morcant's men and his own scouts. "Anything else we should know?" he asked.

"Sources tell us," said Cuffa, "that Aedan and this Priest of Iona intend to travel to Ireland for a council to discuss alliance with the Irish King Aed. They say he could be gone for weeks."

"Oh and who will be left to rule over Dalriada in his absence?"

"Some child," laughed Hussa.

"Child?"

"Yes, a Prince… Arthur, I think?"

"Arthur? Why haven't we heard of him before?"

"He is fourteen, or fifteen, and he is only in his second season, there is nothing to worry about Lord."

"Hmm, really?" he murmured. "Is Morcant saying this?"

"He doesn't know."

The King nodded, "you are probably right but it might be prudent to find out more about him."

Aethelric sank unsteadily to his knees and spread the cloth map across the floor. "We could travel to the north to the Second Wall into Alt Clut and draw the shit out."

Cuffa and Hussa nodded, "about one hundred miles from here," said Cuffa.

"As the crow flies," mumbled Hussa.

"We will have to cut across Gododdin territory," said Cuffa.

"Yes," Aethelric said slowly, "before we do anything we will need to sound them out."

"Might the Gododdin alert Aedan?"

Aethelric puffed out his cheeks and sighed deeply, "so we will have to wait on Morcant."

"We could sail around," offered Cuffa.

"That'll surprise him," laughed Hussa.

"And madness," grunted Aethelric "anyway it's time our friend Morcant did something useful. Incidentally," asked Aethelric, "what news from that slippery toad?"

"What, besides trying to win his lands back?" laughed Hussa.

"He's a treacherous little shit," remarked Cuffa.

"I'm fully aware of that, King Ida would be absolutely incandescent if he knew we were even speaking to the man."

"So why are we?" said Cuffa

"He's a useful idiot," Aethelric responded simply. "He tries to ingratiate himself with everyone but he doesn't have allies, just us and he's frightened of us. To survive he needs others to stand up to us for him and he can't rely on anyone. Let's be clear, it is money and influence that drives Morcant, there's no honour in him." He paused thoughtfully and continued, "Hussa, my friend, make arrangements. Let's be ready,"

"Of course it will be done," Hussa said stiffly.

"And Hussa."

"Yes Lord?"

"Beware of this boy…Arthur. We probably think he is a no one but Aedan has chosen him as his second and we can't ignore that. This Aedan is known for his cunning and that frightens me. And feeling frightened is something I don't like."

There was a moment of silence between the three of them. Then Aethelric nodded gruffly and pointed toward the feasting hall, "perhaps we can have some Ale and ponder things further. I could also do with a piss!"

It had been a number of days since their discussion and subsequent over indulgence with the King. Hussa and Cuffa sat with their captains around a small fire as the sun began to set over the Northern Sea. There had been no news and they were growing restless. Now they waited for Aethelric to join them to discuss their preparations and they knew he would not be happy.

Aethelric was growing more uneasy. His sources had informed him that the Gododdin were becoming suspicious of the Angles and there was rumour that they might ally with the western alliance. Angle dominance of first Deira and then Bernicia had unnerved the Gododdin despite the all too frequent assurances given to them by Aethelric. Aedan's accession and his ambition had seen the development of an unbroken anti-Angle land bridge stretching from East to West. His mood had not improved when the news was brought to him that Morcant was attending Aedan's coronation and marriage to an Alt Clut princess.

The lack of concrete intelligence had made Aethelric uncertain and his prevarications had begun to unsettle his warriors. Aethelric needed to be sure he wouldn't be facing every British kingdom as one. This lack of intelligence had delayed Hussa's enterprise and as time went on the level of risk and direction needed had to be reassessed. Speed, everyone knew, was paramount and a laboured march would give the British time to prepare.

Aethelric's anger at his own uncertainty and how he should proceed against the backdrop of accelerating constant change was the primary reason for calling this gathering. Aethelric wanted answers but no one, even Hussa, wanted or dared deliver bad news and unless something significant changed everyone knew it was unlikely that they would march.

As the amount of ale being consumed increased the more sombre everyone became. Hussa stood and hurled his cup across the camp. FUCK, he roared. He stormed towards the guards at the entrance of the camp with no intention than to dress down any poor soul who had the misfortune to cross his path.

Luckily for everyone, his attention was drawn to two horsemen galloping towards the entrance of the camp. Hussa marvelled at the horsemen's control as they were challenged by Angle guards. They must be Britons he concluded, if only Angles could ride like that, they could advance so much more quickly. He sighed but he consoled himself that Angle foot formations and a strong shield wall would always carry the day against a rabble of undisciplined and wild horsemen.

Their strong accents floated on the wind which confirmed that they were Britons, probably part of Morcant's scouting network. That man was a piece of work, a lying cheating bastard who Aethelric appeared to trust. Hussa considered this to be folly and he would much prefer to slit the little shit's throat.

The horsemen were uttering Hussa's name and demanded they speak to him. He stood far enough away to be unnoticed but close enough to hear the conservations being had. Initially he had little or no inclination to speak to these men but the mention of Aedan mac Gabrain and Dalriada was enough to peek his interest. Rolling his shoulders he stepped forward, "I am Hussa," he boomed, "what is your business? State it now and be gone."

The older of the two horsemen turned his gaze towards Hussa and held his stare for some moments. "You are Lord Hussa?" he said doubtfully.

"I am," Hussa responded patiently, "my men will vouch for me."

He glanced at the sentry, who nodded in return.

"Very well. I am Ruairdri, I am Morcant's man and I bring news from him."

"Yes I recognise your name Master Ruairdri," Hussa acknowledged, "what message do you bring and please say it slowly, your accent is... difficult to understand," he said raising his eyebrow.

Ruairdri's jaw tightened at the perceived insult and then shrugged, "of course," he said with exaggerated slowness.

"Do hurry up man," snapped Hussa whose notorious lack of patience was beginning to fray.

Ruairdri noted the threatening change of tone, he stifled a smile, nodded and continued, "Lord Hussa, the Lord Morcant sends greetings. My Lord has asked me to tell you he is returning to Dun Eidyn having attended the coronation of his overlord King Aedan. He wishes the Lord Hussa to know that Aedan will be travelling to meet with his Irish brethren at Drumceatt on the island of Ireland. He will be away from the great Fort of Dunadd for a number of months."

"Will he now," said Hussa flatly.

"My Lord has also asked me to inform you, because he felt you would be interested, that the Lord Aedan has left his daughter, the Lady Muirgein, to administer his land and his son Arthur has been given command of his army under the guidance of the Lord Gwallog. The Lord Morcant advises that the British forces are dispersed and Dalriada's eastern borders are without defences. The Lord Morcant believes this will remain the case until Aedan's return. Lord Morcant believes you have an opportunity to damage any potential British alliance now before they have time to conclude any agreement."

"Why travel to Ireland before agreeing any alliance?" asked Hussa

"My belief, Lord, is that Aedan believes he can act independently without Irish interference. He will also have more influence." responded Ruairdri.

"He is a man blinded by power," smiled Hussa.

"Yes Lord Hussa."

"Excellent news my friend. What trail will you or the Lord Morcant recommend to us?" asked Hussa.

"We believe that the Gododdin are inclined towards the rising power of Dalriada and even though they fear Aedan's motives they trust you less. So the Lord Morcant believes you should avoid their lands and skirt towards the south, marching eastward before driving north along the borders of Alt Clut."

"Hmm, and how far is that?"

"Some one hundred and twenty miles?"

"A week's march."

"Yes Lord but most of it will be beyond Aedan's gaze so you could reach the borders of Dalriada before any significant arrangements for defence can be made. You will deal them a heavy blow and split the Britons. Defeating Dalriada will surely push them towards an accommodation with you or," Ruairdri continued, "give you time to gather an army of invasion while they are weak."

Hussa nodded, his lips curling into a smile. "I was going to send you away," he continued, but in view of your news, perhaps you might appreciate some refreshment?"

"Thank you, you are too kind Lord." replied Ruairdri with exaggerated precision.

Hussa rolled his eyes and instructed the guards to find someone to look after the horses and to feed their tired guests. He nodded toward the two Britons and returned to where Cuffa and his Captains sat.

They watched him approach with some anxiety but to their surprise Hussa was smiling. "Gentlemen. I don't care what it takes, who gets hurt, I want five hundred men ready to march with provisions for a week the day after next."

"How so?" asked Cuffa confused.

"We have the intelligence we need and news the Lord Aethelric has been waiting for," Hussa announced.

"That old goat Morcant has sent word I assume," mumbled Cuffa with a thin lipped smile, "and not before time."

Chapter 26

A Mother's Advice and a Sister's Respect

The great Fort of Dunadd felt suddenly very empty after all the guests had left. The little pathways leading down to the lower gates were strangely subdued. Arthur's temper, following his father's decision to leave his sister Muirgein to administer his lands and Gwallog to oversee him, was close to boiling over. It was only because of Bedwyr's intervention that Arthur had resisted confronting his father. Even Columba had taken the young man aside to point out that he was still young and had much to learn. Worst still, Gwenhwyfar had not spoken to him, in fact he hadn't even seen or heard from her since the Coronation banquet. He'd seen Galahad but nothing had been said.

The day after the banquet, Arthur had gone for his run hoping to run into Gwenhwyfar. He was very much aware of the warning she had given him not to fawn after her and to leave the next contact to her. Why was it so hard? He had met so many beautiful women but despite being a hero they all seemed to make it so hard for him. He had watched Cai grab the servant girls who, on the whole, had been all too very willing to oblige his wandering hands. What was he doing wrong?

Arthur cut a very gloomy figure as he watched Bedwyr, Drystan and Cai taking the Men of Manau through their paces. He watched the horsemen move in perfect harmony together, it reminded him of the murmurations that offered a majestic spectacle from the top of Dunadd. The dance moves taught just two years before were, being transferred to a field filled with horses and were a joy to watch. He thought of the Sarmatian knights in whose shoes they were following and how the great Cunedda had re-established them in Manau. He knew the Sarmatians and Cunedda would approve of what Arthur was building. But he then groaned at the thought of

Cunedda being an ancestor of Gwenhwyfar. He hurled a stone at a nearby rock. Where was she?

It was some hours before Arthur permitted his men to rest. He decided to visit his mother who had chosen to stay at the Fort until Gwallog was in a position to take her to Loch Lomond. He wondered slowly until he reached her lodgings. His stomach was in knots, it felt almost painful. He must be sickening with something. The only way he could find any relief seemed through running.

The place his mother was staying was a surprisingly large structure. Apparently it had been Dunchaid's residence before Delgon. He stood on the threshold for a few minutes wondering if he should share his feelings with his mother. He was about to turn away when the door flap flew open and found himself face to face with Taliesin.

"Arthur! What a pleasure to see you my boy," he said warmly.

"My old friend," Arthur responded with surprise. "Why do I find you here?" he asked.

"To visit your mother of course. I have not seen her since you were both at Lake Tegid."

"You miss her?"

"Of course, your Mother will always be the love of my life," he shrugged.

"Really? Does she know?"

"Of course."

"Why are you not… with her?"

Taliesin sighed, "because there are more important things. I am a follower of the Cauldron and your mother is a Priestess of the Cauldron. We have other responsibilities. Our lives have taken different paths. It's all part of growing up I'm afraid my boy."

"Do you wish it wasn't so?" Arthur asked

"Don't we all," he shrugged, "there's no point considering that question my boy, it is as it is. Your mother's life belongs to the Cauldron, she guides many and there is no room for lovers."

Arthur considered this for a moment. So many people, he was beginning to realise, were unable to have what they wanted. Taliesin, his mother, Gwallog and even Muirgein, he supposed even Aedan to a certain extent. He was married to Domelch when he was Arthur's age and he wanted Arthur's mother but could not keep hold of her. Would he suffer the same fate? His stomach knotted even tighter.

Taliesin regarded him closely, "what ails you Arthur?" he eventually asked.

"Nothing," Arthur lied

"Really?"

"Nothing of relevance anyway,"

"My advice to you my boy is to confide in your mother, she is wise and whatever it is that pains you she will help you find solace. You must trust people sometimes, reach out and ask for help. People are generally good and will always help if you reach out. You learned this as a member of the Cauldron."

Arthur grunted. "Trust? Who?" he said.

"No one can tell you that my boy. You trust Bedwyr, Drystan, Cai, Gwallog and your uncle Cynon don't you?"

"Yes' Arthur said tentatively.

"And me?"

"Of course," Arthur said defensively.

Taliesin laughed, "don't be defensive my boy. Just trust your judgement."

Arthur looked sceptical and Taliesin shrugged. "Well, anyway, I am detaining you, go in and see your mother; she will be delighted to see you."

Taliesin clapped Arthur on the shoulder and turned towards the lower slopes of the Fort.

Arthur watched Taliesin walk down the slope until he was out of sight. He sighed, turned, and stepped inside. It was dark and it took him a moment for his eyes to adjust. There was a sweet smell of spices emanating from the centre of the residence and he made his way towards the scent.

"Mother?" he called

"Is that you Arthur my lovely," came a response.

"Yes of course it is Mama."

His mother skipped forward her arms wide and welcoming, "come in my darling boy," Crierwy said with undisguised delight.

Despite his embarrassment at his mother's affection, he could fall into Crierwy's arms. They stood in each other's embrace for what seemed an age. Arthur had tried, on a couple of occasions, to pull away but his mother would not let go. She was surprisingly strong, he reflected, and so he acquiesced.

"Come," she said eventually and beckoned to him to sit next to her. "I am so pleased to see you, I thought you would be too busy to see me."

"I will always find time to see you," he lied. "I'm just so sorry it's taken so long to see you again. I never intended it should be so long."

"I hope you're not too embarrassed of me," she chided.

"Of course not," he lied again.

Crierwy sighed deeply and her demeanour became melancholy and her eyes moistened. She composed herself and smiled weakly, "it's not your fault Arthur. We live in violent times and someone of your intelligence and talent for battle could never remain with his mother.

"Is it what you wished for? Me staying with you I mean," he asked.

"I suspect all mothers do," she responded.

Arthur smiled but before the conversation could continue Crierwy changed the subject. "It's the way of world my boy. Now Arthur let us talk of something else. Tell me what has happened in the two years since we lived on Lake Tegid."

Arthur was relieved to talk about other things and spoke enthusiastically of his training, his falling out with Cai, the Battle of Arderydd, his part on the Glein and finally his battle exploits at Delgon. He also blurted how he had almost, fatally, fallen out with Aedan. His mother was at once overwhelmed at her son's deeds and horrified at the dangers he had experienced.

Again tears welled in Crierwy's eyes. Arthur reached over and held her hands in his. It was easy to forget how much had happened in those years they were apart. He had left as a child with a child's emotions and now he was a man but probably still with a boy's emotions. His head dropped and he looked at his lap.

Crierwy could see there was a sadness in Arthur and she gently cupped his chin and raised up his face so that she looked directly at him. "You're sad Arthur?"

Arthur said nothing but then nodded, "I shouldn't be burdening you, you have already paid a big enough price." He started to rise but Crierwy grabbed his arm.

"I don't quite know what you mean by that but one thing you must know. No matter what and when, as a parent, you are always there for your child. It is something you will find out if you are blessed with children."

"Not all parents," Arthur protested

"Indeed not," Crierwy admitted, "some will always find reasons not to take responsibility. To have a child is an adult's greatest responsibility. You can always seek solace in me, speak to me, ask for advice no matter how embarrassing that might feel. Remember Arthur I will never judge you, to err is to be human."

"Thank you Mama," Arthur smiled meekly.

"But before you tell me your worries, I must apologise to you."

"Apologise?" he repeated.

"I embarrassed you in front of your sister. I was wrong. I wanted to protect you not humiliate you."

Arthur blushed, "by all the Gods and Goddesses, please Mama don't ever do that to me again, I wanted to dig a hole and jump into it," he blustered.

"Yes, I know, as I say, I'm sorry." Crierwy soothed, "I have also apologised to Muirgein."

"You did! What did she say?"

"Let's say we reached an understanding. We… understood each other," she continued tentatively.

"Good grief," said Arthur, "I think I'll ask no more." After a couple of beats they laughed,

"Am I forgiven?" asked Crierwy.

"Of course," he replied, "but no more eh?"

They continued to talk about all and sundry until Arthur had prepared himself for the reason of his visit.

"Mama, I need your advice."

"Is this about Muirgein?"

"You'll be pleased to know, no. I can't deny I am furious that Aedan has appointed her ruler in his stead but that's something different."

"Is it someone else?"

Arthur coloured up and nodded, "yes."

"Ah, is this the pretty girl you were deep in conversation with the other night?"

"Gwenhwyfar, yes."

"Have you…"

"No we haven't although… I want to," he admitted, barely above a whisper.

She smiled, "I see, I suppose it is to be expected. So what troubles you?"

"Well she said that I wasn't to… chase her but she hasn't contacted me since. I just, just," he stuttered. "I just don't know what to do. And I have… feelings."

Crierwy eyebrow arched, "feelings? What kind of feelings, can you describe them?"

"I am in pain. My insides are inside out, my stomach feels knotted, I struggle to sleep, to eat. I can't concentrate on anything, nothing feels…"

"Important?" Crierwy interjected.

"Yes, important."

"I suppose many would say that it is an illness you are suffering." Crierwy said kindly. "It is an illness that sadly too many people, if not all people before you have suffered from. You are in love my boy or perhaps in lust!"

"But what about her? Why does she ignore me?"

"She's ignoring you?"

"She doesn't visit me," he protested.

"Some women need space, perhaps it's a test. A woman may need time to decide whether they want a relationship. If that is the case you should consider yourself lucky that you have met a woman of maturity. What did she actually say?"

"She said and promised that she would make contact with me and I was not to chase her."

"My guess is she wants you to act like a grown up. If she wishes to see you again it must be as equals and that her feelings for you mirror yours. All I can say to you is be patient. Look Arthur, I know this is hard but if this is meant to be, it will be."

Arthur's eyes lowered again, "I suppose I will have to be satisfied with that," he murmured.

Crierwy again lifted Arthur's chin despite him trying to turn away, "look at me Arthur, I know it's hard but you have a responsibility to your men, I have a feeling we will all need you before too long. Be with them, spend time with Bedwyr and Drystan and even Cai if he has become more mature and less aggressive. When you are next facing an enemy on a faraway field it will be the love and loyalty of your men that will protect you and not the hope of bedding a woman. Rest assured, this Gwenhwyfar will play a significant part in all our futures.

A more light-hearted Arthur walked briskly to where his men were barracked and headed toward his small hut and lay on the straw covered cot. He breathed deeply, and for the first time in a couple of days he closed his eyes and let sleep take him.

Almost immediately, however, Bedwyr entered casting back the door covering and allowing the late afternoon light shine brightly in. "For fuck sake," he groaned, I have just this minute lain down.

"Sorry Lord."

"What is it? And don't call me Lord, Bedwyr, how many more times? Oh and shut that bloody curtain my bloody eyes are boiling." he remonstrated.

"You're wanted Arthur?"

"Who?" he moaned

"The Lady Muirgein, Arthur."

Arthur lifted his head, "really? Why?"

"I don't know, but freshen yourself up, the Lord Gwallog will collect you anytime now."

"Oh great," he fell back.

"Are you all right?" Bedwyr asked.

"I will be," Arthur murmured.

"Do you need company?"

Arthur considered the words of his mother and marvelled at how quickly the opportunity to bond with friends had presented itself. He nodded cheerfully, "yes my friend but maybe later. Some ale with friends will be what's needed me thinks. I have a feeling I'm going to need my wits about me for the next hour or so."

"I can help there my friend. We'll speak later."

Arthur waved Bedwyr off. He put his hands behind his head and thought of Gwenhwyfar. Well why not he thought she was something to admire after all. I'm in love apparently, he thought, it was painful for sure but exciting too.

As he drifted into a daydream the curtain across his door was flung back plunging his lodgings into searing brightness. "Bedwyr told me you were here," boomed Gwallog cheerfully.

"Are you here to assassinate me or blind me? Give me strength."

"My Prince, the Lady Muirgein summons us," smiled Gwallog

"Summons us," repeated Arthur, "I have swapped one King with a Queen and me the second for what it's worth."

"Ah!" Gwallog said, "you're unhappy with the arrangements?"

"You summarise my position succinctly as usual," Arthur said sarcastically.

"I'm not here to defend your father or your sister for that matter."

"Yes I know," Arthur conceded grudgingly.

"He believes you too young, what else can I say?" Gwallog shrugged.

Arthur said nothing, instead he levered himself off his bed. He grasped Gwallog's offered hand and allowed himself to be pulled upright. "You know I have nothing against you," Arthur confided.

"Glad to hear it, I have tried to protect your mother, your sister and yes even you. I am not your enemy Arthur and nor is your sister. She loves you and wants you to be safe. You know this and you know why.

Arthur nodded and beckoned Gwallog to lead the way towards where Muirgein was waiting for them. They walked side by side in silence. Arthur was deep in thought, his emotions bouncing from juvenile angst for being overlooked and undervalued and feelings he now realised were yearnings for Gwenhwyfar.

As they walked passed the many faces, he still envied the people that milled about him going about their business who seemingly had no worries or responsibilities except for getting through the day. He sighed loudly, and with each step he dreaded having to speak to his sister.

They arrived at the gates of the royal residence at the peak of Dunadd where two guards acknowledged them and a third beckoned them to follow him to where Muirgein, Galahad and Bors were already waiting. Arthur was surprised and a little irritated that whatever needed to be discussed had to involve so many people. They crossed the room and were announced rather pompously.

"Ah my dear brother and Gwallog. Thank you for coming." Muirgein welcomed them effusively.

"That was all rather formal," grunted Gwallog.

Muirgein smiled broadly, "It'll settle down I'm sure. Come let's sit, the round table has been made ready."

"What of the others, I assume there will be others?" jibed Arthur.

"Soon enough," Muirgein responded, "I wanted your thoughts about some information that has just been delivered by one of Morcant's men."

"Morcant?" growled Gwallog, "What is that treacherous shit up to?"

"That's rather cynical Lord Gwallog," Muirgein said slowly.

"And for good reason," Gwallog responded, "anything he says is poison. Whatever he's involved in, there is always treachery of some kind."

Muirgein sighed deeply. "Fine' she said eventually, "I am fully aware of your history but before we dismiss anything out of hand, any information given to us, for whatever reason, we should still consider possible consequences for not acting upon it."

"Lady Muirgein is right," Galahad said, "we must consider the information first."

Bors nodded in agreement as did Arthur.

"Very well," rejoined Gwallog, "but don't let that man's orificial sunshine blind you."

Arthur couldn't help laugh at that.

"Good!" affirmed Muirgein with a slight smirk, "Bors, if you would, please share with us the information you have in your possession?"

Bors cleared his throat and sat forward clasping his hands in his lap. "We have been made aware that a party of Angles, possibly five hundred men, set out from the east coast of Bryneich near Lindisfarena heading west along the borders of the Gododdin. Our informant has told us that they are intent on turning north with the intention of raiding our eastern borders."

"Why now?" asked Galahad.

"That's obvious," said Muirgein, "we have been involved in civil war and the Lord Aedan has gone to Ireland leaving a girl and her baby brother in charge. If you were them, wouldn't you?"

"That makes sense," said Gwallog "but why would Morcant warn us? I don't understand it, there must be something in it for him... some advantage," he said sceptically.

"Because he fears us as well as the Angles," said Arthur quietly. "That man probably killed my grandfather and now he wishes to ingratiate himself with us in the event of our expansion through Manau. The Picts too will be a threat to him and the Gododdin are finally recognising the dangers of having Angles for their neighbours. "Our self-styled Prince Morcant is running out of friends." added Galahad.

"So do we take this seriously?" asked Muirgein.

"We cannot afford not to," responded Arthur.

"The King must be told," interrupted Gwallog.

"Is there time?" countered Arthur, "and if we are wrong how will he react?"

"He will be unhappy at best," said Galahad, "on the other hand if we go against a force larger than ours and lose..." Galahad didn't need to finish the sentence; they all knew that the choices before them were impossible.

Arthur cleared his throat, "I propose we protect our eastern borders. If we were to lose, which we won't, Dunadd is defensible and messages can be sent out to Aedan to return with his men. They have five hundred men, there aren't enough of them to make a serious land grab. Their only purpose is to threaten, undermine and separate. If they succeed it will embolden the Pictish tribes and will no doubt lead to an alliance that will seek to carve us up. Our success, however, will persuade our neighbours to either remain passive or join with us. Only then will we succeed in pushing their kind back."

Gwallog snorted but said nothing. Galahad glanced at Bors but there was no disagreement. "Good," said Muirgein, "we will discuss this with Bedwyr, Cai and Drystan to agree the next steps in the morning. Agreed?"

Everyone nodded

"Arthur," Muirgein turned to her brother. "You my dear little brother will lead our response."

"Father has taught you well Muirgein," Arthur said evidently impressed

"Really?"

"Aye."

"Well you will need to make sure you don't fail. So when we meet tomorrow give me your plan."

Arthur grunted

Muirgein leaned forward and whispered in Arthur's ear, "my dear brother, I chose you because you are the best man for the job and I trust no one more than you. I am not father and if you fail in this enterprise so do I. It would appear that our fate will be forever intertwined. I need you and I fear you need me. Trust might be a problem for you Arthur but sometimes you have to pick a side and live with the consequences of that choice. I have chosen and now so must you."

Arthur nodded. He knew what he had to do.

"We'll meet first light, let the others know," Muirgein said before she turned and retired towards her personal chambers. Gwallog, Arthur noticed, started to walk with her but Muirgein shook her head.

They, including a slightly put out Gwallog, streamed out in single file and when they were outside Bors swung around with a beaming smile, "I think we should have a cold drink to celebrate the opportunity of killing Angle dogs."

Gwallog laughed, "How are you able to drink so much without falling over unconscious."

"I don't know, I haven't tried it. Perhaps today is the day," Bors grinned

"I'll tell you what," Gwallog said, "if we survive the coming battle we will find out together."

"Me too," Galahad chirped in.

Arthur shook his head and wandered back towards his lodgings. "Time to put the men through their paces again."

"At this hour?" moaned Galahad

"In case we have to fight in the dark," Arthur called back.

Arthur woke to a heavy leaden sky. The clouds clung to the nearby hills surrounding Dunadd. Summer it would seem was already behind them. He groaned and wanted to lie there but he gritted his teeth and levered himself

upright. No, he had his routine to follow. He stepped outside his tent, stretched and set off for his run around the perimeter of the Fort and finished by plunging into the nearby River Add. The shock of the water as he broke the surface took his breath away but his drowsiness from yet another poor night's sleep was swept away from him and he clambered out feeling re-invigorated.

He wore only a short tunic as he crossed the camp towards his lodgings where he dressed and drank water from a large cup. He stretched and made his way to the entrance and breathed in the cool damp air. He had stayed awake into the early hours considering what tactics he would use. One thing he was certain of is that it would be a fight between horsemen and foot soldiers. Speed, he knew, was his greatest asset and he knew his foe would reach the place of battle having marched on foot for well over a week. He would get there in two days and choose the place of battle to the north of the River Clyde.

The Angles presented Arthur with a different challenge. They were tough, violent men, well used to combat on foot with a highly effective shield wall which would be a match for any army of horsemen. His men and their horses were brave, but faced by a wall of bristling steel they were unlikely to stay engaged. Arthur knew he needed to find a place where the Angle formations would be tested to the limit and their flanks exposed to his horsemen. He would use his hammer and anvil tactic once again.

He stretched again and decided to make his own way up to the Royal Palace he would soon see what people felt particularly Cai who, as usual, would be the bait. Arthur grinned ruefully, he was continually surprised at Cai's almost unnatural lack of fear. Since their conflict two years before Cai seemed determined to over compensate for the shortcomings he had when he was younger. He was now twenty years of age and stood a head taller than anyone else in the army. Arthur didn't fancy his chances if they were to fight again. Cai frightened Arthur but for all that he must be a thing of dread to his enemies.

Arthur reached the palace and wasn't surprised to find Gwallog already waiting to be shown in. Arthur nodded a greeting to them. The Guard guided them into the room where the round table was set in preparation. Water was available and Arthur set himself opposite to where Muirgein would sit. He leaned back and shut his eyes to calm the nerves that were growing in his stomach. Well at least his discomfort wasn't anything to do with Gwenhwyfar Arthur reflected ruefully. He sensed someone sit next to him. Guessing it was Gwallog he swung round prepared to counter Gwallog's attempt to persuade him not to embark on this venture. But to his surprise, it was Galahad.

"Good morning Galahad," Arthur said jovially, very much relieved he didn't have to be careful of his words

"Lord Arthur, I hope you are well this morning. You look refreshed, you slept well?"

"If only," Arthur moaned, "it's the river that refreshes me not my sleep."

"Sorry to hear that. Oh, my cousin, the Lady Gwenhwyfar sends her regards and hopes the stresses of leadership are not too onerous."

Arthur stiffened, "Lady Gwenhwyfar? I haven't seen her. I was beginning to think she had left with Collen."

"A bone of contention that, Collen would have liked to have spirited her home because he doesn't approve of Gwenhwyfar's interest in the old ways."

"Really?" Arthur was surprised, "he was initiated when I was. Has he been turned by Columba and his minions?"

"Who knows," Galahad grinned, "he has the personality of a damp sack of leather and his conversation is no better."

Arthur laughed, "oh dear. What has she been up to," he said with as much disinterest as he could muster.

"Oh, she has been spending time with your mother and the Lady Muirgein," Galahad said carelessly.

Arthur's blood suddenly ran cold "my Mother and Sister?" he said incredulously.

Galahad waved his hands for Arthur to quieten. "Indeed. It makes sense I would say."

"Make sense?" Arthur asked.

"They are both Priestesses after all," he shrugged.

"I suppose so," Arthur breathed.

Before they could continue the conversation, Bedwyr, Cai and Drystan entered the room and settled themselves alongside a rather dishevelled Bors. Clearly, Arthur grinned, Bors had made a start in finding a state of alcohol induced unconsciousness. Bors nodded towards Arthur who smiled widely in return. Bors rolled his eyes and massaged his temples. Arthur glanced over toward Gwallog who was also watching Bors with some amusement.

At that moment Muirgein entered the room with Taliesin and a priest in tow. "It would seem," she said with more than a hint of annoyance "that for meetings such as these, the Dove of God has instructed that one of his followers should be in attendance. I was going to introduce you to the priest formally but I really can't be bothered."

She was met with laughter.

But for balance," she waived at Taliesin, "I have invited someone you all know."

Taliesin nodded and bowed expansively to everyone, the priest just scowled!

"Gentlemen I bid you sit," Muirgein continued and let's start our council."

She invited Bors to repeat what he had said the previous day about Angle movements to their south east. Bors was able to give more information as scouts had returned during the night. Despite their feelings towards Morcant it did appear that the information they had received was indeed accurate. Gwallog was left to put to the Round table the decision to confront the enemy subject to agreement from all those in attendance. To Arthur's surprise no mention of consulting or waiting for Aedan to return was forthcoming so when Arthur was invited to outline his plans for the forthcoming campaign he was confident of pushing at an open door.

"Friends," he began confidently belying his tender years, "The Angles under the leadership of the Lord Hussa, no less, is currently skirting the lands of the Gododdin, and as Bors tells us, they are expected to turn north to avoid any confrontation with Alt Clut. I believe they will be at our borders in four days. They are on foot so when they reach our borders they will be tired and they will be at the end of their provisions which means they will be foraging.

He glanced around the table and was greeted with nods of agreement. Gwallog, however, sat impassively. He ploughed on.

"My plan is to take a force of two hundred and fifty horsemen leaving at dawn tomorrow. A horse can travel more than fifty miles per day with the right number of water breaks and cooling down time. So I expect to be at the Crooked Fairy rocks where they are bounded by the Campsie Hills by late morning on the second day. I anticipate the Angles arrival, at the earliest, some twenty four hours later and in that time we will harry them, we will snipe at them, we will not let them rest and we will bring them to battle."

There was a murmur of approval as Arthur continued. "They will have an advantage of around two to one so firstly we need to make them think that they have an even bigger advantage than that. They are arrogant, over confident, bastards.

"We know they fight as a single unit with a shield wall and bristling spear points that our horses will be desperate to avoid. We must find any opportunity to break that formation down. So Gentlemen I aim to fight them at Craigmaddie, the Rock of Prayers, the ground is rocky, there is a Burn which will compress their ranks."

"So you want me to lure them in I suppose?' laughed Cai.

"You are the best of our men," Arthur responded.

Bedwyr raised his hand and asked the obvious question, "this is similar to our fight at Delgon, won't the Angles be ready for us?"

"That is a risk," conceded Arthur, "but having thought things through, I would be very surprised if they are aware of our previous battle tactics. They will think that a fifteen year old upstart will show all the skills of a fifteen your old upstart."

"They're probably laughing at you now," chimed in Drystan

"We are going to give them a surprise they won't forget in a long while."

"Our victory has to be so decisive," said Cai "so they will not try again."

"Not for a while at least," cautioned Bedwyr, "you've seen what they have done to our south east. Bernicia? Deira? Some say that they will call it North Humber Land."

"They will never go away," sighed Muirgein

"I agree," said Arthur

"You don't know that," argued the still grey looking Bors.

"It is the way of history," shrugged Galahad.

"We must carve out our own history," said Cai

"We need to unite," said Galahad.

"And that must be our goal," rejoined Muirgein, "our problem is making the other kingdoms feel as equals."

"That will harder than beating the Angles and Saxons," groaned Galahad.

"Yes but we have the makings of an alliance with Rheged and Alt Clut and if the Gododdin were amenable we might find ourselves in a position of strength."

"But there's a problem," muttered Arthur

"I know," sighed Muirgein, "they don't trust Aedan."

"They may not trust King Aedan but they may trust his son," suggested Drystan.

Arthur was embarrassed and flattered in the same instance by Drystan's comment and waived aside the suggestion. "Whoever it is," interrupted Muirgein "he needs to be someone they respect. We are talking about Kings giving power over to a single man. That needs great courage."

"That will need Aedan's agreement," grunted Gwallog.

"Indeed," agreed Muirgein.

The talks continued but Arthur noticed that Gwallog remained quiet and contributed little or nothing to those discussions. Eventually, Arthur stood up and wandered around the circle and whispered in Muirgein's ear. She nodded and she leaned back glancing at Gwallog.

After another ten minutes or so Muirgein announced, "I want to break for a few moments of reflection after which we will concentrate on logistics. Perhaps you might discuss this while I am away?" She paused, looking around the table. "But before we break," she continued, "can we first confirm our agreement of the plans as set down by Arthur?"

"Aye," came the response in unison.

Muirgein smiled, stood and beckoned Gwallog to follow her.

"What can I help you with Lady?" asked Gwallog warily.

When they were out of earshot, they sat together in a small antechamber. Muirgein then turned to him, "you are not the most vocal of men in council but your silence this morning is almost deafening. You obviously do not agree with the will of the council, can you explain to me why?"

"What difference does it make what I think, I am in a minority of one."

"Enlighten me," she smiled sweetly.

"We should not act without Aedan's agreement."

"And how do we get that?"

"I will follow him to Ireland."

"And tell him we are being invaded?"

"Yes."

"And what would he say Lord Gwallog? Perhaps he would say, send a force to check the Angles?"

"And?"

"How long would it take?" Muirgein pressed. "Will we be surrounded by then?"

"You exaggerate," Gwallog retorted.

"Perhaps, but we can't wait around for the Angles to ravage our country. To swear fealty to our people and to then leave them defenceless seems to me to be treacherous at best."

"That's not..." began Gwallog but Muirgein cut him off.

"Your views are noted but I reject them completely and it is me and not you that will be accountable if this goes wrong. If you are unhappy, I suggest you travel to Ireland and I will find someone else to serve the needs of the Council. So make your decision Lord Gwallog. You are either with me or against me. Let me be plain, I will not have someone advising me who is a discontent. I hope I am clear she smiled coolly. Please leave, I need to refresh myself, and I shall rejoin you shortly."

At that she stood and beckoned him towards the door. Gwallog lingered for a moment in anticipation of Muirgein making light of what she had just said but she remained silent. She just stared with a determination he had seldom seen. His mouth opened and shut but he knew this was not purely a matter of fighting the Angles but a battle of pre-eminence within a family that suspected each other's motives and feared the repercussions of doing too much or too little. Gwallog had served these people for so long but in that moment he realised that he was serving as a servant not a confidant. Too long had he been held in by promises including the Muirgein's hand in marriage. In that instance he was reminded of his folly. The evidence had always been there, he had admitted as much to Arthur when the young Prince had questioned his feelings towards the boy's sister and his acceptance of his position. He was the Lord of Lomond, his father was revered and an ancestor of Coel and yet here he was. He was honour bound, what could he do? Being a man of honour, he reflected, seemed to be something to be advantage of.

Muirgein saw the pain in his eyes, she had a lot to thank this man and so did Arthur. But she could not be seen to show any weakness. At that moment they were both painfully aware of each other's predicament.

Gwallog, bowed his head, sighed deeply, turned and left the room. His instinct was to walk away and leave this nest of vipers to their games. He hovered near the door to the outside until sense, or was it guilt, dragged him back. He realised there was nothing to be gained by any grand gesture. He mustn't give way to childish petulance. And after all, what would become of him, murdered in the middle of the night by some unseen assassin. Surely that shouldn't be his fate.

Gwallog stood looking at the doorway. He flexed his neck muscles and closed his eyes. Sighing, he turned on his heels and strode purposefully back to the round table where he took his seat and looked on impassively at the others who were still milling around in amiable conversation.

Muirgein walked back into the room and sat back in her seat. She waited patiently for everyone to settle and when silence finally descended her eyes settled on Arthur. "Have you discussed your needs Brother?"

"Yes," he replied confidently. "Bedwyr will make the necessary arrangements."

"May I interrupt," chimed in Gwallog.

Muirgein looked at him suspiciously but welcomed him to address the group. "We need to protect Dunadd in the unlikely event of failure. I think you know my concerns and I recognise my appointment as military overseer means that there are too many commanders and that can only lead to catastrophe. Can I propose that I take command of the defences of Dunadd. I will take the responsibility for keeping the King appraised but I can assure you that my actions will in no way seek to undermine the will of this council. We all need to protect ourselves in case there is any... ... misunderstanding. In the meantime can I suggest you send scouts out today to gather the intelligence you need?"

There were nods around the table and there was visible relief from both Bors and Galahad. Muirgein too appeared satisfied. Arthur looked up and looked directly at Gwallog. "Are you certain my friend even though I am still inexperienced?"

Gwallog smiled, "Yes Arthur. You have earned your chance. I have heard your plans and can find no reason to disagree with them. My being there would make no difference. I have fought with you before my friend and I know your value."

"I am grateful for your confidence," acknowledged Arthur.

"Bedwyr, can we send out scouts?" asked Arthur.

"It will be done," he responded.

The meeting ended and Arthur hung around until it was only himself and Muirgein. "Is there something you wish to discuss?' asked Muirgein

Arthur remained silent for a few beats and then tentatively asked, "I'm told Gwen has been in your company?"

"Gwen?"

"Gwenhwyfar," Arthur confirmed

"Ah! My little Brother, do you have an interest?"

"Don't mock me," Arthur responded irritably

"It's my prerogative, I am your older sister after all."

"I was just being... ..."

"Nosey," Muirgein jumped in.

"Maybe," Arthur shrugged

"Not that it's your business but your young lady is interested in joining the Sisterhood of the Goddess. She is very talented for one so young," Muirgein continued.

"Did she?" Arthur started.

"Mention you?" Muirgein smiled broadly, "your name was mentioned if memory serves."

"Really?" Arthur perked up.

"She wanted to know about our family and our relationship."

"Why would she do that?"

"I leave that to your imagination," Muirgein said conspiratorially.

Muirgein let the words hang and swiftly changed subject. "What do you think of Gwallog's words? He has positioned himself well don't you think. He keeps his hands clean and he keeps his loyalty to Aedan."

"Well we better make this work," Arthur grunted, a little disappointed that the conversation was at an end.

"Yes you better otherwise are lives will be considerably shortened. Are you as confident as you sound?" Muirgein said quietly.

"Yes Sister. Speed is a necessity of course. If I could leave now I would but tomorrow before dawn will leave us time."

"Then be quick brother, Dalriada is relying on you."

"I will."

"Good," Muirgein rejoined, "now brother, hug me and I will wish you well."

They stood there in a long embrace and Arthur rested his head on her shoulder. She kissed him tenderly on the cheek, "Come back safe Arthur my dearest brother."

At that Muirgein pulled herself away and stroked his face with the back of her hand. She smiled sadly and left without another word.

Chapter 27

The Pieces Move

The crossing had been deeply uncomfortable, it might have only been ten miles but the seas were heavy and even the hardiest of the men struggled with the swell much to the amusement of the sailors. They might be brethren but the Dalriadan Scots had apparently become land loving second class citizens. Aedan reflected that the heavy seas were probably a blessing and aided in the avoidance of confrontations between the differing factions.

The Irish coast was invisible under the black skies as it came down to hug the sea. Aedan stood rigid next to the boat's captain who, much to Aedan's annoyance, appeared to be enjoying every moment of this torment. Aedan glanced over at Columba who sat unmoving under his great cloak. He had not uttered a word throughout the crossing which was both a concern and a blessing.

Aedan shrugged and shouted at the Captain as the rain again began to get harder and stung as it mercilessly slapped his face, "how long will it be?"

"Before we land?" the Captain roared back

"Absolutely,"

"Another couple of hours Lord, this weather is slowing us up."

"The faster we break our ties the better, my guts can't take this," Aedan groaned

"What was that?" called the Captain.

"No matter. Just get us there safe."

"Aye I will."

Aedan snorted and walked away to what looked a safe place from the weather and the Priest.

A couple of hours were an underestimation and it was dawn before the fleet of ships sailed into Murlach Bay. Miraculously no boats were lost.

They set off towards the South-West. It was some forty miles to Drumceatt and they set off, to the surprise of many, in pleasant sunshine. "Typical," grunted Aedan. Aedan and Columba walked in silence together at the front of the column through the rolling hills. Many, Aedan reflected, had been puzzled by his decision to bring Columba to the Convention but few realised that Columba was a distant cousin of Aed mac Ainmuirech and his reputation with the Irish nobles was such that he might have some leverage in any discussions. Aedan knew Columba was uniquely qualified to act as a possible arbiter or bridge between the two factions. After all Columba was a Cenel Conaill Prince. The most important thing to Aedan, and he would use whatever was at his disposal to achieve it, was an independent kingdom of the Scots.

Aedan had his reasons but Columba's reasons for attending he couldn't fathom although he suspected that Columba was probably playing a clever long term political game. But whatever he was hoping to achieve, Aedan would be there to ensure it wouldn't come to fruition in his life time. What was important, he kept reminding himself, was a Scottish Kingdom. Columba had committed himself to pleading the cause of patriotism but also of religion, literature, music and poetry. Aedan had concluded that Columba's defence of the Bardic tradition was founded in misunderstanding as, by implication, it supported the traditions of the old way. If that was true, Aedan decided it was best to keep quiet.

Aedan had been bemused by Columba swearing he would never return to Ireland after this trip and he had even decided that he would not even let himself see the Irish coastline and had instructed his monks to place a white scarf over his eyes which he would not remove until he reached Drumceatt.

"What a strange man he is," Aedan was heard to say.

They moved at a leisurely pace and reached Drumceatt on the fifth day. After a couple of days of rest and recuperation as well as bathing in the Red River, so named it was said because of its iron content, Aedan made his way in to the hall for the first day of the Convention. To his amusement Columba still wore the white scarf, so theatrically wrapped around his head whilst still out at sea. Nonetheless, it wasn't lost on Aedan the symbolism of Columba being led into the hall still blindfolded.

It was an ostentatious display Aedan knew and the reaction from the Kings and Princes in attendance, as the scarf was removed, was almost awe. Aedan knew the symbolism was also not lost on anyone that the spirit of Patrick had returned. Aedan smiled.

Hussa led his men away from their coastal camp southward towards the Great Wall. They then followed the wall westward. The weather was fine and the mood cheerful.

As anticipated the road for the Angles was long and hard but generally flat. Most of the steep inclines were avoided which added time to their march. Angle scouts brought no news from their south but reports of a Gododdin force shadowing their progress to their north was regularly received. As this territory represented the Gododdin's Southern borders it probably wasn't too surprising that the Gododdin had decided to keep a close eye on Angle forces. What surprised Hussa was how quickly the Angle route was picked up. It felt as if the Gododdin King, Cynfelyn, knew in advance the route the Angle Army would take. They seemed too well equipped and battle ready to have reacted so quickly. Nonetheless, the Gododdin made no attempt to threaten the Angle force and reports from the Angle scouts seemed to bear that assumption out. Hussa, however, was becoming uneasy and he felt obliged to post significantly more guards to screen his advance.

After three days Hussa could hardly contain his anxiety, Cuffa tried to calm him, it was, he argued, highly unlikely they would face an attack because they were a force of five hundred battle hardened warriors, and any confrontation would surely result in heavy losses. Hussa knew his colleague was right but for his own peace of mind he still needed to know what their intentions were. To this end Hussa decided to make contact with the Gododdin force but despite his best efforts, the Gododdin rejected all his attempts to have any dialogue.

When the Angles finally turned north, the Gododdin also turned north still being careful not to provoke a confrontation, but shortly after, to Hussa's relief news came from his scouts that the Gododdin force had pulled back. However, Hussa's relief was short lived when it became clear that a different force was now tracking him to the west. Hussa with Cuffa's reassurance decided that Alt Clut were probably simply guarding their borders as well. Hussa concluded that if Alt Clut and the Gododdin knew of their movements so must the Dalriadan Scots. But what could they do he reasoned? Aedan was in Ireland and would never get back in time so surely they would be hamstrung, awaiting instructions. And even if they acted without Aedan's direct command, they were supposedly led, by an inexperienced boy barely detached from his mother's tit.

As time passed Hussa received reports that the Alt Clut forces had also drawn back. Hussa now confidently concluded that no threat was forthcoming, his numbers had been the deterrent Cuffa had told him they would be. He decided to press on.

Cuffa's scouts had moved forward and the information he had received from them suggested that Dalriadan Scottish scouts were roaming some thirty or so miles ahead of them. Cuffa's men had threatened a confrontation but the Scots appeared more than happy to keep their distance. Perhaps they weren't that stupid after all Hussa reflected.

Hussa looked about him, now that the immediate threats appeared to have disappeared his men's mood had become more cheerful and was now generally in good spirits. Through Cuffa's promptings the possibility of plunder now stood front and centre of their minds. They were persuaded that there would be easy pickings and the Angles would be making a statement that they were more than capable of conquering, maybe not straight away, but it was only a matter of time. Angle success would undoubtedly give their Pictish allies, as far as anyone could call them allies, the perfect opportunity to attack the Scots from the north. Hussa smiled to himself, yes putting the Scots to the sword in their own lands made him and everyone excited for battle. Any moans of wear and tear to their feet would soon be forgotten.

Food, however, was becoming sparse and rations were imposed but with the time for fighting was almost upon them the Angle force was confident that they could find the provisions they needed.

Cuffa joined Hussa that night and gave him the news he had been waiting for. The Scots would, more than likely confront them. That was good, that was very good.

"How many are there?" Hussa asked.

"Our scouts are saying between one hundred and fifty and two hundred men," grunted Cuffa

"Is that all?" replied Hussa incredulously.

Cuffa shrugged, "yes but they are on horseback so, I guess, they must believe that they have the advantage of mobility."

"Ha!" Hussa laughed derisively, "we've come all this way to slaughter two hundred men?"

"And they are spread out," grinned Cuffa, "so the Scots will take a long time to concentrate and deploy which will allow us time to choose our own ground and at our leisure."

"I feel almost sorry for them," guffawed Hussa.

As the sun set, Arthur wondered the camp making final checks on equipment and men. He chatted amiably to everyone he came across. He allowed his men to eat and drink what they wanted which cheered Bors but the threat of dumping any hungover men, naked, into the River Add before they set off would be a deterrent to most.

He sat with Bedwyr, Drystan and Cai deep into the evening discussing tactics but as was the norm after a few cups of ale discussion turned to strange and outlandish deeds and of course to the many conquests of the women of Dunadd and the villages beyond. At that Arthur stood and harrumphed in a good humour. "You're a disgrace, all of you," he said

"You're only jealous," called Cai.

"Bah, fuck off," he responded waving his arm dismissively.

"You're not swimming?" said Drystan.

"Of course I am. I have to cool down after that conversation," he shouted back

A laugh greeted that and the others carried on their conversation.

Arthur got to the bank at the place he normally used to bathe. Stripping off he plunged in and gasped as he submerged himself in the cold water. He stayed there for what must have been some thirty minutes sitting on the bank going over his plan in his head.

When he finally got up he washed himself again and strolled back naked through the now quiet camp to his lodgings. He stepped inside and settled down under a sheepskin blanket. He lay back and breathed deeply. He closed his eyes and put his hands behind his head.

After a few moments he became aware of rustling near the door. He slowly opened his eyes and saw a figure wrapped in a cloak. Reaching for his sword he challenged the intruder, "who is it? Make yourself known."

"A friend," came the response.

It took a moment for Arthur to realise it was a women's voice. "Who is it?" he demanded.

"You don't recognise my voice after only a few days?"

"Gwen?" Arthur sat up.

"Shush, of course, who else would it be?" she responded playfully.

"What are you doing here, it's the middle of the night?"

"Yes, I know. I wouldn't want to be like other women. I did expect a better welcome though."

Arthur laughed, "you don't ask for much. Sit down, I'll get up and find some refreshment."

"No Arthur no need," she whispered, "stay where you are."

At that she took off her cloak revealing a linen garment with decorative clasps at each shoulder. Arthur couldn't help gawp as Gwenhwyfar unclipped the clasps and let her dress slip from her shoulders revealing her nakedness. His breathe became shallow as we watched her. It was dark so he could only glimpse her by the moonlight flooding through doorway. She was tall, her figure was slim and wirier than he thought, she crossed to where he lay and slid in next to him resting her head on his chest and wrapping her arm around his ribcage. Her touch brought goose bumps to his flesh and he let out an involuntary gasp.

He felt her naked flesh against his, her skin felt cool and smooth like silk. He couldn't help himself stroking her back. He smiled to himself as he heard her sigh in response.

"Your sister tells me you can't sleep?" she whispered.

He sighed, "have you come here to help?"

"May be. Just close your eyes and let me relax you," she continued.

She kissed his chest gently, her lips caressing his skin. Her hand drifted lower to stroke his belly. Arthur groaned as his manhood began to swell.

Her hand drifted lower and his breathing became more and more shallow. Her fingers tickled his skin and her hand drifted lower until her wrist touched the tip of his erect manhood. Arthur gasped and began to say something but Gwenhwyfar removed her hand and placed a finger on his lips, "Shhh, I want you to remember this moment so you'll want to come back."

Arthur groaned and said no more as her hand again drifted down his chest over his belly and down to his pubic hair. Her fingers circled his manhood for a few beats making Arthur's back arch and then her hand was holding him. As his passion threatened to overflow her hand began to move up and down along the length of his penis. At that he shuddered uncontrollably and gave out a cry of pleasure. His body became rigid and he ejaculated as Gwenhwyfar continued to stroke him.

As Arthur's manhood subsided and his body relaxed, Gwenhwyfar lifted her wet hand up to his belly. "Rest now my Prince, close your eyes and dream sweet dreams." Arthur closed his eyes, and despite himself, he drifted in and out of sleep.

When Bedwyr came to wake him, Arthur found that he was alone, Gwenhwyfar had gone. Had it been a dream? Well, if it had, it had been a good one."

"Did you sleep well my friend," asked Bedwyr

"The best sleep ever and dreams to match."

"Really?" Bedwyr laughed, "you look as if you've been deflowered."

"And what does that look like?"

"Just a thing," Bedwyr shrugged, "come on let's eat before we set off."

To Bedwyr's surprise Arthur ate what looked like his own weight in food, it even drew the attention of Gwallog who had come to see them off. "Good grief," said Gwallog, "I hope you have brought enough food? With an appetite like that you won't last the day,"

Drystan looked on amused, "perhaps Arthur would like to share something?"

"More bread Drystan," Arthur called choosing to ignore the taunt.

"Get him out of here," said Gwallog chuckling.

When all was cleared away and the horses prepared, the horsemen formed lines across the camp grounds. Arthur, Bedwyr and Cai trotted slowly along the lines of horsemen sharing words of motivation.

When he was satisfied he trotted forward and looking east, Arthur could see the sun caressing the tops of the nearby hills as he climbed onto his mount. Gwallog walked up to Arthur's horse, and patted its mane. "Good luck Arthur."

Arthur looked down at the older man, "I will return victorious, be in no doubt. There is much to come back for," he grinned, "and I will not let you down. Look after my sister, she loves you despite the machinations of others."

Gwallog stood back as Arthur looked back over his shoulder at his fellow horsemen, raised his arm and swung it forward. "To destiny!' he shouted and they set off at a canter out of the camp. Bedwyr rode at Arthur's side followed close behind by Cai and Drystan. Bors and Galahad tucked themselves into the middle of the column. They rode through the valley of the Add, below the mount of Badden and turned east.

The column meandered along the edge of the hills and when Dunadd was a distant landmark they spurred their horses into a gallop. Arthur would reach the Rock of prayers well ahead of time. He laughed aloud as they rode towards their fate.

Chapter 28

Becoming Pendragon

Arthur had pushed his men and horses hard and reached the moor of the Rock of Prayers in the early hours. The horses were corralled near the Craigmaddie Burn fed and watered. It was too dark to scope out the ground so Arthur decided to make camp. He issued instructions not to light any fires in order to mask his forces arrival in the event of being seen by enemy scouts he knew were in the vicinity.

It was dry and unseasonably mild so his orders were accepted with a stoic shrug by many. Arthur called over Bors, Galahad and Bedwyr and instructed them to send out scouts to the east and south to determine the exact position of the Angle forces. Once he was satisfied he mounted his horse and trotted forward beyond the Burn. It was dark and he knew he would glean next to nothing but his desire for space and peace drove him further out than he intended and within a short period of time he realised that he was hopelessly lost.

"Shit," he muttered to himself before sliding off his horse. He recognised the folly of not lighting fires as he looked about him trying to identify any points of reference. When he was satisfied he was completely alone, he sat himself down on the grass next to a rock which he used to prop himself against. He laughed then at his predicament and promised himself not to repeat his actions should the occasion arise. Putting his hands behind his head he closed his eyes and drifted into a troubled sleep.

At daybreak Arthur woke with a start as he heard men calling after him. At least they noticed his absence he concluded ruefully. Standing up he considered whether he ought to come up with some excuse but he knew he would have to accept a couple of days of remorseless ribbing anyway so the truth was as good as anything. He groaned at the thought. He waved in the direction of the calls and the first person to approach him was, to his dismay, Cai.

"Ah Arthur, what are you doing out here? We thought you might have gotten lost. It was dark after all."

"Yes it was dark," Arthur said evenly.

A smile crept across Cai's face, "you did get lost!" This was followed by hysterical laughter.

Arthur rolled his eyes, "yes I got lost. It could have happened to anyone."

"Aye, that's true," Cai coughed, "even the leader of the army. You know what they'll say,"

"No, well maybe yes! Just fuck off," he grunted.

Cai feigned hurt but said no more as Arthur swung himself onto his horse. "Get me back to camp, we have work to do."

"If I can find it," Cai said innocently.

Arthur's jaw tightened but even he had to smirk while Cai continued to laugh.

As Arthur anticipated he was the butt of jokes for a number of hours and not only from his commanders but he took it in good grace although it was all wearing a bit thin by the time they rested after digging trenches and the setting of defensive stakes.

The scouts continued to file in at regular intervals and Arthur was soon made aware that the Angles were still a couple of days away. "They have clearly slowed," Bedwyr pointed out

"Over confident," murmured Arthur.

"Sounds like it," piped in Cai.

"What guarantee do we have," asked Galahad "that they will come to us?"

"Because they will think they outnumber us."

"They do."

"Two to one probably," confirmed Arthur "but we will hide at least a third of our force around to the north."

"Surely they will know we are here," asked Cai

"Maybe but our scouts have confirmed that no one has been seen this far north."

"What are your plans Arthur asked Drystan? The ground doesn't allow us to outflank them as we hoped."

"Agreed," said Arthur. "We will harry them to start with," he continued. "I want you Drystan to attack their lines and their camp. They mustn't have time to rest and foraging must be disrupted. The plan otherwise remains the same except part of our force will be hidden by those trees yonder to the north."

"So you will only show them what they want to see," nodded Drystan with a smile of satisfaction.

"Indeed my friend, they will be enraged and people who are enraged do not think straight." He turned to Bedwyr, "you will take control of horsemen on the left and I will attack once Cai suckers them in and breaks. As soon as their formation comes apart we will destroy them." Arthur looked from one commander to the next, "any questions?"

There were none. "Good," he continued, "I will take one in three men and we will camp to the north two or three miles from here. Galahad will be our link man."

"Fires?" laughed Drystan

"We have drawn the short straw I'm afraid," grumbled Arthur

"Don't get lost," said Cai

"Fuck off!"

Arthur stood, "Good luck my friends and remember harry them. Good hunting."

Hussa's temper was becoming frayed. Night time was becoming intolerable. Flaming arrows continued to rain down on his men. Fires were constantly being extinguished and scouts were coming back having constantly been chased by their Scots counterparts.

What was becoming clear was that a Dalriadan force was waiting for them on moors to their north. Hussa could not understand how they had got there so quickly. All indications had been that he would be first to arrive and he would be the one choose the land on which to fight. Nonetheless, despite much discussion, Hussa was adamant; it didn't matter where they fought. The Dalriadan Scots needed to be confronted and he would slaughter them wherever they were. How dare they swarm about him like the midges of this wretched country.

Cuffa's scouts had reported a force of less than two hundred horsemen, probably closer to around one hundred and seventy. Cuffa, however, was clearly nervous. "I cannot believe that they have so few, it feels wrong, I don't like it Lord."

"You worry too much Cuffa," Hussa grunted, realising the irony of his comments, "even if another army is following them, we still have too many well-armed warriors."

"But if this Arthur of theirs is as clever they say... ..."

"He's just a boy Cuffa, he knows nothing of war. He is talked up to scare us. We are a force of which he has never faced. He is in for an unpleasant shock my friend."

"Yes Lord, I hope you're right," Cuffa mumbled uncertainly.

"I am right, I will teach this upstart a lesson he will take to halls of his ancestors," Hussa grinned viciously.

They reached land to the east of the Scottish campfires very late. Men stumbled over the broken ground and the number of twisted ankles left the Angle soldiers in a sour mood. Things didn't improve when rain swept across the moor and soaked them as they tried to establish their camp.

The march had been horrendous, and morale was hit hard. Dalriadan horsemen continued to approach the column and forcing the Angles into continuous defensive formations. After showers of arrows rained down on the Angle warriors, the horsemen would then just melt away.

The night too was sleepless as fire arrows continued to be shot into the camp and as the sun began to rise the following morning, the Scots attacked the camp, picking off the guards before galloping off. The heads of foragers thrown into the centre of the Angle camp by the horsemen was a constant reminder of the growing feeling of isolation they felt in this miserable featureless land.

Hussa's screams of frustration could be heard clearly by Drystan's horsemen once they settled on a ridge overlooking the Angle position. Drystan laughed at the warrior who strode to the edge of the Angle camp to face them, throwing numerous insults none of which the Scots could understand but knew the sentiments all too well.

As morning broke after another wakeful night, Hussa and Cuffa ordered preparations for battle. Their men were at a low ebb, they were tired, damp and hungry. The initial excitement at dealing the Scots a blow had dissipated. The men were more interested in getting this over and done with and to retreat home to lick their wounds. Hussa realised that victory, which he believed was still assured, would probably not lead to the destabilisation and humiliation of his foes that was hoped for. He fumed with impotent rage.

Doubt had crept over Arthur while he and his men had huddled under trees and bushes safely to the north of the intended battlefield. It wasn't until Galahad relayed to Arthur the news that he had hoped for that he began to realise that success was within his grasp. No Scots had been killed or wounded whereas thirty or forty Angles were thought to have been killed. The Angles would be tired and miserable. Hussa, their leader would be incandescent by now Arthur knew. He may be a great warrior but an angry warrior was an ineffective warrior. The Angles would face a foe completely different than what they were used to. Horsemen who were quick and flexible versus men on foot who were static and cumbersome. "Good," said Arthur, "let's prepare for battle."

Galahad rode back to Cai who immediately moved his men towards a position opposite the centre of the Angle lines. Drystan arrayed his horsemen to the right and Bedwyr to Cai's left. They advanced beyond the Burn making sure they avoided the rugged stony land.

Seeing the Scots lining up in front of him, Hussa lined his men up three lines deep seeking to ensure his lines stretched further than those of the Scots. The Angles were always aware of being flanked and refused their lines at a ninety degree angle but Hussa decided this wasn't necessary.

Hussa and Cuffa pushed themselves into the centre of the front line. At Hussa's command, shields were raised and locked.

The Dalriadan horsemen galloped forward but refused to tackle the shield wall head on. Instead they rode in close, threw spears into the Angle lines and swerved away. In response the Angles started to move forward with a great guttural roar.

From Arthur's vantage point he could see the Angle line advance shouting insults and clashing swords against shields. Cai's men began to move forward and more horsemen ineffectually charged directly at the shield wall. Some horsemen struck home but many others swung away as reluctant horses refused to race into the swarm of steel points awaiting them. Drystan and Bedwyr continued to snipe at the flanks as the Angles continued their inexorable advance. Gradually the men of Dalriada were driven back to the burn. It was at this moment when Cai gave the order to fight on foot.

Hussa saw the Scots dismounting and urged the Angles warriors forward but the rocky terrain was causing difficulties in maintaining coherence. The Scots, to Hussa's surprise, formed their own shield wall as the Angles came on. The clash of metal on metal was ear-splitting. The Scots were sent reeling back although somehow their lines held. Drystan and Bedwyr charged into the Angle flanks again and again slowing their momentum but they were beginning to take casualties; making their position untenable.

More of the Scots were dismounting now and joining Cai's men in a desperate attempt to hold the bowing lines. Cai ordered a retreat across the Burn. It was a well ordered withdrawal but with the number of horsemen reducing, the Angle flanks began to surge forward with greater confidence. It was Cai's turn to fear his flanks were being exposed as superior numbers began to tell. Again, Cai ordered a retreat, this time the Scots lines were fragmenting. Roars of triumph came from the Angle warriors as their momentum quickened.

Arthur could see now that Cai's lines were near collapse. He trotted forward as Galahad joined him along with Bors. He turned to his horsemen and boomed. "You are the pride of Manau, the children of Sarmatian knights. See there," he pointed, "our men, our friends are in need. So ride with me, ride now for glory and ride for death!"

The Horsemen roared and Arthur again called, "ride with me. Death to the Angle bastards."

"Death!" came the response as the horsemen began to move forward, firstly at a trot, then a canter and finally a gallop as Arthur screamed, "Charge!"

The Horsemen swarmed down the gradual gradient and closed the gap to Cai's desperate men extraordinarily quickly with spears levelled as they hurtled towards the Angle force.

Unbeknownst to both Arthur and Hussa were the approaching forces of Rheged and Llywarch of the Gododdin who had been shadowing the Angle force. They had gathered on reverse slopes to the south of the battlefield and upon seeing Arthur's force descend on the Angles they had concluded that the Dalriadans were going to win the battle and moved forward.

Hussa was immediately aware of the shouted warnings coming from his right and then from his left. He recognised that his men had left the safety of the shield wall as they began to chase the fleeing Scots. The danger was obvious and Hussa called for his men to gather about him. Panic suddenly spread like wildfire as Arthur's horsemen were almost upon them. But it was too late. Arthur's horsemen sliced through the rear ranks of the Angles with great slaughter. The grass was slick with blood and human detritus as Angle warriors were cut down without mercy.

Cai's men regrouped and reformed a new shield wall and marched back into the fray joined now by the men of Rheged. Hussa was surrounded, his men were being cut down mercilessly. He looked down as he tried to step over bodies and he saw the frozen face of Cuffa staring lifelessly up at him. Hussa swung his mighty sword with savage rage and when that was broken, he used a huge axe which he aimed at all and sundry. Within just a few minutes Hussa stood with just a handful of men about him bloodied and breathing hard. He challenged the Scots to finish him but Arthur had called a halt. The horsemen formed a circle around the remaining Angles and lowered their spears. Hussa's men dropped their swords and shields in submission despite Hussa's continued belligerence.

The horsemen opened their ranks and allowed Arthur to make his way through on his mount. He sat impassively on his mount in front of the vanquished Angles. At first he said nothing, he just stared at the remaining men. "Who are you?" Hussa called out proudly.

Arthur said nothing for a few beats. He removed his helmet and looked coldly into Hussa's eyes. A slight smile crossed his face, "And you must be Hussa?" he said quietly.

"I am."

"Hmm," Arthur grunted, "I thought so."

"And you are?"

"I am Arthur of Dalriada and Prince of Manau, son of Aedan." He paused a moment, "and I will have your surrender."

"I will kill many before you kill me."

Arthur nodded and called for the horsemen to produce their bows, "no you won't. You will die like a dog. A sad end I would say,"

Hussa said nothing, he looked about him and knew his time was up. All he could hope for was a warrior's death so that he might join his ancestors in the great Halls. He dropped his axe and removed his helmet before dropping it to the ground.

"Good," said Arthur. He called over Bedwyr, "find me five horses."

Bedwyr was surprised, "why Arthur?"

"I'm sending Hussa and his men home," Arthur said evenly

Hussa and his men looked dumbfounded, "you are sparing us?" asked one.

"You have been brave and done everything required of you. I cannot see any point in killing you in such an inglorious way. You will go back to Bernicia and you can tell King Aethelric that today you met Arthur and his men and you were beaten. You may have beaten my British brothers but you will come no further. Should you try again, I'll be waiting for you and next time none of you will return."

"You cannot stop us forever," Hussa shot back

"Maybe not, who knows what will happen when we are both dead. But I will come for you and I will push you out of this island. So go now, no one will attack you although I cannot speak for the men of Rheged and the Gododdin. Farewell, Lord Hussa, until next time."

"I will return, you know that."

Arthur smiled, "I'm counting it," he said.

Arthur greeted his unexpected allies. He recognised Urien and welcomed him with the reverence befitting a King as was Llywarch of the Gododdin. They had known that Arthur was about to win the battle but this would be useful propaganda for their subjects. The three men sat together. "What has brought you here?" asked Arthur

"We have been following Hussa's force," responded Llywarch and your attack on them was our reason for joining you. These dogs," he spat "have for too long flouted our borders. You showed us what could be done and I couldn't hold my men back."

Arthur smiled, "I am grateful and flattered."

"No," said Urien, "we are grateful. You showed us that these Angles can be beaten. When we picked up their trail as they skirted Gododdin territory, we had suspected treachery and Llywarch here invited us to join him."

"I hope," started Arthur that this is the beginning of a fruitful partnership."

"Indeed," my friend said Urien. He paused and his eyebrows knitted together. "Tell me something Arthur, why did you let Hussa go? You have done this before and I doubt you are thinking straight and can't believe he will be an ally."

"We killed almost all his force Lord Urien, our point was made," Arthur replied evenly.

"I'm not sure that's a reason," put in Llywarch.

Arthur nodded, "I wanted to humiliate him, he will go back now and tell his king he was defeated by a boy. They will think twice before trying that again and Hussa will not be considered the warrior they thought he was."

"Humiliation eh." mused Urien, "that's worse than being killed."

"That's what I'm counting on. And should he try to redeem himself he will be reckless and recklessness will be his undoing."

Urien glanced at Llywarch with raised eyebrows. This Arthur was someone to be respected, and yes, feared. Urien was a renowned warrior, his stature made him a fearsome sight but strategically, he recognised, he was possibly lacking. But this Arthur was something else, he maybe a boy but he fought and thought in a new way and Urien couldn't help wondering what an unleashed Arthur would be capable of doing. Urien did not trust Aedan and until Rhydderch was confirmed as King of Alt Clut he couldn't be relied upon. Urien knew as well as anyone that a united front would be needed against the Angles if their land aspirations were to be frustrated. He considered himself as the man to lead the Britons but political intrigue would inevitably undermine an alliance no matter what a potent leader he was. Could Arthur be this man? He had shown flexibility and independence at Arderydd and let Peredur go. He decided to probe further.

"Your father has travelled to Ireland?" Urien asked

"Yes Lord to meet with Aed."

"Indeed. I'm surprised he left knowing the Angles were on the move."

"He didn't know."

"Really! So why are you here?"

"It was unlikely we could contact him in time to get his agreement so Muirgein and I decided to act."

"Muirgein?"

"Yes Lord, your... ...."

"My ex-wife," Urien said flatly

"Yes Lord, she is acting regent until the Lord Aedan returns."

"Well, well, who would have guessed," Urien laughed out loud, throwing his head back.

To Arthur, Urien's laugh sounded like a hound barking but its infectious tones soon had him and Llywarch laughing along until Urien suddenly stopped as did everyone else. "Perhaps I should have kept hold of her," he grunted.

Arthur smiled without humour then added, "your loss is Dalriada's gain and mine."

Urien's cheek twitched threateningly but he fought to regain control despite Arthur's look of triumph. He breathed hard and continued, "yes I suppose so, it's always good to have new meat to feed this," he pointed at his crotch.

Llywarch laughed, "you're so right Lord Urien."

Urien grinned at Arthur, satisfied that he had outsmarted the arrogant pup, "so Aedan doesn't know..."

"Yet," put in Arthur, "I expect Gwallog will have got a message to him by now though."

"Are you not fearful of what your father might say or... do?"

"When it's a matter of necessity, I will decide for myself what is right. If my father disapproves there is little I can do. I stand on my success or failure."

Urien nodded and smiled, "you have shown good judgment and bravery. Most of all, my friend, you have shown independence and you have proven here that you are not afraid. Your valour and your trustworthiness is something I can work with." He glanced at Llywarch who nodded in agreement. "As far as I am concerned we have found our new Dux Bellorum. The new Pendragon. Do you accept?"

Arthur's jaw dropped, "Dux Bellorum? But what of my father?"

Urien laughed, "he'll accept and he'll try to manipulate you but I trust that you will plough your own furrow. If you don't..." Urien let the words hang.

Arthur looked from one man to the other, "if Alt Clut and Dalriada agree then, of course, yes!"

"Dux Bellorum," saluted Llywarch, "let it be so."

The forces of Rheged and the Gododdin left with little ceremony. Both forces moved off south and chose to follow Hussa before separating and making for their respective homes.

The battlefield needed to be cleared, it was a grim business and the euphoria felt by all quickly dissipated as friends and foe alike were identified as the rain began to fall once again. The field of battle made Arthur retch as he forced himself to look about him remembering the gruesome task he had overseen at Delgon just a few short weeks before.

He was being hailed Dux Bellorum, the Pendragon. He shook his head in disbelief. What would this mean, what of his father? He swallowed hard and acknowledged the chanting of his army and their allies with trepidation.

It was sometime later that he began to ponder his decision to release Hussa and his surviving men. No one had said anything to him but Cai, in particular, was, he noticed, finding it hard to conceal his annoyance. It wasn't overly surprising as Cai had taken the brunt of the Angle attack. Would Arthur have felt the same if he were in Cai's position, probably he would. He sighed deeply, he found slaughtering men who did their duty by their Lord ugly. Hussa was another issue, he knew, but he was sending a message that he was not an adolescent upstart and that he was a man to be reckoned with. He was certain the Angles wouldn't be coming back any time soon but he also knew they would come back soon enough and in bigger numbers. Would Hussa's death change that? He doubted it.

Arthur strolled over to his horse and patted his mane. He walked the horse forward to where the Angle camp had been situated. He wanted time to think about what came next, he craved peace and quiet above all else. He knew Bedwyr would ensure he was left alone. Tonight would be a time to celebrate again but for now it was time for grieving. Grieving for the men he had lost, grieving for their wives and girlfriends, mothers and fathers and children. He put his hands on his hips and looked to the sky before beginning to weep.

That night the melancholy began to lift. The finding of ale in the enemy camp had had its effect on spirits. Arthur, after being too long without warmth, could sit by a roaring fire and share the celebrations and despite himself joined in with the laughter and telling of great tales of otherworldly deeds of daring and valour. Arthur mentally totted up the numbers of Angles killed from the stories told and found, to his amusement, that the force they had defeated was at least three times bigger than it actually was. It was amazing that the horror of the previous hours could be so easily washed away by Ale no matter how poor it was.

The revelry continued late into the night despite the frequent rain showers and it was almost dawn by the time quiet spread across the victor's camp. Only Arthur and Bedwyr appeared to be awake, Cai was sleeping with his head against Bedwyr's shoulder snoring loudly. Arthur grinned at Bedwyr's predicament as he tried, and failed, to shift Cai's lifeless body off him.

"You can laugh," groaned Bedwyr

"At least he's at peace now," Arthur smiled

"Hmm, he wasn't very happy earlier," Bedwyr sighed.

"I know. He didn't approve of my letting Hussa go."

"That's an understatement."

Arthur chuckled, "Killing for the sake of it is wrong and anyway, I wanted the news of this battle to go back to their King. Anyway why see any more of our men fall? There has been too much slaughter."

Bedwyr nodded, "I will smooth the feathers of the others."

"Others?"

"Cai wasn't alone. Collen too and…"

"I don't want to know, it can't be helped. I will never satisfy everyone. Collen, I think is a Christian and he wants every heathen dead."

"I better slit my own wrists," laughed Arthur.

"I'm not sure it's a laughing matter. Can you trust him?"

Arthur was quiet for a moment, Bedwyr's comment, no matter its context or Bedwyr's personal view, stung him. Was this someone else to look out for? He shrugged "besides being a Christian, is there any reason why I should distrust him."

Bedwyr was aware of the tension in Arthur's voice and sought to defuse the situation by shrugging off his comment. "He is a bit strange don't you think?"

They both laughed, "time will tell I suppose."

Arthur's mood lightened again. "So," said Bedwyr, "you are the Pendragon now? Your father will be pleased."

Arthur groaned and invited Bedwyr to kill himself.

The news of Arthur's victory at the Moor of Rocky prayers spread swiftly. Messengers were sent out in all directions, as far as Ebruac to the south and to King Bruide of the Picts to the North, to spread the news. The slaughter of the Angle army had made Arthur a celebrity and a man to be reckoned with and possibly someone who might become the leader of a new British alliance.

When news of the victory had reached Dunadd there was great celebration. Muirgein had walked through the dwellings of the settlement accepting the cheers of the populace. Her brother had succeeded but that success would bring its own challenges. Somehow the victory would be even more problematic than the decision to send an expedition to Dalriada's eastern borders.

Muirgein knew it was important to ensure the news was taken to Aedan urgently and in a form that would placate him and ensure he did not feel threatened. Reluctantly she turned to Gwallog and requested that he immediately set off to inform Aedan of what had transpired and the news of Arthur's success against the Angles. To Muirgein's relief, Gwallog recognised immediately that there was an opportunity for all the British Kingdoms to unite around a single man, a man who was respected by all and was not seen as a threat to any of them. Urien and Llywarch had seen it and Arthur had their support. From his dealings with Rhydderch he was certain Alt Clut would be supportive and remembering Arthur's treatment of Peredur and his brother it was likely that Eliffer would also be supportive. The likes of the Angles and the Picts would be deterred from attacking any of the British Kingdoms if an alliance could be formed.

Gwallog had already sent word to Aedan about Arthur's advance on the Angles but it was unlikely that Aedan would have received his message so speed was of the essence so he made his way south as quickly as possible. Nonetheless, there was also danger, it was one thing saying Arthur had defeated the Angles independent of Aedan's authority it was a completely different thing to tell Aedan that his son was now being touted as the Pendragon. Arthur wasn't just the Prince of Dalriada but he was Dux Bellorum and as the Lord of Battles he would command all the armies north of the Humber, a power base potentially to rival Aedan. Could Aedan accept it? The trip to Ireland would be a hazardous one.

Chapter 29

Kingdom of the Scots

Columba's performance, for that was what it was, had been a stunning piece of theatre. Taliesin at his best could not have beguiled the people in attendance any more.

Aedan's sole priority was to secure independence from his Irish cousins. Aed was all too aware of Aedan's military threat and there was no appetite for conflict. The Dalriadan cousins had already been in conflict and the spoils had been shared but Aedan was much more powerful now and with his son at this side it seemed an appropriate time to sever the link.

Aed had been initially unwilling to accept independence but his advisors and the promptings of Columba had softened him. His considerations instead turned to what type of relationship might exist and what rights and responsibilities would be acceptable to all parties.

The negotiations had been exhausting. Aedan hadn't realised how difficult discussions would be without the threat of force. As he looked out over the Red River, watching the water glide by he heard a call from the Halls. It was dusk and Aedan could hardly see the man but the voice came closer and Aedan responded. "I'm here, who calls for me."

"Lord," the man gasped, "I have a message from the Lord Gwallog."

"Gwallog?" Aedan responded

"Yes Lord, the Lord Gwallog, instructs me to tell you that Dalriada is under attack."

"Attack? Who from?" Aedan said with agitation.

"The Angles."

"What else man, what have Gwallog and the Lady Muirgein done?"

"Your son Arthur has gone out to face them at the place of Rocky Prayers and Muirgein has ordered that Dunadd by prepared for attack."

"And they decided to do this without my agreement?"

The man swallowed hard, "Lord Gwallog has told me to tell you that he advised against the action until you were made aware but that the Lady Muirgein and Lord Arthur were determined on their path."

"Shit!!" shouted Aedan. He closed his eyes for a moment and breathed heavily, willing himself to calm his escalating alarm. He scowled at the messenger who stood there with fear etched across his face. "I would dearly like to kill the messenger," he muttered grimly. He frowned and sighed, he looked at the man and groaned. "Leave me," he said quietly.

"Do you have a message?" the messenger asked with obvious relief.

"I will think on it," he grunted. "Make yourself known inside and they will feed you and find you lodgings. I will call for you in due course."

The messenger nodded, "your will Lord."

Aedan squatted on the dewy grass. The dampness soaking his trews felt strangely comforting. He dispelled the thought from his mind, embarrassed by himself. The message he had received was probably two or three days old and it was likely that his son would have already confronted the Angles in battle. Even if Arthur had lost, it would take the Angles almost a week to advance on Dunadd, and he reflected, there was no chance of the Fort being taken. He concluded that the Angles would probably try to hold any land they would have taken and set up a bridge head for further attacks into Dalriada. He comforted himself with the worst possible scenario. What was important, he decided, was to conclude the negotiations here at Drumceatt. If he could gain independence from his Irish brethren and forge some sort of alliance with his neighbouring kingdoms, no matter how loose, to dissuade the western Picts from threatening his northern borders, he might even be able to gather his forces to directly confront the Angles.

Despite his strong desire to be at the head of any alliance he wasn't naive to think he would be allowed. His reputation for being "Wily," and his attack on Alt Clut would not be forgotten and any hope of over lordship could not be fulfilled without direct military action and he certainly wasn't strong enough for that, particularly if Arthur had been defeated.

He would have to sit tight and conclude his business or, at least, he would until further news was received from Dunadd. It was unlikely this could be kept quiet for any length of time but he would try nonetheless.

The next couple of days would be painful for Aedan whose attention was being pulled in two directions. He was relieved and glad for Columba's help although he knew that this could, at some stage, come at a significant cost. Columba continued to cajole and bully the Irish Dalriadans into finding a resolution and his machinations were beginning to bear fruit when Aed finally agreed to the independence of the Scots but only if Aedan guaranteed to give naval assistance in the event of Pictish incursion on the northern coasts. This was readily agreed by Aedan who realised this was a mere sop and the likelihood of being held to this condition was slim. He recognised too that Aed was painfully aware that any alliances with Rheged and Alt Clut would place him at a huge disadvantage.

The thorny issue of protecting his own borders was Aedan's final goal. He recognised the issue was close to everyone's heart, and much to everyone's surprise, Aedan's ace was produced in the person of Fiachna mac Baetan, a Pictish Chieftain.

Aedan scanned the room, "Fiachna will be useful ally and what is the best way to cement an alliance?" he asked. "A marriage of course."

Aed looked puzzled, "and who do you propose?"

"My daughter of course."

"The Lady Muirgein?" Aed was surprised.

"Wasn't she promised to Urien or was it Gwallog?"

"Both," Aedan admitted, "the Britons of the north have longed been tied by marriage. And it will always be so. Urien has moved on to another strumpet so Muirgein is... available."

"I see," Aed said sceptically, "shall I assume, my dear Aedan, that they are both... aware of your plans?

"Fiachna is, yes," he responded

"Really?"

"He will be."

"And Muirgein?" he said arching his eyebrows.

"She will," Aedan said confidently but then paused. A smile then spread across his face, "in fact," he continued "we could make it joint wedding, Igraine and I and Fiachna and Muirgein. That would be a fine event."

"And this is your oath Aedan?" Aed said slightly amused.

"Yes, absolutely," Aedan affirmed.

Aed held out his hand, "very well, we are in accord."
Aedan clasped Aed's arm, "Yes we are."
"May we remain cousins and allies," Aed smiled.
"Aye!" came the collective response.
"Tonight we celebrate," announced Aed

It was dawn when Gwallog landed on Irish soil. The voyage had been relatively pleasant, the softly rolling ship helping his slumber. Needless to say there was a fine rain and he had awoken sodden. He ruefully reflected that his trip south to Drumceatt would probably help dry his clothes although the leaden skies above him quickly stole that hope away.

He took breakfast before procuring a horse and set off through the rolling green hills. He would be quick despite the rather scrawny and underfed horse he was riding. As the sun reached its zenith the Hall of Drumceatt came into view with the Red River beyond. He paused momentarily on the crest of the hill overlooking the complex, took a deep breath, and after taking in the view he spurred his horse forward.

Gwallog was surprised to hear merriment as he entered the hall. He was immediately ushered into a side room by Cormons, the ever present menace, where he waited for his audience with Aedan. He sat for some time on his own although he could hear men outside in the passageway close to the door.

After what seemed an age Aedan slipped into the room and offered his hand to clasp Gwallog's arm. "Good to see you my friend," he said barely above a whisper, "what news?"

"It is very good Lord, Arthur was successful and repelled the Angles. Word received at Dunadd suggests that he received support from King Urien and the Gododdin although he would have probably prevailed anyway."

"Urien and the Gododdin? How did that come to pass?"

"I'm not sure," Gwallog grunted "but I am assuming that the Gododdin were shadowing the Angle force and Urien had received intelligence of

Angle movements. What I would say Lord is that everyone seems to have received the same intelligence, almost as if the whole thing was contrived."

"Who did that?" Aedan asked

"I believe it was Morcant," Gwallog breathed.

"That old dog," smiled Aedan, "we will need to watch him very carefully."

"Indeed Lord," Gwallog agreed.

"Excellent," Aedan sighed with relief, "what were Arthur's casualties?" he added.

"Between fifty and seventy five, I believe. It was a hard won battle."

"And he is uninjured?"

"Yes, he's fine," Gwallog said but stopped from saying any more.

"What else Gwallog?" Aedan quizzed.

"Well Arthur is clearly building quite a reputation. He is being called Dux Bellorum and Pendragon."

"Who were calling him that?" Aedan interrupted. "Our men?"

"Yes and those of our Allies, Lord?"

"Urien?"

"Yes Lord."

Aedan paused for a few beats, deep in thought. Was this good for him or not. He suspected that he, Aedan, would never be allowed to lead an alliance against the Angles and the Picts. He knew he was distrusted. The question for Aedan was could he trust Arthur? Would Arthur's popularity endanger him, would he be able to control Arthur in such a position? He looked at Gwallog intently and then asked, "should I be concerned Gwallog?"

Gwallog thought a moment and sighed, "no Lord, I don't believe so."

"Hmm," Aedan nodded, "very well, let's see what Urien and Rhydderch say. But I want you to keep me appraised. You know him and he trusts you. I am relying on you to… contain him."

Gwallog bowed slightly, "Your will Lord."

"Good," Aedan said perking up, "let's put that aside. We have a lot to celebrate."

"Success Lord?

"Most definitely,"

"That is wonderful news Lord."

"Yes Gwallog, we are independent at last. Even that grubby little shit Columba did his bit!" said Aedan grinning.

"Wonders will never cease."

"Indeed my friend, but at what cost?" Aedan shrugged. "Come let's drink to all our health," he continued.

Gwallog followed Aedan into the Hall where dozens of people were milling about including Columba who was enjoying the attention being given him by the many nobles. Gwallog reflected that the alcohol being consumed had also helped Columba's mood and smiled broadly. Perhaps the priest was not as big a prick as Gwallog had first believed. He wandered around pressing the flesh with Irish Lords but he was ill at ease following his discussions with Aedan. This bloody family were causing him a great deal of angst, he closed his eyes and groaned to himself.

His confrontation with Muirgein still grated and she was now unlikely to trust him which meant Arthur would also be on his guard. And for good measure, he was expected to spy on Arthur and by association Muirgein so he would be doing something he wasn't doing but they probably thought he was. His head began to ache.

At that moment he thought again of Loch Lomond, its beauty, its serenity and its distance from court intrigue. Just maybe, he mused, he could lie low for a while assuming there were no further conflicts. He would now be close to Crierwy. His heart leapt at the thought but he soon returned to reality. All of it was just pie in the sky, some hopes, he thought. He laughed out loud which attracted some attention to him. He blushed with embarrassment and automatically raised his cup in toast.

Arthur returned to Dunadd with depleted but victorious forces. People lined the route across the marshes, chanting his name, Arthur Pendragon, as well as the new title he been rewarded, Dux Bellorum.

He waived with a sense of embarrassment but reached down to touch the hands of those men and women who reached out to him and there were many. He was followed by Bedwyr and then Cai and Drystan, who in complete contrast, drank in the adulation.

As Arthur approached the gates his progress was greatly slowed and he decided that his best chance of moving forward towards where his sister was waiting was to climb down from his mount and walk. Bedwyr quickly followed with two warriors who shepherded Arthur through the throng.

As they finally broke through the crowd and into the open, Muirgein strode forward and they embraced with great affection. "You are uninjured?" she whispered in his ear. Arthur nodded, just a scratch or two. At that she hugged him closer.

Breaking the hold, Muirgein turned to the crowd. "Friends," she called with a surprisingly loud voice, "we welcome home the Prince Arthur." Her words were followed by a roar from all and sundry and she found herself waiving her arms to try and gain some quiet. "Yes, we welcome home our hero, the Pendragon," there was another roar. "He has," she continued, "vanquished the Angle scum. They will think twice before they try and invade our lands again."

The roars came again with great gusto and although Muirgein wanted to say more she decided that it would be pointless. Instead she lifted Arthur's arm, and together, they waved and soaked up the adulation. "This is for you Brother… Dux Bellorum," she said with a wry smile.

"News travels fast," he shrugged. "The King will no doubt become aware," he continued.

"Gwallog has already departed to take the news to him," Muirgein said without expression.

"I wonder what he'll make of all this?" Arthur mused.

"He'll, no doubt, consider how or if this strengthens or weakens him," Muirgein responded simply.

"Everything is a calculation," Arthur said sadly.

Muirgein smiled, "that is always the problem when you plot against others, you always think that everyone is plotting against you."

"Are there murmurings of discontent or criticism from Aedan's loyalists?" Arthur asked anxiously.

Muirgein said nothing at first but then turned to Arthur. "All I will say to that is never worry about criticism from people you would never take advice from."

"Poetic my dear Sister, poetic," he laughed.

They walked away from the crowd arm in arm. Arthur's chiefs chose not to follow and it was Bors who suggested what they were all thinking. Time to drink and whore, what say you?" There was no disagreement.

Muirgein and Arthur sat together in the quiet of what was the Lords enclosure.

"When will father return?" asked Arthur without any enthusiasm.

"I don't know, he will know of our decision to send you east and probably your success there. Gwallog will have reached him by now. I assume a lot will depend on what comes to pass a Drumceatt. All I can say is that Aedan will weigh things up very carefully before making a decision on our fate."

Arthur groaned, "our fate," he repeated, "I... we have saved his kingdom and we are here worrying about fate! That is fucking outrageous," Arthur said with rising fury.

"Let's not jump to any conclusions yet." Muirgein soothed, "you have a lot of friends it would appear and so do I. Father will know that. He might be paranoid but he isn't stupid. And then there's Gwallog."

"Can Gwallog be trusted?" asked Arthur

"Gwallog is many things but he is not dishonest, in fact he is the most honourable man, I suspect, either of us will ever know. Whether he approves of what we do or not will not mean he will betray us if he believes our motives are true and non-threatening to our Father."

"And he believes?"

"Yes I think so, at least I hope so. One thing is for certain he has probably had a belly fully of all of us by now."

Arthur shrugged, "is there something to drink?" he groaned.

"Of course," said Muirgein. "actually," she continued "I have something you may never have tasted before. The Romans used to drink it before they found Ale and Mead."

"I'll try it," Arthur said as Muirgein poured a rich red liquid into a pot. "What's in it?" he said as he raised the cup to his lips and sniffed.

"Grapes."

"Grapes?" he repeated, "hmmm... let's see what our former masters enjoyed." He lifted his cup and tilted his head backward letting the surprisingly rich and slightly tart liquid slip over his tongue."

"Well?" Muirgein said.

"It's not what I expected, a bit strong perhaps. Can it be watered down?"

"Let's try," Muirgein said reaching for a jug of water and pouring some into each cup. She drank the new liquid first and nodded approvingly. "Not as good perhaps but at least we'll still be standing."

Arthur laughed, "I'll drink to that."

They chatted amiably while the volume of alcohol loosened their tongues. Arthur could feel a sensation of dizziness, his eyes were heavy and the need for sleep became overwhelming. He lay down and put his head in Muirgein's lap where he dozed as she stroked his hair.

He slept fitfully and when he finally awoke he was alone under some skins. His head ached and he groaned. His mouth too was dry and sour and he looked around for some water. He was partially clothed but his modesty was intact when a servant poked her head around the door and asked after his health before offering him a large jug of water, half of which he drank the rest he poured over his head. She stood close by and when he looked at her, all he could do was grimace before handing the jug back. She was a pretty red head he noticed and despite himself his manhood stirred. The girl took the jug and left smirking. All Arthur could do was slip back down and groan.

Shortly after Muirgein re-appeared, "you slept Brother?"

"I don't want to talk about it," Arthur grunted, "all I can say is that the Roman's must have been tough bastards to drink that stuff."

"I'll get you some food," she laughed.

Arthur looked up and reached for her arm, "where's Gwen?"

Muirgein grinned, "the young lady has taken your fancy? How quickly you cast your sister aside," she teased.

Arthur blushed furiously, "I..I..." he stuttered

"I jest little brother. Anyway, I'm told she is in the company of your mother."

"My mother?"

"They set out for Lomond yesterday when news of your success filtered through. Gwallog made arrangements before his departure for Ulster."

"Why is everything so bloody hard?" Arthur said irritably to no one in particular.

"It is as it should be my dear Brother. Go visit once Father returns, assuming of course he doesn't have us disposed of first," she laughed.

"Your sense of humour leaves a lot to be desired dear Muirgein.

Aedan remained at Drumceatt for a number of days that stretched into weeks basking in the glory of his success. He was now the King of the Scots, and much to his delight, was being acknowledged as such by the dwindling number of nobles and priests. He paid little or no attention to arrangements to return home to Dalriada, leaving everything to the increasingly cantankerous and irritable Gwallog. Aedan did notice this deteriorating mood but chose to ignore it. He had broken the news of his plans for Muirgein to Gwallog who took things remarkably well but Gwallog's mood, he concluded, must have been linked to this news. Aedan knew he had not been fair to Gwallog who had faithfully served him but at the same time Aedan's decision had been best for the country he now reigned over. Unsurprisingly Gwallog thought very differently.

Eventually as the leaves began to turn brown and following many warnings that the crossings back to the mainland would become more treacherous the later it was left, Aedan raised himself to order the return home.

To Aedan's amusement, Columba once more had his eyes bound and was led by the plethora of priests in his service. Noticing Gwallog's confusion, Aedan advised him of Columba's promise never to see his homeland again on their initial crossing. Gwallog shrugged and shook his head which prompted Aedan to bark with laughter.

The procession was leisurely and they were accompanied by Aed who had chosen to waive off his new "ally," and probably to make sure that he was finally rid of this irritating man. The infrequent exchanges of conversation was polite if a little stilted and it was with relief that they reached the port.

As always, there was a drizzle but mercifully winds were light and whilst the Captain advised that there was a bit of a swell the sailing was expected to be relatively comfortable. After the ships were loaded, Aedan and Aed embraced. It was a valuable propaganda moment and it raised cheers from both Irish, and now, Scots warriors. As the ships slipped their moorings Aedan made sure he stood and waived. It was ostentatious, it was hypocritical, Gwallog reflected, but it was brilliant. How could it be any other way?

Mid crossing did find the sea a little rough but it was short lived and it was with relief and much triumph that the coast of Kintyre became large enough to clearly make out the land and cottages on its shores.

Gwallog and Aedan stood in silence at the bow of their ship as it cut through the last waves before reaching the flatness of the waters of the bay. Aedan patted Gwallog on the arm and pointed at their destination place where there was a large welcoming committee lined up along the shore. The crowd on the beach roared its approval as the ships came to rest and Aedan was helped down from the ship and on to beach. The sun had finally broken through the clouds and Aedan enjoyed the heat on his face. He then straightened and walked towards where Muirgein stood. He noticed that Arthur stood a couple of paces behind her.

He first embraced his daughter and then Arthur warmly. "You have been busy," he smiled dangerously, "Gwallog told me all about your deliberations and your decisions."

Arthur glanced at Gwallog but didn't catch his eye, "Father," he said, "we had to make a decision to act and could not wait. The Angles…"

Aedan held up his hand stopping Arthur in mid flow. "Calm yourself my boy, you did the right thing as it turned out. The Gods were and are smiling on you Arthur or should it now be Dux Bellorum."

"Thank you Father," Arthur grunted looking at his feet.

"All I will say is don't do it again son, and that goes for you too Muirgein."

Muirgein nodded. After a beat she straightened "Congratulations Father," she said as effusively as possible.

"Yes Father," Arthur chimed in, "congratulations! You have made Dalriada a kingdom."

"Thank you, I am now free to do as I choose."

Muirgein and Arthur bowed, "your people await you," Muirgein said without expression and pointed towards the awaiting crowd. Aedan nodded in return and acknowledged the throng. He stepped onto on a large flat topped rock and held up his arms. "My fellow Dalriadans or should I says Scots," he began, "these are historic times." He paused until the clapping and roaring died down. "We are now an Independent nation and this is our home, the roots we have tried to put down are now permanent. We have shown all the kingdoms around us that we are a force to be reckoned with, the leaders of the resistance against the Angles and the Picts. And we have a new hero, my son Arthur who has served me and you well in defeating the Angle hordes. We all owe him a debt of gratitude and he has rightly been nominated Dux Bellorum. He will be my mouthpiece and my general on the battlefields of the future."

More mad cheering followed as Aedan climbed down and was ushered to his mount on which he began the ride north towards Dunadd. Arthur sighed with relief, he was safe for now. His father had clearly shown his superiority despite Arthur being the Pendragon. As Arthur rode just behind his father and sister he knew that his life would never be peaceful but at least his new position might enable him to put some distance between him and his father. After so many years wanting to know his father he wished he'd never met him.